OUTRAGE

ALSO BY JOHN SANDFORD

LUCAS DAVENPORT NOVELS

Rules of Prey
Shadow Prey
Eyes of Prey
Silent Prey
Winter Prey
Night Prey
Mind Prey
Sudden Prey
Secret Prey
Certain Prey
Easy Prey
Chosen Prey
Mortal Prey
Naked Prey
Hidden Prey
Broken Prey
Invisible Prey
Phantom Prey
Wicked Prey
Storm Prey
Buried Prey
Stolen Prey
Silken Prey
Field of Prey
Gathering Prey

VIRGIL FLOWERS NOVELS

Dark of the Moon
Heat Lightning
Rough Country
Bad Blood
Shock Wave
Mad River
Storm Front
Deadline

KIDD NOVELS

The Fool's Run
The Empress File
The Devil's Code
The Hanged Man's Song

OTHER NOVELS

The Night Crew
Dead Watch

BY JOHN SANDFORD & MICHELE COOK

THE SINGULAR MENACE

Uncaged

THE SINGULAR MENACE • BOOK 2

OUTRAGE

JOHN SANDFORD
& MICHELE COOK

ALFRED A. KNOPF ⬩ NEW YORK

THIS IS A BORZOI BOOK PUBLISHED BY ALFRED A. KNOPF

All rights reserved. Published in the United States by Alfred A. Knopf, an imprint of Random House Children's Books, a division of Penguin Random House LLC, New York.

Knopf, Borzoi Books, and the colophon are registered trademarks of Penguin Random House LLC.

Visit us on the Web! randomhouseteens.com

Educators and librarians, for a variety of teaching tools, visit us at RHTeachersLibrarians.com

Library of Congress Cataloging-in-Publication Data is available upon request.
ISBN 978-0-385-75309-8 (trade) — ISBN 978-0-385-75310-4 (lib. bdg.) —
ISBN 978-0-385-75312-8 (ebook)

The text of this book is set in 11-point Simoncini Garamond.

Printed in the United States of America
July 2015
10 9 8 7 6 5 4 3 2 1

First Edition

OUTRAGE

PROLOGUE

She stalked across the Home Depot parking lot: a West Coast punk with brutally cropped black hair, a black tank top, muscles in her shoulders and arms, wearing jeans and lace-up boots. At her knee, a wolf-dog wearing a phony "service" tag.

Like a raven-haired, bad news version of Alice in Wonderland, she led the animal through the store, past shelves that rose to the ceiling: cleaning liquids, paper towels, paint, insect killers, tree trimmers, and tools—walls of wrenches, hammers, pliers, screwdrivers, tape measures . . . and bolt cutters.

Everything from hand-sized cable nippers to four-foot-long monster jaws that could slice through the roof of a truck. Momentarily bewildered by the choices, she reached up and selected a tough-looking twenty-four-inch H. K. Porter general-purpose bolt cutter for $44.97.

She had plenty, she thought. She slipped the fingers of her right hand into her jeans pocket and touched the wad of bills there . . .

and her fingers came away with the sticky, rusty stains of drying blood.

The sight of the blood struck her like a thunderbolt. She brought her hand close to her face, could smell the coppery scent of blood and death—and was instantly transported to a makeshift prison a hundred and thirty miles away, back in time by half a day, a bleak, concrete box of locks and bars and tiny cells, screaming, desperate, mutilated inmates, the stink of torture and human waste. . . .

The images tumbled through sixteen-year-old Shay Remby's mind: her brother Odin's beaten face, the torture room with its tub and hoses, the Asian girl with the grotesquely wired-up scalp. Beneath all those thoughts, the image of a handsome black man, Marcus West, lying in a pool of his own blood. Down the hall, in another puddle of blood, the man he'd shot in self-defense.

West still had a gun in one hand. Shay was kneeling by his side, trying to lift him, while he pleaded with her to run. There were armed men coming, he said, killers who'd shoot her as well. Then Cruz pulled her from the floor, away from West, and half carried, half dragged her out into the night.

Then it started over again, like a bad film loop playing through her mind. . . .

Shay had no idea how long she stood there, frozen by the images. She came back from the nightmare and found X anxiously licking her left hand—her right hand, the one with the blood, was still crooked in front of her face.

She whispered, *"Shit, shit,"* and looked down at her pocket: she hadn't seen it earlier, but there was a palm-sized bloodstain on the denim. The contact point with West's bleeding rib cage. Down her leg, she saw more of the rusty blood spots.

She shuddered, put the bolt cutters back in their bin, and looked wildly around, then hurried X down the aisle toward the back of the store. The restrooms were always in the back of the store. . . .

The ladies' room was big and clean but not quite empty—an elderly woman was pushing a walker from the handicapped stall to the sink. She flinched away from the punk and her tethered wolf, and made straight for the exit; Shay heard the yellow tennis balls on the walker's front legs swishing. She locked herself and the dog into the stall at the end of the row and pulled the money out of her pocket.

A wad of fifties, and every bill had been touched with West's blood. For some, the blood extended into Ulysses S. Grant's bearded face. Others had only minor stains.

She stuffed the bloodiest bills into her left front pocket and took the rest to the sink. The blood had been nearly dry, but the water seemed to reanimate it, a thin red stream that seeped out of the bills and curled down her fingers. She teared up as she worked, watching West's blood flow down the drain.

X whimpered at her, and when the water finally ran clean, she dried the bills as best she could by blotting them against paper towels, then carried them to the hand dryer to blast them with hot air. The bills came out limp, but clean. She took a second to throw cold water on her face and said to X, "Let's go."

She went back to the bolt cutter aisle, got the H. K. Porters, and carried them to the self-checkout counter. She kept the blood-dappled side of her jeans to the counter, nodded to the woman supervising the checkouts, and went out to the Jeep.

West's Jeep . . . She opened the door and saw a smear of dried blood on the driver's seat, where she'd been sitting. She dug into the backseat, found a pack of insect-repellant wipes, pulled one out, and used it to scrub the blood off the gray leather. She dropped the wipe in the parking lot and turned the leather key fob in her hand as she was about to start the ignition. More damn blood: West had been clutching his side and laid down a complete thumbprint when he thrust the keys at her. . . .

She flashed back to the basement again, could see her own face reflected in the shine of West's brown eyes . . . desperate to get her moving, thinking only about her safety, not about himself. Insisting that the wound wasn't fatal—he knew that from his past as a soldier. He said the police would get him to a hospital and into surgery. . . .

And then, when she'd landed back safely with her friends, they'd given her the bad news. West had died.

The anger came suddenly, bursting over the sadness, the guilt at leaving him behind. Singular had murdered him, and the anger enveloped her, and she began to tremble, to shake, until she had to grip the steering wheel to keep herself from shaking to pieces.

Then the trembling subsided, and she started the truck.

"No mercy," she vowed to her wolf. "No mercy."

1

Odin Remby held a rolled-up washcloth in the young woman's mouth as she thrashed in chains on the narrow motel bed. Cade Holt had thrown his torso across her bucking legs, and Cruz Perez was trying to restrain her flailing arms. The harder she struggled against her bindings, the more she'd bleed, and the yellowed sheets were already striped with blood.

"Careful, careful, let's not make it worse," said Twist. He was standing back from the bed, leaning on a gold-headed cane, watching the struggle. The curtains were drawn, and the TV was turned up. "It's okay, sweetheart, you're almost through it."

Another seven or eight seconds, and the woman's thrashing limbs began to slow. She went still for a moment, then began to tremble, went still again, suffered another fit of trembling, and finally went still and stayed that way.

She was wearing a gray hospital smock and sweating heavily, and the stink of her sweat saturated the room. When he was sure the fit had ended, Odin pulled the washcloth from between her teeth. Her lips were crossed with healing wounds made when she'd bitten herself in earlier, unprotected fits. Cade and Cruz both backed away.

Twist looked at Odin. "We've got to get the chains off her. Where in the hell is your sister?"

"She'll be back," Odin said. He was thin and pale, breathing heavily. There were vicious purple bruises across his cheeks and hands, as if he'd been patiently and thoroughly and repeatedly beaten—as he had been.

"She's been gone for almost an hour," said Twist. "If she needed to cry, that's fine—but we've got things to do and crying's a luxury right now. We don't know what Singular's doing, we don't have any communications, we—"

A key rattled in the lock, and the door banged open. Shay was there with X, backlit by the Reno sun, carrying an orange Home Depot bag. She kicked the door shut with the heel of her boot and pulled a heavy set of bolt cutters from the sack. Her eyes were dry.

"Let's cut her loose," she said to the men in the room, who were all thinking a version of the same thing: the red-haired, camera-friendly beauty of a week ago was gone. Standing before them was a fugitive with a harsh black hack job of a haircut and a smoldering fury in her hazel stare.

Twist tipped the head of his cane toward her. "Don't leave us in the lurch like that."

They locked eyes, and after a few seconds, she nodded, snapped open the blades of the bolt cutters, didn't bother to apologize. "We've got things to do."

"Like what?" asked Cade. He was a tall, tanned kid, seventeen, with shoulder-length Jesus hair.

"Like revenge."

For a long moment, everyone in the room just looked at her.

Then Odin slowly stood, body stiff, moving as though his bones hurt, and did something he hadn't done in weeks—he smiled.

Cruz, the ex–gang member from East L.A., simply held out his hand, and Shay passed him the bolt cutters.

"These'll work," Cruz said, snapping the heavy jaws.

Shay was studying the woman on the bed. She was Asian, with delicate features gone gaunt from months of stress and pain. "She looks worse than when I left."

"She had another seizure," Odin said. "They're so violent. That was the third since—"

The chained woman was coming around: she tilted her head up at Odin and whispered, "Water." Odin grabbed a cup off the night-stand and held it to the woman's lips. She drank it all, greedily, then lay back on the bed.

"Where're we cutting?" Twist asked.

The woman was bound in a twelve-foot chain, a cold metal boa constrictor that circled her slender waist and looped like handcuffs around her wrists and ankles. Each set of loops was cinched with a U-shaped padlock.

"Start at her waist," Shay said to Cruz. Shay pulled the chain as far off the woman's body as she could, about three inches, and Cruz carefully gripped a link in the blades and squeezed. It broke in half with a quiet pop.

Twist: "Cade, pick up the chain and the padlocks, wipe them, stick them in a pillowcase. We'll dump it in the trash somewhere."

Cade grabbed a pillow, and Cruz moved on to the woman's wrists and then ankles.

"Please don't move," Cruz said, positioning the blades on the chain. "I don't wanna cut you. . . ."

When the woman's chafed and bloodied wrists were free, she groaned in relief and said, "Thank you" and "More water, please?"

Odin got her another cup of water. Twist packed a pillow behind her back and said, "Better?"

She took another long drink and looked around the bed at the six of them: four men, a girl, and a dog with mismatched yellow and blue eyes. The dog sat away from her, but his nose was working hard, sniffing at the blood on her ankles.

As a group, her rescuers looked more than a little tattered: teenagers, mostly, the girl had a swollen lip, the long-haired kid had recently been hit in the face, the heavily muscled Hispanic had a bandage wrapped around one hand, the older man, perhaps thirty, was leaning on a cane. Her grateful gaze settled on Odin—Odin, the boy with gingery whiskers who'd been imprisoned in the same Singular warehouse. He'd cradled her head in the back of a truck as they'd fled from the scene. Now he patted her arm awkwardly and said, "You're safe."

Twist asked, "Can you talk?"

She nodded and put the cup down. "Yes."

Shay: "What did they do to you?"

"They put an American woman into my mind," she said in precise, heavily accented English.

"Into your mind? You mean . . . What do you mean?" Twist asked. He sat on the end of the bed, his cane between his knees.

The woman rubbed at her sore wrists and said: "I have memories that are not my life, I know things that are not my knowing. . . . I am unable to think only for myself."

The rescuers looked at each other, and Twist said, "They're that close. This is science fiction."

"It's depraved," Odin said. "They drilled into her head just like they did all those poor monkeys—"

"Monkeys?" the woman asked.

Shay gave her brother a look that said *not now,* but the woman had a flicker of understanding.

"Yes, I think I am like a monkey—an experiment," she said. "But I do not think the experiment worked. Not completely. If the experiment worked, she would have taken over my brain and driven me out. I think only pieces were successful. I do not know. . . . There is much confusion."

They'd all been staring—and trying not to stare—at the woman's horribly mutilated head. Now, as if suddenly realizing what it meant to have her hands free, she reached up and probed her skull. Spread across the whole dome of her depilated scalp were dozens of tiny brass caps, each sprouting a wire as thin as thread. The wires swept back and ended in pigtail-like connectors at the back of her neck.

"I have not felt my head since before the operation," she said, answering their faces. "I was chained, to keep me from pulling these things out. Please, may I see a mirror?"

Twist didn't think that was a good idea, not now or for the rest of her life.

"Why don't you wait until you've rested," he said.

She arched her eyebrow and said: "I am not so afraid that I cannot see the truth."

An iPad belonging to West, sticking out of his leather briefcase, pinged. Shay said, "Just a second," and stepped over to the table to check it, then turned back to the others, agitated. "It's a note on BlackWallpaper." That was the Facebook account West had set up to communicate with them—but obviously it wasn't West posting. . . .

"From them?" Cade asked. He went over to view the screen and nodded. "Yeah. Singular."

Last night can be forgotten. Return the copied flash drives and we're done.

A warning: You are associating with a Chinese spy who came here illegally to attack government officials. If you help her, you will be equally guilty of espionage. The FBI is looking for her and won't stop until she's in custody.

"Last night can be forgotten?" Shay seethed. "They murdered West. They murdered him. They think we're going to let them forget it?"

Twist put a hand on her shoulder. "Let me show it to . . ." He turned to the girl on the bed. "I don't even know your name."

"Fenfang."

"Let me show it to Fenfang," Twist said. "Can you read English?"

"Of course."

She took the slate, frowned as she read the message. "I am not a spy! I am a university student. My cousin Liko and I, they . . . they . . ." She touched her head again, and her eyes began twitching and then rolled upward. Twist said, "She's seizing again. Get the washcloth. . . ."

Fenfang fell back on the bed, shivering, her teeth beginning to chatter, and she moaned as if someone was indeed fighting her from inside.

Odin knelt next to her, grabbed the washcloth off the nightstand, and thrust it between her teeth. She began to gnaw at it and struggle, and he said, "Help, hold her arms. . . ."

The spasm went on for two minutes, peaking a minute after it started and gradually subsiding. When it ended, she opened her eyes and said, "I can't . . ." She closed her eyes and seemed to fall asleep.

Odin, staring at the woman's scalp, sickened by it, said, "We need to get her some kind of treatment."

"What kind would that be?" Shay asked. The anger was thick in her voice. "They made her into a lab rat. If she's like those monkeys you turned loose, or like X, her brain is full of wires. Where do you go to get that fixed?"

"I don't know," Odin said. "But leaving her like this is not an option. We've got to do something."

Fenfang's eyes fluttered: she'd been unconscious for no more than a few seconds. She said, "You cannot cure me. I think I will die soon. Or I will kill myself."

Odin crouched beside her. "Don't give up. Please. Don't."

Fenfang focused her eyes, which were dark brown, almost black. "I have no control. These things they put in my head . . . I see things. I do things. They connect me to a machine."

"No machine here," Cade said.

"No machine ever again," said Odin.

Twist leaned in. "The note from Singular said you're a Chinese spy. . . ."

"I am not a spy."

"We're under the impression Singular might be dealing with North Koreans. Are you Chinese or Korean?"

"I am Chinese, from Dandong," she said. "I was a university student there. My cousin, Liko, and I, we studied together."

Cade's fingers rapped across the keyboard of his laptop, and he checked a map. "Dandong is on the border, across the Yalu River from North Korea."

"Yes. We made money for school, trading with North Koreans," Fenfang said. "Then an American man came, he was a Christian man. He wanted to go across to do research on the suffering, and we took him. On the third night, we were captured."

There was a flurry of glances between Shay and the others. One of the videos from the encrypted flash drive Odin had cracked showed a robotic Asian man speaking as though he were an American Christian aid worker who'd gone missing a year earlier along the Chinese–North Korean border.

"Was it Robert G. Morris?" Cade asked. "Robert G. Morris from St. Louis?"

The young woman seemed startled when she heard the name. "Yes. You know Robert?"

"No," Twist said. "But we found . . . evidence of him on a Singular video. We also found news reports that no one had seen him for months."

Cruz, who'd stepped back and was petting X, asked, "How did you get from North Korea to here?"

"On a ship," she said, her voice trembling with effort. "There were other people with me, also experiments. One of them was my cousin. Everything was clouds. They gave me drugs, all of us had drugs, to keep us quiet, almost to the end. The last four or five days, they did not give us drugs because they wanted our blood to be clean for the examinations. One man died when we were on the ship. We were in a metal box, he was sick, and then he did not move, and they came and took him out. We never saw him again."

Shay jumped in: "Fenfang, we don't know who the other prisoners were at the facility we broke into last night. Do you?"

The young woman squeezed her eyes shut, as if trying to see inside the cells where Shay and West had spied several catatonic men in the moments before they found Odin.

"No," she said. "I heard crying, but I only ever saw Odin."

Odin said, "They were dragging me down the hall to my cell after waterboarding me. I couldn't walk, I was just hanging off them. Fenfang was being taken the other way. One of the guards said, 'Water Boy meets the Girl with Two Brains,' and the other guards laughed."

"Not laughing now," Cruz said.

Fenfang nodded and looked at the group again, scrutinizing each of their faces: Shay, Twist, Odin, Cade, Cruz, and X. Then she asked, "Who are you?"

Shay said, "That's a complicated story."

"I am a good listener," Fenfang said.

Odin ran his hands through his hair and started at the beginning: "I don't like animal experimentation in research laboratories. Most of the time, it's unnecessary and cruel, and if you'd seen the messed-up monkeys with their heads cut—"

Shay squeezed Odin's arm, gave him a quick shake of her head that said *spare her the details*. "My brother's got a very kind heart, but basically, what happened is, he and some extreme animal rights people raided a lab to wreck their experiments, and they got away with a lot of computer files and our dog here. Turns out the company that owns the lab wasn't just experimenting on animals, they were experimenting on people, like you. We think they're trying to find a way to make people . . . immortal."

Odin broke in: "The problem is, they can't create a brain or a body, so they have to use one that already exists. They kidnap a living person, try to erase her memories, and then they try to move the mind of another person into her brain."

"And that is me," Fenfang said.

Odin nodded. "It makes me so angry. The worst thing you can do is kill a living being; they killed hundreds of animals trying to figure out how to do it, the monkeys I was telling you about—"

Shay touched his arm again: "Anyway, Odin and his friends stole computer records, and the company, it's called Singular, went after them, trying to get back the files."

"And the dog," Odin said, nodding at X. "He was one of their experiments, and I took him, but God, I forgot the poor little three-legged rat. Then Shay came looking for me and met Twist—"

"I'm Twist," Twist said.

Odin continued: "And I gave her the dog and copies of the files I stole, and then Singular kidnapped me."

"We put some of the files Odin gave me on the Internet," Shay said, "and we caused them some trouble." She smiled ruefully. "One of the Singular people, a man named West, changed sides to help us. He was with us when we found you and Odin, and they killed him. . . . And that's where we are. We got Odin back, and you, and we lost West."

"And now?"

"We fight," said Twist.

"They'll be coming for us," Shay added. "They know we can expose what they are really doing—so they've got to get rid of us."

Fenfang had questions, lots of them: how Odin got into the lab, how Cade and Cruz got involved. They explained about Twist—an affluent artist who lived and worked in a hotel of sorts that sheltered street kids in Los Angeles. Shay had been lucky to land there in her search for Odin, as Cade and Cruz had been when they'd needed shelter from their own messy lives.

When Fenfang asked how long they'd been fighting Singular, Shay was stunned to realize that it had been less than two months. These people who'd helped her rescue her brother, these people she'd lay down her life for—she'd known them less than two months.

Fenfang said, "I would kill myself rather than go back there. Are we secure now?"

Twist said, "Maybe. When we ran out of Sacramento, we were

acting almost randomly. We didn't know where we were going—so I don't know how Singular could know."

Odin shook his head at Twist. "Don't underestimate them. They found me and the group I worked with after we trashed the lab, and we were really careful. They're probably doing psych studies on us, and who knows what other resources they have? All kinds of places have license plate scanners, and if they can tap into that . . . Shay came here in West's Jeep."

Twist nodded then. "We need to move soon. We're too close to Sacramento."

"Where to?" Shay asked.

"We should talk about that," Twist said. He looked at Fenfang and then Odin. "First . . . you guys must be hungry."

"I hadn't thought about it, but I am," said Odin. "They never gave me anything to eat except some rice and biscuits."

Fenfang nodded. "I would eat anything. But steamed fish and zongzi especially."

"Zongzi?" Cruz asked.

"Hmm . . . rice that is wrapped in bamboo leaves? You know? With maybe salted duck eggs or pork bellies."

"I don't know if Reno does Chinese that authentic, but we'll see what we can find," Twist said. "We can talk about where to go while we eat."

Suddenly Fenfang's eyelids began to flutter, and she slipped back on the bed and began to shake. Twist said, "Oh, Jesus, here she goes again. . . ."

But after less than a minute, the shaking stopped, and her eyes popped open, with a disoriented look that slowly came to focus on the group.

"That wasn't so bad," Cade said.

"Maybe they're subsiding . . . the fits," Twist said.

Fenfang rubbed her forehead, as if thinking over the possibility. "Maybe."

There was a loud slapping noise, and Shay turned to see that her brother was flapping his arms, something he'd done since childhood when he was upset. His face grew flushed, and one of his legs started to stomp in time with his arms.

"Odin, everything's all right," Shay said, trying to soothe him. "Odin—"

"I—I—I can't stand what they did! What they did to Fenfang, and to the monkeys, and to the rats, and to X, and to the Xs they hurt before him. He's X-5, that's what they tattooed on his ear— what if they started with *A* and they experimented on ten or fifty or a hundred dogs for every letter? *X* is the twenty-fourth letter—"

"Odin, stop," Shay said, and turned him away from Fenfang to mouth more emphatically, *You're scaring her, stop.* That got Odin's attention, and his face screwed up with effort as he pulled in his arms and unclenched his fists.

Shay turned back to Fenfang, expecting to have to explain, but instead, Fenfang was busy propping herself up against the pillow. Twist reached in to assist her, and she said, "I want to stand up."

Shay: "Are you sure?"

"Yes."

Twist pulled a hundred-dollar bill out of his pocket and handed it to Cade. "You and Cruz hit a Chinese takeout. Shay and Odin and I will stay with Fenfang."

Cade and Cruz went out, and Shay and Odin helped Fenfang to her feet and walked her around the motel room. Eventually—there was no avoiding it—she stopped and looked at herself in the tall dresser mirror, Shay and Odin reflected on either side.

"This isn't how I thought it would be," she said, almost to herself. "I'd like to see the back." She turned sideways and sighed at the cap of wires and the bundle at her neck. Then she turned again, toward the center of the room, done.

"If you don't mind," she said, and unhooked her elbows from Shay and Odin, "I can do this myself." She started another loop around the room, solid enough on her feet to not fall down, though always using a chair, a bed, or a wall to keep herself upright. She sat down a few times and stood up and touched her head, the connectors sparkling in the overhead lights.

Shay said to Twist, "I can tell you one thing: she needs a wig. Like, right now."

"We need to find one of those cancer places," Odin said.

Shay took a prepaid phone out of her back jeans pocket, and the knife she'd carried since Eugene out of her waistband. She tossed them both on the opposite bed and then sat down with West's iPad to search for a wig shop.

While Twist and Odin watched over her shoulder, Fenfang picked up a motel guide from the desktop. "Where are we?" she asked.

Shay answered, "Reno, Nevada. Where there are a surprising number of wig shops. Let's figure out which one is the closest."

Fenfang said, "I need to . . . ," and walked carefully toward the bathroom.

Twist told Shay and Odin he'd been thinking of calling Lou, one of the two women he'd left in charge of his hotel for street kids. He had a stash of cash hidden in his studio, and he was trying to figure out how Lou could get it to them.

Shay put a finger to her lips. "Listen."

Faintly, they could hear Fenfang in the bathroom, talking in a low voice. Shay looked over at the other bed and said, "She's got my phone . . . and my knife."

She jumped off the bed and stepped over to the door, Twist right behind her. Together, they heard the young woman they'd rescued saying:

"Hurry. Something bad is happening to this body, you have to hurry. Get me away from these people. . . ."

"What the hell?" Twist said, and rapped his cane on the door. "Fenfang? Open up."

She didn't answer him, but went on talking, her voice going to a whisper. Shay reached out to try the knob—"Is it locked?"—and when it turned, she pushed inside. . . .

"Careful," Twist said from behind, "the knife . . ."

Fenfang, sitting on the toilet lid, tried to get to her feet but staggered, nearly losing her balance. Shay lunged for the phone, but Fenfang swung her other arm around with the knife, and Shay jumped back just enough to avoid being slashed, then Twist hooked Fenfang's knife arm and wrenched it until she screamed in pain and dropped the knife. Shay snatched the phone.

"Who'd you call?" Twist asked as he held Fenfang from behind, pinning her arms.

"I won't tell you a thing," she sneered.

Shay, checking her phone and the last number dialed, said, "It's a California number, the same area code as West's phone number. The same prefix . . . Did she call Singular?"

"Jesus," Twist said. "Fenfang, did you call Singular? Fenfang?"

"It's *not* Fenfang," said Odin, who'd come up behind them. "Don't you get it? The other woman made the call. The one fighting for control."

The young woman looked up at Odin and smiled. She said, "And I have—"

Then her eyes rolled back in her head, and she started thrashing against Twist's arms.

2

When Sync and Harmon entered the suite at the Four Seasons in San Francisco, Thorne was standing at the living room window, staring out over the city, hands in his pants pockets. Micah Cartwell, the CEO of Singular, was sitting on an easy chair in the bedroom, behind closed French doors, talking on a cell phone with military grade scrambling software.

Sync, Harmon, and Thorne were big men with scars showing lives of conflict—they might have been professional athletes, tall, tough, competent. Cartwell was shorter and rounder, but had the same alpha-male aura. Sync was Singular's security chief, and worked directly for Cartwell. Harmon was an intelligence coordinator, Thorne ran the enforcement section, and both reported to Sync.

A silver tray of carefully cut triangle sandwiches sat on a round table at one side of the room, with a half-dozen bottles of Perrier in a silver ice bucket. The room had been rented for one night with a credit card that would bill Boeing Aircraft, though Boeing didn't know about it, and never would.

Sync nodded at Thorne and said, "Where are we in Sacramento?"

Thorne stepped away from the window. Early thirties, with close-cropped hair and narrow-set pale eyes, he was at least a decade younger than the other men, and aggressively ambitious. He was limping, but his expression gave nothing to the lingering pain in his leg.

"Basement's remodeled and scrubbed, new doors up and down the hallways," he said. "As soon as the cops left, we brought in a couple of semitrucks full of lab equipment and some door plaques from Staples that say SECURE STORAGE. Some smart-ass on the crime scene crew wanted to keep us out of the lobby for a while, but we talked to his boss. . . ."

"The cops didn't hear anything from the Rembys?"

Thorne shook his head. "No. Nobody's heard from them. If they'd told the cops that the shootings were down in the basement, and not up in the lobby, and the cops had gone down there and found the cells . . . we'd be toast."

"But now?"

"We're good for now," Thorne said. "We're blaming everything on West. He had a drug problem, result of his war wounds, went a little crazy. . . . The media's buying it. We might have trouble with his father, but his father doesn't know anything about the media. We can send out signals about the grieving father being a bit unbalanced, and contain that."

Sync nodded and said, "Good. That's good. We've started playing down the Remby connection. We don't want the wrong cops picking them up, especially not if the Chinese girl is with them."

Thorne kept talking: "We've got to come up with another solution for the experimental subjects. This was too close. We survived by the skin of our teeth."

Sync asked, "How in the hell could a couple of kids and some flaky artist pull us under?"

Thorne bristled: "We can't think of them that way. They're not kids or flakes; they're the enemy. Same mistake we made when we went into the Twist Hotel and got our asses kicked."

The fight in the hotel had given Thorne the gimpy leg.

"That might be overcooking it a little," Harmon said. Harmon was wearing a conventional blue business suit and dress loafers, in place of his usual jeans and cowboy boots. Here, two blocks from the financial district, the idea was to look like everyone else, even if Harmon, with his desert-weathered face and hands, and the mirrored aviators, looked like a stockbroker who could pull your arms off.

"Maybe what we need is negotiation," Sync offered. "If we can talk to them, impress them with how unbeatable we are, every resource on our side, maybe we can get the flash drives and make them go away. Without any outside proof, anything they could tell the police would sound like a fantasy."

Cartwell had gotten off the phone and pushed through the French doors in time to hear the last of Sync's suggestion. He was wearing a thin pair of reading glasses, which he took off and slipped into the breast pocket of his suit. "You're half right," he said. "We need to find them and the experimental subject, and do what we can—anything we can—to get the flash drives. We know that Odin Remby cracked at least one. Now that he's back with them, they might be able to crack the rest. So, if they'll talk, we'll talk. If they'll negotiate, we'll negotiate. If they won't do any of that, we'll hunt them down."

Thorne: "How can we trust them? Odin Remby's an animal

rights maniac, and he has some pretty heavy computer skills. If he has the chance to get more videos out there, he'll do it. He's a hard case: didn't even crack under the waterboarding."

Cartwell broke in, impatient: "We don't trust them, not a god-damn inch. We talk if we can, we negotiate if we can. We promise them everything they ask for, and we get the drives, and then we get rid of them."

This was why they'd rented the room with the Boeing credit card: so nobody, ever, could put them here, together, talking about murder.

After a moment of silence, Harmon said, "That might be prob-lematic."

Cartwell snapped: "You going soft on us, Harmon? Like West did?"

Harmon had been a Special Forces sergeant in Afghanistan. There was nothing soft about him, and the comment burned. West had been a good man, a soldier who lost his legs in the same crappy war.

"I'm not soft on anybody," Harmon said. "But killing people—a whole group of people—is not easy to pass off in this country. If it's not done all at once, the survivors will be screaming bloody murder to the press. You might have noticed, they've got some media skills, too. The artist does. On the other hand, if you kill them all at once, we're talking about a massacre. That tends to catch the eye."

Cartwell waved a hand at him. "You guys get paid to sort these things out. We almost got our ship sunk this morning. This group—the enemy—they're dangerous. We can't leave them out there."

Sync said, "I agree they've got to go. It'll take some staging, but we can work it out. A van goes into a canyon, the artist maybe over-doses. . . . It can be done."

Thorne nodded. "First we've got to find them."

Harmon started to speak, "I'm not so—" but Sync cut him off: "About those flash drives, the copies that Odin Remby made. The originals were DARPA specials, which is about the only thing Janes got right. They have two levels of encryption—Remby got lucky with one level when he found the decryption software on Janes's office computer. The second level he broke with . . . well, he somehow worked through Janes's personal password.

"But the files are embedded in software that only allows one copy. So, if we get the copies they have, there won't be any more of them. That threat would be over. Janes said that at least three of the flash drives had been copied once, so those are already dead."

"That helps," Cartwell said.

Sync continued, "There's a possibility, a remote possibility, that they'll contact Janes to try to break the other passwords if they can't do it themselves. We can't put full-time surveillance on Janes's house, because of where he lives—it'd be noticed by the neighbors and there'd be questions. But if the Rembys go there, we've set up a little surprise for them."

They talked about that, and Cartwell asked, "What about this Chinese girl? If anybody outside the company stuck her head in an X-ray machine, we'd have a problem. If the Chinese government ever found out that the Koreans had kidnapped Chinese citizens and used them as lab subjects . . . the problem might be unstoppable."

Sync said, "I've been working on that. We've got no direct control over her, so my thought is, we build a backtrail for her. One that doesn't involve us. We've got her Chinese passport. We fly it into Canada with a look-alike, with an appointment with a neurosurgeon. Then she tries to walk it across the border to the U.S., without the right documents. They turn her around and she disappears. Maybe leaves some personal stuff in a Canadian hotel room. If she turns up here, it'll look like she crossed the border illegally—"

"The point being?" Cartwell asked.

"The point being that we didn't have her and never did. She'll have a trail that the cops can follow. If she turns up with the Rembys or this Twist character, and they try to connect her to us, we'll have evidence that they hooked up long after Sacramento. That we had nothing to do with the shit in her head."

Cartwell peered at him and scraped his top teeth over his lower lip a few times, a nervous tic. Then he said, "That's not optimal, but it's better than anything else I've heard. Get that going."

"I already have," Sync said. "A Chinese woman will fly into Vancouver tomorrow morning with the girl's passport. If you need to veto it, you've got about"—he checked his watch—"two hours. She should be heading for the Hong Kong airport about now."

Cartwell nodded. "Good. Go with it." He turned to Harmon. "What are we doing to locate them?"

"We're looking for West's Jeep. We're looking at the phone numbers we know, but they're staying off the phones. And we're doing all the other routine checks for credit cards and Internet accounts that they're known to use. The problem is, we don't know which way they went. I figure they either headed back to Los Angeles, where they've got support, or they just took off. If they just took off, it's most likely they headed for Nevada. It would be a logical move for them, if they thought the police were looking for them, to get across a state line or two."

"You think it's possible that they headed back to Oregon?" Thorne asked.

"Possible, but less likely," Harmon said. "Our early research showed that the Rembys didn't have the kind of personal connections that would provide them with hideouts, other than Odin Remby's connection to Storm. Most of the group's members are now in jail, except for Rachel Wharton, and she hasn't gone back to Oregon. No, I think they went east or south. I've got guys watching the Twist Hotel, and depending on what we decide here, I could send some men to Nevada or wherever else they might turn up. Right now, my guys are mostly looking at computer screens."

Cartwell: "Computer screens. What about this website they set up, Mindkill?"

"We blocked it," said Sync. "They can get it back up, but they haven't, yet. Our problem is, they ran it through a Swedish Web provider that mostly supports pirate sites. The provider has very tight controls. We don't have the technical ability or the political clout to eliminate the site altogether. But we can keep messing with it."

Cartwell said, "Okay. We've sealed off the Sacramento problem, we're distancing ourselves from the missing experimental subject, we're hunting down the Rembys. Now, what are we going to do about the other experimental subjects? We need a secure facility."

They'd been standing up as they talked, and now they moved to the chairs, and Cartwell and Sync picked up sandwiches. Sync said, "There are a whole lot of conflicting requirements when you start talking about a dedicated holding facility. First of all, you need anonymity. There are a couple of different ways you can go with that. . . ."

They talked about it as the sun went down, running the company, and the search, from their encrypted cell phones. Since the holding facility would function as a disguised prison, and would require armed guards to move the experimental subjects when needed, Cartwell delegated the search for a new facility to Thorne, who would run it, with oversight from Sync. Sync suggested that Thorne look closely at Stockton, California, a large but nearly bankrupt city with a tiny police force. Stockton was convenient to Singular's San Francisco–area headquarters, as well as the Sacramento research center.

They were still talking about it when Cartwell's phone buzzed. He looked at the screen of his secure phone and frowned: the number was unknown. That just didn't happen. He hesitated, then punched answer. "Hello."

A woman's voice, weak, thready, tentative. "This is Charlotte. Help me. Help me."

Cartwell said, "Who is this?"

He listened for another twenty seconds, heard commotion on the other end, and then the connection broke off.

Cartwell said, "Jesus," and stared at the phone.

Sync: "What?"

Cartwell looked at the others. "She said she was Charlotte Dash. Dash has this number—but it wasn't her. She sounded foreign."

Sync blurted, "It's the Chinese girl! She was implanted with the Dash persona. We know some of it took; the whole reason we brought her here was to try to figure out how much."

"But she's—"

Harmon: "With the Rembys. Could the implanted personality have enough control to call us? Or is that crazy?"

Cartwell said, "It's somewhat crazy, but not entirely. We've had hints of things like this. Oh, Christ, she said something about her bones. . . ."

Harmon said, "Give it to us, word for word. Best you can."

"She was so damn hard to understand. She said she was Charlotte, but she sounded . . . Mandarin," Cartwell said. "But she would . . . wouldn't she?"

Sync nodded. "Language and accent are separate. . . ."

"Then she said 'Help' or 'Help me,' " Cartwell said. "She said that a couple of times. And then something about . . . her bones? The bones? Something like that."

"Bones," Thorne repeated. "Could that be code for something?"

Cartwell cocked his head. "Code? I don't know, maybe. Nothing I know about. But we know the girl has seizures—maybe she's hurt."

Sync pressed his hands together. "This could be a break."

Cartwell was less certain. "If it really was this escapee . . . can we figure out where she was calling from?"

Harmon said, "Give me ten minutes." He took Cartwell's phone and walked into the bedroom, pulling a laptop from his briefcase.

Cartwell turned to Sync. "Should I call Charlotte?"

"You know her better than I do," Sync said. "If she knew there was a Dash double out there, how would she react?"

Cartwell rubbed the side of his face, thinking, then said, "I don't know. She's got half a billion dollars with us so far, and she's already had two rounds of chemo, so she knows we're working on her as a priority. But the reality of what that means—"

"Is she stable?" Sync asked. "Mentally stable?"

"She's got a lot going on. The cancer, the stink from her husband's hedge fund, and trying to work out his estate . . ." He did the lip-scraping thing again, then: "Maybe we'll let it go for now. Admitting we lost the girl won't inspire a lot of confidence."

They were still talking about it when Harmon came in from the bedroom and handed Cartwell his phone back. "She's in Reno," he said. "The Bones Motel and Casino. Some kind of low-rent place on the edge of town."

Sync: "The Bones?"

"Like in 'rolling the bones'—rolling the dice," Harmon said.

Thorne punched the air with his fist, then looked past Sync and Harmon at Cartwell. "Give me the jet, Micah, I can have a team there in two hours."

"You've got it," Cartwell said. "Let's get this done."

"We will," Thorne said, and walked away, already on his phone.

3

The seizure on the bathroom floor lasted ninety seconds, with Twist holding Fenfang's wire-plaited head in his lap and twice taking a bony elbow to the windpipe: like getting hit with a fire poker. Both jabs hurt, and when she finally went still and her eyelids fluttered, he croaked, "What'd you tell Singular? Are they coming?"

"I . . . What?" she said. Her eyes were cloudy, dazed. "How am I here?"

Odin, crouched to one side of her with the spit-soaked washcloth, looked back and forth between Twist and his sister, who'd held down the young woman's legs, and said, "She didn't make the call, okay? It's not her fault."

Shay said, "Hey! Odin! Singular murdered our friend. They tortured you, and you almost died. I don't want to hear any crap about whose fault is whose. If she's on their side, we're gonna drop her in a ditch and keep going."

"I am on *your* side," she said softly.

Shay glared at the Chinese girl and held out her recovered knife. "Yeah? Who used my phone? Who tried to stab me?"

Cade and Cruz came crashing through the door, called back by Shay during the seizure. Fenfang struggled with her question and said, "I do not know about a knife. I would not hurt you; it is my promise. This must be Charlotte. I am Fenfang."

Odin, his face reddening, tried again. "It's like when that beaten-down Asian guy on File 12 says he's Robert G. Morris of St. Louis—that's who he is. Whether he exists as himself anymore, or they killed those memories, we don't know. One thing we do know"—he touched the center of the young woman's forehead—"Fenfang from Dandong is still here."

Fenfang clasped his hand in gratitude. "Yes," she said.

Twist said, "All right. But . . . who is Charlotte?"

Fenfang turned toward him. "I do not know. I know Charlotte. I know some things about her, but they are more facts than memories. Names . . . and many numbers . . . she is one hundred thirty-six pounds, her house is 524. I know her house security codes, her business security codes; she has passwords, she has telephone numbers."

Odin took Shay's phone out of her hands, found the last outgoing call, and showed it to Fenfang: "You know this number?"

She squinted at it and said, "I know the name with it: Cartwell."

Twist said, "Cartwell is Singular's CEO. She went right to the top." Cade glanced at the door and said, "We gotta get out of here."

"Yes, but not in two minutes," Cruz said. "We have a little time before he could do anything."

Twist said, "If she's got all these security measures, if she's talking to Cartwell, she's probably one of Singular's backers."

"I do not know this Cartwell, only the number," Fenfang said. "I know another important number has the name White. Another important number is Jackson. I know eight of these numbers with names."

Cade opened his laptop. "Fenfang, give me those phone numbers."

She was getting some strength back and pushed herself up on her elbows and rattled off a string of eight phone numbers. Cade typed them, and Odin went to stand over his shoulder. Odin asked, "Where are you?"

"Twenty-two Hornet," Cade said.

Odin patted his shoulder. "Okay."

A minute later, as Twist and Shay got Fenfang to her feet, Cade said, "That White number? That's the office phone for Harry White, the U.S. Senate majority leader."

"Shit," Twist said.

"Got her," Cade said. "Charlotte Coulter Dash . . ."

"Holy cats," Twist said. "*Senator* Dash?"

"Yup," said Cade, who was already skimming her Wiki page. "Charlotte Coulter Dash is the senior U.S. senator from New Mexico. Second-term Democrat, age forty-eight. Her husband, Huck Dash, ran a hedge fund called Hondo Investments until last December, when he croaked. Dude was like the forty-ninth-richest human on the planet. Says she's a member of the Senate Select Committee on Intelligence; there's a photo of her on Fox News."

Twist slapped his forehead. "She's in charge of our spies."

"Merry Christmas and happy birthday," Cruz said. "Now let's get out of here before the FBI arrives." He surveyed the room. "If you guys pack, I'll wipe everything down."

Fenfang: "Wipe?"

"Fingerprints," he said. He turned to Shay and asked, "Where's the phone she used?"

"It's the one I bought this morning," Shay said.

Cruz took it from her, got the steel bolt cutters, and used them to snap it in half. The others watched, caught a little off guard by the destruction, though X, standing next to Cruz, seemed completely calm about it. Cruz said, "We won't make the mistake of using it again."

"Where we going?" Odin asked.

Twist was already on the iPad, looking at maps. "Las Vegas. We can be there in seven hours."

"Why Vegas?" Cade asked as he began gathering up computer gear.

"Because it's big and it's full of tourists coming and going and it has about a million motels," said Twist. "Plus, it's only about four hours from L.A., where we've got help if we need it."

"Maybe we should dump the Jeep," Cade said. "West's plates could give us away."

"I'd like to keep it if we can," said Shay, and Twist heard the slight choke in her voice. "It's got some capabilities you don't have in a Camry. No offense, Toyota."

Cruz caught Shay's eye and spoke to her directly: "Plates won't be a problem. I'll take care of it."

They were ready to go in ten minutes. Cruz, the tattooed, muscular ex–gang member, sounding like a mom—"Don't touch that. Don't touch that, *Jesucristo,* don't touch that!"—and wiping behind them.

"Fenfang's awfully visible," Odin said. The Chinese girl was watching them all from the bed, still barefoot and wrapped in the dead-gray hospital smock.

"Wig shop," Shay said. "I'll go in; her head's about the same size as mine. Then we'll stop at a mall—I saw one on my way here. Anybody needs anything, we can get it there."

"I'll need to swing by the airport," said Cruz.

Shay tilted her head at him, but Twist understood the purpose right away and answered: "Plates." Cruz nodded and Twist said, "Okay, then, who's driving what?"

Cruz, X, and Shay took the Jeep, headed for Reno-Tahoe International, while the others, in the sedan and the pickup, drove to the mall.

The second level of the airport garage was long-term parking; Shay cruised it until they spotted another Jeep Rubicon, but Cruz said, "Keep going."

"Why?"

"Because it has Nevada plates. If we look, we'll find one from California."

"Why California?"

"Because we've got California plates," he said. "If we stick with the same state, it'll take the owner of the other car longer to notice the change."

They found a California Rubicon in the next row. Cruz changed out the plates and climbed back in.

The next stop was fast and expensive. They paid four hundred dollars for a jet-black natural-hair wig that fit snugly over Shay's thick, chin-length hair. Shay said that her mother had lost her hair to chemotherapy and didn't want to go anywhere until she had some hair back.

"She doesn't have to be embarrassed, honey," said the nice lady who ran the shop. "We deal with this all the time. We've put wigs on the showgirls here, and nobody ever knew."

• • •

When they got to the shopping center, they found Cade, Odin, and Twist leaning against the pickup. Cruz pulled into a parking space as close as he could, and Shay and X climbed out, with Cruz a few steps behind them. "Where's Fenfang?" Shay asked.

Twist poked a thumb toward the Camry. "Trying her new clothes."

Shay leaned toward him. "There're no phones in there?"

"No. We made sure of that."

Behind them, the back door of the Camry opened, and Fenfang, wearing a yellow shirt, khaki pants, and red high-tops, struggled to get out. Odin hurried over to help, and she told him, "My legs . . . the nerves . . . something is not correct."

"Hey, don't get out yet," Shay called. Fenfang sat with her legs dangling out of the door, and Shay helped her with the wig. After a few twists and tugs, they got it in place, and Fenfang, straight, shiny hair falling to her shoulders, said, "Yes?"

Shay stepped back. "Yes."

Fenfang rubbed a lock between her fingers and said, "It is only a costume, but . . . I feel better."

"I'm glad," Shay said.

Odin gave a thumbs-up over Shay's shoulder, and for the first time, Fenfang smiled.

Cruz said he needed to grab something inside the mall. Cade nudged Shay and asked, "When was the last time you ate anything? Like, maybe, yesterday morning?" Shay shrugged: since losing West, she hadn't thought about food except to get a burger for her dog.

"C'mon," Cade said. "You won't be any good to us if you don't put something in your stomach." Shay reluctantly agreed to go to the food court with him, they'd get sandwiches for everybody. Odin said he was coming, too, that Shay wouldn't know a vegetarian sandwich "if it bit her in the butt."

Twist said he'd keep Fenfang company and took charge of X's leash.

"You wanna sit or you wanna practice walking a bit with a gimp and a mutt?" Twist asked Fenfang. Fenfang pushed herself off the backseat and said she'd like to walk. Twist worked the leash and cane in one hand and offered her the crook of his other elbow. She held on lightly and asked, "What is your problem for this cane? You had it when you saved us, so it is from before, yes?"

"Yes, but it's nothing, really. An old . . . sports injury," he said. "Now let's talk about you."

They took a lap around the parking lot, with Twist gently probing about her life back in China. She told him that she'd grown up working seven days a week with her parents on the family rice farm, that they'd never been more than a few months out of debt. There'd been a brother, the firstborn, but he'd died as a toddler. She'd been studying computer science at university and hoped to get a "dream job" with an American-based company in Dandong that would pay her enough that her parents could retire.

"We live with my grandparents, my other relations, too. My best friend from when I was little is always Liko. We were born on the same day."

Twist had been preoccupied with so many details about the raid and their escape over the last few hours, it hadn't occurred to him that Fenfang might have family back in China that they should contact. He stopped and turned to her.

"Your parents—is there a way to contact them? Email? Phone?" He held up his phone. "We'd have to get you a different phone, one that allows international calls."

Fenfang let go of Twist, and after some serious thought, she said,

35

"My family will think I am dead, it has been so long. If I contact them now . . . I do not want to make danger for them."

Twist nodded. "I understand. But . . . think about it. You might send them a message of some sort to ease their minds. Let them know you're alive."

Fenfang looked at him and said, "We will see how my life develops."

She took his arm to walk again, and turned the conversation back on Twist. "It is very strange that you should be with Shay and Odin. As if they are *your* family. But you do not know each other long."

Twist was taken aback by Fenfang's directness—but liked it.

"You're right. It is very strange, but Shay isn't somebody you brush off. Never met anyone quite like her. She's got a nose like granite."

"Granite?"

"It's a rock."

"I do not understand your idiom," Fenfang said.

"She's tough. She's made herself tough. Odin . . . he's what is called a high-functioning autistic. That means—"

"I know this," Fenfang said. "That may be true with me, also."

"Okay. Well, their parents got killed, and they were taken in by their grandmother, and when she died, they were moved along to a state agency that takes care of orphans. Odin got involved with computers as a child, and with that peculiar focus that autistic kids can bring to their interests, he's . . . sort of a genius, I guess. But he's not very socially adept. Shay had always looked out for him, you know, and when he took off after the raid on the lab, she worried he couldn't handle it out in the world, especially not in hiding from Singular. She followed him to L.A., and that's where I met her. They are very unusual people. Both of them."

"I think you are, too," Fenfang said.

"Weird's more like it," said Twist. "I don't try to be, but that's just the way it is. If you're weird, you gotta live with it."

"I think I am also weird."

"Good," said Twist. "Because you know what? When any worthwhile thing is done in the world, it's usually done by somebody weird."

Fifteen minutes later, Cade, Cruz, Shay, and Odin were back at their cars with bags of food, a pillow, and an evolving plan. Cade would leave the group and drive to Salt Lake City, where he would send a reply to the message on the BlackWallpaper Facebook page. Singular's security experts would track it and, with any luck, conclude that the Rembys, the artist from L.A., and the girl with two brains were hiding out in Salt Lake.

"Need to decide exactly what we want to say," Cade said.

Shay scowled. "What's there to say besides 'Go to hell'?"

"I'm not sure it matters what we say," said Twist. "The point is just to ping them from a state we're not in."

Cade said, "They were careful and cryptic in their note to us because they're afraid we'll go to the police, and they want deniability. We should think the same way."

"No. Tell them the truth," Odin broke in. "Tell them I'm going to crack all the flash drives and spam the FBI and the CIA and the networks with them."

"Let's not do that just yet," said Twist. "We need to think about what we'll do next. So, Cade, let's string them along in this first contact. Like Odin says, we tell them the truth, something that they'll buy—tell them we need time to think things over."

Cade raised an eyebrow at Shay, and she shrugged. "Yeah, sure, tell 'em that."

"Gotta fly," Cruz said, and jingled a set of keys.

"Who's the pillow for?" Twist asked, eyeing a bag in Cruz's hand.

Cruz tipped his head at Shay. "She's gotta sleep sooner or later."

Cade would take the pickup; Twist, Odin, and Fenfang, the car; and Shay, Cruz, and X would go in the Jeep. After a round of hugs, they drove in a convoy back to I-80, then east on I-80 to Fernley, where Cade went his lonesome way up the interstate and the others turned south on Highway 95.

Cruz and Shay talked about Singular for a while, and about Fenfang, then Shay yawned and said, "You got me figured out. Where's that pillow?"

She hadn't slept in two days, and when her head hit the pillow, scrunched against the window, she was out. But not in peace. The scene in the prison, with West bleeding on the floor, looking up at her, pain in his eyes, urging her to save herself, ran through her subconscious like a tangled loop of film, in full Technicolor and surround sound.

She moaned in her sleep, and shook, and Cruz was tempted to wake her, but he didn't; he rested a hand on her leg and drove on. When Shay opened her eyes, finally, it was to more Technicolor and surround sound. This time, for real.

X was in the back, looking out the window. He'd slept as soundly as Shay. He yawned at her, turned again to the window, and yipped at all the brilliant lights outside.

Vegas.

4

Twist called a few minutes after Shay woke up, said he'd found a place: the Moulin Rose, a dumpy casino a couple of blocks off the Strip. It was a squat six-story structure with a lonely valet out front, looking for cars. "How does Twist find these places?" Shay asked.

Cruz shook his head. "He's got a talent for it. He's rich enough for Beverly Hills, but he lives in a Hollywood fleabag."

The lobby of the Moulin Rose smelled like lilac perfume and beer, the carpet tacky underfoot. When they walked in, X was on his leash, the phony service-dog tag clipped to his collar. The guy behind the desk didn't blink, and Shay got the impression they could've come in with an alligator.

Twist had managed to find three rooms in a row, with connecting doors from one to the next. Also uniting them was an easy-wash vinyl décor, from the furniture to the garish floral wallpaper. Odin was sitting on a brown vinyl couch in an end room, looking at Twist's laptop. He had one of the stolen flash drives plugged into a USB port and was probing it. He did not look happy.

"Hey, bro," Shay said as she crossed the room, relieved to have Odin in her sights again. "Where's Fenfang?"

"Down at the other end," Odin said. "C'mon next door." They moved into the center room, where Twist was reading a newspaper.

"Nothing in the news about Sacramento," he said.

Cruz flopped onto the room's red vinyl couch. "This'll work."

He'd let Shay sleep the entire way, and Shay said, "Yeah, your turn—we'll get out of your way."

Odin said, "I have the first four letters of the password on drive six. *Y-E-L-L,* like in *yellow,* or *yells.*"

"Do we know how many letters?" Shay asked.

"Sixteen," he said. He looked at her expectantly.

"What?"

"C'mon. You're the one that does this," he said. "What is it?"

"Yellow Rose of Texas?" Twist suggested.

"Too many letters," Shay said.

"How do you know? Let's count them off," Twist said. He counted them on his fingers and came up with seventeen.

"You're sure it's not seventeen?" he asked Odin.

"It's sixteen," Odin said patiently. "That's an entirely different number than seventeen."

"All right, smart-asses, you figure it out," Twist said.

"We will, but later," Shay said. "Now, if you two don't mind, I want to take a shower."

"Go," Twist said. He said to Odin, "I'll take the other end room. The Twister doesn't share. One of the beds here is yours; Cade and Cruz can work out who gets the other bed, who takes the couch."

"Looks like Cruz already has the couch," Shay said.

She turned toward the room where Fenfang was sleeping, and Odin said, "Hang on a minute."

"Mmm?"

"Fenfang doesn't have a phone. If Dash takes over again, she might try to run for it, so, without telling her, I wired your door shut—the chain on the door," Odin said. "If she tries to get out that way, she'll make some noise. You've got to be listening for it."

Shay nodded. "We've made her a prisoner again."

"Yeah, and I hate it," Odin said. "Fenfang's a nice person, but Dash is ruthless. We can't forget."

Shay took her shower and let hot water pour down on the back of her neck for five minutes. She'd left the door open so she could see Fenfang on the bed, still sleeping. She washed her hair, or what was left of it. She hardly felt like herself without her long red mane. It'd grow back—that piece of her could be the same again someday. She wondered about the other pieces.

As she was toweling off, she closed her eyes, lined up sixteen boxes in her mind. She'd been running the password problem somewhere beneath all her other thoughts. She counted letters.

Sixteen.

When she was dressed again, she watched Fenfang softly snoring for a moment, then knocked quietly on the connecting door. There was no answer, and when she went through, Cruz was asleep on the couch. She could faintly hear men's voices from the other end room, knocked quietly on that door, and heard Odin say, "Yeah?"

She pushed through, nodded at Twist, and sat next to her brother on the bed. "Where's the password block?"

Odin touched a couple of keys, and it came up. She typed in the words that had appeared in the boxes in her mind; the flash drive opened up.

Odin said, "I got the first part of that. . . ."

Shay said, "Willamette Valley—spelled backward."

Odin nodded. "Should have thought of that." The man who'd thought up the passwords lived in the Willamette Valley, in Oregon, as had Odin and Shay.

Twist, who'd been sewing a button back on his sport coat, cut the thread with his teeth and said, "Willamette Valley, spelled backward. That's so obvious, we all should have thought of it."

"I know," Odin said. "I've been sort of preoccupied—"

"I was joking, Odin," Twist said.

"Oh." Odin was mystified: didn't see the joke.

Twist shook his head. "You know, you guys really do scare the shit out of me sometimes."

Shay said, "Whatever. Let's see what's on the drive—"

Odin clicked a few keys, got a list: 1,124 files.

"Gonna take a while," Odin said. He began clicking through the files and found experimental reports, some only a paragraph long, others several pages long, all in dense scientific language—some pure chemistry, others on cellular biology, more on electrochemical reactions. None of it comprehensible to the three of them.

"Gotta be important—but we'd have to get specialists to look at it," Odin said. "Tell you what, I'll go through these, see if there's anything here that's a plain-language report. When we go public, we could dump these on the Mindkill site and crowd-source the interpretation. If we could get enough people interested, we could probably pull together a good interpretation in a few days."

"That's all fine, except . . . maybe we don't want people to know the details?" Twist said. "If we put too much of this research out there, are we inviting somebody else to pick up where Singular left off?"

Shay exchanged a look with Odin, and they both nodded. "That is a problem. I never thought of it quite like that," Odin said.

"We need a few people we can trust to go through it," Shay said. "I don't know where we'd find them, though."

"Maybe it's for later," Twist said. "We don't need the research data right now. We need something that screams at people, that you'd see on YouTube and the television networks—like when Shay rappelled down that building, like when we hijacked the Hollywood sign. This research—this will hang them in the end, but right now we're looking for photos and video that'll go viral overnight."

Odin nodded. "Here's another problem: I'm not operating at full strength—I need to get my computer back. My girlfriend . . . well, my ex, anyway . . . Rachel probably has it. When everything was getting crazy, I was afraid we'd get separated, so I put a program on her computer that will let me pinpoint her, if she's using it. If I can get back on the Net, I think I could find her."

"We could wait to use Cade's computer, or we could go out and get any kind of computer you need—" Twist began.

Odin shook his head. "Mine's got years of software on it. Tools. That software's a major resource. The problem is, Singular could be watching Rachel, waiting for me to get in touch. It's a risk."

"And you're not sure she even has your computer?"

"Well, we know she didn't get picked up by the feds, and if she's running, she would have taken it. I really need the software."

"By software, you mean hacker stuff," Twist said.

"Tools. We'll have invisible access to lots of powerful databases. Like, if Singular is tracking us and flies its people to Vegas . . . I've got the airline databases, and I've got all the car rental companies."

"All right, we'll get a laptop and you can take a look," Twist said. "If she's anywhere close by, we'll see what we can do."

They talked for a while longer, then Cruz came in, yawned, scratched his chest, and said, "That nap sucked. What are we doing?"

"Going shopping," Twist said.

Twist and Cruz went out to get a computer, pizzas, and Pepsi, and Odin and Shay moved into the middle room, where they could hear Fenfang if she woke.

Odin continued digging through the newly opened flash drive, and Shay went through West's briefcase. Before they'd attacked the Singular prison, they'd left anything that Singular might find useful—phones, laptops, iPads, wallets—in the getaway cars, in case they should be captured.

Shay opened West's wallet, and the first thing she saw was his driver's license. His intelligent brown eyes looked straight at her, just as they had in their first meeting at her foster parents' house, back when the future seemed so simple. Finish school, go to college, get a job. . . . She'd liked West, though she hadn't wanted to at the time.

The rest of the wallet was routine—credit cards, membership cards to a couple of San Francisco museums, and a key card. Shay tossed it over to Odin, who examined it and said, "Not been used much. Probably for a parking structure. Could be for an office door, but that's unlikely. Could be useful. I'll keep it."

Shay nodded; if there was one thing Odin knew how to manipulate to spectacular effect, it was a key card. It was how he'd helped Storm break into the Singular lab—the raid that had started this whole thing. Shay said, "You know, if you hadn't had Mom's cards . . ."

"I've thought all about that. If I hadn't had the cards, we wouldn't be here—but we need to be here. Here is the right place to be."

They'd been in elementary school when their mother, a young scientist, went to work at a laboratory in Eugene, Oregon. Something related to Parkinson's research, she'd told her family, a brain disease that made people lose control of their bodies. What had interested young Odin more was the security fence around the lab. The gates opened with key cards that changed every month. He had collected his mother's discarded cards, had learned how they worked, and had discovered the algorithm by which the codes got updated.

At the time, it had been simple nerd curiosity, but years later, after their mother had died, and Odin had joined a radical animal rights group, it became crucial. The radicals had used his knowledge to break into that laboratory in Eugene—a Singular laboratory as it turned out. And what they found there led to the widening conflict.

Shay looked at West's briefcase and sighed. "Sometimes I wonder if Mom really wanted to be a mom. It seems like Dad took care of us most of the time, until he died, and after that, it was Grandma. Mom was always so preoccupied with her work."

"She loved us, but she loved the work, too," Odin said, clicking through screen after screen of research text. "Dad wasn't as deep into his job, so he made more time for us."

Shay's expression said she didn't entirely buy it. "You think she cooperated with Singular?"

Now Odin looked up. "From what I've been able to get from the records, it looks like Singular really was doing a lot of nerve and brain research aimed at helping crippled people. You know, funded by the military and the government. That's what she was doing—

that's why she was working in an animal lab. From what I've read, it seems like Singular began to swerve away from that about the time she died."

Shay scratched her forehead, then asked the question: "Do you think Singular was involved? In her death?"

"I don't know," Odin said, "but I've thought about it a lot. I mean, I can't help wondering what that whole trip was about. Scuba diving? Australia? The Great Barrier Reef? I don't remember her talking about those kinds of things. That seemed more like something Dad might do, but neither one of them was all that big on water sports. Dad liked the mountains. Mom liked the library and the lab. So . . . I don't know."

They both sat for a moment, then Odin said, "Let's not talk about it anymore. We take these assholes down." Shay nodded, and pulled West's laptop out of the briefcase. "This could have good stuff on it, but it's protected with a password."

"Macs, I can crack," Odin said. "Of course, he might have encrypted everything inside it, like they did with the flash drives."

Shay reached back into the case for one last thing: a small external hard drive. Odin looked at it and said, "Interesting. You don't usually carry those around in a briefcase."

"West told us about it," Shay said. "He copied files from their logistics department. He figured out where the Singular prison was by finding out where they were sending food."

"Smart," Odin said.

West had a USB cable in the briefcase, and they'd just plugged the drive into Shay's laptop when Fenfang woke up. They heard a soft moan, and Odin set the laptop aside, and they went into the next room, where they found the Chinese girl sitting on the bed with her head in her hands. The wig was on the nightstand.

Odin crouched beside her and asked, "Problems?"

"Memories," Fenfang said. She met Odin's eyes. "I wish to know what happened to Liko. Is he dead? Is he here?" She gingerly touched her head. "Have they done this to him?"

"Do you have any reason to think they did?" Shay asked.

"They took us at the same time, and I last saw him in the laboratory in North Korea," she said.

"What about Charlotte?" Shay asked. "Is she still there?"

"There is a feeling, yes. It feels like somebody else is there, hiding."

"That's got to be strange," Odin said. "We need to see if we can do anything about it. . . . Kick the bitch to the curb."

Fenfang squinted at him, not knowing the expression. Odin rephrased: "Force the mean female out of your head."

"Ah. Yes. I do not think she will go. She feels stronger when I am tired. When I am weak."

"Then we need to keep you rested," Odin said.

X had been lying on the floor near Shay, but now he stood and pointed at the door with his nose: someone coming. A moment later, the door in the next room popped open and Twist and Cruz walked in.

"Got two slightly ancient Sony Vaios on sale," Twist said. "Plus four pizzas and something for the dog. Let's eat and talk."

"Wish Cade were here," Shay said.

"So do I," said Twist. "Even though he tries to be unreliable, he's pretty useful."

They considered their position as they ate:

Were they safe? For how long? What kinds of resources did Singular really have? They needed time to work, and the first priority was to crack as many of the flash drives as they could.

Twist asked Odin, "How big a problem are the phones? Can they track us, even if they're prepaid and we use fake names?"

"Sort of depends on who's doing the tracking. The police and the FBI have to know the numbers you're using, so throwaway phones will beat them. But the NSA has voice-recognition software that's so good, it can pick up voice files anywhere in the world and figure out who it is," Odin said. "If they recorded us anywhere along the line, or me, really, and I used any phone, even if it's clean . . . Senator Dash is on the Intelligence Committee, so she may have help from the NSA."

Twist said, "Okay. So no phone for you. How about the computers?"

Odin said, "If we do too many searches on Singular, or North Korea and brain research, the NSA could spot us."

"Credit cards . . . ," Shay said.

Odin shook his head. "Absolutely not. If it was a real emergency, and you had to use one, you'd have to get as far away as you could as fast as you could right after. Everyone tracks purchases. Verizon and AT&T track purchases and know where you're at."

"We're going to need more cash," Twist said.

Shay said, "There was a thousand dollars in West's wallet, and I had the money you gave me. I spent like a hundred bucks on a motel room, plus hair dye and a phone and some food for X and the bolt cutters—"

She pulled the cash out of her pocket, some of it still dappled with dried blood. "It's got some blood on it, from West," she said. "We should rinse it off. God . . . that's just awful."

"I'll take care of it," Twist said. He slipped the money in his jacket. "It's good enough for a while, but these three rooms are costing us five hundred bucks a day. I've got a stash back in L.A., and

I'm thinking of going down to get it tomorrow afternoon, after Cade gets back. Cruz and I could run down, be back in ten or twelve."

Cruz nodded. "I know where we can pick up some cold plates for West's Jeep, and some good-looking registration and insurance papers. Then the Jeep really would be ours."

"How will you get into your hotel?" Shay asked. "They'll be watching for us."

"I got an idea for that," Cruz said, breaking out a wicked grin.

"I'm not going to ask . . . yet," said Twist.

Odin had been tapping along on one of the Sonys and said, "Guess what? Rachel's been using the Wi-Fi at the Pasadena Public Library on Hill Avenue, always in the evening. She's in L.A."

"If you really need your old laptop," Twist said, "you could come with Cruz and me, we could see if we can find her."

"I think I will," Odin said. "We really could use my tools."

They'd talked about taking the night off, but it was impossible. They were a restless bunch. Shay poked through West's external drive and found thousands of files, all apparently from Singular's logistics department.

"It's like reading the Yellow Pages," Shay grumbled.

"There must be stuff in here that we can use," Odin said. "You read, I'm going to crack his laptop."

They worked on the files long after midnight—Odin cracked the laptop in a few minutes, working around the password, and found that West had encrypted some files, but most were not. Unfortunately, the open files weren't particularly interesting.

Twist and Fenfang did what they could to help, and at one point, Cruz went out to a twenty-four-hour office supply store and bought a small printer so they could move some files to paper, the easier to read. But eventually, they began to drift away from the computers: files were coming up, all good evidence, someday, maybe, but nothing that would break Singular right now. And they were tired: too much running, for too long.

They went to bed.

And dreamed of hard times. Shay, of the shooting that left West on a basement floor; Odin and Fenfang, of their treatment at the hands of Singular; Twist and Cruz, of gang fights from their past—Cruz, the barrio war that killed his brother; Twist, a beating years before that nearly left him dead and that he never discussed.

In the morning, still tired and anxious, they went down to the hotel restaurant, ate breakfast, went back to the rooms, and read more files.

"It's like going into a library and trying to find a book by the last sentence in it," Odin told Twist. "You can go through all the books, one at a time, but if the library is large enough, it'd take forever. We don't have forever."

"I'll think about it," Shay said.

She did. She kept coming back with ideas, and Odin kept saying, "I thought of that."

"Listen, do you want me to keep working or not?" Shay asked.

"Yeah, yeah, don't get all snarly. Just don't think the same things I do."

They sniped some more, like brother and sister, with X showing a little anxiety about it, but they gave him a three-way group hug, which he liked. As he walked away from them to turn in a circle and lie down, Shay noticed that one of his hind legs seemed to get momentarily tangled with the other one.

Shay stooped next to him and scratched his head—he liked a firm fingernail scratch right between the ears. His artificial blue eye—implanted by Singular—wasn't right: Shay thought it looked faded, unsharp. "Dammit. I think he needs a charge."

She'd explained to Odin how they'd recharged X's brain battery, and now he said, "That's a little scary. Plugging something into a living brain."

"I know," she said. "But the last time, he almost died before we plugged him in."

They looked at the dog for a long time, in silence, then Odin said, "It's your call: he's your dog now."

Shay got her laptop, and the Thunderbolt cable, and got X to lie down. He knew what was coming and seemed willing enough: he stretched out on the floor, his jaw between his front paws, with his eyes closed. She plugged him in.

"How long?" Odin asked.

"I don't know," Shay said. "Last time, it took at least an hour, but I wasn't watching the clock. His battery was totally flat back then."

"Interesting," Odin said. "Freakin' Frankenstein science, but . . . interesting."

Shay looked up at Odin, and then at Fenfang, and at Twist, and it was Twist who asked, "What?"

"We keep saying we need something dramatic."

Twist said, "Right."

"Well, we've got Fenfang," Shay said. "And we've got Dr. Girard. And you're going to L.A."

Twist said, "Oh . . . jeez. Where's my head been?"

Odin asked, "What?"

Twist said, "Girard's a friend of mine. He runs a clinic in L.A., and he's got an X-ray machine. He X-rayed the dog for us."

Fenfang said, "Then he could"—she gestured at her head—"X-ray this?"

"That would be great on Mindkill," Shay said. "You don't have

51

to be a doctor to look at an X-ray showing hundreds of wires stuck in a brain and know it's a problem."

Fenfang nodded and said, "I will do it."

An hour later, X's eye was dark blue again, and his tail thumped against the floor. Shay unplugged him, and he licked her hand and rolled onto his back for a belly rub.

Cade arrived in Las Vegas at noon, having left Salt Lake at dawn. "They should be all over Salt Lake," he said. "I left several difficult-to-find clues that they'll find, if they're competent."

"They're competent," Odin said.

Cade was carrying a bag from Cabela's. Twist said, "You're not old enough to buy a gun, there's no place to fish. . . ."

Cade emptied the bag on a table. Six Motorola walkie-talkies and a pack of batteries fell out. "We can talk to each other without using cell phones. We choose the frequency, good for a mile or so. You'd have to know we were using them, where we were, and what frequency we were on, to intercept."

"Old tech, but useful," Odin said. "We'll take them with us this afternoon."

"What's this afternoon?" Cade asked.

Twist briefed him on the proposed run into Los Angeles.

"They're probably watching the hotel," Cade said.

"Yeah, we thought of that, not being complete morons," Twist said. "We can handle it."

"What am I doing?" Cade asked.

"Computer files—you and Shay will be trying to find more stuff we can use to hang Singular," Twist said. "We'll be out of L.A. and back here before morning."

"I'm worried about the hotel. Not everybody in there can be trusted," Cade said to Twist. "They ain't a bunch of little snow-flakes. If I were Singular, I'd call up some rap sheets to see who might be bought. Some of them could be. If they see you, and make a quick call, you're trapped."

"I can get in and out," Twist said. "Cruz has a plan." He turned to face a mirror, looked himself over admiringly, from his sleek brown pompadour to his polished black boots, and sighed.

5

Once the others had left, Shay told Cade about searching the hard drive. Cade shook his head. "That sounds like the next thing to hopeless."

"What else are we gonna do?" Shay asked.

"Here's the thing," Cade said. "When I'm looking at a computer screen, I can't think. We should turn the computers off."

"Pretty radical for a computer punk," Shay said.

"I'm not *just* a computer punk," Cade said. He flicked his hair. "I'm also *very* good-looking."

In fact, he was, Shay thought. His phony-real vanity made her smile.

The four travelers made one stop in Vegas, at a Ross Dress for Less, then sped across the desert in a shifting clutch of cars and semi-trucks, all headed for L.A. They were slowed on the mountain down into San Bernardino, where a traffic accident pushed everybody into a bottleneck in the left lanes, and they got caught in the evening rush on the 210. Still, they were in Pasadena before seven o'clock.

"Doesn't look like L.A.," Odin said. "At least not the parts I've seen." In the weeks he'd been hiding out in Los Angeles with Rachel and the other members of Storm, they'd never made it to the suburbs.

"More like an actual town," said Twist. "You know, a downtown area, surrounded by houses."

They parked behind a McDonald's, divided up the walkie-talkies, then walked to a Starbucks. Odin signed onto the Wi-Fi and did a Google image search for Rachel Wharton. He hadn't wanted to do that in Las Vegas, in case her name might be a trip wire that Singular was watching.

He found a dozen pictures of Rachel, stretching back to her high school days. Cruz, Twist, and Fenfang studied the pictures, then Odin shut down the computer and they left. Cruz and Fenfang went ahead, aiming for the library, while Odin and Twist walked down the opposite side of the street. They were all carrying backpacks— they were near Pasadena City College and were going for a student vibe.

Cruz went into the library, swept through it once, didn't see anyone who resembled the photographs of Rachel. He went back out the front, took a left, said "Nobody" to Fenfang. They walked along Hill Avenue, arm in arm, brushed past Odin and Twist, who'd come across after them, and Cruz muttered, "Not there. Don't see anybody watching."

Twist and Odin split up, Twist walking down to Green Street, while Odin leaned inside the library's door, as if waiting for a date. Fenfang and Cruz walked around the block, looking for people watching them, saw nobody, then went into the library, where they found seats at a long reading table.

And they waited. They'd decided to wait until nine o'clock—Rachel had always signed on before then—and if she didn't come, they'd head down to Hollywood and the Twist Hotel.

Rachel showed up just before eight.

Twist saw her coming and walked past her on Green Street, to check; when he was fairly certain that the woman was Rachel Wharton, he beeped Odin and said, "Coming your way. Nobody with her."

Odin went into the library, got behind some bookshelves, out of sight. She'd most likely go to one of the big tables, he thought, where she could use her laptop.

She stepped into the library a minute later, and Odin's heart skipped a beat: she was pretty, wild-haired, his first girlfriend, the first woman he'd ever slept with, someone who was willing to trash a lab on behalf of tortured animals. . . .

As Odin watched, she headed straight for a study area. He used the walkie-talkie, said, "Got her. Watch for me."

Cruz and Fenfang got up and left the library; with Twist, they'd watch the place from three different angles, looking for Singular operators. Odin waited, back in the books, looking for anyone who was paying attention to Rachel. Nobody was. She settled behind the laptop and started typing.

She was still working ten minutes later when Odin settled into a chair across from her. Her eyes flicked up, back down to the laptop, then, startled, back up. She blurted, "Oh, Jesus."

He asked, "Got a minute?" He tipped his head toward the books. She pushed down the lid of her laptop, got her pack, and followed him into the stacks.

"You got away! How'd you find me?" she whispered.

"I put a tracker on your laptop," he said. "In case we got separated."

She frowned, a wrinkle between her eyes: didn't like the idea of being tracked. "We're the only two still out," she said. "The cops got the others."

"I know," Odin said. "Listen, the Singular people are way, way worse than you can believe."

"I saw the videos on that Mindkill site—they were from the flash drives, weren't they?"

Odin nodded. "It's bad. Really bad. You should get out of here, at least for a while."

"Yeah . . . What about New York?" she asked. "Nobody knows me there. I've still got some money. . . . I could get to Paris, maybe, one of my old girlfriends lives there, they'd never know about her."

"Using your passport could be risky. New York maybe. But go fast. I've got a name and email address for you—he's the CEO of Singular. I suggest you send him an email. Don't let him know where you are or where you're going, but tell him you don't have any of the flash drives they're looking for, tell him that you don't want to have anything to do with him or with Singular, that you're quitting the animal rights movement, that you're going away and they'll never hear from you again. You gotta do this, Rachel."

"What happened to your face? What'd they do to you?"

"That would take a while to explain, and I don't want to be here that long," Odin said, glancing around the room. "We're trying to expose them before they get us. You don't want the details, but believe me: they will kill you if they think you're a danger to them."

"All right," she said. "But you didn't just come here to talk. If you saw me signing on, you could have sent me an email. You want your laptop."

"Do you have it?"

"Yeah, I do." She put her pack between her feet, unzipped the top, and pulled his laptop out. "I was afraid to turn it on, in case Singular or the cops could trace you."

"Thanks." He took out his wallet, found a slip of paper, and said, "This is the Singular guy's email. Send that message one minute before you leave Los Angeles. Then get lost."

"What about you?" she asked.

"We're running until it's settled. If they get us, you probably won't hear. If we get them, you definitely will."

She reached out and clutched his forearm, and tears trickled down her cheeks. "Odin, be careful."

"I will," he said. "I gotta go."

"Wait," she said, and pulled him into a hug. "I know what you think about me, but you're wrong: I really liked you."

"And I liked you." He let go of her and stepped away. "Rachel: have a good life. Seriously. Have a good one."

Odin was out the door and walking down the alley. Twist and Cruz were hidden at the end of it, should anyone be following. Fenfang was back at the McDonald's, watching the car. When the men came up, she nodded and they all climbed in, and as they pulled out of the parking lot, Odin got out a tiny tool kit and began taking the laptop apart.

When he'd gotten the clamshell off, Cruz shone a flashlight on the inner workings and asked, "See anything?"

"Nothing here. It's clean," Odin said after a moment.

Twist: "You're sure?"

"I know every molecule of this thing. Nothing's been moved or added or subtracted. I gotta look at the software. . . ."

"We'll leave you at Dave's Chicken and Flapjacks," Twist said. "I know Dave, he'll let you and Fenfang sit in a booth as long as you want."

At thirteen, Cruz had been running with the gang his older brother belonged to, although he'd not yet been accepted as a full member. After his brother was shot to death, Cruz dropped out at his mother's urging, just before she was deported back to Mexico. In the months that followed, he'd found his way to the Twist Hotel and a different kind of life, but he still had contacts, and they were coming through for him now.

Dave's Chicken and Flapjacks was a greasy spoon three blocks from the Twist Hotel. Twist had spent a significant part of his life in the place and led the way straight into the back, where a man named Al was nursing a Coke in a red plastic glass. When he saw Cruz, he stood up, and they hugged, and he passed a package to him. "Plates and papers for a Jeep Rubicon."

Cruz nodded and cued Twist, who took an envelope from the interior pocket in his sport coat and handed it over. "As agreed," he said.

Al nodded and put the money away without counting it. "There are two watchers, all the time. One watches the front, the other watches the back and the south side. Can't see the north side so well. They dress like people in the neighborhood, but their haircuts are wrong, and they are too much like soldiers. Big vibes."

"That's them," Twist said.

"You want us to move them along?" Al asked.

"No, no," Cruz said. "When we go in, if you see them make a move, call us. But that's all."

"This we can do."

Cruz said, "*Gracias, Alejandro. Mándale saludos a tu mamá de mi parte.*"

Cruz and Twist left Odin and Fenfang in the restaurant, working on his laptop. Twist did a quick change of clothes in the car while Cruz changed the license plates, and then they walked down to the hotel. A block away, Twist asked Cruz, "Do you still have that .45?"

"In the car. Why?"

"If we were stopped by the cops or anyone else, I'd want you to shoot me," Twist said.

Cruz laughed and said, "I think you're cute."

"Cruz . . ."

"I'm lying. You got ugly legs. Ugly."

"Thank you."

They went in the hotel's north door, which opened with a key that only a few people had, and straight up the back stairs to the rooms that housed Dum and Dee, the hotel's enforcers. They saw nobody on the way up. When Dum opened his door, he stared at Twist for a moment, then broke into a spasm of soundless laughter.

Twist said, "Yeah, yeah, let me in so I can get out of this dress. . . ." He was wearing a yellow dress with a puffy skirt, of a kind popular in parts of the L.A. Hispanic culture, and an orange silk scarf tied around his head; he was carrying a wicker tote and a pink umbrella, instead of his cane.

"Ugly legs," Cruz said.

Twist went into Dum's bathroom with the tote and changed into his regular black T-shirt, black jeans, and high-tops.

Sitting on the toilet, lacing up the shoes, he realized how much he'd missed the place: since getting involved with Shay, he'd literally been driven from his home.

As crazy as the hotel was, he loved it. Though it ran right on the edge of chaos, somehow it had always held together, and the kids who lived there seemed to grow into an extended family—in some cases, the only family they'd ever had. Even the cops would come around to chat, knowing that the hotel was a good thing. Now he was like a hunted animal, always looking over his shoulder. Couldn't turn back. He picked up the dress, went back out into Dum's room.

Dum got his twin brother, Dee, and Lou, Twist's second-in-command, and Emily, a girl who'd been Shay's roommate during her short stay at the hotel and who'd been there at the start of the conflict with Singular.

Twist started with Lou: "Any problems?"

"People are wondering where you are," she said in her soft Somalian accent. "With Dum and Dee, I can keep the lid on for a while, but if you're not around, people are going to start getting . . . pushy."

"Anybody in particular?"

"Barbara Hemme comes to mind. I've been getting a lot of lip from her. That guy Tucker, who calls himself Duke, he's been throwing some bullshit around about the place going straight."

"You are a little too straight," Twist laughed. "I'll jack those two up and the word will get around."

Lou handed Twist a brown paper sack and said, "This is all there is."

"How much?"

"A little over twenty thousand," Lou said.

"It'll have to do. Listen, has anybody been upstairs, in my studio? Anybody at all, besides you?"

She shook her head. "Nobody. I took a cot up there and started sleeping near the elevator, just in case."

"Thanks," Twist said. "Did you call Danny Dill?"

"Yes. He's still there, still operating," Lou said.

Emily asked, "How's Shay?"

"She got her brother back," Twist said. "We're all in trouble. I wanted to talk to you, see if it might be possible for you to move in with your mother. Probably only be a couple of weeks, or a month."

He explained that they were worried about residents of the hotel being paid to betray them to Singular: "If they know you were Shay's roommate, and there are people here who could tell them that, they might think you're still in touch. They could try to come in after you."

"I'm safer here than I would be with my mom," she said. Emily's mother was a lifelong alcoholic, and her devotion to bad choices was why Emily had left home at fourteen. "I've got Dum and Dee right downstairs; they'd have to get past them to get to me."

"What about when you're working?" Twist asked.

Emily was a "picker," who found items that looked like junk but could be sold for more than she paid for them. "Well . . . I've got a whole pile of crap down in the basement, in that old coal bin, that I've been meaning to inventory. I can stay inside here for a couple of days doing that and put all the numbers on my spreadsheet. That would limit their opportunities."

Twist thought about it, then asked Dum and Dee, "Can you watch her?"

They both nodded.

"All right," Twist said. "I'm going to go show my face around—talk to Miz Hemme and Mr. Duke, give them some advice about their personal conduct. Knock on a couple more doors."

"Only ten minutes, in case somebody snitches," Cruz said.

Emily picked up the dress that Twist had thrown on Dum's couch and shook it out. "This is your dress? This? I could have done you a lot better. Let me see what I've got in my room. Something that would make your shoulders narrower, but still show off your butt. . . ."

"Dum, kill her," Twist said, and Dum and Dee did their silent laughing thing, and Twist went out the door to kick some ass. Enjoyed every minute of it: slapped backs, snarled at Hemme and Duke, got a sandwich from the kitchen. Took too long doing it.

But nobody made a call, as far as they could tell. Nobody followed them from the hotel.

By the time they got back to Dave's Chicken and Flapjacks, Odin had determined that his software had not been touched, that nothing had been added.

One more stop. Driving across town, Twist told the others about Dr. Girard and the covert medical practice he'd operated for years.

Odin, sitting beside Fenfang in the backseat, said he liked the idea of having X-rays done but wasn't sure he wanted to put Fenfang in the hands of an unlicensed doctor.

"How do we know he's not going to blast her with about ten thousand times too much radiation because he doesn't know any better or his X-ray machine is screwed up?"

"Nothing unmodern about the clinic or the doc," Twist said. "It's just that he's illegal in this country, and there's no way for him to get legal. I'm not the only one who knows—but nobody else is doing his kind of work with street people and the poor, so everybody pretends he's, you know, a branch of the Mayo Clinic."

"I'm gonna want to take a look at it first," Odin said.

"You're smart, Odin, but everything you know about a modern medical clinic could be written on the back of a postage stamp with a paintbrush," Twist said. "I don't know any more than you do—but I know Girard, and he's a good guy."

Fenfang, looking out at the passing shops and people on Cesar Chavez Avenue, said only: "A doctor with no license is little trouble for me now."

A CLOSED sign hung in the window of the botanica that fronted for the clinic, but the lights were on, and Girard himself met them at the door.

"Twist," the slender, middle-aged doctor said, and the men shook hands. "I'm not so sure that I like these midnight meetings." Twist and Shay had visited him late at night when they thought X was dying, and after restarting the dog's heart with a shot of adrenaline, he'd confirmed Singular's experiments with X-rays.

"All we need from you is another set of X-rays," Twist said. "You don't have to identify yourself, and we won't give you up, either."

"C'mon, then," Girard said, and they followed him down a dark aisle, past tall handblown bottles of herbs and religious candles, and through a blue-painted door. Inside was a modern, brightly lit clinic. Wasting no time, Fenfang peeled off her wig, and Girard groaned, in lightly accented English, "Oh my God. They . . . like the dog."

"Yes," she said. "X and I . . . we are the same."

Girard made the guys sit in plastic waiting chairs while he took

Fenfang into an exam room. Twenty minutes later, he reemerged, sat opposite them, and rubbed his face with his hands.

"You can see the X-rays when she's done using the restroom," he said. "I'll tell you privately, Twist, you boys, that there are several wires coming down from each of the nodes on top of her skull— like spider legs. The wires are very thin, but . . . it appears to me that they've done some damage to her brain. I doubt that it can be contained or reversed—but I'm not a brain expert. I've told her that she needs to get to an advanced medical center as soon as she can. She's resistant. She has a rather paranoid fantasy that the forces of evil will somehow get to her there—"

"Not paranoid," Odin said.

"You can get her somewhere. Somewhere they can't reach."

"Tell us where," Odin said. "Not where you *think* she might be safe—but where you *know* she can be safe from some of the highest people in the government. People with guns. People who can make the FBI work for them. Where would that be?"

Girard threw up his hands. "You're overstating—"

"No, I'm not," Odin interrupted. "I'm telling you what we know for sure."

Fenfang came out; she was carrying the wig, which she tried to pull on as they watched, and Odin jumped up to help her.

Girard asked, "What will you do next?"

"I don't know," Twist said.

The two men stared at each other, then Fenfang smoothed down her hair and said, "Ready." Girard and Twist stood, and Girard said, "I'm so sorry for what these people have done to you. And that I . . . that I can't fix you."

Fenfang nodded politely and patted him on the arm. "I think you are a good man," she said. "Can we have the pictures, please?"

• • •

At five in the morning, they were back in Vegas with the damning images of Fenfang's brain, a sack full of money, Odin's computer, and clean plates and papers for the Jeep.

Twist led the weary group up to the rooms, and Shay met them at the door, wide awake and wearing a dangerous smile: "We've got a plan."

6

Twist wanted to hear the plan, but first he wanted to show Shay and Cade the X-rays of Fenfang's head.

Girard had given them a flash drive with the images. Odin called them up; each of the nodes on Fenfang's scalp did, in fact, look like the body of a spider, with long, thin legs leading down into her brain. There were hundreds of them.

Shay, standing beside Fenfang, reached out and grasped her hand. "We're gonna figure this out, we're gonna find someone to help you."

Fenfang shook her head. "We do not know who to trust. I am afraid that if I see a doctor, he will call in police and the police will call the CIA and then I will be taken away and everything would be buried. This is what I fear the most—that this will be buried. That it will be confused . . . that the Singular leaders will all disappear and come back somewhere else. Immortality is a very powerful desire, if you think you might be a person who can get it."

"But—" Cade started to say.

"There's only one possibility—that we put Singular on public trial before all of this can be buried," Twist said. "We need to get everything out at once."

"That's our plan," Shay said. She was nervous: Twist hadn't seen that before, not like this. "Let me give you the overall concept. First: we're not going to take Singular down by shooting people."

"Knew that," Twist said.

"So we have to get at Singular in some other way," Shay said.

Cade picked up: "We have to get at Singular from inside—but most of Singular is too protected. The corporation itself, the laboratories. They've got those ex-soldiers working security."

Shay: "But they don't know that we know about Senator Dash. And they think we're in California, or maybe Utah. Running. Scared. Hiding. We know two places that might be unprotected, where we might get the kind of evidence that'll let us expose them: Senator Dash's house and Dr. Janes's house up in Eugene."

Twist frowned. "You want to break into a U.S. senator's house? That's a plan, all right. The kind that gets us sent to federal prison."

Shay shook her head. "Fenfang knows her alarm codes, so I don't think, technically speaking, we'd be breaking in."

Twist rolled his eyes, and Cade said: "Listen, we know from Fenfang that Dash has already tried to do the mind transfer. If we can get her talking, we can show people that this is actually going on. Can you think of anything more explosive? A senator looking to buy a new brain? Let me show you something. . . ."

He walked into the end room and brought back two boxes, popped one of them open, and took out a tiny movie camera. "Went out and bought these. Sony Action Cam Mini. It's a high-res video camera."

The front of the camera was about an inch wide and an inch and a half high. Cade had figured out how to secure the camera on his upper arm—below his armpit and between his arm and his body—using a black elastic band.

"If we can get to Dash and Janes, we film them," Shay said. "Cade and I have been practicing with the cameras. The video and sound are good, and if you're wearing a black shirt, you can't really see the camera. We might be able to get more direct evidence or documents from either Dash or Janes, but even if we don't, we can dump the video onto Mindkill."

Fenfang clapped her hands together and said, almost gleefully, "We get video of Charlotte's head!"

Everyone, including the dog, looked at her, but only Odin caught the implication. "I hadn't thought about that, you're saying—"

"Yes, I think her head must have had operation, too," said Fenfang.

"That's *exactly* what we need on camera," Cade said. He took the camera off his arm and handed it to Twist, who turned it in his hands. It was half the size of a pack of cigarettes and fit easily in his palm. "Man, if it actually worked, if we could find a way to get them talking on this thing . . ."

"Yeah. That's why instead of looking at twenty-seven thousand files that are probably outdated, we looked at Janes and Dash," Cade said. "We were careful about it, we routed through Sweden."

They'd found working schedules on Dash's U.S. Senate website. "We think she's at home through the weekend, and all those numbers Fenfang's got in her head should get us past her security and into the house," Shay said. They'd also gotten addresses and satellite photos of the two houses from Google: Dash's in Santa Fe, New Mexico, and Janes's in Eugene, Oregon.

Cade brought up side-by-side photos of Janes and Dash on his laptop screen and turned it to Fenfang. "Have you ever seen these people?"

"The woman . . ." She shook her head. "No. But the man, I see him. I see him in the prison. I am on a chair, the kind that tips, and he is looking in my face and asking questions. I answer. I do not know why, but I answer. I feel . . . unusual?"

"I understand," Odin said. "You'd been given some drugs."

"I do not know about that, but his face, I know that." She touched the screen. "Who is this woman?"

Cade said, "This is Charlotte Dash."

"This is she? This old woman in my head?" Fenfang stared at the senator's face for so long, her own face so contorted, that eventually Odin stepped up and put an arm around her shoulder and said, "Enough of this," and Cade shut down the screen.

Cruz had his arm around X's shoulders. "What will we get from Janes?" he asked.

"Probably documents. I bet he takes some of his work home," Cade said. "And maybe the passwords for the flash drives we can't open. He's the one who made up the passwords, so he should be able to get us into all of them. And when we're talking to him, that's on film, too."

Odin liked the idea, but for different reasons. "We need to make him tell us how to undo the shit they did to Fenfang. There has to be a drug, something that'll stop the seizures, right? You can't sell someone's body to some rich bitch and have it going spastic, now, can you?"

Shay signaled Odin to take it down a notch, then continued making the pitch. "Their houses are both somewhat isolated—especially Dash's. We split up, do the raids at the same time."

Now Twist raised his voice: "Split up? Whoa, uh-uh, I don't know about that—"

"Have to," Cade said. "After one home invasion, they'd be on high alert for others."

"Cade and I wrote out a minute-by-minute plan," Shay said. "We want all of you to look over the details, tell us what you think. But, Twist: it's doable."

Twist stared at Shay, already very much thinking, and Odin asked, "The few things you found in the computer files . . . anything really good?"

Cade shook his head. "No. Got some personnel information on Singular, but I don't know how we'd use it. There's a guy named Thorne, who seems to be in charge of the Singular security people. He's probably in charge of the goons who ran the prison. That's what it looks like his job is, from all the requisition slips for supplies he signed. There's another guy, Thorne's boss Sync, and we've got pictures of him. He's the guy we saw on television when they were showing off those prosthetics. And we've got pictures of the top boss, Micah Cartwell, and the company's top lawyer, and a few other people. But less than you'd think—not much in the way of photos or even basic information that wasn't written by one of their own PR guys."

"Did you see Liko's name?" Fenfang asked.

Shay shook her head. "Didn't find anything on where they might be keeping the experimental subjects."

Odin: "Nothing else about the experiments at all?"

"Sorry, man," Cade said.

Twist put the tiny camera under his armpit, swiveled, then stood up and studied himself in a dressing mirror. The camera was virtually invisible. "Dash and Janes," he said slowly. "Say cheese?"

They all slept for a few hours, got up at noon, and spent the rest of the day talking about how—if they were going to do it—it would be done. Two raids at the same time: Twist, Odin, and Cade hitting Janes; Shay, Fenfang, and Cruz going after Dash.

"We have a real opportunity with Dash, because she must be crucial to the company, with her government position," Shay explained. "And Fenfang knows the codes for all the locks."

"And the words for the dogs," Fenfang added.

Not something Shay or the others had heard about yet. Twist raised an eyebrow and asked, "You mean guard dogs?"

"Yes, they are made for attack," Fenfang said.

Cade went to the computer and found a photograph of Dash flanked by two black-and-tan German shepherds, the dogs looking larger and more muscular than lions.

"Bred in Germany, trained in Germany," he said, reading a Facebook entry from a German breeder boasting about their placement with a U.S. senator. "Actually, trained in their native tongue."

Twist: "The dogs talk German?"

"I know the words—the words that make them stop and stay," Fenfang insisted.

"You hope," said Twist.

"*Platz, sitz, bleip*—down, sit, stay . . . I know them."

"Just teach me 'Don't bite,'" said Cruz.

"*Nein packen!*" Fenfang shouted.

Cruz smiled. "For real? *Nein packen?*"

"Yes. The words will work. I can see them in my mind's eye, like they are written on my brain. I can hear them working: I hear them in the voice of Charlotte herself."

Shay took Cade's computer out of his lap and handed it to Fenfang. "Type every command you know in German and what it means in English, and we'll start practicing."

Before they went to bed that night, Shay took Odin by the arm and said, "Come walk with me." They went out, and she walked down the hall to the end room. She knocked and said to the door, "Shay."

Twist opened it. "What's up?"

"Need to talk—you and Odin," Shay said. "I didn't want the others to hear this."

"Well . . . come on in."

Shay sat on the bed. "I found something in the Willamette Valley drive. There's a memo in there—if you search for 561-A, you'll find it. It says that experimental subjects almost always die within four to six weeks after the onset of seizures."

"Oh, shit," Odin blurted. To Twist: "Girard said it looked like there was serious damage."

Shay nodded. "The memo says that the leads—the wires in her brain—cause irreversible brain deterioration. That the actual insertion of the wires does the damage. That future experiments have to focus on much smaller wires that are put in place quickly and quickly removed. I was careful about it, but I asked Fenfang how long she'd been having the seizures, and she said they started about two weeks ago."

"Got to get them out," Odin said.

"Doesn't help," said Shay. "You've got to read the memo. Taking the wires out, after they've been implanted for a long time, causes even faster deterioration."

"Ah, Jesus," Twist said, rubbing his face.

"I didn't tell her. But we should . . . shouldn't we?" Shay said.

"More to think about," Twist said. "It's a goddamn disaster."

"Not much time to think," Shay said.

Late that night, with Cruz and Cade sound asleep, Odin began to relive the waterboarding: a dream, but no less real than the actual assault. He moaned once, then again. The other two guys never moved. But Fenfang, in the next room, heard a sound that she knew from the trip across the Pacific: another prisoner in pain.

She slipped out of bed, careful not to wake Shay, and listened for a moment at the connecting door. Odin moaned again, and Fenfang pushed the door open. There was little light, but she moved softly to his bedside, sat down next to him, brushed hair out of his face, and whispered, "It is all right, Odin, you are with your friends. Odin . . ."

Though he was asleep, and dreaming, he reached out to her and caught her by the wrist; she whispered, "You are safe, you are with me." She lay down beside him and wrapped an arm around his shoulders. He moaned some more, and she held him tighter, and the nightmare faded away; a few minutes later, they were both asleep again, side by side.

In the morning, Shay and Cade worked with the cameras, doing videos of the others as they talked. They shot in more light than was recommended, then in less, seeing what would work. The front of the camera was a matte black. Twist went out to a department store and got two long-sleeved black shirts; the cameras disappeared.

"Remember," Odin said, "we can edit the video before we put it online. . . . So, if we say something, you know, threatening . . . we can cut it out later."

They broke for a fast lunch of Subway sandwiches, since Twist said he couldn't look another pizza in the face.

While they were eating, Cade said, "We're gonna need a hideout after this. Like a missile silo or something."

Twist said, "Got one. A hideout."

"Not L.A.?" Cade asked.

"Not L.A.," Twist said. "You remember Danny Dill? You met him that time—"

"Down at the Salton Sea," Cade finished. "Danny Dill. All right. He's in Northern California somewhere, right? Or he was. . . ."

"Still is," Twist said. "Lou's talked to him. Given the situation, he has the best possible security. I don't think Singular could find us there. If they did, we'd see them coming."

"Danny Dill," Cade said. "Hope he's still a criminal."

"Oh, yeah," Twist said.

Late in the afternoon, they agreed that they'd have to move soon if they were going to pull off the raids.

"The longer we wait, the longer Singular has to search for us, and the tighter they can get their security," Odin said.

Twist said, "Vote. How many think we move now?"

Every hand went up, Twist's last. He said, "Once we do this, there won't be any more possibility of negotiation. This is it."

"Yes," Shay said. "It is."

They were all still sitting there, after the vote, when the fur on X's spine went up and he let out a warning growl a second before a knock at the door: not a hotel-maid knock with a key—too late in the afternoon for that—but a knuckle.

They all looked at each other, then Cruz said, "I'm the one nobody knows. I'll answer."

Twist said, "Get out of sight. Everybody but Cruz."

Another knock. Cruz moved to the door, left the chain on,

opened the door, and peered through the crack. None of the others could see the man outside the door, but they could hear his voice: "I need to talk to a Mr. Twist."

Twist frowned and mouthed, *What the hell?* Twist moved over to the door, and Shay followed behind him, hand on her knife, staying out of sight.

The man in the hall was wearing khaki shorts, an olive-drab T-shirt, and running shoes. He was slender and broad shouldered, with a sunburned face; he was hard and leathery, like a bicycle racer. He looked at Twist and said, "You're Twist."

"Who are you?"

"I'm the guy you owe five hundred dollars to," he said.

Twist said, "Excuse me?"

"I've got a message for you. The guy who is sending it said you'd pay me five hundred, up front, to deliver it. Hand it over."

Twist didn't hesitate. He dug in his pocket, pulled out a roll of bills, and stripped off ten of them.

The man took them, zipped them in a pocket, then said, with no sign of emotion, "Get out. Singular is coming. You have two hours. . . ." He looked at his watch. "Well, I got here quick. You got two hours and fifteen minutes."

He walked away.

Twist called after him, "Hey, wait! There's more money!"

The guy shook his head without turning around. "That's all I got."

Twist shut the door and said, "You heard the man."

Cade said, "Who was he?"

"Who cares?" Cruz said. "He knew Twist, he knew where we were hiding, he knows Singular."

"We go," Fenfang said. "We go now."

Cade asked, "How was he dressed? How—"

Twist shrugged. "Khaki shorts, olive T-shirt."

Cade was at the door. "What'd he look like? Quick! Quick!"

Twist said, "Broad shouldered, thin, looked . . . military. Or maybe like an athlete, a coach. Buzz cut."

Cade said, "Wipe the place," and he was out the door.

The man had said two hours, but Twist gave them fifteen minutes. Cruz suggested that they wipe last, when everybody was ready to walk out. Five or six minutes later, Cade was back, breathing hard.

Twist: "Where the hell . . . ?"

"Parking structure," Cade said. "I caught him getting into his car, walked on past and up the stairs. But, dude: I got his tag number."

Odin: "Oh, yes! Yes! That gets us everything."

"Keep packing," Twist said. "I gotta tell you, Cade, you've picked up some smarts since you started hanging out with me."

"Humble thanks, sensei."

Everything was packed and ready to go in fifteen minutes, and even neatly packed. Cruz handed out paper towels and passed around a bottle of Windex, and they started erasing fingerprints.

"This just cuts a day off the schedule," Twist said as they worked. "We're ready to do it; we were getting our guts up."

"We need to run that license plate soon as we can," Shay said from the bathroom, where she was wiping every hard surface she could find. "We need to know where the warning's coming from. We're either heading into a trap or we've got an ally within Singular who could help us a lot—somebody who knows what Singular is doing."

Cruz started stripping the sheets from a bed. "You think they might be doing this to break us into the open?"

"That doesn't make any sense," Odin said. He was wiping electrical outlets. "If they knew where we were, they could watch us, and sooner or later, we'd *be* in the open. They could go after us without any warning at all."

"You're right," Twist said. "This is critical—we need to figure this out. The other thing, of course, is that they found us, and pretty fast. Didn't even bite on Cade being in Salt Lake, as far as we know. How'd they do that?"

Odin said, "We've been out on the street. There are cameras *everywhere,* and Dash has access to the intelligence community. They could have run a face-recognition program on us."

"If that's it, us guys ought to start working on beards," Cade said. "We should all wear caps when we're on the street. Or cowboy hats."

"They're narrowing down what we can do," Shay said. "They're limiting our movement. The more they limit us, the easier we'll be to find."

"Be quiet. Wipe faster," Fenfang said. She was walking on the edge of panic. "They are coming."

Shay, Cruz, Fenfang, and X would go in the Jeep to Santa Fe. Cade, Odin, and Twist would take the truck to Eugene after leaving the Camry at the airport. "I'll have somebody from the hotel take the bus up here and drive the car back," Twist said. "We might need another cold car later."

He picked up his bag and said, "We're not checking out, so everybody down the back stairwell into the garage. For God's sake, be careful. Shay, careful. Cruz, careful. Fenfang—"

"I know, careful," Fenfang said. "We go, go." She was out the door.

Twist said, "X . . . take care of them."

X yipped back at him.

Shay kissed her brother on the cheek and clung to him for a moment. "Do not get killed."

"I'll give it a shot," he said.

That almost made her laugh.

7

They were moving, fleeing Vegas.

Singular was also moving.

That morning, Thorne had checked in with Sync. "I think we've found what we're looking for. It's an older freighter, brought in a year ago for refurbishing, and the owners ran out of money. The engines have been rebuilt, the diesel tanks have been replaced; there was quite a bit of work done on the crew quarters, where we could put our guys. There're toilets, a good-sized kitchen. The cargo holds are good for the experimental subjects. Since the walls of the holds, and the hull, are solid steel, there's no way anyone could break out."

"What about security?" Sync asked. He was standing over his desk in the San Francisco office, talking on a speaker and chugging some Singular-concocted green juice that was supposed to help him live longer; it tasted like a mixture of egg white and sagebrush. "We'd be moving them back and forth, not always sedated."

"My idea is, we put vinyl stickers on the panel vans that say, you know, RAY'S PAINTING or some such. The owners have been working on the boat off and on for a year, so there've been trucks coming and going. Where it's tied up, it's all by itself. Not much else around."

"How long to buy it?"

"We can get it now and at a good price," Thorne said. "Here's the clincher: if there's trouble, we can move it. Given twelve hours' notice, we can move it a hundred and fifty miles. Given five minutes' notice, we could move it a mile, and off-road. Hell, we could move it to North Korea if we need to do that. Korea's two weeks from San Francisco."

"How long before we can move the subjects in?" Sync asked.

"We could start putting them in the hold right away. A bunch of cots, weld some steel rings to the floor for ankle cuffs, if we think we need them. If we want some isolation cells, we could just bring in a bunch of used shipping containers—steel, lockable from the outside—you can buy good used ones for two grand. And the boat is built to take them."

"I'll talk to Cartwell," Sync said. "If he says okay, we'll buy the boat with one of the front companies. I think he'll go for it, so do whatever you need to get the wheels turning."

Ten minutes later, Cartwell said, "Yes."

The experimental subjects, fifteen of them, were being held in three rented RVs parked in a corner of an obscure private campground in the Valley. There were two armed Singular security people with each RV.

The leader of the detail, who reported to Thorne, said, "We can't keep this going much longer. There's always somebody who's snoopy. We're sitting here doing nothing, but if some snoop thought we were strange and called the cops . . . we'd have a problem. And we are a little strange."

"I'll find another campground," Thorne said. "You can move along in a couple hours."

"That'll help, but what we really need is to get the subjects out of sight altogether. If we ever do this again, we need some women working with us. It'd be better if the campground people saw some couples out here, instead of a bunch of guys who look like ex-SEALs."

"I hear you," Thorne said. "We're working on it."

And they were working on finding Shay, Twist, and the other people who'd attacked the Sacramento facility.

The day before, Cartwell had called Singular's secret ally on the U.S. Senate Select Committee on Intelligence, Senator Charlotte Dash, to make a request . . . a careful request.

"We need this," he told her. "But not if we put you at any risk."

"I could do it as a test of the system; they run the tests all the time," Dash said from the back of a limousine, heading for a youth-empowerment luncheon at George Washington University. "Send me the photos."

Cartwell had Sync send along good digital photos of Twist, Shay, and Odin. What he hadn't done yet—and was hoping he'd never have to—was tell the senator that some of the contents of her brain were on the loose with an escaped Chinese prisoner.

Six hours later, Dash called Cartwell back. "They're in Las Vegas. They identified the Twist person and Odin Remby on the Strip, at a pizza parlor. No question on the identification. They were on foot, the artist with a cane, the kid limping like he'd been injured. We followed them with street cameras walking past Caesars and the Mirage to Treasure Island, then lost them. This is with law enforcement cameras. There should be more cameras run by the casinos, but I didn't want to ask to get into those, because it would have required a search warrant. Since they were on foot, and carrying pizza boxes, they won't have been going far. This was yesterday afternoon, twenty-four hours ago."

Cartwell smiled into the phone and said, "Madam Senator, you do know how to get things done."

"Yes, I do," she said. "Oh: we never had this conversation."

Sync called Harmon: "Find them."

"Las Vegas has one of the densest concentrations of surveillance cameras in the world. Nothing happens there that's not on video," Harmon said. "We should be able to crack those casino cameras easily enough. I'll get back to you."

An hour later, Harmon and the computer jocks watched on a monitor as Twist and Odin carried the stack of pizza boxes into the Moulin Rose twenty-five hours earlier.

Harmon called Sync, and Sync said, "Excellent. We'll take care of this once and for all."

"What's the plan?" Harmon asked. "You heard what I told Cartwell. . . . I'd say this is where we bring in the cops; I've got a contact in the Phoenix FBI office—I could leak this to him. . . ."

"No, no. You're done for now. We'll take care of it."

Sync said to Thorne: "Take them down."

"I'm over at the boat. It'll take a couple of hours before we're ready to roll," Thorne said. "We need to get one of our lawyers over here to sign the papers on the purchase."

"I'll take care of it," Sync said, and hung up.

Thorne and four of his men "gunned up," as they called it. They all had concealed-carry permits that were good in Nevada, though the permits didn't cover the extended magazines and silencers that went in the duffel bags with the pistols. They reserved three cars at Hertz and flew out of Sacramento in a private jet with the sun low on their right wing.

"Have to isolate them, figure out what we can do to make all the hits look either accidental or explainable and definitely separate," Thorne told the group as they huddled over bottled Perrier and pretzels. "Some of them could just disappear, and nobody'll come looking."

"Lot of empty desert around Las Vegas," somebody said. Out the window, the view was changing from the Central Valley to the mountains and then the desert.

"Like old times," Thorne said to everybody in general.

When they got to the Moulin Rose, Thorne pushed some cash across the desk to the manager, who didn't touch it. "I'd like to take it, but they're gone. One of the maids saw them loading up in the parking garage. Two hours ago, maybe. Seemed like they were in a hurry. I guess that was because of you guys?"

"Yeah, we've got some paper on them," Thorne said. "If we can find them, we'll hold them for the cops on California warrants. They are very bad people, trying to crack the major banks. Hackers."

"Well, I didn't know," the manager said. "The guy with the cane said they were here for a sci-fi convention up the Strip."

Thorne pushed the money farther across the desk. "You mind if we take a peek at the rooms?"

"Go ahead. Won't be cleaned until tomorrow, so maybe they left something," the manager said. He gathered up the money, got Thorne a key card, and said, "You can go on up on your own. Throw the key away when you leave."

"Thank you," Thorne said.

Three of his men were still waiting in the cars, engines running to keep the air-conditioning working. Thorne went out, told them that the targets had apparently checked out, and said, "Move around a little, keep an eye out. They might still be close."

Thorne and his top assistant, whose name was Red, went up to the rooms, walked through them. There was nothing: no hair in the sink, no dirty towels, no bedding. Red squatted next to a bedside table, turned on the lamp, and squinted at the glass top. "They took the time to wipe the place," he said. "You can see the streaks on the glass."

He stood, walked around to a glass-topped desk, squatted again, checked the glass. "Yup. It's been wiped."

Everything had been wiped: the sinks, the toilet handles, the doorknobs, every surface that might take a fingerprint.

"Nothing here," Thorne said, and led the way back out through the first room.

In the hallway, they met a maid pushing a laundry cart. Red asked her, "These people just checked out. Did you take the towels out, the sheets and bedcovers?"

She shook her head. "Nah. I don't know what's going on. I had an empty cart parked up the hall. When I come out of the room I was cleaning, it was full. If they's gone from here, that must be where the linens come from. That don't happen. First time, for me, anyway. But it's all down the chute now."

Down the chute: already mixed up with the other sheets from the hotel. Unfindable.

As they walked away, the two men put on their sunglasses, and Thorne looked back at the line of doors that led into the rooms that the targets had used. "It's almost like they knew we were coming for them," he said.

Red nodded. "Yeah. Exactly like that."

Outside, in the open, Thorne got on the phone and called Sync. "I got some bad news and I've got some worse news."

"Give it to me," Sync said.

"They're gone and they've wiped the rooms, so we won't be able to ID whoever's with them," Thorne said.

"Is that the bad news," Sync asked, "or the worse news?"

"That's the bad news."

"What's the worse news?"

"We maybe got a leak," Thorne said. "And it's somewhere near the top."

Each of the two cars carried a phone that they believed was safe to use, especially if they stayed away from key words like *Singular* or *Shay* or *Odin* or *Twist,* words that a big intelligence agency might be able to pull out of the air and attach to a phone number.

Odin also worried about voice recognition and suggested that only Cruz and Cade make the calls because he didn't believe Singular would have identified either of them.

"Gonna be a long haul, man," said Cade, who was sitting up front with Twist driving. "Fourteen hours, if we don't stop."

"My leg won't last that long," Twist replied. "I'll need to get out and walk a couple times."

From the back, Odin asked, "What happened to your leg?" as he unfolded a road map they were using instead of the phone GPS.

"Broke it," Twist said in a tone that suggested end of story. At least it did to Cade, who looked over his shoulder at Odin and gave him a quick headshake, but Odin was lousy at subtext. He instead persisted:

"An accident, one presumes? Car? Ski jump? Banana peel? The limp appears to me to be a minor hitch in the ball and socket. . . . You really need the cane?"

Twist checked Odin's reflection in the rearview mirror, and Odin sort of smiled at him. That got him: a bruised and sincere kid. He decided not to bite his head off.

"I can manage without the cane if I have to, but it relieves some pressure along an old fracture. There are some secondary uses for a gold-weighted cane, which Cade will likely, behind my back, explain later. Okay, then? Let's drive."

Odin nodded in the mirror and said, "Give me one of the phones. We paid for some data on that, right?"

Cade fumbled in his pockets, then passed it back. "Watch out for key words."

"Not gonna use many words," Odin said. He turned the phone on, typed with his thumbs for a few seconds, waited, got into another rush of thumb-typing, then waited some more. Cade said, "You've been on that for a while."

"Not giving anything away, though—went through Sweden to AfghanistanBananaStand, and . . . we're in."

"In what?" Twist asked.

"Nevada DMV. The winner is . . . Jerry Kulicek. . . . Let's see if we can find his photo. . . . And there we are."

He passed the phone over the front seat to Twist. "This the guy you gave five hundred dollars to?"

Twist: "That's him."

Odin said, "Saving his name, address, car tag numbers, license plates. With this, we can get anything we want."

"How about a phone number?" Twist asked.

"That, too, but it'll take a little more research than I want to do on a cell phone. We can get that when we're done with Janes."

The sun was dropping low in the sky, south of Hoover Dam, when Shay woke up from a hard nap, feeling unprepared.

"If I'm going to threaten a U.S. senator with a gun, I need to look like I know what I'm doing," she said, squeezing the pillow from Cruz to her chest. "Plus, I should probably learn where that safety thing is. You know, learn how *not* to shoot somebody."

"You've never handled a gun?" asked Cruz, draining a can of Coke and holding his highway speed to a law-abiding seventy-five.

"Nope."

"Then we best find ourselves some wide, wide open space," he said.

They were over the Nevada border and fifteen miles into Arizona Red Rock Country, where about the only living things were lizards, buzzards, and small packs of bony wild horses. Cruz swerved off the highway at the next exit—one shuttered gas station—and took another quick turn down a ranch road that showed a thin sheen of gravel over the tan desert soil. Fenfang and X, dozing beside each other in the backseat, felt the change of texture and woke up.

"Where are we?" Fenfang asked.

"Out in the desert," Cruz said. "We're going to shoot the gun."

"Why?"

Shay turned her head. "In case I ever have to."

Two or three miles in, Cruz found a shallow arroyo with a cut bank that would work for target practice. He drove on for another mile, making sure that they weren't close to a ranch house, then turned back to the arroyo, and they all climbed out. As X sniffed around for the perfect place to pee, Cruz walked his Coke can down the arroyo maybe twenty feet and braced it against the weedy bank.

Then he went to get the .45 from the truck, a chunk of black steel that smelled of oil and something else, something sharper and metallic. West had given him the gun in the minutes before the raid on the Singular prison, and while he'd pulled it out of his waistband when the gunfire between West and a guard erupted, he hadn't fired it. Instead, at West's urging, he'd pulled Shay out of the building to safety—and been left to wonder if he might have saved them both if only . . .

Back to the gun:

"These are very simple machines," he said, holding it up in front of the girls' faces. X stood between Shay and Fenfang, looking up at the gun, his head cocked to one side. "There's a barrel, there's a chamber to hold the bullet, there's a hammer that hits the firing pin that hits the primer, which is a little metal button on the back of the cartridge, and that shoots off a spark that fires the gunpowder that shoots the slug out the barrel."

The butt of the gun held a magazine, which in turn held seven cartridges with copper-plated slugs that each had a bowl-shaped indentation in the tip.

He popped a cartridge out of the magazine and showed them the primer, the small round silver cap in the center of the back end of the cartridge. "The firing pin hits this, and boom."

"But they're safe to handle?" Shay asked.

"Sure. You could walk around with them loose in your pants pocket and it'd be really weird if one of them went off—not that I think you should do that," Cruz said as he thumbed the cartridge back into the magazine. He smacked the magazine back into the grip.

"You hold the gun with both hands," he said. "Think about pointing it, rather than aiming it. Think about pointing your finger."

He gave the gun to Shay, who pointed it at the can. "Not as heavy as I thought it would be," she said. She touched the trigger with her index finger. "Shoot now?"

"No. This kind of gun you need to cock before you can fire," Cruz said. He took the gun back and showed them how that was done, pushing the slide back so they could see the cartridge ready to load into the gun's firing chamber, then letting the slide slam forward.

"Now it's loaded and ready to fire." He pointed the gun at the can and said, "Click off the safety here. . . ." He did that. "And fire. . . ."

BANG!

The shot was loud, and Shay and Fenfang both jumped. They saw a puff of dirt as the slug hit a few inches left of the can. X snorted at the faint odor of gunpowder, then set his eye on Shay, as if trouble might be coming.

"After the first shot, the gun loads automatically, which is why they call it an automatic," Cruz said. "It's ready to fire again. You can fire as fast as you can pull the trigger, until you run out of ammo."

He pulled the trigger. *BANG!*

He missed the can again, but was close. He asked Shay, "You ready to try?"

"Yes," she said.

He clicked the safety on, she took the gun, and he stood behind her, wrapping his arms around her, adjusting her grip. "Look down over the barrel, but don't worry so much about aiming. Just point it at the can. Click the safety off."

She did, and he said, "It's hot, it's ready to fire. Pull the trigger when you're ready. Don't yank on it, just squeeze. . . ."

BANG!

The gun jumped in her hand . . . but not that much. She had it back on target in a half second and pulled the trigger again. *BANG!*

They had two boxes holding twenty cartridges each. Shay had found them in West's Jeep, stashed under the seat. Cruz suggested they hold back one box, "just in case." Shay found she liked the rush of trying to hit the can, and wondered if twenty shots would be enough "to get good."

"Shay," Cruz said with a smile that was just a little condescending, "you're a certified badass, but you're not going to hit the can on your first time out. No offense."

Shay was neither offended nor deterred; she just lined up her next shot. After a couple more rounds, the bullets hitting high and wide on the bank wall, Cruz showed her how to pull the magazine and unload the auto-loaded shell that was already in the chamber.

He then had her reload the gun, jack a shell into the chamber, click off the safety, and fire. And do it all again. And again. And again. Shay didn't hit the can, but she was hitting within a few inches of it a lot of the time. She paused to rest her arms for a bit, and Cruz walked back to the Jeep for a bottle of water.

Fenfang grinned at Shay. "You are becoming like a cowboy."

"Cowgirl," Shay said. "You wanna try?"

As soon as the words were out of her mouth, she realized their stupidity: Fenfang, the girl without a mind of her own, could certainly not be entrusted with a loaded weapon. Dash might ambush them.

"Ah, I . . . ," Shay stammered.

Fenfang put up a hand to stop her. "I understand," she said.

Shay was relieved to hear that, but it wasn't only out on a shooting range that she and Cruz might need to be on the lookout for Dash; it could be at Dash's house itself. Shay thought about that for a few moments and said, "Maybe what we need is a code word, something you could say, or some answer you could give, when we really need to be sure you're . . . you. Would that be okay with you?"

"I think that would make us all feel better. We make a code in my language because this lady does not know Chinese . . . only maybe some Spanish."

"That sounds smart," said Shay, and they quickly settled on a simple exchange they would rely on anytime Shay or the others felt a need to check Fenfang's ID:

"Are you okay?"

"Háixíng."

I am okay.

When they were down to the last seven cartridges from the first box, Cruz had Shay fire three shots quickly, trying to repoint after each shot. With the next three, he had her pull the trigger as quickly as she could: the shots were all over the place. "If you take just one extra tenth of a second to steady yourself, you'll shoot a lot better than when you're just pulling the trigger as fast as you can," he said. "If you ever have to pull the trigger, remember that. You probably won't, but try."

"I'll do that," Shay said.

From behind them, Fenfang said, "You should practice once with your words, too, Shay. When you make the lady think you will shoot her—so she will do what we want."

"Good idea," Shay said. Back at the hotel, she and Twist had written scripts for the two groups to follow when they confronted Dash and Janes. Clicking on the safety, she handed the gun back to Cruz, who put it in his waistband, and they started from the top.

"Give me the gun," Shay said in a stone-cold voice.

Cruz pulled the gun out and handed it to her. Shay thumbed off the safety with a dramatic flourish, held the pistol upright in front of her face, and took aim.

"What are you doing?" Cruz asked in mock alarm.

Shay shook her head and lowered the gun. "The line is, 'What are you going to do?' "

"Sorry. . . . What are you going to do?"

Shay widened her stance and again took aim. "I'm gonna kill the bitch. Say good-bye to Senator Dash."

BANG!

The can flew through the air like a hockey puck.

Feeling slightly more prepared, they continued south to Kingman, Arizona, stopped to use the bathrooms and buy water and some snacks, and then headed east on I-40, rolling along at an efficient eighty miles an hour. The Jeep wasn't the most comfortable vehicle in the world, but out in the desert, it felt seriously competent.

They passed the time explaining the word *snack* to Fenfang, in both verb and noun forms.

"So I snack on a snack?" she asked.

"Yes," Shay said. "My brother once said he felt a little snacky— meaning he wanted to snack on a snack."

Cruz said, "You can get snack cakes . . . so that's like an adjective. If you're feeling a little snacky, you could snack on snack-cake snacks."

"Could you snack on a dinner?"

"No, because a dinner is a meal . . . so you eat a dinner. Of course, you can also eat a snack. . . ."

Cruz and Shay traded off driving every couple hours. Whoever wasn't driving sat in the backseat with Fenfang to help her if she had a seizure and monitor her for signs of Dash. They were nearly nine hours out of Vegas without a seizure, and all of them were starting to privately brace for trouble.

As they approached the lights of a huge casino at Acoma Pueblo, New Mexico, X, sitting up front with Cruz, suddenly stood, leaned over the seat, and pointed his nose at Fenfang. She was in the midst of telling Shay and Cruz about Internet blackouts by the government in China, and how she and her university friends got around them, but the dog's nose, two inches from her own, made her stop.

"Don't be rude, X," Shay said, and pushed him back over the seat. Fenfang resumed speaking, but the dog came back at her with his nose, sniffing at her. Suddenly Fenfang stiffened, and then her eyes rolled up and she started to thrash.

"She's seizing!" Shay said, and threw herself across Fenfang, trying to hold her away from the hard surfaces in the car, things that could hurt her. Fenfang's back arched, and she began to rhythmically shake as Cruz pulled to the side of the road.

When the Jeep was stopped, Cruz knelt on the front seat and asked, "What can I do?"

"Nothing, unless . . . she gets out of control, but I think I have her. . . ."

Ninety seconds after the seizure started, Fenfang began to relax and her eyes opened, and she said something in Chinese and looked at Shay as though she didn't recognize her. She turned her head away and said something else in Chinese, then turned back to Shay and said, "Shay?"

"Are you okay?"

"I think I am okay."

"What's the word?"

"*Háixíng.*"

"Okay. You're back."

"I have . . ." Fenfang touched her head. "Pain inside. How do you call it?"

"I don't know, maybe we need to find a hotel. . . ."

"No, no . . . this is, mmm, normal pain. Is that correct? Like when you study too hard? I need, mmm, aspirin."

"That, we've got," Cruz said. "Check in my backpack."

During the seizure, X had been intently focused on Fenfang, almost like a hunting dog focused on its prey; now he relaxed and settled back in his seat.

Fenfang said, "X knew I was going to have a seizure before I did. His nose . . . that was what he was telling me."

Shay looked at X and said, "I think you're right." She reached out and gave him a scratch between the ears. "Now we'll have to pay even *more* attention to you." The dog panted and hung his tongue out.

Twist, Odin, and Cade stopped in a state forest in Northern California, in the dark, Twist hobbling off to stretch his legs. Cade aimed Odin the opposite way and told him why Twist needed a cane.

"What happened was, he nearly got beaten to death when he was twenty by some drunk assholes," Cade said. "Twist was living in a warehouse, illegally, getting started as an artist, and he was walking back there when he ran into these three rednecks who thought he looked homeless and jumped him for fun. They beat him up and kicked him senseless. Broke both his legs and cracked his pelvis and left him for dead. Never were caught. When he got out of the hospital, he bought a pistol, legally, and carried it with him, waiting for them to come back. Lucky for Twist, they never did, because he was going to kill them."

"Lucky for them, too," Odin said.

"I guess, but that's not the way I think about it," Cade said. " 'Cause I didn't care what happened to them after I read the police file. Dead was okay with me. But it would have been a tragedy if Twist had been sent off to prison and there never was a Twist Hotel. Dude's helped a lot of kids."

"Like you?"

"Yes."

"And Shay."

"Yes. But hey, don't ask him a lot of personal stuff. Man gets edgy."

"All I was asking was why he limps, and he can't be maniacally private if he let you read that police file. . . ."

"He didn't *let* me read any files, Odin," Cade said. "He's totally stonewalled me on every personal thing I've ever asked him. So I went looking for myself."

"Police files are so easy," Odin said.

Cade smiled at that and gave him a fist bump.

They traded hacking stories until Twist came ambling back to the car, carrying his cane. Back on the freeway, Cade and Twist talked for a while about the hotel, and every few minutes, one of them would throw out an improbable theory about the warning they'd gotten from the mystery man in Vegas.

Odin, who was driving, had the only one they couldn't refute: "When Storm did the raid on the laboratory that started all of this, we had an insider. I don't know who it was—but it's possible that he's still in place, and that he might have heard something."

"He happened to know where we were, and also know someone

in Vegas who could warn us?" Twist asked. He didn't even bother to sound skeptical.

"Better idea than any you have," Odin said.

"That's true. Mine are all about a one on a one-to-ten scale. Yours is a two."

Eight hours after the gun lesson, past the Meteor Crater, past the Painted Desert, past the Petrified Forest, Shay, Cruz, Fenfang, and X pulled into the Bandolero Motel in Albuquerque, New Mexico.

"This has got the look," Shay said. The look of a place that would take cash and not ask questions. "I'll get the rooms."

"Better that I do it," Cruz said.

"Why?"

"Because *bandolero* is Spanish, and there are five beat-up trucks with Spanish bumper stickers in the parking lot. This is a Mexican motel. And as you might have noticed . . ." Cruz patted his chest.

"You look Mexican. Go ahead."

He got out and walked into the motel's office, and Fenfang asked, "He is Mexican?"

"No, he's an American, but his parents were Mexican. Though it's not incorrect to say he's Mexican American. . . . It's kind of complicated to explain."

"No, I understand this. It is not at all complicated like snacky snacks."

Cruz paid in advance for two rooms for two days. They were all asleep before two o'clock and didn't get going until ten the next morning. Cruz woke first, knocked on the girls' door, and found that Shay had wired it shut to contain Fenfang if Dash emerged. Shay undid the clothes hanger she'd bent around the chain lock and slipped outside.

"She had a seizure around four this morning," Shay said. "Two, actually, they were back to back, about a minute in between."

"You should have gotten me up to help you."

"You needed to sleep," Shay said. "You've been doing most of the driving, you never nap, you get up before everyone else. . . . Wait, you're not a vampire, are you?"

He tapped his teeth together noisily, then bent to her throat and gave her a little nip. Shay responded with an "Ooo, ow!" that sounded awfully real; Cruz was mortified. "Jeez, I'm sorry—did I hurt you?"

"Not my neck—my feet," she said. "The sun's already so hot, the pavement's like a skillet."

He looked down at her prancing feet, understanding the problem now, and scooped her up in his arms. "I rescue girls with hot feet," he said. That made her laugh.

Cruz said, "It's nice when you smile." Her arms were around his neck, and they looked at each other for a moment before Cruz opened the door and set her down on the grungy green carpet.

"See you in twenty minutes," he said. "The vampire needs an Egg McMuffin."

Shay shut the door with a grin still on her face, and they all got cleaned up and went to find a drive-thru.

At noon, they rolled into Santa Fe, an hour north of the motel. The city was the oddest Shay had ever seen, mud-colored adobe houses everywhere, many surrounded by high walls. There was a feeling of being paused in some earlier time, with dozens of Indians selling jewelry on blankets in the plaza downtown, and gravel roads all over the place, even a couple of blocks from the state capitol.

And it was dry: hard, high desert. The sign coming into town said the city was 7,199 feet above sea level, which was a couple thousand feet higher than Denver, and in places, it almost seemed like you could reach up and touch the cottony clouds.

Senator Charlotte Dash lived on the edge of the city, up a low, scrub-covered mountain, inside a walled compound—one they knew from satellite and aerial photographs downloaded in Vegas. Those photos had also shown Sun Mountain, a huge rounded hill that hung over the east side of the city. In the photos, they could see the thin thread of a hiking trail up the mountain.

They got binoculars at an REI store and sandwiches and water at a deli, and by two o'clock, they were settled on a dusty cutout in the mountain trail and looking down at Dash's mansion, a half mile away and three hundred feet below.

Cruz said, "Look at all that green grass. More green grass than anybody."

"Is that bad?" Shay asked.

"If you live in L.A. or any other desert, water hogs are not appreciated," Cruz said. He handed her the binoculars.

Shay brought them to her eyes, looked at Dash's house and her lush gardens, and after a minute, said, "She's also got the highest walls."

"She has much to hide," Fenfang said. "It is the same in China. Houses with walls to hide things."

"We can take that small street up the hill and park in that grassy place until we get the gate open. Nobody will see," Cruz said, pointing. "We go over the wall right next to the car, you see the greenhouse. . . ."

They worked out a variety of possible approaches, taking turns looking at the house. Ten minutes later, Cruz said, "When the sun hits that side wall, it sparkles along the top. Here, take a look."

Shay looked and said, "I see it. You're right. What is it?"

Cruz: "If it's like it is in Mexico, could be broken glass. You know, to discourage thieves."

"Or angry teenagers," said Shay.

Twist, Odin, and Cade had taken turns sleeping in the truck, best as they could, but were tired when they checked into the Triple-A Motel on the edge of Eugene. Twist got two rooms—he still didn't share—and paid for two days. They probably wouldn't stay that long, but he wanted a bolt-hole in case of trouble.

The Triple-A, which apparently hoped to be confused with motels approved by the American Automobile Association, was a Twist special: a place with a roof that probably didn't leak too much, toilets that mostly flushed, and beds that smelled funny, but not too funny. The guy in the office who took the cash was a guy who wouldn't ask questions, or even think of any.

At seven o'clock in the morning, they were all asleep. At two o'clock in the afternoon, they were up again, eating pancakes, quietly reviewing what they needed most from Janes and how they intended to get it.

When Shay, Cruz, Fenfang, and X began their watch, there were two cars and a truck parked behind a steel gate in Dash's front wall. The truck, which belonged to a gardener, left at three o'clock. One of the cars left an hour later. "Maid," Cruz grunted, watching through the binoculars.

The other car left a few minutes after—a well-dressed woman in heels, not Dash. They hadn't seen Dash at all.

At five o'clock, a garage door rolled up, and a huge white

Suburban backed carefully out. When it turned, they could see the driver. Shay, who had the binoculars, said, "There she is. That's Dash."

As the SUV rolled slowly up to the gate, a back window dropped and a German shepherd stuck its head out in the open air and sniffed.

"That ain't no poodle," said Cruz, who'd taken the binoculars.

He passed them to Fenfang, who said, "It is good I know the control words."

"Let's hope we don't forget them in the heat of the moment," said Shay. "Else we're gonna be somebody's lunch."

"Midnight snack, I think," Cruz said.

"Enough of these snacks," Fenfang said, peering through the binoculars.

"Nein packen," said Cruz.

Fenfang went over the German commands for the dogs again, and that night they practiced them as they headed back up the mountain. Shay was wearing the black shirt, with the Sony camera tucked into her armpit. As Cruz drove, she shot a few seconds of video to make sure the camera's lens wasn't blocked by a fold in the sleeve.

The video was fine; she just had to remember to keep aiming at Dash once the action got rolling.

Five minutes out, Cruz called Cade: "We're going."

Cade said, "Yes. We are, too. Good luck."

"You too," Cruz said, and jammed the phone in his pocket.

9

They parked out of sight, off the road, twenty feet from Dash's perimeter wall. They left X locked in the Jeep and slipped past the desert brush. Shay unhooked a thick blue yoga mat from her backpack, shook it out. Cruz crouched next to the adobe wall, and Shay settled on his shoulders, her legs dangling down his chest. "Lift."

Cruz caught her by the feet and stood up. Shay couldn't quite reach the top: Cruz did a forearm curl, lifting until she could step on his shoulders, her gloved hands against the rough plaster. When she was upright, she tested her balance, then felt along the top of the wall, where she found the embedded glass shards they'd seen from the hillside.

They were sharp, but manageable, meant to defeat bare-handed intruders. She threw the yoga mat over the wall, then carefully shifted her weight onto it until she was sure that none of the glass would penetrate.

Fenfang stood ten feet away, at the edge of the passing road, watching for cars. There was no moon, but about a million stars, and a gritty wind rustled her long hair and made her blink. She half turned to the other two and whispered, "I see nobody."

Shay hoisted herself onto the mat and then waited atop the wall for a minute, listening, watching the darkened house. She heard a faint toll of church bells from the old cathedral downtown—midnight—and dug inside her pants pocket for the small banded stone Cade had given her for luck the night she'd rappelled off an office building in downtown L.A. She rubbed the stone between her fingers, said a silent wish that no harm would come to any of them in the next hour, and dropped to the other side.

She was behind a four-foot-tall clump of scrubby plantings called chamisa. Again, she listened. After a few seconds, she took a coiled rope from her pack, held on to one end, and threw the rope back across the wall. On the other side, Cruz tied it to a homemade rope ladder. He called quietly, "Okay."

Shay pulled on her end of the rope until the ladder curled just over the top of the wall, then tied it to the base of a piñon tree and gave the rope a tug.

Cruz picked up his backpack, pulled it on, turned, and whispered, "Now." Fenfang took a last look down the road, then hurried to the wall and awkwardly climbed the rope ladder as Cruz held it steady. She clambered atop the mat, sat down, and dropped inside.

Cruz followed a few seconds later. When they were all together, they pulled down the rope and ladder, huddled behind the piñon, and bundled the gear into Shay's backpack. And heard the crunch of a car's wheels on gravel . . .

They all ducked, then felt silly, because neither they nor the passing motorist could possibly see each other with the eight-foot wall between them. "We're idiots," Shay whispered with a smile.

"Pure reflex," Cruz said. He took the black .45 out of his pack and pushed it under his waistband, at the small of his back. All three of them were wearing ski masks rolled up as watch caps; now they pulled them down over their faces and adjusted the eyeholes.

Shay touched Fenfang on the shoulder. "You still with us?"

Fenfang nodded, and part of a smile showed through the breathing hole, but Shay needed reassurance. "The word, please . . ."

"Oh, right . . . *Háixíng.*"

"Good. C'mon."

Fenfang and Cruz fell in line as Shay took them through a formal garden, carefully avoiding the crunchy gravel pathways and the spotlighted bronzes—two life-sized buffalo, an Indian maiden, and several nineteenth-century cavalrymen, crouching with rifles—to the back of an elaborate greenhouse.

As Fenfang had predicted, the greenhouse door was locked and protected by an alarm. Cruz illuminated a keypad with a thread-thin beam from a flashlight with a tape-covered lens. Fenfang reached out and tapped five numbers into the keypad, and they heard the lock snap open.

Shay whispered, "Okay," and opened the door.

The greenhouse was filled with orchids, barely visible as fragile gray shapes against the general darkness, and they wrinkled their noses at the chemical odors—fertilizer, insecticide, fungicide. A wide bench ran down the middle of the greenhouse, with narrower benches at the side. Shay turned on her flashlight, which had a red LED option, less visible than the white LEDs; it was just luminous enough to get them down the greenhouse aisle.

The greenhouse connected to the underground wine cellar of the main house, but only through the trapdoor hidden beneath the rag rug in the northwest corner. Fenfang kicked away the rug to reveal the steel door in the concrete floor. It, too, was protected by an alarm and another keypad lock. She stooped and punched in four numbers. The lock popped, and they were in.

They went down seven flagstone steps and, in the thin light of the taped flashlights, walked past wall-to-wall coolers stacked with thousands of glistening bottles of wine. They continued out through a set of French doors, past a mechanical room with two big boilers to heat the sprawling house above, and up another set of steps to the kitchen entrance, where they paused and listened.

They heard the scrabbling claws of the dogs advancing on the brick floors on the other side of the door. The dogs didn't bark, because that would give them away. They were like drone missiles, unseen until they exploded. They knew there were intruders in the cellar, because the dogs could hear a fly walking across a window.

Cruz said, "If it doesn't work, stand back." He had the gun in his hand.

"Don't shoot one of us," Shay said. She opened the door just a crack, and the dogs were right there, teeth flashing in the ambient light above them.

Shay called, *"Zurücktreten!"* The dogs stood down at once, though they kept their attention on the intruders. Shay said, *"Still halten!"* The dogs obediently dropped to their bellies and froze in place.

The three teens eased past into the kitchen, the dogs following them only with their eyes. The kitchen didn't smell of food at all—it smelled of disinfectant. They passed an eight-burner stove and four wall-mounted commercial ovens and a stainless steel refrigerator that could have held a whole cow. They crept down a short corridor to a dining room and through the dining room to a living room. The living room and the corridor beyond were illuminated with dim cove lighting and decorated with cowboy paintings and Navajo rugs. They were halfway to the target bedroom at the end of the hall when a woman's voice, both shrill and commanding, yelled: "Somebody there? Who's there? Otto? Karl? *Herkommen!*"

"Calling the dogs," Shay muttered. She went running up a short flight of wide stairs for the bedroom.

Too late. In the next second, the door to the safe room was activated, a bank-vault-caliber steel panel bursting from a hidden slide and slamming shut.

No need for subtlety now. Shay wheeled around and shouted, "Fenfang!" and saw that Fenfang was already groping behind a mounted pronghorn skull. Cruz ripped the tape off his flashlight and shone it at the wall, and Fenfang found the keypad behind the left horn and entered the code: 71717. The safe room door rolled back with a scraping sound as the dogs breached the hall.

"Zurücktreten!" Shay shouted, and again the dogs stopped on a dime, though now they looked uncertain, confused.

Shay swung her light into the bedroom, and there, reaching across a four-poster bed for a hardwired phone on a nightstand, was Senator Charlotte Dash. She fumbled off the receiver.

"Stop right there!" Shay yelled.

"Don't hurt me. Don't hurt—" Dash put her hands up beside her head, as though to fend off a blow.

"Shut up," Shay snapped. She stalked over to the senator, who was dressed in a white nightgown, and ripped the phone out of the wall. "You have a contract with Singular Corp. What are they going to do for you? When are they going to do it?"

As she asked the questions, she cocked her right arm a bit to the side: filming.

Dash—her blond hair coiffed in a lacquered flip—said,

"Singular? I don't know what you're talking about." She braced herself against the headboard. "How did you get in here? Do you know who I am?"

Fenfang stepped forward—Shay pivoting to catch her on camera—and said: "I let them in. I gave them the security codes. And the dogs' commands."

"What? Who are you?"

Fenfang reached out to her right and flipped on the bedroom lights. She continued over to the nightstand, opened the top drawer, and found the remote control where she expected it to be. Shay stepped back so she could catch both women on the video at the same time.

Dash, pulling away from Fenfang, was almost as indignant as she was frightened. "What the hell are you doing?"

Tapping several numbers on the keypad, Fenfang said, "I am opening the front gate."

"You can't know that. . . . I've never written it down. Who are you?"

With one hand, Fenfang peeled off the mask and, in the same motion, her long black wig. Her wired-up scalp, peppered with pin-heads, glittered in the light of the crystal chandelier.

"You know who I am," she said. "Because I am in part . . . you."

The senator's hand went to her throat. "No! They said it didn't work."

Shay stepped closer. "We need to know three things now. How far does this go? We know you're involved. What about the CIA, the military, other politicians? Who, besides you, is paying Singular? We need the names now. And we need to know how many people are like our friend. How many human copies have you made?"

Dash said, "You're crazy. I'm not saying a thing." She shouted, "Otto! Karl! *Herkommen!*"

Cruz slammed the bedroom door, locking the dogs out.

Shay said, "We need—"

"Not a thing!" Dash shouted. "Nothing! Never!"

Shay turned to Cruz and said, "Give me the gun."

He slipped it out of his waistband and handed it to her. "What are you going to do?"

Shay took the gun and thumbed the safety off with a metallic click. Didn't worry about covering the camera, because they'd edit this part out, anyway.

"I'm gonna kill the bitch," she said. She raised the gun. "Say good-bye to Senator Dash."

Something in her voice was both cold and convincing.

"Don't! Please." Dash did not want to die. She'd been going to great lengths to avoid that. . . .

Cruz: "Let her talk."

"Too late," Shay said, her voice climbing. "They murdered West. Turned Fenfang into a lab rat. Too late . . ."

It was acting, they'd written the script with Twist back in Las Vegas, but also . . . it wasn't.

"No!" Dash raised her hands in front of her face as if they might deflect the .45 hollow points. "Whatever you want! Whatever you want!"

Cruz had the next line: he put out a hand toward the gun, but without touching it, and said, "Give her this chance. Jus' one. She bullshits us, we kill the *gabacha*."

Fenfang, out of Dash's line of sight, had pulled a hardcover novel off a shelf and raised it over her head the way they'd practiced, and in the next second, she threw it down on the hardwood floor. *BANG!*

Dash's hands flew away from her face, and she looked down at her chest and probed her stomach to see if she'd been shot. "Still cocked," Shay said coolly, and the senator looked up to find the gun still pointed at her head. Shay angled the camera at Fenfang and asked, "What do you want to do?"

Fenfang, clutching the wig and mask she'd peeled off in her dramatic reveal, regarded Dash for a long moment, then said, "What she did to me . . . I will die from this. If she talks, maybe we can save other people. If she lies, then . . . I have no pity."

"I won't lie," Dash said urgently. "Whatever you want."

"I want to know how many there are like her," Shay said, nodding at Fenfang. "How many others have had your memories implanted in their brains?"

"I . . . I don't know," stammered Dash.

"Who else is involved? The NSA? CIA? Other politicians?" Shay demanded.

Dash was shaking her head. "No. No one."

"She's lying," Shay spat. "I'm going to—"

Cruz broke in: "Take us to the safe."

Dash cut her eyes away from them.

"You want to live? Take us to the safe," he repeated.

"I'll show it to you, but it won't do any good." She got out of bed, found some slippers on the floor. "It's my husband's safe, and he's dead."

Dash shuffled out of the room, cutting a wide circle around Fenfang. Cruz stepped behind Shay and said, under his breath, "Don't let the dogs see the gun."

Shay dropped her gun hand to her side and concentrated on filming as Dash led the way down the hall past the two black-and-tan German shepherds, still frozen in place. Shay had thought X was large at seventy-five pounds, but these dogs were half again as big, with killer eyes as cold as marbles.

Dash muttered, "Worthless mutts. Ten thousand dollars each, and they sit there."

Dash took them to a utility closet filled with brooms, mops, and other cleaning supplies. She reached out and grabbed the middle shelf and pulled. It came out from the wall to reveal the solid steel door of an embedded safe.

"That's all I know," she said. "My husband had the combination."

Fenfang shook her head: "No, she knows the combination. So do I." She stepped forward and pushed 7415963, which made an N shape on the keypad. She turned the handle, and the safe popped open. It was stuffed with documents in brown file folders and stacks of bundled hundred-dollar bills.

Dash crossed her arms tightly in front of her and said, "That money can be traced."

"I doubt it," said Cruz, "but we're not thieves." He took a plastic garbage bag out of his hip pocket, and he and Fenfang tossed in the files, ignoring the cash.

Shay said, "Now—the other safe. The one with the good stuff."

Dash was beginning to panic. She shot a look down the hall at the dogs. Shay touched the woman's pale cheek with the muzzle of the gun, and Dash flinched. She said, "Okay, okay. But you don't know what you're getting into here. There are secret government papers. Every government agent in the country will be searching for you."

"I suppose," Shay said. "If you're alive to tell them."

The second safe was in a wet bar off the living room, the last place an intruder might look for it. The floor was covered with wooden parquet tiles, and when Dash put her feet on two of them in an out-of-the-way corner, they both sank almost imperceptibly into the floor, and when she stepped off them, a two-by-two-foot section of the floor retracted into the wall, exposing the steel face of the safe.

Cruz said, "I'm gonna get the car. You got this covered?"

"I do," Shay said. She was six feet from Dash, the gun leveled at the woman's chest.

"Don't kill her unless you have to," Cruz said. "If we kill her, the local cops get involved and then the feds. If we don't kill her, maybe she keeps her mouth shut."

"Not likely," Shay said. "After that torture palace in Sacramento, after what they did to my brother, and with her money . . ." She was goading Dash into talking, keeping the camera on her face.

"I did nothing!" Dash said. "I paid for medical care."

Shay was about to press her—to get her to say on camera what she'd paid Singular for—but then Fenfang was screaming.

"I am medical care? This is medical care? This is murder! I am a human person; I am not a laboratory rat!"

Cruz rushed back to them, putting himself between Fenfang and Dash. He looked into Fenfang's eyes and said quietly, "Hold it together. We're nearly there."

Finally, Fenfang nodded. *"Háixíng."*

"You guys clean out the safe; I'll bring the car around."

Fenfang got the combination right but wasn't strong enough to lift the heavy safe door. Shay wagged the gun at Dash and said, "Help her."

With both Fenfang and Dash pulling up on the door, they got it upright, and they all peered into the safe, set like a small square well in the floor. More documents, more cash, and gold.

Fenfang stared down at the contents.

Shay gestured at Dash with the gun barrel: "Over there, sit on the red couch." She did. And to Fenfang: "Get the files and any computer stuff."

As Shay filmed the scene, Fenfang knelt next to the safe and began pulling the contents out onto the floor. Files, envelopes, and four thick manuscripts bound in brown covers stamped TOP-SECRET. "It is too much for the bag. We need something stronger."

"Right. Here," Shay said. She pulled out her street knife, walked to the couch where Dash was sitting, picked up one of the pillows, and slashed it open. With the foam pads removed, the pillowcase made a heavy cloth bag. Fenfang began filling it up with paper. Beneath the files and the cash were bars and bars of gold. Fenfang lifted one out. It was almost as long as the palm of her hand, and she said, "One kilo. It says 999 PURE." The bar was a dull yellow with an oddly crude surface.

Shay looked back at Fenfang, who was fixated on the gold, and said, "Fenfang. We need to—"

Fenfang shook her head in a gesture that imitated Dash's gesture a few seconds earlier, and Shay felt a chill. "Fenfang!"

Fenfang put her hands to her head and said, her voice grating, "She is trying . . ."

"Fight it! Fight it!"

"I fight. I think of Liko! I think of my mother!"

. X galloped through the front door and into the living room, followed by Cruz. They both looked at Fenfang, and Shay said, "Get her to the car. Dash is trying to get into her head."

Fenfang said, "No, I am winning. I push her back."

Cruz said, "We need the code."

Fenfang got shakily to her feet. *"Háixíng."*

Shay turned and handed the gun to Cruz. "If she gives you any shit . . ."

"Might be fun to break all her bones."

"Your call," Shay said. "I want to cruise the house, see what I can see."

She didn't do that. Instead, she ran up the stairs into Dash's bedroom, looked around—and found Dash's laptop. A cell phone was there, too, plugged into a charger, and though her fingers twitched with temptation, Odin had warned against taking it because of possible GPS tracking. Shay stripped a linen pillowcase off one of the bed pillows and stuffed the laptop inside.

When she came back out, she found X standing in the hallway, staring at the two huge dogs. The hair was standing up on the backs of all three animals, and Shay gave X a hand motion to stay as she edged around the German shepherds. She hooked a finger through X's leather collar and took him with her down the stairs.

Cruz asked, "What about the gold?"

Shay: "We couldn't spend it—it looks like it all has serial numbers."

"It does," Dash said, from the couch.

"Is that how you pay Singular?" Shay asked as she aimed the camera back at Dash.

"For my brain!" Fenfang said sharply. "Money you pay for my young brain!"

Dash just sat with her shoulders hunched and shook her head.

"We could take it with us and bury it in the desert," Shay said with indifference.

Cruz said, "If she told us one useful thing, we could leave the gold. . . ." Baiting her.

Dash, who hadn't gotten to the Senate by being a sissy, sat up straight and scowled. "I'll tell you something—Singular will kill you. I know who you are: you're the people who did the Mindkill website. They will hunt you down."

114

Cruz and Shay, both still wearing the black ski masks over their faces, exchanged a glance, then Shay said, "Not if we take them down first. If you don't talk, if you don't send the police after us, we won't drag you out in front of the television cameras when we take Singular down. This will be our little secret."

Dash stood up. "Most of those papers are secret material from the Intelligence Committee. I can't hide the fact that they were taken away from me: I have to return them when I get back to Washington, I have to account for every page. They can't be copied."

Shay ignored her and said to Cruz, "One more thing. We need the skull shot of the senator."

Fenfang said, "Yes!"

Dash backed away and said, "Don't you touch me."

Cruz handed the gun to Shay, then stepped behind the senator and wrapped his arms around her, pinning her arms. "Get it," he said.

Shay moved in close, and Fenfang, like a woman crazed, stepped over to the struggling woman.

"Your hair is wig, too?" Fenfang asked. The senator's shoulder-length flip had hardly moved since they'd pulled her out of bed. With Cruz still holding tight and the senator shouting expletives, Fenfang raked a hand back and forth through the woman's scalp— "Is not wig"—and then, suddenly, she stopped. "Here is something," she said.

Shay bent close and Fenfang spread apart the hair on one side of Dash's head, and there it was: a bump, a plastic cap the size of a quarter.

"You people are so sick," Shay said to Dash. She was filming it but realized that they still didn't want Dash to know that. Improvising quickly, she took out her cell phone and pulled up a camera app and said, "Smile for the camera."

Dash's face had gone scarlet: she was angry enough to kill them with her bare hands.

"Got it," Shay said. Fenfang, nodding, stepped away and pulled her wig back on over her wired head. Cruz released Dash, who sank to the floor.

Fenfang scowled at the woman. "I am not sorry," she said, then put the ski mask back on, rolling the knit fabric over her face, and went out of the room, carrying the garbage bag of files.

Cruz said to Shay, "Look at X."

The dog was pointing his nose after Fenfang, and Cruz said, "That's not good."

Shay: "Stick with her, take X—X, go with them, buddy." Cruz grabbed the heavier bag of files and ran after Fenfang.

"You're all dead," Dash said again to Shay. "They're far too big to be hurt by a bunch of teenagers."

Shay opened her mouth to respond, to get in the last word, but Cruz began shouting from the yard: "Shay! Shay!"

Shay backed away from Dash, still pointing the gun, and said, "Stay there."

She stepped through the door, slammed it shut, then turned and ran down the front steps toward Cruz, who was crouched over Fenfang. The girl was on the ground, shaking, seizing, the bag of documents on the ground beside her. Shay shouted, "Get her in the Jeep, I'll get the bag. . . ."

Cruz was looking past her and snapped, "Look out, look out. . . ."

Dash had come out on the steps with the two huge shepherds, and she clapped at them and shouted, *"Orkan! Orkan! Orkan!"*

The two huge dogs were coming, like panthers.

Shay shouted *"Zurücktreten!"*—stand down—but the dogs ignored her, and two seconds after Dash screamed at them, the first of the dogs was hurtling through the air at Shay's face—

And was hit in the side of the neck by X—a missile taking down a fighter plane.

The second dog went for Cruz, and the three dogs and Cruz tumbled over each other in a swirling, snarling fight, and then Shay, hoping to distract them, fired the .45 in the air, and the two German shepherds spun out of the fight, some built-in training that made them focus on a gun. One of them launched itself at Shay but was intercepted by X, and Cruz grabbed the other dog's collar and lifted him most of the way off the ground, the dog's hind feet scrabbling against the brick driveway while X bit the first dog's throat. The dog howled and twisted away, and X whirled and launched himself at the exposed stomach of the dog that Cruz was holding and ripped it open. Cruz threw the dog away from himself, and X pounced again, pinning the yelping dog by its throat.

Cruz shouted, "Get Fenfang in the Jeep!"

Shay picked Fenfang off the ground, her limbs still flailing with the seizure, and carried her to the Jeep. She lay Fenfang on the backseat and turned to see Cruz pulling X away from the badly injured second shepherd. He shouted, "Call X, get him and the bag in the Jeep," and he ran toward the front steps of the house, where Dash had frozen in horror.

"Where are you going?" Shay screamed.

"Start the car!"

Cruz ran up the stairs and smashed his fist through Dash's face. She went down, screaming, her front teeth, broken, spewing out across the porch.

Cruz squatted next to her. "You think you can do whatever you want, *kill* whoever you want? You think nothing can touch you?"

Dash lay on the ground, one hand covering her bleeding mouth, the other shoving at Cruz's bloody arm, trying to push him away. Cruz added, "You better find an excuse for the broken teeth that doesn't involve us, or we'll send your top-secret papers to every TV station in the country."

He turned and went down the steps past the bleeding shepherds and climbed into the passenger seat and said, "We gotta go. That gunshot, someone might have called the cops."

The ignition was already running, and Shay hit the gas and went down the driveway and through the front gates that Fenfang had opened with Dash's bedside remote. They turned onto a gravel road that went swirling down the mountainside. Shay pulled her mask off and glanced over at Cruz and his bleeding arm and said, "How bad? How bad are you?"

"Hurts," he said. "But not too bad. I'm more worried about X—I know he got bit."

The dog was sitting on the backseat next to Fenfang and seemed calm enough, his tongue hanging out in its usual *I'm cool* expression. There was blood from the other dogs caked on his muzzle.

"We'll check him. What happened back there? With Dash?"

Cruz hesitated. "I lost my shit for a minute."

"You hurt her?"

"Maybe," he said, and yanked off his mask. Then: "Yeah, I broke a couple of her teeth. Whatever she was yelling at those dogs must have been some kind of override command. Without X, we'd have been hamburger."

Shay said nothing for a moment as she drove through the tangle of streets out to the main road, then: "Broke her teeth. Good. She deserved it. She's a monster. She knows what Singular is doing— God, she's paying for it."

The road intersected with Old Santa Fe Trail, which they took toward town, then swerved onto a side street over to Old Pecos Trail, and then onto the I-25. In the backseat, Fenfang was stirring.

"Code word," Shay said.

"Háixíng," Fenfang said. "Are you two all right?"

"Cruz got an arm bit up. X got some bites, too," Shay said.

Fenfang asked Shay to switch on the interior lights. She found the Jeep's first-aid kit and said to Cruz, "Give me your arm."

Cruz took off his T-shirt and turned and extended his arm, and Fenfang washed it as best she could with an alcohol swab. When Cruz flinched, she said, "Do not be a baby."

Shay asked, again, "How bad?"

"He was not so much bitten as cut. He has teeth cuts and he bleeds, but there is no, mmm, heart-pumping wounds. . . ."

"No arterial bleeding," Shay said. "That's good."

"He might need to be sewn. . . ." Fenfang rifled through the first-aid kit and said, "There are some bandages here that should work."

"We need to go to an emergency room, but not here," Shay said. "Albuquerque."

"Not for me—I've been hurt worse than this. But we might need a vet for X," Cruz said.

Fenfang pulled a long strip of gauze off a roll, folded it over several times, put on some disinfectant cream, and taped it over Cruz's wounds. Then she turned to the dog, carefully parting the thick hair along his neck where she could see blood. "X has bites, not cuts. Holes. The skin is ripped on his legs but is bleeding only a little. . . . It looks . . . It should be bone, but it looks like metal?"

"His back legs aren't the originals," Shay said. "Singular replaced them with prosthetics. Part of their experiments."

"Poor boy," Fenfang said. "But also brave."

Shay reached over and touched Cruz on the thigh. "You too. I couldn't believe what you were doing—what you did to help X. Thank you."

"De nada," Cruz said, and looked away from her, from the intensity of the moment, but he was pleased.

He turned to Fenfang. "What about you? How bad was the seizure?"

"Not so bad," Fenfang said, but she was sweating, the shine glinting off her chin and cheeks. "I fight her with my thinking, with my memories, with *my* brain."

10

The three men were twenty minutes from Janes's house.

Janes lived in the south end of Eugene, on a narrow lane off Spring Boulevard, in an area of long, curving streets with nice houses set in a heavily wooded landscape. Odin hadn't known the area existed until he joined Storm. One of the group's leaders had grown up in an overcooked Swiss chalet about a quarter mile from Janes, as the crow flies, although the streets were so rambling, the driving distance was almost a mile.

"That's another problem," said Twist when Odin mentioned the chalet. "It'd be easy to get lost out there, but the cops will know the streets. We need a couple escape routes."

Odin had mapped two routes using one of the clean laptops and the pancake house Wi-Fi, and Twist copied them on a page in his sketchbook. From studying satellite photos, they'd decided they would park on the main street, cut through one of the wooded areas, and approach Janes's house from the side. From there, they'd try to spot the best entry.

As they left the pancake house, Twist taped the sketchbook page to the truck's dash. "We need to rehearse the escape routes," he said.

When they got to Janes's neighborhood, though, it was clear that their basic plan wouldn't work: the side approach, which appeared heavily wooded from the satellite views, was wide open to a house with a deck next door. If they were seen walking through the trees by a crime-stopper type, the police would be there in four minutes.

"Now what?" Cade asked.

Twist: "How often have I said to you that when you have eliminated the impossible, whatever remains, however improbable, must be the truth?"

"What?"

Odin said, "It's a quote from Sherlock Holmes. The question is, what's the truth?"

"The truth is, we can't sneak up on him," Twist said. "We're gonna have to pull into his driveway and knock on the door. Let's figure out the best way to do that."

They rehearsed their escape routes and made another pass on the main road, which gave them a glimpse of Janes's house. No lights. "You know, he could be out of town," Twist said.

"That would bite," Cade said. "Maybe we should call his lab and ask for him."

"Let's hold off on that," Twist said.

They made another pass. The house was still dark. Then another . . . and there were lights. Cade: "Are we going?"

"Yeah."

"Once around the neighborhood to check for cops," Twist said.

• • •

As Twist drove the neighborhood, Cade changed into the black filming shirt and mounted the camera under his arm. "Remember to keep his eyes off me as much as you can: you guys are the drama queens."

"I can do that," Twist said.

"Yeah, I know."

"Let's just get it going," Odin said.

They headed back to Janes's house, but at the turnoff from the main street, Twist swerved into the parking lot of a pizza place called Slice and parked between two pizza delivery cars.

"Man, I could use a slice before we do this," Cade said. "How about mushroom and sausage and pepperoni?"

"I'm going to buy whatever they've got ready," Twist said. "When I stick my head out the door and wave at you, that means the coast is clear. The signs on the delivery cars are magnetic. Pull one off and stick it in the back of the truck. You see how this works?"

"I do," said Cade.

The simple plan worked well. Twist waved; Odin pulled the pizza sign off the roof of the farthest delivery car and stashed it in the back of the truck. Cade moved into the driver's seat. As far as they could tell, they'd attracted no attention at all. Three minutes later, Twist came out with a pizza box in his hand.

"We're now a pizza delivery service," Cade said as he pulled into traffic and eyed Twist in the rearview mirror. "Your brain is more deviant than mine."

"Maybe."

They ate a veggie pizza as they drove—Twist hadn't forgotten Odin's stance against meat—but they could all feel the stress building as they rolled back down Spring Boulevard. They drove past the entrance to Janes's side road one last time and could see a light in the front window.

"Time to put the sign on the roof," Twist said, and Cade pulled to the curb.

The sign was lit by a battery-powered LED with an external switch. Odin put it on the roof, turned on the light, and got back in the truck.

"We go straight in," Twist said as they made a U-turn. "Cade: you have your softball bat?"

"Check."

"When he opens the door, you gotta get right on top of him," Twist said.

"I got it, I got it," Cade said.

"When Cade's in . . ."

"You follow him to make sure Janes is under control, and I take the pizza sign off the truck roof and follow you," Odin said to Twist. "I got it, I got it."

"If we pull into the driveway and somebody else comes to the window or the door . . ."

"We tell them we got the wrong address," Cade said.

"Let's just do it," Odin said impatiently. "This is nothing like what Shay's looking at."

They pulled into the driveway, their headlights sweeping over the windows at the front of the house. A few seconds later, they saw Janes come to the window and peer out at them. He was a narrow-shouldered, soft-looking man with thinning brown hair and oval glasses, still wearing a white shirt and a tie. "That's him," Odin said.

"I don't see anybody else," Cade said. "Give me the pizza box."

"Are you running the video?" Odin asked.

"Yes," Cade said. He got out of the car with the bat in one hand, hanging down along his street-side leg, and the pizza box in the other. He walked up to the door.

"Got more balls than I do," Odin said, watching him go. He had his pack between his legs and pulled it over his shoulders.

"He has a history," Twist said. "And say, didn't you break into a lab that had an armed guard who actually shot somebody?"

"Yeah, yeah. You ready?"

"Yeah."

They unlatched their car doors, and Twist added, "Don't run."

Cade was in front of the house and held up the pizza box so Janes could see it through the window. Janes moved toward the door, and Cade, standing in front of it, put the pizza box on the stone stoop. When Janes began to open the door, Cade leaned back, picked one foot up off the ground, and kicked it all the way open, plowing ahead with his bat.

"Go!" Twist said.

Odin pulled the sign off the roof and followed Twist up the walk and through the door. Inside, they found Janes flat on his back, his glasses down on his chin. Cade was standing over him, threatening him with the softball bat. "He says he's alone. I haven't heard any-one else."

Twist turned to Odin and said, "Grab the pizza box and close the door."

Janes, still on the floor, said, "I know who you are—and you don't know how much trouble you're in."

Twist sauntered over to him, taking his time. "Yes, we do." He put the tip of his cane on Janes's breastbone, as though he were about to punch a hole through to his heart. "Our friend Fenfang had four hundred holes drilled in her skull so you guys could stick wires in her brain, and she's dying from the aftereffects. We know exactly what you people are capable of, but I suspect you don't know what *we* are capable of." He pressed the cane harder. "You're a multiple murderer, and we can prove it. The feds still execute people for that."

"I did not kill anyone—"

"We've seen your experiments," Cade spat. "Don't give me that 'didn't do it' shit." He leaned close to Janes so the scientist's face would loom large in the video.

"I did not—"

"Don't be modest," Twist said, pushing down on the cane. "You're a leading figure in a criminal conspiracy that's murdered dozens of innocent people. You're a prime candidate for the needle."

Odin came back and bent over Janes, staring down at him with a look so scorching that Janes winced. Twist waved his cane to get Janes's attention back. "You're a scientist, so you should know a little about physics: This gold head is as heavy as a hammer. The handle is twice as long as a hammer handle. If I hit you with it, you won't have to worry about the needle. The same with my friend's softball bat. So don't mess with us. Where's your office?"

"There's nothing in it," Janes whined.

"Oh, I imagine there's *something* in it," Twist said. "Get up."

As Janes started to get up, Odin said to Cade, "If he tries to run, break his legs. He won't fight if his legs are broken."

"Maybe I should break them now," Cade said. "Then he won't be able to run."

"Don't hurt me, don't . . ."

They needed to keep him scared, and their evident anger gave the threats the weight of the truth.

Janes had a large, bland office, converted from a bedroom. There was a tower-style computer at the side of the desk and a wide high-res screen on top. "Look at this," Odin said. He pointed to a small square appliance with a glass face, sitting next to the computer screen. "A thumb pad."

"Excellent," Cade said. He turned in a circle, taking in the office, more fodder for the video.

They made Janes sit in a reclining chair and recline so he couldn't easily get up. "I'm going to take a stroll through the rest of the house, see what I can see," Twist said. "Remember—"

"Legs," Cade said as Twist walked out of the room.

Janes said, "I don't bring my work home. That's forbidden."

"Really?" Odin said. "Why do you need a thumb pad, then?"

Odin sat at the desk, took a nylon envelope out of his backpack, and shook the flash drives onto the desk.

"Are those . . . ?" Janes asked.

"Yes, they are," Odin said. He poked the power switch on the computer and waited as it came up.

"Ah . . . you don't—"

"Know what we're into," Cade finished for him. "But, dude—we do. We keep telling you that, but you just won't believe."

"Doesn't believe what?" Twist said, coming back to the office. He shook his head once at Cade: no one else in the house.

Odin was peering at the computer screen. "We need a thumb," he said.

Cade reached over and grabbed Janes by the necktie and pulled him out of the chair. "If we don't get the correct thumb, we'll smash the wrong one with my bat to remind us which one is right."

"Goddamn thugs, you're no better—"

"We're better than cold-blooded murderers," Odin said. "Thumb."

With Janes's thumb on the pad, the computer opened like a flower blossom.

"What do you think—will we need to take the thumb with us?" Twist asked.

"Gimme a minute to think about that," Odin said. "If we did, we'd need to keep it fresh. Get some ice, or something. . . ."

Twist poked Janes back into the recliner with his cane. "We have questions. You can enlighten us. Fenfang is having seizures, and periodically the second personality emerges and tries to take control. How do we stop that?"

Janes peered at him for a moment, then asked, "How thoroughly does the second personality take control? I mean, would you say fifty percent?"

Twist waved the gold head of his cane in front of Janes's nose. "Eh-eh. I'm not here to help your research."

"We knew we had an incomplete conversion," Janes said.

"Is that what you call it?" Odin snarled, turning away from the computer. "Incomplete conversion? How about brain murder?"

Cade was looming over Janes, filming his answers, but Janes was focused on Odin.

Twist leaned into Janes. "Focus, please. The seizures. How do we stop them?"

"We've found that carbamazepine can be effective," Janes said, shrinking back. "Sometimes supplemented with gabapentin."

"What dosages?"

He gave them several dosage possibilities, then said, "About the alternative personality—"

"How do we get rid of it?" Twist asked.

Janes shook his head. "It will never go away entirely. What will most likely happen is that as the primary personality overlays the implant with more recent experiences, both intellectual and sensory, the implant will tend to fade. Eventually, it'll have the status of old memories."

128

"What would you do to hurry that along?" Twist asked.

"If I were treating her, I'd prescribe . . . I don't know . . . music lessons on an unfamiliar instrument, dance lessons, perhaps, if she's never taken dance. I would have her memorize lists of names from history, but not contemporary history. Unfamiliar names."

"Do you know who her alternate personality is?" Cade asked.

"No, no . . ."

"The doctor's lying," Twist said. "Break some ribs."

"No, no, no . . . All right, all right, it's . . ." He paused. "But you know. I can see it in your face. That means that . . . she's talked to you? The alternate?"

"You're answering the questions, not me," Twist said. He rapped Janes's forehead with the gold head, and Janes said, "Ahhhh!" and covered his forehead with one hand. "That hurt. That really hurt."

"Yes, I know," Twist said. "Look at me, Dr. Janes."

Janes looked at him, and Twist nodded at Odin. "You see the bruises on this kid? That's what your Singular security team did to him. Then they nearly drowned him with a shitty little technique called waterboarding, which is condemned by the United Nations and every civilized country. When we went in to save him, your colleagues murdered one of their own. Flat-out cold-blooded murder."

"I'm a scientist—"

"I don't think a jury will see it that way," Twist said. Cade stood next to Twist's shoulder, filming. "Now, who is the alternate? Who is it?"

Janes muttered, "Charlotte Dash."

"Who?"

"Dash. Senator Charlotte Dash. You knew that."

"We just wanted to know if you knew. But of course you would, you're the chief scientist on this murder crew, aren't you?"

"It's not murder," Janes said. "It's important research—"

Odin cut him off. "Passwords. For these flash drives that came from your lab. Sit there and write them out."

Janes said, "They'll kill me."

"Probably, eventually. But not because you spilled some passwords," Twist said. "They're going to kill you because you know too much. Give us the passwords and we'll pretend that we decoded them on our own. We already decoded some of them, so you know we can do it; we're just pressed for time."

Janes stared down at the floor for a long ten seconds, then said, "There's a copy on my hard drive. There's a hidden file."

Odin peered at him. "That's unusual. Why would they be here when the flash drives were at the lab?"

Janes shrugged. "Security. If I needed a code, I'd just link in here. If some goofy ecoterrorists raided the lab and stole the flash drives and the computer . . . there wouldn't be a file on the stolen computer to open the second level of security on the flash drives."

"That's really hilarious; pretend like I'm laughing," Odin said. "How does it work?"

"You won't tell Singular?" Janes asked with a pleading note.

Twist: "Not if you're straight with us."

Janes said, "Plug a drive into a USB port. You'll get a password box. Type in 2jcqo6h, and you'll open a file of passwords. You didn't keep the file folders that the flash drives were in, so there's no way to tell which is which. You just select codes until one opens. You can make as many attempts as you have to."

Odin said to Twist, "If he's lying, hit him with the cane again."

"With pleasure," Twist said.

Odin lined up the flash drives, plugged one in, and a password box popped up on the computer screen. "Give me the code again."

Janes gave him the password, and when Odin entered it, a file opened, showing twenty-five or thirty codes. "We didn't get all the drives when we hit the lab," he muttered to no one in particular.

He began clicking on the codes: the eighth click opened the flash drive. "All right," Cade said. "Let me write that one down."

With Cade looking over his shoulder, Odin paged through what seemed like an endless list of scientific papers and photos. In the next five minutes, they opened all the remaining drives. Odin marked each of the drives with a number, and Cade noted each number next to his list of passwords.

When they'd done that, Odin got out an external hard drive and started copying Janes's drives onto it.

Twist, facing Janes, said, "Now tell us about the dog. Why is the dog so important?"

Janes shook his head.

"C'mon. . . ." Twist waved the cane in front of his nose.

"Because our research suggests that we could create some interesting biomechanical enhancements for our clients. You've seen some of the research with direct nerve-electronic connections in our prosthetics. But prosthetics are prosthetics. If we could actually replace bone and tissue with better-quality structural elements, we could make . . . better people."

"You mean like that guy in the movies?" Cade asked. "Wolverine?"

Janes waved him off. "That's a fantasy. We don't deal in fantasies. But you could say that the concept is similar. Without all the angst. Perfect hearts, new livers, replacement pancreases. It'll all be available in twenty years, if our research is allowed to continue. If not, maybe not for another hundred."

"So the dog is . . . bionic."

"Biomechanical. Yes. I understand you've figured out how to charge it."

Cade: "The artificial eye—can it see in the dark?"

"Yes. That was one of the primary enhancements. The animal can't see in pure darkness, of course: he needs a bit of light. His vision system was fitted with what amounts to a starlight scope, with the electronics fused to the optic nerve."

Cade glanced at Odin. "How much longer?"

Odin said, "Nearly there." Then he turned on Janes. "You said twenty years if the research continues, a hundred if it doesn't. You mean research using human subjects. Right?"

Janes looked away. Cade stepped closer with the hidden camera. "Right?"

Janes said, "You don't understand. This is critical research. Sometimes you do things that seem . . . extreme . . . to outsiders."

"Like turning humans into lab rats," Odin blurted.

"We're not the first. How do you think yellow fever was cured—the scientist infected himself. Sometimes you need to use humans—"

"Only when they volunteer," Odin said. "You don't kidnap a Chinese girl and drill a thousand holes in her skull. . . ."

"I have nothing to do with the acquisition of experimental subjects— Ow!"

Twist had hit him on the head with his cane again.

"Where are the subjects now? Where'd you take them after Sacramento?" Twist asked.

"I don't know—they don't trust me with information anymore," Janes whined.

"We should get out of here," Cade said. "It's a rule. Something bad happens if you stay too long."

They were ready to go in two minutes: Cade picked up the pizza box, and Odin gathered up the flash drives and pulled the external drive when the copy was complete.

Janes stared at Odin. "You look like her, you know. Your mother."

Odin froze. "You knew my mother?"

"Kathleen Carter," Janes said. "Yes, brilliant woman. Brilliant biochemist, brilliant theorist."

Odin's brain was exploding—the thing he hadn't wanted to believe. Could his mother have really been working for Singular? Cade crowded up next to him, prodded Odin with his elbow: he was filming. "Did Singular kill her?" Odin blurted. "Did they send somebody out there to sabotage that dive?"

Janes looked at him, clearly knowing what Odin meant: the diving accident in Australia that had killed his mother. Janes shook his head. "I'm not even sure she's dead."

"What?"

"I'm not sure—"

Odin grabbed Cade's bat and surged toward him, Cade still filming.

Janes held up his hands defensively. "I had nothing to do with any of that. If I had known that the company was thinking of doing something about her, I would have resisted with all my might."

Odin held the bat over his shoulder, ready to bring it down like an ax. "What happened? Why don't you think she's dead?"

"I was shocked by your mother's death. As a friend. Then, maybe a year after she supposedly died, I got a copy of a paper written in English from one of our North Korean facilities. There was no author identification on it—there's no identification on any of our papers—but people have signature writing styles. Even on scientific papers. This paper had Kathleen's style of writing, the way she expressed herself. I was sure it was her. There have been several more papers over the years that I thought might be hers, concerning nerve grafts. There hasn't been one for a while. So, I don't know if she's alive anymore. But I'm not sure she's dead, either."

"But you thought they might have killed her," Odin pressed. "Why?"

Janes hesitated, and Twist whacked him on the knees with his cane. Janes buckled over in pain, and Twist said, "Answer the question."

"She was doing animal-based work—which she was perfectly willing to do," Janes said quickly. "But when she found out that other parts of the company had moved to human research, she began to have doubts. Began to ask questions. I pleaded with her: don't make trouble. I thought her work was too valuable for the company to . . . to . . ."

"Kill her," Cade said.

"Well, too valuable to kill her, yes, but also too valuable to let her go."

The three of them stared at Janes, then Odin said, "Sonofabitch."

The epithet was not aimed at Janes, but at the world in general.

"We should go," Twist said, pulling at Odin's sleeve. "Say goodbye to Dr. Janes."

Odin raised the bat over his head and glared at the cowering scientist. Twist watched, no sign of disapproval. . . .

"No! I helped you!" Janes wailed.

In the next instant, Odin swung the bat around and into the side of the chair. The impact knocked it over and Janes fell on his belly. Before he could push up off the floor, Odin had a shoe on his back.

"I don't believe in killing anything," Odin said. "But when you get the needle, I'll have a very hard time feeling bad about it, you evil piece of shit."

. . .

Then they were gone.

Janes remained huddled by the chair for nearly a minute, heard the truck pull away from the driveway. Eventually, he dragged himself to his feet and found his cell phone. He called up a contact list and pressed one of the numbers.

A man's voice: "Sync."

Janes identified himself and said, "Your hundred-to-one shot just came in. They were here. I was afraid they were going to kill me."

Sync, his voice gone hoarse, asked, "Did you give them the passwords for the drives?"

"Yes, and they opened them all right here."

"Yes! Oh, Jesus, that's better than sex."

"I risked my neck to do it," Janes said. He didn't mention the thumbprint decrypt or the stolen hard drive.

Sync laughed. "All right: Dr. Janes, you are *the Man*."

"I need to tell you something serious," Janes said. "You say all of our conversations are encrypted. Could the NSA be listening to us now?"

"No. They are not." Sync sounded very sure of that.

"Then I'll tell you. These people need to be . . . eliminated. Immediately."

"Oh, yes," Sync said with another laugh. "They surely do."

11

They ran like bank robbers, both teams, getting as far away from their crimes as they could, as quickly as they could, one bunch scrambling south across the Oregon-California border, while the other stopped briefly in Albuquerque, decided that Cruz's and X's wounds would hold for a while, and headed west.

Shay was behind the wheel, her hair wet from a shower to get the stench of Dash off her skin and to loosen up for the ten-hour drive to Barstow, California. The plan was to get halfway to their final destination, check into a motel, re-dress Cruz's wounds, and get some sleep.

"You gotta pull over if you so much as yawn," Cruz said from the backseat, where his throbbing left arm was propped on the pillow he'd bought for Shay. Beside him, X was licking lightly at the Ace bandages Fenfang had used to cover the gauze wrappings on his legs.

"Won't be a problem," Shay said. "I'm wide awake."

"Me also," said Fenfang, who was rocking back and forth in the passenger seat, still amped up from the confrontation. She twisted the cap off a warm bottle of Pepsi and took a long drink.

"You know what caffeine is, right?" Shay asked her. "You should probably try to sleep; cola won't help."

Fenfang shook her head. "I am too much thinking about the dragon lady to sleep," she said. She burped. "I will be your company instead."

"All right. Just remember, Dash's thoughts seem to take over when you're tired."

"I feel strong enough to beat her down now. You made me feel that way tonight, Shay. You and Cruz, you made me feel I can beat her down every time."

Shay and Cruz checked in with each other in the rearview mirror: neither felt the same optimism. Shay reached out and patted the young woman's small hand.

"We're proud of you, Fenfang. You really kicked some dragon-lady butt."

"Did I kick her butt? I do not recall that. I would have liked to—"

Shay stopped her. "It's more of a saying, 'kick her butt.' Not that you actually kicked Dash's butt, but that it felt like you kicked Dash's butt. Does that make sense?"

"Yes. I feel that. I feel your American saying very much."

"You kicked butt," Cruz said.

"All of us," Fenfang said, and turned inside her seat belt to pet X. "You are one awesome kick-butting dog."

The attacks had been synchronized to go off at the same time, and unless something had gone terribly wrong, Shay was to call Twist at 3:00 a.m. mountain time. Thirty miles west of Albuquerque, she punched in the number.

"Tell me you're okay," Twist said.

"The girls are okay, the two boys got some dog bites. We're headed toward the meeting place."

"Tell the truth. How bad?"

Shay held the phone up over her shoulder and said to Cruz, "He wants to know how bad?"

The bandage on Cruz's arm was stained with new blood, but he said only, "One to ten, maybe a three. Everyday stuff where I'm from." He pushed the phone back at Shay. "Tell him about the video."

"We parted her hair, got great video; it was all there," Shay said. "About the bigger boy: I'd say it's a six, not a three. It's not an everyday thing, even where he comes from."

"Did you get to a hospital?"

"No, we think it can wait," Shay said.

"I gotta leave the call to you," Twist said.

"How'd you do?" Shay asked.

"Your kin is a genius. The other guy's pretty frickin' smart, too. We got the stuff that should unlock the other stuff . . . good, good stuff. And he named names. He mentioned the cooperating country by name. It's all on video."

"Hug your guys for me. Hug yourself. See you soon."

"Wait . . . you think she'll call the police?" Twist asked.

"No. You think he will?"

"No. But the other side knows by now, so you and your codriver need to stay focused and watch your back; get to the meeting place as fast as you can but without driving more than seven miles over the posted speed limits, use the cruise control to be sure—"

"Can you please stop worrying?"

"No. I can't."

"Bye."

All rolling toward the hideout in Arcata, California.

Twist, Odin, and Cade were ninety minutes into what for them was only a six-hour drive. Odin had been anxious to look at the decrypted drives, but Twist had urged him to wait until they made it to the Arcata safe house. Now, with all of them jacked up by Shay's call, they decided to pause at a brightly lit truck stop, get some Cokes and junk food, and allow Odin a few minutes to do his thing. Twist and Cade got out of the car, while Odin stared into the white light of his laptop.

"We'll bring you some veggie-type thing to eat," Twist said.

"A Ding Dong, a Sno Ball, a fried cherry pie—I'm a vegetarian, not a lunatic," Odin said.

"Back in ten."

They were back in eight and could hear Odin shouting through the closed windows, "Shit! Shit!"

Twist opened the passenger door. "What?"

"The flash drive files. Something happened, and it's not good. Wait, let me . . ."

Cade opened the back door and scooted in alongside Odin, and his face went dark as he saw the jumbled nonsense on the computer screen. Odin fumbled another flash drive out of his backpack and plugged it into the USB port.

"Garbage! It's all garbage. Janes . . . the passwords were a trap. It's all gone!" Odin said.

He plugged in another flash drive: more garbage.

"What's happening?" Twist asked them, bent over the seat but not able to see what was on Odin's screen.

"They set us up, man," Cade said. "They figured we might be coming. They gave us a program that ate our evidence."

Twist didn't understand the mechanisms of hacking, but his paranoia was still working. "The immediate question is, are they tracking us somehow?"

"No," said Odin. "The drives might have been used to plant something in my computer that would contact them through the Net when I plug in. But I haven't plugged in, and I can sterilize it."

"You sure?"

"Of course," Odin said. "The problem is, we lost the flash drives. I mean, Janes stuck it to us. I never saw it coming. Never even got a hint of it; I thought we had broken him. He punked us! The sonofabitch punked us!"

"What's one thing we know for sure about Singular?" Twist asked, not quite rhetorically.

Cade caught it. "Yeah. They're smart."

Odin looked up. "We still have the video of Janes. And his hard drive. The trip wasn't a total loss. . . ."

Odin checked all the flash drives and found garbage in all of them. He worked them for a while, trying to find out if a recovery was possible, but eventually gave up. "I can't work in the car. This is too complicated," he said.

"You've sterilized your machine?" Cade asked.

"It's done," Odin said.

They rode most of the rest of the way in silence and rolled into Arcata just before eight o'clock in the morning.

Twist was driving, and he threaded his way through the eastern part of town, then out on a gravel road into the forest. Four miles farther along, he pointed the truck up a narrow strip of yellow dirt.

At the end of the dirt road, they found a rambling house built of redwood, glass, and fieldstone perched on a steep slope and surrounded by a stone fence. A six-car garage sat at the bottom of the slope, next to a gravel trail that led to the house.

"Growing weed must pay good," Cade said as they bumped across some corrugated ruts to the parking area. "I guess I knew that."

"He's got a trust fund," Twist said. "His grandfather ran a pharmaceutical company out east. Growing weed is a hobby."

Odin: "Check out that stone fence—there're no holes that you can get a vehicle through. You couldn't even get a trail bike through the gate. Anybody who comes to the house is going to be walking."

"I noticed that fence when I was here before, how it was kind of weird, but never thought about it," Twist said, scanning the stone wall. "You're right, though. If the cops show up, you could run out the back door before they got to the front, and get lost in the trees."

"Where does he grow the weed?" Odin asked.

"Out in the woods—last time I was here, he said he had eight hundred plants," Twist said. "He breeds hybrids. He told me he was looking for a mellow, full-body high. He talks about it like it's wine."

They climbed out of the truck, and Twist said, "Take it slow. Give him a chance to check us out."

Two of the garage doors were open, and they could see a powerful Mercedes-Benz G-Wagen in one of the bays and a Volvo in another. A third bay was empty, but they could see a couple of ATVs and a utility vehicle, like an undersized pickup truck, to the far side and a pile of athletic equipment at the back. "Think he's gone?" Odin asked.

"Nah. That's where his girlfriend parks," Twist said. "She has a Lexus."

The stone fence around the yard had an opening wide enough for a man to walk through, but built in a zigzag pattern with two tight changes of direction. There were flowerpots and garden gnomes on the fence, so it all looked decorative, but Odin was right: it would be difficult to get even a trail bike through.

As they walked up to the house, a door slid back, and a tall, thin man stepped out on the front deck, squinted against the sun, and called, "Hey, Twist. Who's that with you?"

"Friends from L.A.," Twist called back. "They're cool."

"Come on up. Great to see you, man. And hey: I remember the tall guy—what is it?—Cade?"

"That's me," Cade said as they climbed the last few feet to the house and then up a redwood stairway to the deck.

Danny Dill was twenty-six, with reddish-brown hair twisted into rough, unkempt dreadlocks. He had a week-old beard and was wearing circular gold-rimmed glasses and a T-shirt that read MOLON LABE. He said to Twist, "How's the art, man?"

"Down in L.A.," Twist said. "You see us on TV?"

"I did. That Hollywood action and the one on the building with the redheaded chick," Danny said. He greeted Twist with a hug, bumped knuckles with Cade, nodded at Odin. "You didn't bring the chick along?"

"She'll be here later," Twist said.

"Great. I mean, like, looking at her ass when she was swinging across that building, that was like seeing the sun come up," Danny said.

Twist said, "Yeah, thank you for that observation. She's sixteen— and I'd like you to meet her brother, Odin."

Danny faked a flinch, grinned at Odin, and said, "You got a cool-looking sister, man." And to Twist: "You guys on the run?"

"Exactly."

"Hey, *mi casa es su casa*. I owe you big." He looked at Odin again. "What happened to your face? Somebody beat the shit out of you?"

"Insight like that, you could have been an astrologer," Odin said.

That made Danny laugh, and he said, "Been there, dude. Hey, you guys want breakfast? I get some crazy rad eggs from a neighbor, man. He feeds his chickens on weed seed, like an egg sandwich gets you just a very light, mellow high to get the day started. . . ."

"Already had breakfast, Danny," Twist said. "And thanks, we really need a place to lay up for a while. We've been careful, we won't drag anybody in here."

"No need to worry," Danny said. "I got the town wired. Anybody comes looking for this place, I'll get a call."

"Where's Cindy?" Twist asked.

"Cindy." Danny scratched his beard. "She, you know, chose to take a different path through life. She's been gone for three months."

"Did the path involve the Lexus?" Cade asked.

"It did, man," Danny said. "She had this insight: the name Lexus is part of this constellation of words—*Lexus, plexus, nexus*—that pointed her out of here, on her own road, to her own reality, rather than my own, mmm, what she said was my phallocentric universe."

"Sounds like a heartbreak," Twist said.

"Yeah, she was majorly cool," Danny said. "Even if she did clean out my number two safe before she split. Hey, c'mon in, tell me your story."

They went inside, drank green tea and honey, and told Danny about Singular and their dual hits on Janes and Dash overnight. When they were done, Danny said, "Man, that is totally negative. These

dudes have gotta go down. Go down. We gotta fight them. I'm signing up. I'm signing up. They're so rank . . . gotta fight."

"Excuse me for pointing out the obvious, but you're too stoned
to fight the frickin' tooth fairy," Odin said.

"Odin lacks some social skills," Twist said to Danny.

"But he's right," Danny said, though he seemed a little wounded.
"I'm not stoned so much anymore. I'm more interested in the plants
than in the effects. I get things done when I gotta. What do you guys
need? I got lawyers, guns, and money, like in the song, and I got
cars, uh, I got weed. . . ."

"We mostly need to stay out of sight," said Twist. "We've got
three more people coming, along with a dog."

"Then you came to the right place," Danny said. "When the
crop is ready, I get friends to come up and help with the harvest, so
I got rooms. Nice ones, too, but we oughta freshen up the sheets."

Shay had driven from Albuquerque to Barstow, California. Cruz
volunteered to change off with her, but his arm was obviously hurting, though he wouldn't admit it. Fenfang said she drove an electric
scooter in China, and while she would be willing to try to drive the
car, she might not be very good at it. . . .

So Shay had stayed with it, and shortly before one in the afternoon, they found a motel in Barstow that would take cash. The room
had one lumpy queen-sized bed and a wobbly cot, and they slept,
badly, into the evening; Cruz moaned in his sleep, his re-dressed
arm stretched out to the side.

At six o'clock, he woke up for good, and X, who heard him moving around, woke up Shay. She was sharing the bed with Fenfang,
who was curled on her side, still asleep.

Shay crept away from the bed and over to the door—chain lock in place, curtains drawn—to talk with Cruz. "Still hurt?" she asked in a low voice.

"I took some aspirin."

"I gotta know the truth, Cruz," she said.

He shrugged with his good shoulder and said, "Well, I think you should get some more sleep, because you'll be driving again."

"I can do it."

Cruz smiled. "I know, that's the thing about you . . . or one of the things. . . ."

"Oh, really?" Shay said, and pushed some of the black bed-head hair out of her eyes. "Name two more."

"Nah. I'm gonna make you wait."

"I don't like to wait."

"I know. That's another thing."

"Hey!"

Cruz put a finger to her lips, reminding her of Fenfang.

"Go lie down, try to sleep a bit longer," he said softly. "I'll wake you in an hour."

"All right."

At seven o'clock that night, they were all out of bed, getting ready to move again. Shay walked by herself to a gas station and bought a bottle of orange juice.

Walking back to the motel, toward a wounded guy and dog and a wired-up girl who was probably dying, she suddenly felt overwhelmed by it all. She thought foster care had made her tough, but she could barely keep up with all the disturbing things she'd seen and experienced the last few weeks. Didn't know that rich women were protected by giant German-trained dogs and had safes full of gold bricks and stacks of cash. Didn't really know about criminal corporations, immoral scientists, or guns. Didn't know that someone might torture her brother. Might kill him—or her—for what they knew.

If things had worked out differently back at Dash's house, she could be dead. At sixteen, dead and gone. She could still be dead and gone at sixteen, if Singular won.

Couldn't let that happen. She drank her orange juice and took deep breaths.

Could. Not. Let. That. Happen.

12

At eleven o'clock in the morning after the attack on Dash, Harmon looked out over the wing of the company jet and said, "God's country."

"Not a hell of a lot of people would agree with you," Sync said. "Looks like that piece of the 'stan down west of Hyderabad."

"Yeah, it does, a little," Harmon agreed. "I liked it there, too."

The plane was five hundred feet above the tan-and-yellow desert, dropping into the airport at Santa Fe. There were five of them aboard: Cartwell, the CEO; Sync, the senior vice president and head of security; Harmon, the intelligence chief; and two tough former Delta Company fighters retrained to be bodyguards and whatever else they had to be, or do, with guns.

Sync was on his cell phone when they landed; he clicked it off and said, "Thorne said the RVs have had to move—some redneck at the trailer park tried to get friendly. They're out on the highway again, looking for a new spot."

The airport terminal was the size of an average high school

cafeteria, with rental car agencies at one end, a diner at the other, and the ticket and luggage desks in the middle. Cartwell led the way through to Hertz. Two SUVs were waiting just outside the door, and five minutes after they landed, they were on their way toward town and up Charlotte Dash's mountain.

Harmon drove, Sync beside him, Cartwell in the backseat. Cartwell said, "The last time I was here, Charlotte was recovering from some intracranial mapping we did as part of the prep. The dogs had only recently arrived from Germany, but it didn't matter—those mutts would jump out a third-story window if she used the right command."

Sync said, "They sound like soldiers."

Harmon, from behind his mirrored aviators, said in a neutral voice, "Robotic ones, maybe. I mean, if they answered to both Dash and Remby . . . where's the loyalty?"

Cartwell made a face in the rearview—*Who cares?*—and asked Harmon impatiently: "You think Remby's still around?"

"No," he said. "My guess is, she's crossing back into Nevada or California about now. Getting lost in another city."

Cartwell's eyebrows went up. "Let's be clear: when we speak with the senator, there's no 'guessing.' We are closing in and we are eliminating the problem."

The gravel road up the mountain was bumpy, which got some more grumbling from Cartwell, and maybe a little extra boot on the accelerator from Harmon. The gravel ended the instant they drove through Dash's front gate.

Inside, they found a pleasant garden full of flowers and a circular parking area of silk-smooth brick. And three cars: a limousine and two black Tahoes with dark glass all around. Three men in suits were facing the gate as they drove in. One of the men held a submachine gun by his side.

"This doesn't necessarily look good," Harmon said.

One of the three men put up a hand, and they stopped.

Cartwell said, "Oh, Jesus. I think I know . . ."

Harmon rolled down his window, and the man who'd held up a hand came over and said, "U.S. Secret Service. You are Misters Cartwell, Sync, and Harmon here to visit Senator Dash with two bodyguards."

"Yes."

"Please leave any weapons in the car, if you're carrying. All weapons, including personal knives."

Sync, Harmon, and the two bodyguards were all carrying pistols, and Harmon had a switchblade. They got out, put the weapons on the car seats.

"That's it?"

"That's it," Sync said. "How's Senator Dash?"

"She's hurting," the agent said. "You're Mr. Sync?"

"Yes. How'd you know that?"

"They're waiting inside," was all the agent said.

Cartwell told the two bodyguards to wait with the Secret Service agents, and as he, Sync, and Harmon were going up the steps to the mansion, Harmon muttered, "I didn't know the Secret Service guarded senators."

"They don't," Cartwell said. "But they protect the vice president of the United States."

"What?"

Inside, in a cool, darkened living room, they found Dash propped up on a velveteen chaise. Sitting across from her was a tall, gray-haired man in a blue suit: Lawton Jeffers, the vice president of the United States. He was wearing the kind of glasses that turn dark when exposed to sunlight, and though there was no sunlight in the room, they shadowed his eyes so that nobody could quite make them out.

Jeffers stood up, shook hands with Cartwell. He said, "Micah. This is a disaster."

"I know. How long have you been here?"

"Half an hour. I was in Phoenix for a speech, stopped on my way back to Washington when I heard about this . . . incident." The vice president sat down again, and Cartwell quickly introduced Sync and Harmon, with their job titles. Jeffers nodded but didn't offer to shake hands. Dash looked at Cartwell and said, "They beat me up, Micah. They broke into my home."

Cartwell said, "We've brought a couple of our security guys to watch over you. They're outside. They will stay as long as you want."

"Locking the barn door . . ."

"Protecting our friends," Cartwell said. "We don't want them coming back."

Jeffers said, "We need to talk. . . ." And his gaze flickered over to Harmon and Sync.

Cartwell said, "Harmon, could you give us a few minutes here? Sync, I want you to stay."

The four of them waited until Harmon had gone, and then Jeffers said, "This is bullshit, Micah. What the hell have you been doing? They know enough that they go after Charlotte? They're that deep into us? How did they find out about her? Charlotte says an Asian girl . . ."

Cartwell nodded. "Yes. A girl who has some of Senator Dash's . . . knowledge. But it's limited to that girl—there're no documents, no records; it's limited to this one woman's consciousness."

"Not anymore," Dash snapped. "The files they stole include

some of the medical papers I got about the cranial wells, along with some top-secret stuff from the Intelligence Committee. My computer's all encrypted, but there are some Singular emails on it. From you, Micah."

Cartwell scraped his upper teeth over his lower lip, then sat himself down on an ottoman by Dash's legs and said, "Charlotte—start at the beginning. I want to know exactly what happened here."

"You want to see my teeth? I'd show them to you, except I've already got temporaries on them. . . ." She sniffled and looked as though she were about to cry, and she said, "They broke them off, my teeth, they were bloody little stumps. Hit me in the face. They killed one of my ten-thousand-dollar dogs; the other one's at the vet, he's damaged beyond—"

"Charlotte, I don't want to seem unsympathetic, but we know all that," Cartwell said. "What I really need to know is the sequence. How did they get in, what did they say, how much did they seem to know?"

Dash pulled herself together, nodded, and took them through a second-by-second sequence as she experienced it, ending with the intruders taking a photo of her scalp with a cell phone, then the dog fight, the punch in the face, and the last sight of the intruders as they disappeared through her gate in the Jeep.

"They are crazy and violent, and I hate to say it, but they're also smart and they know things. They have to be stopped," she concluded.

"We're tracking them," Sync said from where he was standing in the middle of the room. "We've found them a couple of times, and we'll find them again. You know that we lost some critical flash drives in the original attack in Eugene. Those drives have now been neutralized. That whole threat is gone. We can contain this."

"What about me?" Dash wailed. "There's a girl out there with my memories—who knows everything about me!"

"Not everything about you, Charlotte, not really very much, in fact—" Cartwell began.

Dash, rising from her chaise and shutting down any tears, cut him off: "You told me we were still years away from the transfer. You said we'd pick the young person together. We never did that! I've got six hundred million dollars into your company; I've pulled some very risky strings with Intelligence for you. What's going on? Am I in that girl?"

Cartwell was shaking his head. "No, no. There's not much of you in there. We used some of your recordings for a preliminary test to see what kind of implant response we would get. From what we understand, our Korean associates did manage to implant some things, some information from you—"

"Like all my security codes!" Dash said. "They walked right through all of the alarm systems; they knew the combinations for the safes."

"Yes. Very tight, discrete pieces of information. That seems to be the easiest kind of thing to implant. But we *are* still years away from implanting a full personality and suppressing the former personality. We've made progress, though, and we now believe the implantation and the suppression may be the flip sides of the same coin. The more thoroughly we can wipe the personality of the experimental subject, the more completely the new personality implants. We're pretty excited about some results we've gotten in the last three months."

"In the meantime, there's some woman running around with wires in her scalp and parts of me in her head."

Cartwell said, "That, uh, is a self-resolving situation. The implant antennas are far too crude, we've found. We need to go to much finer gauges. Much finer. You said she was having some kind of seizure before they left. That's happened in other subjects. The seizures will get worse, and then . . . she will die."

There was a long, uncomfortable silence, then Dash said, "What if they drop her body at a hospital? Some pathologist takes a look at her head—"

"We'll find them before then," Sync said. "I promise."

The vice president had been watching the exchange and now said, "I'll tell you, Micah—I don't like the way this has been going. This whole situation should have been resolved weeks ago. I have to start asking myself if the right people are running this company. We're spending billions, and critical material is stolen by teenagers?"

Sync stepped up. "The break-in at the Eugene lab was a freak incident that—"

Jeffers cut him off: "That you have been unable to put a lid on. I don't want excuses. I want it taken care of."

He leaned forward to Micah, still sitting on the ottoman, and tapped him on the knee. "I'm not fooling here, Micah. You're going to find these people and get rid of them, with no comeback, or you're gone. You and your company will disappear like a fart in a whirlwind."

There was a momentary silence after that, then Cartwell nodded, turned back to Dash, and asked quietly, "Who hurt you, Charlotte? Which one?"

"Some big, mean Mexican. But as I said, he and Remby never took off their masks. Do you know who he is?"

"Not yet, but we will," Sync said.

"Actually, I can probably help you with that," she said. The men watched with curiosity as she heaved herself out of the chair, peered toward the door to the kitchen to make sure none of the servants were coming through, then went to a side table, pulled open a drawer, and handed Sync a Ziploc bag with a bloodstained paper towel in it.

"When the kid hit me, I grabbed his arm—he'd been chewed up some by one of the dogs—and got his blood all over my hand. When I got back inside, I wiped it on a paper towel. I thought maybe he'd have a DNA record somewhere."

Sync said, "Hard-core."

Dash: "What?"

"Not one guy in a hundred would have thought of that, in that situation. You are one tough cookie."

"I thank you for the 'cookie' part," Dash said, sinking back into the chair.

The vice president stood up, peered at Sync, then at Cartwell, and said, "I have to go. I hope I've made my position entirely clear."

Cartwell nodded, and the vice president stalked to the front door and out.

Sync said, "Jesus."

Cartwell said, "Get Harmon back in here."

Harmon returned, got a quick synopsis of what Dash had told them, and Dash interjected, "What about the photograph they took of my head, the cranial well where you inserted that activity monitor? What if they put it online?"

"We'll handle it the same way we handled the research videos they dumped on that Mindkill site a couple weeks ago," Cartwell said. "It's nonsense, pure fiction. Photos can be faked. We'll say these extremists are obviously going after politicians now, and the American public is too sophisticated to stand for it."

Dash sighed. "Why's it taking so long to find these kids—and this artist they're working with?"

Harmon leaned in. "The holdup is, they don't use the phones we know about, they don't use credit cards we can track, they're using cars we don't have plates for. We think a lot of that is the work of this Odin Remby, the computer kid."

Dash had heaved herself out of her chair again and gone to the window, where she was looking out through the heavy French-made drapes, a slash of sunlight falling across her shoulders and chest. "Found them fast enough with the face-recognition program," she said. "How'd you manage to lose them?"

"We're hoping to use it again," Cartwell said. "Find out where they went from here. Is that possible? Is there fallout for you from using it?"

Dash turned from the window and said, "The gardener's burying my dog out there. The dog that they have with them . . . it's a killer. I never saw anything like it."

"One of our special projects," Cartwell said. "We need to get it back, too."

After a moment of silence, Dash said, "Two people at the NSA know about my use of the face-recognition program. They did it for me as a favor, didn't ask any questions; they just want to be 'remembered' if they need to be. We can use them again."

"That would be good—" Cartwell began.

"But it's not without risk," Dash interrupted. "What happened the first time? I find them for you, and the next thing I know, they're in my house."

"We're not sure," Sync told her. "It's possible that it was a coincidence. They left Las Vegas about two hours before our people got to their hotel—and the next thing we knew, some of them were here, and the rest of them were in Eugene."

Dash: "Is it possible that there's some other agency involved? That we're not just dealing with some teenagers? They seem too sophisticated—"

Harmon jumped in: "Almost certainly not. They're not sophisticated, not in the sense you'd use that term in the intelligence community. They were involved in animal rights mischief, in political protests, and they learned how to live underground. They learned what resources the law enforcement agencies might use against them and how to avoid detection. But they aren't professionals. So far, they've been smart, but they've also been lucky. The luck's going to run out."

"It better," Dash said. She used a thumb to push on her broken teeth, as if resetting the temporary caps. She winced as her cell phone beeped, and she pressed a button. "Yes, Rosita?" She listened and then said, "One minute."

She turned to the three men and said, "Rosita's got brunch ready for us. I'll be having a milk shake, because I can't chew!"

Cartwell stepped up to her and put an arm around her shoulder. "I'm so sorry this happened. I can't tell you . . ."

"You say you'll get them, I'll take you at your word. For now," she said.

They ate brunch, and after the kitchen crew was out of the way, Dash worried more about the loss of classified government documents from her safe. "If they should dump those on the Internet, there'd be some tough questions about why I had them at all, and how I lost them. If I told the truth, about the raid, that'd tie me to Singular. If I didn't tell the truth, the FBI would be all over the place, looking for spies."

"Are the papers that important?" Harmon asked.

"Well . . . they have some details of NSA data collection that hasn't gone public yet. If it did, we'd have another round of finger-pointing, and some people would probably get fired, but it wouldn't be like the country was going to fall down. It would be pretty damn unpleasant for me and a few other people on the Intelligence Committee."

Cartwell muttered, "These people really stuck us."

"Really stuck *me*," Dash said.

They talked for a while longer, mostly going over the same information.

Harmon looked at a row of Native American pottery that sat atop the dining room china cabinets: shiny black, brown, and red carved clay pots. He said to Dash, "That's a nice collection."

Dash shrugged and said, "I don't know much about them. They were my husband's. The good stuff is in his library. They're called . . ." She rubbed her forehead, remembering. "Mimbres pots? Does that sound right?"

"Yes, exactly," Harmon said. "Would you mind if I take a look? I love those things."

"I'll show you the library," she said. "Maybe you could tell me if they're worth something."

"I'm sure they are," Harmon said.

They finished brunch, and Dash took the three executives and the two Singular bodyguards around the house, showing them how the entry had been made through the underground wine storage connecting to the greenhouse, and what they'd be guarding. "It's the henhouse after the fox has gone," she said.

When they went through the library, Harmon lingered to look at the Mimbres pots: his major interest, outside of work, was South-western archaeology, and he spent his free time roaming the desert Southwest, finding unknown archaeological sites.

While he was doing that, Cartwell and Sync broke away from Dash and the bodyguards and went for a walk in Dash's well-watered garden.

Cartwell asked, "You know what? I want to know the same thing Charlotte does: who warned Remby and the others to get out of Las Vegas?"

Sync shook his head and said, "I don't know. I assume it's not you, and I know it's not me."

Cartwell snapped, "This is no joke."

"I know it isn't," Sync snapped back. "Not many people knew we were sending those guys to Vegas to pick them up. The leak can't be with the guys themselves, because except for Thorne, they didn't know where they were going until they got on the plane. There were only six of us who knew. It wasn't you, it wasn't me. That leaves four people."

Cartwell nodded: "Thorne, Harmon, Denny Jackson, and Imo-gene Stewart."

"Yes. All four know about the Sacramento raid and the evacua-tion of the experimental subjects; of course, Harmon and Jackson didn't know we had human experimental subjects until the Sacra-mento cleanup, but neither of them batted an eyelash. Here's what I'll do. All of them know we're looking for a new site. I'll make sure Thorne doesn't mention the ship to anyone but you and me, then I'm going to tell Harmon that the new site is in Stockton, I'll tell Jackson that it's in Modesto, and Stewart that it's in Merced. I'll fix it so they actually see some addresses. If Remby and her gang of assholes show up at any of those sites, we'll know where the leak is. If nobody shows up at any of them, we'll take a closer look at Thorne. . . . But my gut tells me it's not Thorne."

"Why not?"

Sync snapped off a piece of purple sage and crushed the fragrant little flowers between his fingers. "Because if he was on their side, he wouldn't have shot West—certainly not personally, with witnesses. California is a death penalty state. I doubt that he'd sell us out, because he knows what the payback could be."

Cartwell thought about that for a few seconds, then nodded. "Okay. So Harmon, Jackson, and Jimmie. Christ. Got a favorite?"

"I keep thinking about Jimmie." Jimmie was the nickname for the company attorney, Imogene Stewart. "She can be pretty soft sometimes."

Cartwell grunted and shook his head. "Don't be fooled by the dress. She's got a heart like a half-carat diamond: tiny and hard. Be careful not to misread her."

Sync nodded. "All right."

"Why do you think these goofs would show at whatever site they're fed?"

"Because they asked Janes where the experiments were. Because they're do-gooders who want to save the world. Because their tender hearts won't be able to resist."

Cartwell scraped his upper teeth over his lower lip. "I like it," he said finally. "Use their own insider to pull them in. And we get both."

Harmon let himself out of the library through a pair of French doors and into the back gardens to have a look around. Joaquin, the sun-fried old man with the shovel, was laying the last of the dirt on a grave at the base of a majestic Arizona cypress. The dead hound at least would get some shade.

It took about five minutes to retrace the intruders' steps from the greenhouse to the back wall, where a blue yoga mat remained. He pulled it down and almost chuckled at the simple fix Shay Remby and her friends had used against the security spikes. He admired a creative opponent, hadn't dealt with a truly formidable one since his last tour in Iraq.

From the wall, they'd come down in the chamisa—he fingered some thin broken branches—then worked their way across the garden; it wasn't hard now for him to see where their footfalls had punched down the springy, overwatered grass. They'd avoided the gravel pathways that might have set off the guard dogs before they could use the security commands on them.

He rolled up the mat and started back for the house. Dash was a powerful woman, a bit flaky on Middle East containment strategy, but influential at the highest levels. He hadn't known she was involved with Singular, but then, Sync kept the roster of power brokers and richie-riches close to his vest—as he had the part where the company was kidnapping people, experimenting on people, and killing people. He wondered if he'd been naive to think that Singular's work ended with biomechanics and limb and organ replacement. Brain transfer . . . He could hardly believe they'd gotten as far as they had.

A shiny black stone caught Harmon's eye. He was walking across the lawn and saw it lying on some gravel near the hoof of a bronzed bison. He scooped it up: a pretty little thing with a white stripe running through the center. One of his friends on the Navajo Nation called such linear mineral deposits "spirit lines" and believed they carried some sort of healing power. He didn't know about that, but he'd always kept a small, fluid collection of nifty rocks on his desk at home. He stashed this one in his jeans pocket and went back inside the house.

They gathered on Dash's porch before heading back to the airport. Dash asked Harmon, "So, are my pots worth anything?"

"They're the best Mimbres pots on earth. I'm serious. The collection as a whole . . . sold carefully . . . would probably bring a million and a half, maybe two million."

"Good God, I used to use one of them as an ashtray," she said.

"Don't do that," Harmon said, but in a friendly way. "What you might do, if you're not really interested in them, is give them to a museum or a university. Talk to your accountant: you could get a nice tax write-off and some good PR."

Dash peered at him for a minute and said, "That's an idea . . . when I'm up for reelection."

She turned to Cartwell. "You need to find these people, Micah. Put an end to it."

13

Twist and Cade and Danny Dill were sitting on the front deck, in the early-morning sunshine, while Odin sat at the kitchen table with his laptop, trying to figure a way through the disaster of the damaged flash drives.

Danny was saying, "I don't really need the money, and things are getting tense around here, you know? More and more assholes showing up. I'm thinking maybe I should go on the road. Write a book: *The Legend of Johnny Weedseed: How Danny Dill Took the Stromboni Hybrid to America.*"

"I know some publishers who would go for that," Twist said. "I'll do the dust jacket."

Danny leaned back in his chair and closed his eyes and said, "Man, that would be epic."

"Yeah, well, first you got to drive around America with the weed seed," Cade said.

Odin came out on the porch, looked at them. "It's gone. The data's gone."

"I thought we already knew that," Twist said.

"I was hoping I could figure out a fix."

There was a chirping sound from inside, not loud but attention-getting, like somebody had pulled a hawk's tail. Danny said, "Got somebody coming in."

Danny walked back inside and picked up a remote control and pointed it at a compact television built into a kitchen cabinet. The screen came alive, and they saw a Jeep far down the drive, bouncing toward the camera.

"Shay," Twist said.

The four men went to stand by the deck railing as the Jeep pulled up to the garage. A moment later, Shay climbed out of the driver's seat, and X hopped out after her and walked over to the corner of the garage and peed on it. Cruz and Fenfang got out of the back. They gathered up an assortment of backpacks and bags of stolen stuff, and they all started up the hill to the house.

The last few yards, Shay broke into a jog, ran up the steps, and gave Odin a squeeze, and then Twist and Cade. X was right behind her, and Cruz followed Fenfang up, and after all the hellos and introductions, Twist asked Cruz, "How bad is the arm?"

"It's manageable."

"It's bad," said Shay.

Danny: "Come on inside. Let's look."

Shay: "You're a doctor?"

"Not in the official doctorate-degree sense, but I know some stuff. People got dogs out here, I've seen some bites. . . ."

Something in his voice was convincing, and at the kitchen table, they moved Odin's laptop aside and Danny unwrapped Cruz's arm.

A mess: the flesh ripped and torn, blue bruises now covering his whole lower arm to his wrist, black dried blood coating his forearm muscles.

Twist: "That needs a doctor."

"Yeah. I got a doc in town who won't ask questions," Danny said. "Maybe he'll look at the dog, too—he's a loose kinda doctor."

Odin was standing next to Fenfang and said, "We need a couple of prescription drugs."

Twist to Odin: "We got those recommendations from Janes. What if it's another part of the trap?"

"What trap?" Shay asked.

"Tell you later," Odin said. "I looked up the drugs, and they're really for seizures. Maybe this doctor can give us some."

Danny, Cruz, and X left five minutes later, Danny carrying a black briefcase with two cakes of marijuana inside. "The doc likes to do a little reefer after work," he said.

By the time they got back, Twist, Cade, Odin, Fenfang, and Shay had caught each other up on the details of their raids, what they'd gotten, and what they hadn't.

Cruz's arm was now wrapped in a thick layer of semi-rigid white plastic bandage.

"He'll have some scars, but the muscle damage was minimal, and the doc doesn't think there's any nerve damage," Danny said. "He's got to let the arm heal, though. No rough stuff."

"The doctor said it's going to itch like fire by the end of the week," Cruz said. "It already itches. I'm not supposed to take the cast off for two weeks."

Shay took Cruz's elbow and stood on her tiptoes to kiss him on the cheek. "You saved our butts."

"X saved mine," Cruz said, giving the dog a skritch on the forehead.

"What did the doctor say about him?" Shay asked.

"That he had some bad cuts but wasn't missing muscle," Danny said. "The doc scrubbed him down with topical anesthetic, sprayed on some antiseptic, and sewed up the cuts. He's not sure how the skin will heal because . . . well, X has got metal legs."

They all looked at the dog, standing at attention, his ears erect, and Cruz added, "X knew we were taking care of him. He sat there and took it without a whimper. Kinda reminded me of you."

"Yeah, right," she said, and bumped his hip with hers.

Twist glanced at Cade. He was sitting with a smile on his face, but he was watching Shay and Cruz. *Hope this isn't a problem. . . .*

Odin asked, "Did you get the pills for Fenfang?"

Danny said, "Yeah. They're pretty commonly prescribed for seizures, but they don't just lob them at you. Usually, the patient has to be worked up—"

"You're saying she shouldn't take them?"

"No, I'm saying I don't know and neither does the doc," Danny said. "I had to tell him that she already had a prescription for them but had run out."

"I don't know," Twist said.

"I will think about it," said Fenfang.

While Shay, Fenfang, and Cruz napped, Odin, Cade, and Twist worked through what they had—Odin on Dash's computer, Cade on Janes's, Twist on the documents taken from Dash's house.

For the first hour, Twist said "Shit," "Crap," or "What the . . ." about every five minutes. After that, he read with one hand clamped on top of his head to keep his brain from exploding.

When everyone was back together, he explained: "There are three NSA reports about surveillance on what they call 'Influentials.' We know they watch suspected terrorists, but the Influentials they're looking at in these reports are American reporters and anchors, university professors, and foreign leaders. They're opening the mail of the French president. They're doing surveillance on the *New York Times* and the *Washington Post.*"

Cade said, "If we put that out there . . . that would attract some attention."

"It would," Shay agreed. "And it sucks. But we're not trying to take down Dash or the NSA. We're trying to take down Singular."

Danny: "Should we try to line up a reporter? Give him or her a look at what we've got on the NSA, and tell them we'll deliver the whole package if they help us with Singular?"

Twist: "How do we know which reporters we could trust? Don't they have to go to the people they're accusing and get a reply? That'd tip them off that we were coming."

Danny said, "I'm mostly familiar with San Francisco, and a lot of *Chronicle* reporters are stoners—I could ask some of my people, find out who's both a good investigator and a stoner, make the approach that way. . . ."

Twist dropped his head onto the tabletop and said, "Danny, sometimes . . ."

Odin said, "Maybe hold off on the reporter idea. For now. There's something in that, though."

Shay asked: "Is there anything in Dash's papers to tie her to Singular?"

Twist nodded. "We found an agreement between Singular and

Dash for 'medical treatment.' There's a note from Dash to the Singular CEO—this is printed out, one of the paper files, Odin couldn't find it on her laptop—about money being transferred from a Venezuelan bank to a bank in Russia. Are you kiddin' me? A U.S. senator, from Venezuela to Russia? You know what she wrote—handwrote—on the printout?"

Shay asked, "What?"

"'500m.' I think she transferred five hundred million dollars to Singular. A half-billion dollars."

Nobody said anything for a moment, then Cruz grinned. "That should hang her."

Twist said, "Okay, so we stage an event, get people's attention. We get Mindkill back up and put out the videos of Dash and Janes, and people freak out. Then we tie Dash to Singular with her contract. People freak out again. Then we reveal some research documents, the picture of Dash's head, the X-rays of Fenfang. We keep up the drumbeat."

Cade nodded: "We need to find Singular's new prison. We want a police raid. Pictures of the lab-rat prisoners on network news. Then Mindkill will have the details on how these people were kidnapped and tortured. It goes viral and Singular's done."

Shay looked at Twist, Cade, and Odin and said, "You say Janes doesn't know where they moved the prisoners, but do you really believe him?"

"He made a convincing argument: they don't tell him what he doesn't need to know," said Cade.

Shay shook her head. "We know he was at the Sacramento prison—Fenfang saw him."

"I did," Fenfang said.

"Yeah, but—" Odin started.

Twist thumped his cane like a gavel. "It doesn't matter. If he does know, he didn't tell us."

"We could follow him," Cruz suggested. "See where he goes every day. He could lead us to the lab eventually."

Odin said, "We don't have time for *eventually*."

And Cade added, "Singular will be watching him now—looking for us."

Shay said, "We need to talk to the guy who warned us to get out of Vegas. He's got to be Singular. Odin worked out the phone number of the man he sent to the hotel . . . Jerry Kulicek. He could hook us up with the guy who told him to warn us."

Twist said, "Right. That's good. And something else. What if we made a movie about Fenfang, put it on YouTube, on the website, Facebook. . . ."

Shay said, "Like a documentary . . ."

"Yes," said Twist. "She tells her story—about how she was kidnapped with this American missionary, what they did to both of them, how they smuggled her into the country with a bunch of other human experiments. She shows off her scalp with the implants. We make a Chinese version of it, put it on Chinese sites. I mean, she was a Chinese citizen kidnapped by the North Koreans—that ought to get a few million hits."

Fenfang raised her hand and said, "Hey."

They all looked at Fenfang, realizing they hadn't asked *her*.

"We start now," she said. "Make my message to the world."

That was the agenda:

They'd make a movie with Fenfang. Edit the video of Dash and

Janes. Try to contact Jerry Kulicek. Pull together the most damning computer files and documents to release on Mindkill.

Cade found a bunch of addresses in West's logistics office files. Most led to nothing, but six of them led to possible laboratory or medical testing sites.

Shay found a medical research paper on something called "cranial wells" among Dash's papers that would pair well with the shot of her head.

Twist was rapidly becoming an expert at video editing, while Cade, Odin, and Danny were getting new footage of Fenfang telling her story. Cruz slept.

After five intense hours of work, Danny led them out to a volleyball net on the back lawn. Twist was concerned about Fenfang getting hit in the head, that a ding to the wires might set off some bad and unknowable thing. So Danny found his ex-girlfriend's pink bicycle helmet. Thrilled, Fenfang played gamely for Team Twist, high-fiving "like American winner" after every point, while Cruz managed several impressive spikes with his good arm for Team Shay. Odin, though cheerfully intrepid, missed nearly every ball that came his way.

"I never could do anything physical," he said after the game.

"Because nobody ever taught you," Danny said. "Guys like you don't learn the way other people do: you don't learn by imitation, you learn through words."

"Yeah, right," Odin said.

Danny said, "Really. That's the way it is. Take me: I tried to play musical instruments since I was little, all by imitation. I never got anywhere until somebody said, 'You should read some music theory. Once you understand the theory, you can play the instrument.' They were right. Instead of learning how to play 'Red River Valley,' which bored the shit out of me, I learned the pentatonic scales and went straight into the Chili Peppers."

"I'll think about it," Odin said.

Later, while Fenfang was napping, Shay found Danny, Odin, and Cade sitting on the deck, passing a joint. Twist had declined and was annoyed when the others didn't follow his lead. Shay saw that and said, "I'm with you."

"Glad somebody is," Twist said.

"Two somebodies," Cruz said. He was stretched out on a lounger, half dozing, but decidedly not smoking, either.

Danny said, "Well, I know Twist has his reasons, but they're not the reasons for everybody. But hey . . . you won't get any peer pressure from me."

Twist raised an eyebrow. "We're peers?"

A little later, with the three guys mildly stoned, Danny offered to take Odin out on the road and teach him how to run like a human being. "Now, you run like a chicken. You're all over the place."

Shay started to defend her brother, but Odin waved her off and said, "I do run like a chicken. Let's try it."

Shay and Twist trailed behind as the two of them walked down to the road. Danny told Odin he should start by tying his unlaced shoes, then said, "You're a machine. Your hands shouldn't flap. Your arms should be cocked and go forward and backward in a more or less straight line. Think of your arms being like a link in a bicycle chain. Or like the pistons on a train wheel. Make that little circular movement."

He had Odin stand in place and make the movement with his

arms until he had it. Danny said, "Now, about your legs. Don't throw them out there. They should be catching up with your body, not leading. Lean forward. . . ."

After five minutes of talk, they jogged down the road and out of sight. Odin was still flapping a bit, but was about three hundred percent better than he'd ever been. Shay flashed to the moment when he'd been running up the oceanside highway like an out-of-control marionette, trying and failing to flee from Singular.

"I can't believe Danny just taught him something in five minutes that he wasn't able to learn in eighteen years," she said to Twist.

Twist nodded, and they started back up to the house. "Dan's got some interesting talents. Unfortunately, he's not as motivated as he might be."

"He is pretty laid-back."

Twist shrugged. "Hasn't lived a day in the past ten years without THC in his blood. But then, who am I to judge? He runs a successful small business, files a tax return every April, employs a dozen illegals who might otherwise be working for a meaner breed of drug dealer. . . . I don't know."

"Hmm. So what are your reasons for not smoking?" Shay asked. "Or would that be oversharing?"

Twist stopped walking and looked at Shay for a bit, then said, "My mother was an addict. She used to buy these little balloons of heroin, with me in tow. Then one afternoon, she cut one too many—she OD'd. I found her dead on her bed, all curled up like a puppy, but cold and stiff."

"Aw, Twist, that's awful. How old were you?"

Twist leaned on his cane. "I believe I spent my tenth birthday at the morgue."

Shay sagged but Twist shrugged it off. "Long time ago. And pot is not heroin. But still."

Odin shouted at them, "Hey!"

They turned, and Odin and Danny were jogging toward them, Odin looking like any other runner. The transformation had taken ten minutes and maybe, Shay thought, a little marijuana to reduce Odin's self-consciousness. Her brother trotted up to her, wiped his sweaty face on his sleeve, and said, "Why didn't anyone ever tell me this?"

"You and I practiced, remember that time . . ."

But he was gone again, running harder, and Shay looked at Twist, and they both smiled.

They were heading back to the deck when Cruz shouted, "Hey, hey! Fenfang's having a seizure."

Fenfang had fallen backward on the couch where she'd been reading. Her teeth were chattering and Odin grabbed a sheaf of the papers she'd been reading, rolled them, and pushed the roll between her teeth. Her entire body was shaking, but a minute later, the trembling subsided.

Shay said, "Fenfang . . . Fenfang . . ."

Fenfang looked up at her, her eyes glittering with hate. Cruz said, "Crap. It's Dash."

Fenfang tried to push up from the couch, but Odin restrained her, pushed her down. Danny said, "We should have tried the pills."

"We have to now," Odin said. Fenfang struggled against him, spit out the rolled paper, groaned, shook, and then, suddenly, began seizing again. After a long spasm, Fenfang went limp.

"Who is she now?" Twist asked.

"We have to check," Odin said. "Somebody get my laptop."

Fenfang opened her eyes, which looked cloudy, dazed. Shay asked, "Fenfang . . . are you okay?"

She said, "Yes."

"The code, please," Shay pressed.

"Háixíng."

Cruz handed Odin his laptop. Odin hit a few keys, and a Chinese phrase came up. "Translate this," Odin said.

Fenfang glanced at the laptop screen, then dropped back flat and said, "Forty-five chickens and a dinosaur."

Odin handed the laptop back to Cruz. "She nailed it. This is Fenfang."

"I take the pills, even if there is danger," she said.

They started her on the antiseizure medication as soon as she seemed stable.

Shay was cutting up carrot sticks in the kitchen when she became aware that Odin had come in, silently, in stocking feet, and had been watching her for a while. "What's up?"

"Haven't been able to get you alone," he said. "Wasn't sure I even wanted to."

"Huh?"

Odin said, "Up in Eugene . . . Janes said . . . Mom might not have died on that dive."

Shay dropped the knife on the floor and it clattered away, unnoticed. "What?"

"Janes said—"

"Why didn't you tell me? How did it come up? What exactly did he say?"

Odin held up his hands as if to fend her off. "I've been working up to it. Because . . . well, he doesn't know if she's alive *now*. Just that he didn't think she died in Australia. And you know . . . dead is dead, whenever it happened."

"My God, Odin!" Shay was staring at her brother, stunned.

Odin told her what Janes had said. When he was done, Shay said, "So she could be in North Korea? She *could* be alive?"

"Maybe."

"She really worked for them, then. She really did. Shit."

"I know." Odin nodded.

"We have to find out what happened to her," Shay said.

"Yeah, we do. But I almost don't want to. If she was in North Korea, and hasn't been heard from in a while, and they wanted to get rid of her . . . What if they used her to . . . you know . . ."

"Experiment on? Oh, Jesus!" She put her hands to the sides of her head. "Oh, jeez. Oh my God."

Cade came in, realized he was interrupting, but said, "You better come look at this."

Odin: "Later, man."

"No, really—"

"We got kind of a thing going on here. . . ."

"I found Janes's cover-your-ass file. I think he squirreled some stuff away, in case he needed protection. There's a photo. I mean, maybe it's Photoshopped, but I don't think so. It looks like somebody took it with a hidden camera."

"All right, give us one minute," Odin said. Cade backed away, and Odin turned to Shay and said, "That's everything I know. Everything you might think of, I already have. If we can take Singular apart, maybe we can find something out. That's our best hope."

Shay shook her head, trying to find an objection. Odin picked up the knife she'd dropped and said, "C'mon. Let's see what's got Cade so freaked out."

Shay followed her brother into the living room, where everybody was bent over Cade's laptop.

The photo was of a group of people sitting in a haphazard arrangement around a conference room table scattered with papers, pencils, notepads, coffee cups and soft-drink cans, looking as though they were taking a break during a meeting. The far left side of the photo was obscured, as though the lens had been partly blocked by some kind of fabric; it looked as though it had been taken secretly. The people around the table were well dressed, and all were white, except for three Asian men: one older, two much younger.

Shay peered at it, then said, "Dash," and touched the senator's face in the photo. And then: "We know this guy, too. It's Micah Cartwell, he runs Singular."

Odin touched another face, a tall, gray-haired man. "Is this . . . ? No way. I mean, is this . . . ?"

Twist said, "I think so."

Shay didn't recognize the face immediately. "Who is it?"

"It looks like the vice president," Twist said.

Shay's hand went to her cheek. "You're right. It's Jeffers."

Fenfang touched the image of the older Asian man. "You do not see him without his uniform, but he is very well known in Korea and China. He is Ch'asu Kim Lee Pak . . . mmm . . . I am not sure I say this right, but I think you would say . . . vice marshal of the Korean People's Army."

Twist said, "If the vice president was there, if Dash was there . . . why was a North Korean in the same room? They aren't allowed in America—not at all. So where was this meeting? What were they doing?"

"We know," Fenfang said. "They were talking about people like me. Making the arrangements."

Danny: "Makes you wonder where it stops. A senator, the vice president . . . it's only one more step to the very top."

"I don't believe it," Twist said. "That the president knows."

"Why?"

"Because . . . ," Twist said, looking at each of the young people around him. "Because I voted for him . . . Ah, shit."

14

Air Force Two touched down at Washington National and taxied toward the terminal. As it rolled, Vice President Lawton Jeffers was sitting on the lid of the toilet in his private bathroom, with one sleeve of his dress shirt pulled up over his elbow.

He'd applied a patch to the thin skin below his elbow joint and now sat, with his head down, as the first wave of hormones hit his head and heart. The wave was neither pleasant nor unpleasant, but it was powerful, and in a few minutes, he'd begin to feel sharper, stronger. Hornier, too.

As the wave subsided, he sat another minute, looking out the port at the airport while the plane turned and began to taxi toward a sequestered gate. So many threats out there.

At the end of the minute, he peeled off the patch, stood, lifted the toilet lid, dropped the patch in, and flushed. He'd stepped back into the office and was rolling his sleeve down when a Secret Service agent tapped a call button, and Jeffers said, "Yeah. Come in."

The agent poked his head in and said, "We'll be at the gate in a minute—and your appointment is there."

Jeffers said, "Show him in. We won't be long."

The agent nodded and backed out. The plane rolled smoothly to a stop, and three or four minutes later, there was another knock, and a plump, pink-faced man in a gray suit stepped inside. He wore fashionable steel-rimmed glasses, a blond mustache, and a Minnesota Vikings ball cap. He was carrying a briefcase, and was sweating.

He closed the door behind him and said, "Mr. Vice President."

"Sit down, Earl," Jeffers said. "For Christ's sake, stop calling me that. How long have we known each other? Thirty years? And what's that ridiculous hat all about?"

Earl Denyers blushed and took off the hat. The hair on the top of his head, normally well combed but sparse, looked like it had been worked over with a staple gun. "Uh, actually, I got a hair transplant. That bald shit was making me feel old."

Jeffers shook his head, and Denyers sat down and asked, "What's up?"

"You're aware of the situation with Singular?"

"Hang on a second," Denyers said. He opened his briefcase and took out what looked like a miniature boom box. He put it on the floor and pushed a button. When Jeffers asked, "What's that?" he put up a finger.

A series of letters poked across the device's screen, and Denyers looked up and said, "We're secure."

"Of course we are," Jeffers said. "We're swept before every flight."

"Yeah, with stuff you could buy at RadioShack. But this . . . we're secure," Denyers said. He was the CIA's assistant deputy director of operations, and he didn't take unnecessary chances. "Anyway, yes. I'm aware of the Singular problem. The NSA has processed some requests from Senator Dash, attempting to locate these animal rights kids. From what I'm hearing, the situation is . . . unstable."

"Cartwell and Creighton—Sync—swear they have the situation under control, or soon will have. I think that's possible," Jeffers said. "It's also possible that the whole goddamn thing will go sideways. We need an alternative ending."

Denyers nodded. Before Jeffers had gone into elective politics, he'd been a four-year director of the CIA: he knew how things worked and what resources were available. "Did you have something in mind?" Denyers asked.

Jeffers swiveled in his chair and looked out one of the ports at the tarmac, where he saw nothing interesting. "I think . . . a tragedy. A plane crash, perhaps. We'd want to decapitate the company— Cartwell, Sync, and Stewart for sure, maybe this Harmon guy. But we don't want to lose the researchers. We'd pick them up, quietly, move them to a new operation."

Jeffers rubbed his nose and added, "My sense of this, the timing, is that it's all coming to a head. I believe Singular will find these kids and get rid of them in the next few days. On the other hand, if the kids actually start generating some attention, and they've been good at doing that . . . then we might have to seal the problem off."

Denyers nodded. They sat silently for a moment, then Denyers said, "Hey, Law—you remember how we used to sit around the house and plan out how we'd conquer the world? We've come pretty goddamn close, haven't we?"

Jeffers and Denyers were fraternity brothers at Dartmouth.

Jeffers said, "Heartbeat away, as they say. If it weren't for Berman, we'd own this country. You'd be running the CIA, Travers would be at the NSA, Dash and Banfield in the Senate and House. . . . We could hide Singular so deep that nobody could dig it out. We could live forever, Earl. We're that close."

Terrance Berman was the president, two years into his first term, and popular. He would almost certainly be reelected, which meant that Jeffers was at least six years away from a shot at the top job, and even then, nothing was guaranteed. Berman knew nothing about Singular. Not yet.

Denyers cleared his throat. "I wonder if we should consider the creation of a . . . more direct pathway . . . to your ascension to the presidency?"

Jeffers sat very still for a moment, then said, "I couldn't in any way, not even distantly, be involved in even discussing something like that."

"Neither could I," Denyers said.

Jeffers rubbed his chin and then asked, "Would the game be worth the reward? That's what we always tried to figure out, back when we were working together."

"Law—the reward is *not dying.* I believe Cartwell on that score, when he says they're close, maybe five years away, ten at the outside. If Singular gets shut down, it'll take decades more. We'll be long gone. Immortality—that's a pretty big reward in any game."

"Yes, it is," Jeffers said. He looked at his watch and said, "I'm due home in less than half an hour. It's been good talking this out with you, Earl. We need to get together more often. Too bad about Berman. If he were someone else, I might be able to go to him, ask him if he'd like to ride along. But Berman's a moralist. He'd be shocked, and I'd wind up on a landfill somewhere, giving speeches to the seagulls."

"Then maybe his usefulness is over?"

Jeffers looked at his watch again. "I've really got to go. Why don't you sit here for five minutes or so, have a beer or a Bloody Mary. I'll tell the steward."

"Of course." Denyers understood that they shouldn't be seen together, not by people who couldn't keep their mouths shut. "I'll take that beer."

"A heartbeat," Jeffers said, and he was gone.

A steward brought Denyers a beer, and the CIA man kicked back in his chair and thought about it. They'd known each other since they were teenagers, and he'd been one of Jeffers's top aides in the good old days at the CIA. Denyers knew him well.

In their brief, secret talk about the possibility of stepping up to the top job, the vice president had said a lot of things. Hadn't said others.

Most notably, he'd never said no.

15

Shay, Twist, and the others tried to think of different options, but finally Shay said, "Staging a raid on the new prison is the best plan we've got. Maximum exposure and minimum deniability for them. We need that Singular insider. We should call his messenger. Right now." She pulled out her cell phone.

"Wait. We have a hideout that works. We need this place," Twist said. "Any phone call represents a danger because we know they have heavy-duty intelligence assets. If they spot us again . . ."

Danny said, with a grin, "You guys keep forgetting I'm a drug dealer. I have to call lots of people on a phone I don't want traced."

"They don't have to trace the phone, dude," Cade said. "Locate the cell tower, send in some spies. Game over."

"My cell tower is in orbit," Danny said. "That's exactly how far they can trace it. Wait one." Danny walked back to his home office and emerged a few seconds later with a chunky piece of black machinery, half the size of a brick, with a short, fat folding antenna.

Odin said, "A satellite phone?"

"Yup," Danny said. "My business phone. I had it sent to a PO box in San Francisco three years ago. Once a year, I send the satellite-phone company a postal money order for whatever time I think I need. The money order comes from Mick E. Maus. They cash it, and everybody's happy. The signal never touches a cell tower on our end, and it's fully encrypted."

Cruz nodded his approval. "When we see one in East L.A., we say, 'There's a cartel man.'"

"So we could call from the front porch," Twist said.

"We could," Danny said. "But for the first contact, I'd suggest driving a couple hours away and using a regular cold phone. No reason to think that Singular would know to track calls to a guy named Jerry Kulicek. If the guy calls you back, you can talk to him and then get rid of the phone. We reserve the satphone for more extensive conversations, later on."

Shay: "Sounds like a plan."

Shay and Twist took the Jeep south through Eureka, and then farther south on Highway 101, finally stopping at Willits.

Twist made the call. Kulicek answered with a gruff "Yeah?"

Twist said, "This is the guy who paid you five hundred dollars. We need you to call your friend and tell him to call us. We'll give you a number. Do you have a pencil and paper?"

After a moment, Kulicek asked, "Why should I do that?"

Twist was ready with a rehearsed answer. "Because he's your friend, and we have information he needs. You're just passing on a number. Let him decide if he wants to call it or not."

Another moment of silence, then Kulicek said, "Gimme the number."

Twist gave it to him, and Kulicek said, "Nice talking to you," and hung up.

"That was quick," Shay said. "Now what?"

"Let's drive south. I still don't trust this whole phone thing," Twist said. "If he calls back, and they manage to track the call, at least we'll be even farther from Danny's."

They bought a couple of Diet Cokes and a bag of corn chips and drove, still on the 101. Thirty minutes later, the phone rang. Twist was driving, Shay had the phone. He said, "Put it on speaker. I'll pull over when I can."

Shay did, punching up the call. "Who is this?"

"Let's avoid names," said the man on the other end. He had an easy baritone, with a touch of the South in it. "My friend said you had information."

"We appreciate the help you gave us," Shay said. "We need more. You must know what your company's doing is not right."

"Is this the swinger?" the man asked.

Shay had to think for a second, then Twist muttered, "The building," and she got it—she'd swung across the face of a building during a highly publicized political action for Twist. She said, "Yes."

"You ever climb anything good? Rock?"

"Yes."

"As one climber to another, I'll tell you that I don't like what's going on, but there's damn little chance you'll be able to stop it. Damn little chance that I'd be able to. Too much weight on the other side."

"We know about the weight," Shay said.

"I doubt it. It's not just some corporate guys—"

"We *know* about the weight," Shay said more emphatically. "We have photographs."

"Of?"

"Of weight so big that there might only be one that's bigger," Shay said.

"I'd like to see those pictures," he said.

"Let's meet somewhere. Somewhere we can both be comfortable," Shay suggested.

Twist pulled into a rest area and parked so they could concentrate.

"Can't. Everybody is too tense, everybody's watching everybody else," the man said.

Shay countered: "Did you know West? He was one of your company's own men. He found out about the prison where my brother was being tortured, and then you guys murdered him. He didn't have to die—"

"Don't tell me about West," the man snapped. "He was a friend of mine. If West was still alive, we wouldn't be talking."

"What happened to the people in the cells in Sacramento? I saw at least five people locked up. Where are they now?"

"I don't know that."

"You can find out. You found out that they'd tracked us to Las Vegas; that had to be a secret." The man didn't say anything, so she added, "How did they do that, anyway?"

"Facial recognition program."

Shay looked at Twist. Odin had been right. "We guessed that. We didn't know for sure. Someone must be calling in favors. She's probably not happy about that."

Another moment of silence, then: "Are you still running with Perez?"

Shay frowned at the phone and mouthed to Twist: *Cruz?* Twist nodded, and Shay said into the phone, "How do you know that name?"

"DNA. From that place you visited in New Mexico. The

company got blood samples and ran them against a database. We didn't find him in the database, but we found another guy—long rap sheet, deceased—with DNA so close that your friend had to be a brother."

Shay didn't know what to say, but Twist whispered, "Ask about a meeting again."

"We really need to talk face to face," Shay said.

The man said, "Keep your phone. I might call you back on it."

"No, too much chance you can trace it," Shay said. "We're going to ditch it as soon as you hang up."

"Well, I'm not giving you my number, so I don't know how we'd hook up again," the man said. "I really don't *want* to hook up again. We're talking about my neck."

Twist, speaking to the man for the first time, said, "West had a Facebook page nobody else knows about." He spelled *Gandy-Dancer*. "When you want us to call you, leave a time and a number. We'll check as often as we can, but we're moving around a lot and don't always have Wi-Fi."

Another silence, then: "I can do that. I can't promise I'll call with anything."

Shay broke in: "I'm going to send a picture to this number as soon as we hang up. Can you take a photo?"

"Yes. What is it?"

"One of your lab rats. She's with us now."

Twist said, "We appreciate what you did for us before. You saved our lives. You can't stop fighting now. This thing is evil. There isn't any other word for it. You've got to tell us where the new prison is."

"I called you on an impulse. I was pissed off because of West. I'm going—"

"Wait, wait," Shay blurted. "You know about Robert G. Morris?

He was an American, a missionary from St. Louis. They kidnapped him for practice—to transfer his brain into another man. Look him up—he's missing, and his family won't ever get him back."

"Good-bye," the man said, and he clicked off.

"Shit," said Shay. She fumbled in her pocket and found the phone she'd used to take the picture of Dash's head during the raid. There was a shot of Fenfang on there, too. She sent the photo to the phone they'd just used, then forwarded it to the caller's number, hoping there wasn't some way he could trace it back. She pulled the batteries from both phones and chucked the one they'd talked on out the window.

She rolled the window back up and asked, "What do you think?"

Twist started the car and got back on the highway. "He sounded conflicted. I bet he'll work through it and contact us."

"Really?" Shay wasn't so sure.

"When he jumped on you about West, he sounded sincere. I think West really was a friend of his."

Shay sighed and said: "They've identified Cruz."

"Yeah. That's a kick in the ass," said Twist. "He's not anonymous anymore—jeez, they've got everything. Facial recognition, DNA, we can't mention names because they might be searching phone intercepts. I . . ."

He trailed off, staring at the road ahead.

Shay said, "What?"

"What if we can't handle this? Have you thought about that? That Singular might be too connected?"

"Thought about it, but I don't believe it," Shay said. "They don't believe it, either—that's why they're so frantic to shut us up."

• • •

They got back to Danny's at dusk. As they pulled into the parking area, they saw Fenfang and Odin emerge from the woods at the top of the hill, holding hands. Shay said, "Uh-oh. That won't end well."

"Give them a chance."

"I'd be more than happy to give them a chance," Shay said. "But there's a good possibility that Fenfang will die soon, and my brother has already been pretty beaten up."

"You've got to let him go a bit," Twist said. "It could be a good thing for both of them."

"It's not just the two of them, Twist. There's Dash. If Dash suddenly took over Fenfang's brain and attacked Odin . . . I'm not sure he'd have the heart to fight back," Shay said. She opened the car door, and Odin, still holding on to Fenfang's hand, waved.

They gathered around Danny's kitchen table, and Shay told them about the conversation with the mole from Singular. When she finished, Danny said, "So we don't know whether he'll help again or not."

"No, but he did tell us at least one more useful thing," said Twist. "They've identified Cruz."

Cruz stood up from the table. "How?"

Shay looked at him. "They got DNA from blood at Dash's place. They didn't have a DNA file on you, but they did on your brother. They have your name."

Cruz said, "Shit." And then, scratching at his arm under the cast: "Guess I can't back out now."

Fenfang giggled and Cruz smiled back at her. "At least you get me."

Odin, sitting at Fenfang's elbow and remaining very serious, said, "Cade and I finished the video with Fenfang. It's strong . . . if you know for sure it's not faked."

"The problem is, it *could* be faked," Cade said. "Get a girl to shave her head, glue a bunch of gold beads to her scalp, and there you are. The X-rays help, but—"

"How about this?" Shay broke in. "We drive a long way from here, somewhere there's a big brain-surgery hospital. We find a doctor, someone who seems a little idealistic. We show him Fenfang, we show him Girard's X-ray. We get him to X-ray her head at the hospital. Or do an MRI, or a CAT scan, all of it. Then we take her to another hospital and we do the same thing. And another. We get four or five of these places, then when we go public, we name all the places where they did the scans, scattered all over the country. It wouldn't be like an X-ray from an illegal doctor in L.A. It'd be big-time doctors. Singular couldn't get to all of them to shut them up."

Cade said, "It could work. It would take a long time. All that driving, all that research. But if we got enough people freaked out and then produced the actual living Fenfang . . . it'd be hard to refute."

Fenfang smiled and said, "Even if I die, there will still be my body."

Odin said, "Don't say that! Don't say that!"

Nobody said anything for a while, and then, his hands on the table clenching into fists, Odin said, "All of us . . . first and foremost . . . we need to keep Fenfang safe."

Everyone nodded.

The next morning, Danny and Shay walked down the hill to the garage, and Danny rolled out the John Deere Gator, a utility vehicle with six wheels that looked like a small pickup. They drove up through the forest along a hand-cut trail.

A mile back, they came to a ravine, and Danny said, "This is it."

They got out, and Danny brought along a gym bag full of guns and ammo. A hundred feet in, the ravine curved, and on its far wall, Danny or someone else had driven two steel fence posts into the ground and had stretched a piece of chicken wire between them.

Danny zipped open the gym bag, took out a roll of paper targets, unrolled one, and asked, "You're sure you want to do this?"

Shay nodded. "Cruz showed me how to shoot the .45, but I need more practice. Plus, you've got way more kinds."

"I gotta tell you, I don't know much about guns, except that I have some," Danny said. "I come out here and shoot every once in a while, but if somebody tried to hold me up for my grass . . . I'd give it to them. Nothing's worth the bad shit that comes with killing someone . . . the bad karma."

"Then why have the guns at all?" Shay asked.

Danny took a joint out of his shirt pocket and stuck it between his lips, unlit. "It gets a little scary out here from time to time," he said. "We had these two guys, I guess they were, like, former Green Berets, they were crazy paranoid. Their whole idea was to grow as much grass as quick as they could and shoot anyone who got in their way."

"What happened to them?" Shay asked.

Danny flicked open a lighter, then thought better of it and put it back in his pants pocket. He said: "They grew a lot of grass, but everybody hated them, and was scared of them, so we started sending them letters that if they didn't clear out, we'd tell the feds exactly where they were. Eventually, they split. Before they left, though, you'd run into them out in the trees, and they'd always have these M16s and so on."

"So you got guns, too?"

Danny shrugged. "Everybody did. If you go out and shoot every once in a while, then maybe you're telling somebody not to come after you, because you're a shooter. Even if you aren't."

He held up a finger, then walked over to the fence posts with the chicken wire, clipped the target on it, walked back, and took three pistols and two sets of shooter's earmuffs out of the bag.

One of the guns was a short silver revolver with wooden grips; another was a small but chunky piece of dark blue machinery; the third was a nearly featureless gray weapon that might have been made of plastic.

"A Smith and Wesson revolver, a Beretta automatic made for concealed carry, and a Glock, also an automatic, which a lot of police departments use. How much do you know about handguns?"

"What Cruz showed me."

"Well . . ." Danny looked helplessly at the guns. "I can show you how they load, but I'm a crappy shot. Can't help you with that—you'll just have to practice."

They loaded up the guns, and Shay started shooting. She persisted for an hour, hitting the target more often than not, until Cade showed up on one of Danny's trail bikes. He wasn't smiling, but Shay could see he was pumped about something. She clicked the safety on the Beretta and took off her earmuffs.

"We got a message from the Singular guy," he said. "He thinks he knows where they're keeping the lab rats."

Danny said, "Human beings, man."

"Yeah, yeah," said Cade. "Come on. This is it. We're moving."

Cade roared off, and Danny and Shay hurriedly picked up the empty ammo shells and tossed them back into his bag, and then Danny took a small, flat suede holster out of his bag, put the little Beretta into it, and said, "C'mere."

Shay walked over, and Danny tucked the holster beneath the waistband of her jeans. A metal clip held the holster secure, with the grip extending above her waistband. Shay could reach back and pull the gun free in an instant. When it was in the holster, it was comfortable enough, and no more obvious than the knife she usually carried at the small of her back.

"You're gonna let me use it?" Shay asked.

"I'm giving it to you. But remember—it's only good for one thing, and that's killing somebody. I'm gonna pray you never use it."

"You pray?"

Danny smiled. "I mumble a lot and hope somebody's listening."

Shay smiled back and touched his cheek. "You have a good heart, Danny."

16

When Shay and Danny got back to the house, the rest of the group was looking at GandyDancer on Odin's laptop. Twist stepped back and let Shay in.

The note was simple enough:

I looked at the picture and I'm sorry about your friend. I worry about telling you this—you have to be careful, because something doesn't feel quite right—but after the corporation evacuated that holding place, they rented another that seems to fit the same requirements. I believe they moved the operation there. (I'm being careful with identifying words, you should do the same.) I don't want to put the address here, where it could be caught by a search program. I have a good phone now. Call me. Or not.

Beneath that was a phone number.

Shay glanced around for Danny's satphone, brought it back over to the computer, and started punching in the number.

"Wait," said Cruz.

Shay eyed him impatiently. "We gotta call," she said. "This is happening right now, this prison, these people, their suffering."

"My cousin," said Fenfang.

Cruz said, "Why would this guy talk to us now? He's got to be high up if he knows this—so he must have known what was going on with the experiments. And he suddenly decides he doesn't like it?"

"Could be another sign that they're starting to crack," said Twist. "The guy is trying to bail out before the cops show."

Cruz was still hesitant. "And it could be a trap to lure us in."

Shay finished dialing the number. "We won't know if we don't call."

The man at Singular answered on the first ring and asked, without saying hello or anything else, "Do you have a pencil and paper?"

Shay said, "Yes," and reached for a pen.

The man said, "A satphone. Good idea. I'm going to spell names and address numbers. Individual letters and numbers can't be searched so easily."

Shay said, "Okay."

The man said, "The new facility is in the town of S-T-O-C-K-T-O-N in C-A on C-H-A-M-B-E-R-S Avenue at 1-5-4-7. I don't like the way I got this information. It was mentioned to me in passing. When I went looking for the address, I found it too easily. So you have to take extreme care."

"Any specifics about the threat?" Twist asked over Shay's shoulder.

"Only that the people protecting the facility are professionals. They will be looking for you and they will be prepared."

Shay said, "Okay. We might want to talk to you about that some more."

The man said, "That address. I don't think you should Google it until you get somewhere far from where you're hiding, because the company has a direct connection to the National Sunshine Association through that woman you spoke to a couple days ago, at her house. Do you understand that?"

"Yes," Shay said again.

"I will keep this phone but can't guarantee that I'll answer it. I have your satphone number now. Can I call it anytime?"

"Yes."

"Good luck."

"Hey—how'd you know it was a satphone?"

"I can hear the echo. Good-bye."

And he was gone.

They all looked at each other, weighing what to believe, except for Fenfang, who clapped her hands together and asked, "Can we go today?"

They wrangled over their next move, but they already knew all the arguments, had gone over them endlessly. Fenfang and Odin were adamant that they had to investigate the Stockton building, and do it immediately. Twist, Shay, and Cade mostly agreed. They thought they had to be cautious, but believed that their source was telling the truth. "He even warned us that there might be something flaky about his information," Twist said.

Cruz still sensed a trap: "All the better to reel us in."

Fenfang had heard enough pessimism.

"It is risk we must take," she said, her face gone angry. "When they start to feel threatened, they will get rid of prisoners. Then they will start up somewhere else. Maybe move everything to North Korea. Liko, Robert, the others—they will be gone. Dead."

Shay called the vote. "I'm ready to go take a look at the place, and if we see any sign of human experiments, we bring in the cops. Who's with me?"

Fenfang and Odin, then Twist, Cade, and Danny, raised their hands. Cruz was the lone holdout, but reluctantly raised his plastic cast to make it unanimous. "A *careful* look."

"So we start with Google," said Odin.

"He warned us against—" Cruz began.

"Against Googling the address," Odin said. "We don't do that. We Google San Francisco, which probably gets several million hits a day. Then we scroll over to Stockton, and zoom in until we find the street, and then do a street-view scan until we find the address. We never actually enter *Stockton,* or the street, or the address, into the search field."

"Oughta work," Cade said. "Google was doing more than six billion searches a day, last time I looked. You want to monitor that, you'd need to look for some pretty specific terms."

They found the target address after ten minutes of scanning Google Maps on Danny's oversized desktop screen. It was in an area of manufacturing companies and warehouses, north and west of the city airport. There were residential areas both north and south of the building, and open farm fields to the east.

The target building, which looked like it had been clicked together with huge gray Lego blocks, was set close to the surrounding roads and was wrapped in shallow parking lots. The parking strips, in turn, were surrounded by a fence: on three sides, a five-foot-high barrier of upright steel rods with powered gates at the ends; on the fourth, a chain-link fence, probably eight feet high, with a big sliding double gate at one corner. The back of the building showed seven loading docks and two standard entrance doors at parking-lot level.

There was a main door at the front of the building, and two smaller entries a few yards left and right of the main entrance. Two sides of the building had a small, unmarked door, probably emergency exits. There were a half-dozen light poles on all four sides, lighting the parking lots.

Cruz said, "Like the place in Sacramento, but flat, instead of tall. With those parking lots all around it, there's no way to sneak up on this one."

"In Sacramento, they weren't ready for an attack," Twist said. "Now their security will be better. That's one thing we need to look for: security people and cameras."

"Yeah, except Cruz is right—I don't see any obvious weak points," Odin said. "If you come in at night, you have to cross those empty parking lots. They're all lit up . . . and then, even if you got across, where would you go?"

"Could go up," Shay said. She tapped the roof in the overhead shot. "If we could get up, we could all hide on the roof. . . ."

"One thing you have to be careful of is that old hammer-and-nail thing," Twist said to her. "You know, your only tool is a hammer, so everything looks like a nail. You, Shay, can climb, so you think about climbing everything. But what would we do up there? I can see a lot of what look like ventilation ducts, but I don't see access to the interior."

"Well, if I could get up there—"

"But you can't get up there," Odin said. "Not unless you came in by parachute, and then what would you do?"

"I don't know," Shay admitted as she studied the mostly empty rooftop. "Put on my invisibility cloak?"

"Let's give up the bullshit and figure out what we *can* do," Odin said.

When the others broke for lunch, Shay pulled up a view of the surrounding area, eyeballed it for a while, then called Twist over. "I found a nail."

"What?"

She pulled back the satellite view and touched the roof of a building across a highway from the target building. "Look at the roof on this building."

Twist looked. "There's nothing there. It's emptier than the roof on the Singular building."

"Right. There's no access to the roof from inside the building. No way somebody's going to find you by accident. Now look at this."

She went to the street view and scanned it around to the side of the building. "See this . . . what would you call it? A hut?" A small auxiliary building, a perfect cube, hung on the side of the larger one.

"Yeah, I'd call it a hut."

She touched a door going into the hut. "Check out the door. It looks like a standard door, which means it's probably around six feet, eight inches tall—call it seven feet. The distance from the top of the door to the roof is only about half as high as the door. So the roof is ten feet up. If I stood on Cruz's shoulders, or Cade's, I could climb up there. Then it's about another six feet to the roof of the bigger building. I could do that in one second. From up there, we could watch the building across the street. Heck, we could probably put a tent up there, and if we put it in the middle of the roof, nobody would see us. We could watch the Singular building day and night."

"Probably only have to do the night," Twist said. "That's when we saw delivery trucks at the Sacramento building. But this other building could have some decent security of its own."

"Nope, and here's proof." She scanned around to the front of the building, where a huge sign said UNCLAIMED FREIGHT AUCTION. She tapped a long string of graffiti below the tattered sign. "The writers feel safe enough to do this on the front of the building. That tells me no one's paying much attention to the property. Or even much cares."

Odin and Fenfang drifted over. "What have you got?" Odin asked.

Shay explained, and Odin nodded. "That's something I can get behind. Look, there's this subdivision." He touched the screen. "If you had to run, it's a few hundred yards. The houses look like they're about ten feet apart, and everyone's idea of landscaping is jungle-style. Once you got in there, nobody could find you. If you had to run the other way, there's this bunch of houses to the south. . . ."

The rest of the group had come over to look.

"Lots of cars parked on the street—which means we could have a backup car thirty seconds away, if we needed it," Shay said. "We could reach it with the walkie-talkies."

"We don't know how old the Google pictures are," Cade said. "We'll have to see it for real to decide."

Odin said, "We should go tomorrow morning."

"Not you," Shay said. "They know your face too well. And not Fenfang—we need her safe. She's our final proof, if we really need it." She shook her head at Twist. "I don't think you, either. You're pretty recognizable, and you have trouble running."

"I'm going, but I don't have to climb," Twist said. "I'd be the emergency backup. And I'll monitor the satphone—in case the guy calls back."

"Cade, Cruz, me, and you," Shay said. "I've got to go so I can check out the climb."

"Probably don't really need to climb," Danny said. "I've got an aluminum folding ladder, weighs twenty pounds, unfolds to eight feet. You could run over behind that little building, throw the ladder up, pull it up after you, climb to the top roof. You wouldn't have to go up there alone—you could have somebody with you."

"That'll be me," Cruz said.

"Get the ladder," Twist said. "We'll do some practice here on the front deck."

"I'll still take rope," Shay said. "We could tie it around a vent on the opposite side of the building, so if somebody did see us, we could run across the roof and slide down the rope and take off."

Twist nodded. "So—we go tomorrow morning. Check it out, and when it gets dark, if everything looks right, we'll put two people on the roof."

They spent the afternoon shopping for supplies and the evening talking about all the possibilities, until Odin said, "You know what? We're talking in circles. I'm gonna go work on the Mindkill cache."

"Where you at with that?" Twist asked.

"We're working out all the formatting, and all the pieces we have so far. We want to be able to bring it up in an instant," Odin replied.

Cade said, "We're also prepping a message to all the sites that took us seriously the first time, asking them to mirror us. With any luck, Mindkill will show up on a couple of hundred sites all over the country. Singular would have a helluva time bringing it all down. . . . There's a lot of busywork."

"Alternatively, we could just mellow out, since it's closing in on midnight," Danny said.

"I ain't smokin' nothin'," said Twist.

"Then I'll get you a root beer," Danny said. "But really, I was thinking about some old Seattle sounds. . . ."

He brought up an eighties album from Pearl Jam, and Twist said, "Excellent."

Things didn't mellow out right away: they still couldn't tear themselves away from the talk-and-more-talk. Danny shook his head and said, "I'm gonna have to drop the bomb." A Willie Nelson album came up, and the computer speakers began kicking out *really old* songs, slow ones, beginning with "Stardust."

Danny came up behind Shay and put his arm around her waist and said, "Dance."

Shay pulled back. "What?"

"We're gonna dance. We need to dance."

"You gotta be kidding me," Shay said.

"I'm not," Danny said. He pulled her into the middle of the living room floor, swung her around, and Shay muttered, "This is weird."

And they slow-danced. Shay probably wouldn't have admitted it, but it felt good the way her planning brain faded into some other place as she swayed to the music.

Odin said to Fenfang, "C'mon."

Fenfang blushed and said, "I am a nerd. I do not know how."

Cade smiled and stepped toward her. "One thing you learn in private school is how to dance to old-fart music. C'mon, I'll show you."

"Show us both," Odin said, cutting in front of him. He looked into Fenfang's eyes and said: "You haven't had any seizures since the medicine kicked in. Janes said we might be able to bury Dash's personality if we teach you new things. He even mentioned dancing. So . . . let's both learn how to dance."

Cade got them positioned, and Odin put one arm around her waist and raised one of her hands in his. Then Cade explained the box step.

"This makes perfect sense," Fenfang said, and they both stared down at their feet. Cade started them off, and they made their first small square together.

. . . And they danced.

Cade cut in on Danny for "Georgia on My Mind," and then Cruz cut in on Cade and took Shay for "Blue Skies."

Twist didn't dance, and didn't explain, just sat backward on a dining room chair, grinning at the makeshift ballroom. "I gotta say, I can't believe . . . Cade? Cruz? Odin? Danny? You can all dance. . . . I mean, Cruz, look at you."

Cruz said, "It's my culture." He had a tight grip on Shay, his good arm around her waist, his plastic-cast arm resting on her shoulder, as though he weren't inclined to let go again.

Cade danced with Fenfang, but then Odin cut in again, and then Danny danced with Fenfang, and Odin cut in again, and then everybody got the hint, and Odin and Fenfang edged off by themselves.

Shay muttered to Danny, "I can't believe my brother. My brother can't dance."

"I get the impression that you think your brother can't do a lot of things."

"What? No, I don't—"

"Yes, you do," he said. "When I was teaching him to run right, you were worried that he was going to hurt himself, for God's sake."

"I—"

Danny put a finger to his lips to shush her and said, "Let's find something that rocks a little. . . ."

So they danced faster, and mellowed out more. A party, almost.

A tension break, definitely. Once, when Shay stopped dancing for a while and was wiping her face off with a towel, she noticed that Odin and Fenfang had gone out on the front deck.

Twist followed her gaze and said, "You may want to avert your eyes."

Shay watched as her big brother silenced the laughing girl in his arms with a kiss.

17

The next day, Twist rode with Shay and X down to Stockton, with Cruz and Cade following in the truck. "Six hours of hell," Twist said to Shay as they drove away from Danny's. "For you, anyway, because I plan to talk. You know, about your life, the way you dress, why most current art has no objective correlative, and so on."

Shay rolled her eyes, and he said, "Okay, I'll keep it short: butt out of your brother's love life."

"Twist: she's probably going to die. Soon. He's been through enough pain."

Shay was driving, and Twist was watching the speedometer rise with her emotion.

"Slow down. I agree there's probably pain ahead, but Odin knows that. That's *his* problem. You rescued him from Singular—and that was necessary. Saving him from Fenfang isn't."

"Look, I'm not trying to be a hard-ass," Shay said.

"You are a hard-ass. Too hard for your age. I can't complain about that, because I was the same way. All I'm saying is, it's not your job to protect him from everything. He won't thank you for that."

X was sitting on the backseat, his head going back and forth as they talked, like a ball-obsessed dog watching a tennis match. Now he looked at Shay and made a sound that might have been a whimper had it gone on for more than a half second. As it was, it sounded like a "Yes."

Twist said, "Even X agrees with me."

Six hours on the road, with a stop for water and Cokes and gas and, for Twist, a chance to stretch his legs. Then they were driving through Stockton on I-5. From the beginning of the built-up area, to the airport was twelve or thirteen miles. Cade and Cruz had arrived ahead of them and had spotted both the Singular building and the building that Shay hoped to use as a lookout.

Using cold cell phones, and no names, Cade said, "Might be a problem—might be two problems. First, there's hardly any traffic on the frontage road that goes by the building we're interested in, so if we drive up *that* road, they could get a good look at us through the cameras. Could catch license plate numbers, too."

"They have cameras?" Twist said.

"Several. We didn't want to get too close, so we didn't drive around the building. We stayed on the main drag, lots of traffic there."

"Any good news?"

"Yes. That climb . . . we think it could work. You'll see."

Twist was driving, and Shay began picking up the distance markers they'd pinpointed on Google Maps. Then: "Here we go. Off to the left. Don't slow down."

The Singular building, if it was a Singular building, was completely unmarked.

A nearly blank-faced rectangle, the building had only three obvious entries on its front, and all of them were glass: anyone approaching from the front could be seen coming.

Shay and Twist went on by, Shay turning to look at the side of the building: nothing much had changed from the view on Google Maps.

Twist said, "There's our watchtower."

The Unclaimed Freight building looked abandoned, with not a single car in the front parking lot. The banner with the name drooped dispiritedly over the entrance, and more graffiti had been added since the Google shots.

"We need to cruise it again," Shay said.

Twist took the first exit, and they curled back around. From the left side of the Unclaimed Freight building, and the back, they couldn't see the Singular building at all. As they came out from behind the back, Shay said, "Look at the trees. I didn't even see the trees on Google."

Twist stopped at a stop sign. They could see the small cube-shaped building that would give them a boost to the roof. Shay nodded and scoped out the nearby buildings.

Cruz and Cade were waiting at a McDonald's back on I-5. The day was too hot to leave X in the Jeep, so they gathered at an outdoor table.

"What do you think?" Cade asked when they'd settled in with food.

"I don't see any reason not to," Shay said. "We can do it tonight. We'll just look."

Twist kept his eyes on his burger as Cade and Cruz looked over at him, waiting to hear his take. Eventually, he dabbed his mouth with a napkin and said, "We won't get anything done without taking some risks."

"Then tonight it is," said Cruz. "We need to find a place where we can wait it out."

"I've got just the motel," said Shay as she fed half her hamburger to X. "It's where I cut my hair off. The guy who runs it is probably the president of the National Dirtball Association."

"Sounds perfect," Twist said.

Shay squinted at him, something in the tone of his voice. "There's something else going through your head. What is it?"

"Nope, not going to tell you," Twist said. "Not until we know if the building is Singular or not."

"You ought to tell us now," Cade said, and Cruz nodded.

Twist shook his head. "No, it's only half an idea, and it's just completely ridiculous."

Twist wouldn't budge, and when they finished the food, they all headed across town to the motel. Twist rented the rooms, then came out with three keys and said to Shay, "You have identified the single sleaziest guy in Stockton, running the single scummiest motel. I have no more to teach you."

Shay's room was not the same room she'd rented before, but it was just as disgusting. The cleanest thing on the bed was the bottom sheet, so she pulled all the rest off and threw it on the floor so she could stretch out and close her eyes. X settled on the pile of bedding and closed his eyes.

Shay knew she should nap if she was going to be up most of the night, but her brain was churning, and sleep didn't come easily. What she'd do that night was, technically, a crime. Just as it was when she'd hung Twist's immigrant rights banner off a twelve-story office building, and again when she'd scaled the Hollywood sign and lit it up with MINDKILL.NET.

Both those actions thrilled her in some way, despite the legal consequences, despite the physical danger. Tonight's warehouse climb, looking for Singular, felt different. The actual climb was nothing, really, but the stakes were so much higher. X made a snorting sound, a snore. It made Shay smile, and after a bit more churning, she followed him down.

They moved on the Unclaimed Freight building at ten o'clock. Cruz and Cade, in the pickup, made the first pass. Cruz called on the walkie-talkie: "Looks clear."

The space around the building was darker than Shay had expected, and the flickering of car and truck lights from Route 99, through a fence along the highway, would make it even more difficult to see dark-clothed intruders hurrying across the parking lot. Shay was wearing jeans and a reversible jacket—black side out, the red lining invisible—given to her by Danny.

"Dope dealer trick," he said. "You run with the black side out—but if you think they're going to catch you, if you can't get away, you come strolling down the street with the red side out, like you don't know nothin'. I mean, what sneaky criminal would wear a bright red jacket?"

Shay and Twist approached the back of the building, Shay with her pack, which contained a climbing rope, a flashlight, binoculars, some sandwiches, two bottles of water, and—unknown to Twist—the gun Danny had given her. Twist would drop Shay and keep moving so nobody would see a car loitering behind the building.

She had the walkie-talkie and would warn the others if she ran into anyone. Cruz and Cade would be just behind, so if she did run into interference, she could turn around and pile into the back of the pickup.

There were no other vehicles in sight. Twist said, "Shay."

"I know. Be careful," she said.

Without any more talk, he slowed, and then Shay was out the door, walkie-talkie clutched in her right hand, running through the dark. X watched her go, whining a little when the Jeep's door closed in his face. Twist said, "Say a doggy prayer," and pulled away.

The run to the back of the small building took fifteen seconds, and Shay neither saw nor heard anyone else, though she almost went down when she tripped on a curb at the edge of the parking lot. Recovering, she stumbled up behind the building, put the walkie-talkie to her face, and said, "I'm here."

Less than a minute later, Cruz scrambled into the darkness next to her. "Listen," Shay whispered. They both watched and listened, and heard nothing but traffic. Fianlly she said, "We go up."

They fumbled for a minute with the locking bolts on the ladder, then it was up, and Shay led the way to the first roof. Cruz pulled the ladder up behind them, and propped it against the wall of the main building, and Shay climbed to the top step, and then over onto the roof, which had a foot-high parapet. Cruz was right behind her, and pulled the ladder up, and they sat another minute, listening.

Again, they heard nothing but traffic.

Crouching, they walked to the back of the building, where, in the dim light, they fastened their escape rope to a vent housing and coiled it next to the edge of the roof. If they had to run, they could be down in seconds.

When Shay was sure the rope was secure, she whispered, "Let's go look."

They went halfway back across the roof, then crawled to the edge facing the target building and peeked over the low parapet. The other building showed only the faintest light from the main windows. There were three cars in the parking lot—somebody was inside. The parking lot itself was brightly lit. They were looking at the building from an angle, so they could see all of the front, all of one side, nothing of the other side, and part of the back parking lot, including the gate for truckers.

"Wish we could have scouted the back," Cruz whispered.

"If we don't see anything tonight, maybe we take a shot at it tomorrow," Shay said. "No reason to think they have the plates on your truck."

"We could buy some rakes and shit and throw them in the back of the truck. I could drive it through there and nobody would see anything but another Chicano gardener."

"Yeah, and then we'd have the rakes and shit. Maybe you could get a few yards when this is over."

Cruz laughed, too loud, then clapped a hand on his mouth and said, "Sorry."

Then nothing happened for a long time. Surveillance, Shay found, was tougher than it looked—just sitting up was tough, if you had no back support. They spent some time looking at the stars, which were hazy. Shay knew the names of a few constellations, and Cruz knew a few, too, and told her the names in Spanish.

Cruz, who had his own pack, pulled out a bedspread from the motel, and they took turns lying on it, while the other one watched, fifteen minutes at a time. Every half hour or so, Cade and Twist would check in on the walkie-talkie, quick clicks and then: "Good?"

"Good."

They ate the sandwiches at one o'clock, and by two o'clock, it had gotten quite cool. Shay wrapped the blanket around herself.

At three o'clock she sat up and said, "Wish I'd brought some earphones and music to distract me. How did it get so cold? I wasn't thinking about that."

Cruz said, "C'mon over here."

She settled in beside him, and Cruz pulled the bedspread across their shoulders, and they huddled together, and she eventually warmed up. At three-thirty, Shay was dozing against Cruz's shoulder when he stiffened and muttered, *"Hijueputa,"* and Shay's eyes popped open.

A truck had turned off Route 99 onto the frontage road and then onto the road along the side of the Singular building—a road that went nowhere except around the building and into the parking lot.

Cruz was holding the binoculars, and he whispered, "When I saw it coming, I thought—"

He stopped midsentence as the truck disappeared behind the Singular building.

"Thought what?"

"Take the glasses," he said, and thrust them at her as the truck reappeared at the back gate, which was just visible from their perch.

The lot was brightly lit, and Shay watched through the binoculars as the truck waited until the gate rolled open, then pulled into the lot and turned left, showing its side to them.

"Oh my God, it's the same truck as in Sacramento," she said.

"That's what I thought," said Cruz. "I couldn't exactly remember the name on the truck in Sacramento, but the writing, the colors, they look right. . . ."

"It's either the same truck or one identical to it," Shay said. "It's delivering food for the prisoners. Cruz: we've found them."

18

They called Twist and Cade, retrieved the escape rope, came down off the roof with the ladder, and ran around to the back of the building, where Twist was pulling up, with Cade a hundred feet back in the truck. Shay jumped into the Jeep, and Twist pulled away, with Cade and Cruz right behind them.

"You remember that truck when we raided the Sacramento prison?" Shay asked Twist, her voice pitched with excitement.

"Yeah, the one bringing in the food."

"I didn't pay much attention at the time, but it said something like KENDALL'S KATERING on the side, with *K*s. Well, a Kendall's Katering truck pulled into the back of the building over there. What are the chances that it's a coincidence?"

"Slim and none, and Slim is outta town," Twist said, pounding the steering wheel with his hands. "It's gotta be Singular."

"Now the question is, how do we get in there?"

"I don't think we do. Get in there, I mean," Twist said. "I've got another idea."

"The one you wouldn't talk about?"

"Yeah. Because it's imprudent, preposterous, and highly flammable."

At the motel, Twist said, "The underlying fact is, we can't get in there. So we make them come out. Or we get someone else to go in. Or both."

Cade lifted a finger. "Um, Twist—"

Twist said, "Shut up for a minute. I drove down 99 and took a close look at the fence around that place. It's not much. If you hit that fence with a big enough truck, you'd knock it flat. If you hit it in the middle, you'd be looking at that big glass front door. You could drive a truck—if it was big enough—right through the front doors."

"Then what?" Shay asked. "We yell at them to surrender?"

"No," Twist said. "We throw a bomb at them and let the cops and the fire department clean up."

"What?" the other three asked all at once.

Twist: "Listen. We get a truck. We make some Molotov cocktails. You guys know how to make Molotov cocktails, right?"

Cade said, "Some Beefeater gin, dry vermouth, maybe a twist of lemon . . ."

"That's a martini, you decadent little punk," Twist said. "A Molotov cocktail is made with gasoline and engine oil, mixed in a bottle, with a rag tied around the neck of the bottle, which is the fuse. You light the fuse and throw the bottle, it breaks, the fuse lights the gasoline—"

"But, Twist, if we burn the place, we could incinerate the people we're trying to save," said Shay.

"No, no, no. We call the cops, tell them there's been an explosion at the Singular building, that people inside are hurt. At the same time, we drive the truck into the fence and throw the Molotov cocktails out the windows into the *parking lot*. No one gets burned. Then we drive the truck into the lobby. Doesn't have to be fast, put it in the lowest gear with a brick on the gas pedal. The cops are there in two minutes, the firemen get there a minute later. They see these big fires and the ass end of the truck sticking out of the lobby. Big hole in the front of the building. One of us calls the fire department to say there are a bunch of illegal immigrants in the basement. Somebody else calls the TV stations. The police have to go in and search the building. It's too bizarre not to. Once the cops find the prisoners, the jig is up. They're done. Can't hide it."

Cruz shook his head and said it was crazy, and Cade said he thought it could work, and then the three men all waited on Shay, who said, "It's both things. It's crazy and it could work. But where would we get a truck like that?"

Twist picked up a copy of the local newspaper, called the *Record*, folded it back to the classified ads, and pointed to a circled ad.

> Mack Ten-Yard dump truck. 1976 DM 685, 6/6 manual, 230,000, runs good, Jacobs brakes, newly serviced, fair rubber, everything works, but sold as is. Scale weight 23,000 empty, $5000, call Rod Jurondick at O'Hara's.

"We've got the cash," Twist said. "And Cade, master prep-school car thief, can drive anything."

"That's true," Cade said.

"What if there's a guy right inside the glass door with a machine gun?" Cruz asked.

"That would be a problem," Twist admitted.

"I don't think there is anybody in the lobby. The lights were all real low," Shay said. "If we crashed through there, but were going slow and jumped before it was all the way in, anybody inside would have a lot more to think about than running out to catch us."

Twist was pumped by his plan, twirling his cane between his hands. He said, "It's still a risk, and we have to admit it. But the way I see it, Cade drives, I ride shotgun, Cruz and Shay drive our getaway vehicles. . . ."

"No. Cade drives the Mack, you and Cruz drive the getaways, and I ride shotgun—me and X," said Shay. "If there's trouble, I can run faster than you, and X, well, you had to see X at Dash's house to know what I'm talking about. If X thinks I'm in trouble, then even a machine gunner would have a problem."

For once, they didn't argue. The plan felt right. They all nodded at each other, and Cade said to Twist, "Get ready to lay down your money, O rich person."

Shay said, "We have to work out the sequence just right: attack, call the cops, call the fire department, call the media, one-two-three, really quick sequence. Then we call Odin and press restart on Mind-kill. The video of Fenfang, the X-rays, the secret stuff from Dash's place, and the videos of Dash and Janes . . ."

Twist: "What about the photo of the vice president with the North Koreans?"

"I'd hold that back until the world believes, then put it out there," Shay said, and slung her arm around X. "That'll be the cherry on the cake."

Twist nodded. "Let's call Odin and tell him to be ready."

• • •

They were up at nine o'clock the next morning. Shay woke to a knock at the door and found Twist standing outside. "I'm going to a bagel joint. Give me your order."

She ordered two Diet Cokes and two cinnamon-raisin bagels for herself, then went to get cleaned up. When she got out of the shower, she noticed in the cracked motel mirror that her black hair was showing glints of red, as were her eyebrows. Not much yet, but the hair dye, which had been only semi-permanent, was beginning to fade.

She wasn't too unhappy with that; she missed her red hair, and not only the color, but the length of it. The dye she'd combed randomly through X's coat was holding up, since he wasn't standing in a daily shower. She realized X hadn't had a bath in all the time she'd known him.

"C'mere, boy," she said, and he trotted over from where he was lying in the bathroom entrance. She stuck her nose in his neck and gave him a smell test and declared: "Fresh as a month-old daisy."

She got dressed, gave X a couple of cups of dry dog food and a small can of meat. When he'd finished gulping it down, she washed the bowl, said, "You're excused" when X burped, and then took him outside for a walk.

As she returned to the motel, Twist got back with the bagels. He was starting to feel the stress. "It's like this every time. We get close to doing something, and I get cold feet. Every time. We do it anyway. It's killing my feet."

"We'll worry when that *doesn't* happen," Shay said.

When they knocked on the guys' door, Cruz was on the phone with Rod Jurondick: still speaking English, but with a just-arrived Mexican accent. "Then," he said. "We will see you at noon."

He hung up, checked the time on his phone, and said, "We've got two and a half hours to chicken out."

"Time to eat, talk, and shop," Cade said.

"What are we shopping for?" Shay asked.

"Cruz needs to become your typical underpaid, overworked, undocumented yardman," Cade replied.

"Yes, but I am eager to move up," said Cruz. "I will leave my puny pickup behind, and I will have a dump truck."

They went to the Goodwill. An hour later, Shay was a little embarrassed by the fact they'd built themselves a stereotypical illegal immigrant gardener, complete with a wide-brimmed straw hat and stained blue cotton work trousers. Cruz thought it was hilarious and walked around speaking with a terrible fake accent until Twist told him to knock it off: "You're gonna screw us up."

Cruz said, "Ho, seeeñor, hi don' theenk so. Hi theenk hi fool anybody. . . ."

"Twist's right. You're gonna screw us up," Shay said.

Cruz wriggled his eyebrows at Shay and said, "Ooooh, señorita, you have zee vaary nice maracas, you know what hi say?" He held up a hand, and Cade, who was dressed in worn jeans, a faded Fender T-shirt, and a backward L.A. Dodgers hat, slapped it.

Cade and Cruz took the pickup over to Rod Jurondick's house, a low pink concrete-block rambler, neatly kept with a flagpole in the front yard. A little girl was playing on a Big Wheel in the crescent-shaped driveway, and an orange-and-white Mack dump truck sat at the curb.

Twist and Shay hadn't expected to go, but they were both so curious about the truck negotiation that they'd followed in the Jeep, with X in the back, and parked half a block away to watch.

Cade pulled up in front of the house next door to Jurondick's, and he and Cruz got out of the truck and started up his driveway.

The little girl abandoned her Big Wheel and ran to the front screen door. "Daddy," she called out, "they're here."

Jurondick came out of the house, and Cade and Cruz spent more than half an hour crawling over the truck, starting it, driving it around the block. Finally, they went into the house with Jurondick. "I think they bought it," Twist told Shay.

"Took them long enough."

"Wanted it to feel real," Twist said.

A couple of minutes later, Cade and Cruz came out of the house, Cruz carrying some papers, and Cruz got in the pickup and Cade got up in the dump truck and they drove off down the street.

"Step one," Twist said to Shay, and followed after them.

Cade parked the dump truck on the street outside of the motel. "Jurondick was a nice guy. He made us promise to take care of the 'Mighty Tonka' he always wanted as a kid." They all looked at the beat-up old truck. "Hope he doesn't watch the news when this thing busts through the building, 'cause, man, the dude's gonna cry like he's three all over again."

They did a number of things during the afternoon and evening to prepare for the attack: They went to one Walmart and bought a two-and-a-half-gallon gasoline can and a small bag of quick-setting patching cement. At another, they bought two cans of engine oil and two bungee cords; at a third, they bought four big Ball jars, the kind used for canning vegetables, and a pair of rubber kitchen gloves.

They filled the gas can at a Shell station.

Cade spent an hour in the truck, working out the best way to anchor the steering wheel with the bungee cords so that, after he jumped out, the truck would continue straight ahead. The bag of patching cement was molded around the gas pedal to hold it down, then sprinkled with water to make it retain its shape. Cade would drop it on the gas pedal and let the truck drive itself.

They cruised the Singular building twice, and Cade drove around the building in the dump truck, which they thought would be safe enough: who'd suspect that they'd arrive in a dump truck? He reported two cars and a panel van in the lot behind the building; they'd seen three other cars parked in front.

"Not enough cars," Twist said. "That's a big building for six cars."

"Probably nobody in there but the prisoners and the guards— there weren't that many cars at Sacramento, either," Cruz said.

At nine o'clock, as it was getting dark, they brought the gas, the jars, and the motor oil into a motel room and, being careful not to spill anything, filled the jars with a mixture of gasoline and oil—X sniffing the air like they were in a bakery—and screwed the lids on tight.

"The gas sets it off; the oil keeps it going for a while," Twist said.

When that was done, they tore up the old cotton shirt that Cruz had worn to Jurondick's house and tied the rags around the jars.

"Just before you go crashing through the fence, Cade pulls over to the side. You unscrew one of the lids, dip the rags in the gas, then screw the lids back on. When you crash the fence, you light up the rags and throw three of the jars out the window—as far away from the truck as you can," Twist said. "The fourth jar, you keep in the cab, and after you jump, if you can, you throw that jar back into the cab, hard as you can, so it breaks. We want a fire in the cab when it goes in. Not enough to set the building on fire, but enough to distract anyone inside until the fire department gets there."

"You really think that's necessary?" Shay asked.

"Yes. After Singular identified Cruz with his DNA, I read up on it," Twist said. "Fire kills DNA—even a little fire."

They took the Molotov cocktails out to the Mack truck and wedged them behind the passenger seat.

"What are they going to light the fuses with?" Cruz asked.

Twist's face went blank for an instant, then he grinned and said, "Holy cats. We forgot to get a lighter."

"That would have been a bummer, getting there and no match," Cade said.

Shay looked at Cade and Cruz and asked, semi-seriously, "Do you guys feel like criminals?"

"I do," Cruz said.

"I'm getting there," said Cade.

"We're not criminals, we're outlaws," Twist said. "There's a critical difference."

"Sounds right to me," said Shay, and off they went for Bic lighters to ignite their homemade firebombs.

19

Twist and Cruz went out first, in the Jeep, ferrying Cruz to the Unclaimed Freight building. He'd carry the ladder and one of the video cameras they'd used on the Dash and Janes raids. He'd film the attack and the response, and be in position to warn Cade and Shay if something looked bad on the approach.

Twist would get in position to make the pickup.

They'd all be in touch by walkie-talkie.

When Cruz was settled on the roof, Twist called: "Go."

A heavy chill crawled along Shay's arms as they drove over to the Singular building. She wasn't superstitious, but something felt wrong to her.

She let the premonition go and asked Cade, "What do you think?"

Whenever he spoke to her, he tended to smile, because that's what he did. But as he worked up through the gears in the big truck, he glanced at her, unnaturally serious. "I don't know. This is a tough one."

X was on the floor by Shay's feet, and he, too, seemed to be looking at her with an unusually serious gaze: he knew something was up. She'd recharged him that afternoon, and he was primed to run.

Cade said, "You still got the spirit rock? You might give it a rub."

"Yeah, I . . ." Shay dug in her front pocket, then in the other one, and the back pockets, and she blurted: "It's gone! The rock is gone!"

"Back at Danny's? Or the motel?"

"No, I always keep it in my pocket. I gave it a rub before I went over the wall at Dash's place, and that worked out. . . . Where is it?" She was patting her pockets again, digging into them, looking for it again.

"Hope this isn't a bad omen," Cade said.

Not much traffic. Cade didn't say much more until: "Cop." A police car rolled by, going the other direction. Kept going. A minute later, he said, "Twist is right behind us."

Shay put the walkie-talkie to her face, clicked it, and asked, "Clear?"

Cruz came back: "Yes."

"Then we're going," Cade said, sounding grimmer than his face looked. They were on the frontage road, south of the target building. Cade braked, and for an instant, Shay, forgetting, thought something had happened, but Cade glanced at her and said, "Bombs."

Right. The Molotov cocktails were her responsibility. She turned and fished the four jars out from behind the seat, and as Cade idled the truck at the side of the road, she unscrewed the top of one of the jars, and the air inside the cab was instantly infused with the odor of gasoline and oil. She carefully dipped the rags on each bottle into the gasoline, then screwed the lid back on and said, "Go—and when you take the jar from me, don't fumble it or we die."

"Got it."

Cade reached down and grabbed the ends of the bungee cords that had been fixed to supports in the back of the seats. Another car came up from behind them, honked, and went on by. They were no more than a hundred yards out when Cade said, "I'm shifting down. The weight is right by my foot, push it over."

Shay reached down, found the cement weight, pushed it toward the gas pedal. When Cade lifted his foot, she pushed it onto the pedal, and the truck's engine groaned against the lower gear and picked up a little speed.

They were fifty yards out, twenty yards, and then Cade said, "I'm turning in and going down another gear. Start lighting up the jars. There'll be a bump, so be careful."

Nothing like in the movies: nothing fast and furious. The truck was behaving more like a snowplow, moving slow, but with a heavy authority.

"Here we go," Cade said, and they plowed across the verge of the highway, over a curb. The truck shuddered when they hit the fence, knocking it down; the steel bars of the fence tore along the fenders and made a screaming, ripping sound, but the truck kept plowing forward. X struggled to get up out of the foot well, but Shay shouted, "No! Down!" and he shrank back. She used a Bic lighter to ignite the rag wick on the first of the jars, and then the second one, small flames licking up the glass sides.

She was holding them in her gloved hands, the rubber kitchen gloves, and Cade was chanting "Go, baby, go" to the truck. They lurched into the parking lot, and Shay threw the first jar out the window, and it landed and shattered with a flash of flame ten feet tall, and she handed the second jar to Cade and said, "Don't drop it, don't drop it," and he backhanded it out his window, and another haystack-sized flame blossomed in the parking lot.

"Unlatch the doors," Shay said.

Cade had hooked up the bungee cords that would steer the truck straight ahead, and now he made a few last-second adjustments as they advanced across the parking lot straight toward the front doors of the building, moving at a walking pace. Shay unlatched her door, then lit the last two Molotov cocktails. She threw one of them out her window and handed the other to Cade, who shouted, "Get out now! Get out now!"

She pushed the door open with her knees and was out, with X behind her. She was supposed to run immediately, without looking back, but instead, she slowed to make sure the truck was on course. A fourth explosion bloomed in the cabin of the truck—Cade had thrown the last bomb—and Shay, feeling the heat, turned and ran.

As soon as the first Molotov cocktail exploded, Twist, who was holding one of the cold phones in his hand, punched in 911 and said, "There's been a big explosion in a building down on 99 by the airport. Man, there's just a huge explosion. . . . Man, something just blew right into the building. . . . It looks like a tank just hit the building."

The 911 operator said, "Sir, you say there's been an explosion. Exactly where—"

"I don't know!" Twist shouted. "I'm on 99 down by the airport and—Man, another one just went off! It's like bombs are going off here. You'll see them, you'll see them!"

He could hear the operator talking to someone, and then she said, "Sir, we're getting more reports now, could you—"

Twist hung up.

From the roof across the street, Cruz was talking excitedly, in broken English, to another operator. "*Mucho* explosions, is *infierno*! Bring fire trucks. . . . Me, I'm going!"

Twist was talking to a local TV station, screaming about explosions and tanks, as he drove the Jeep toward the first rendezvous with Shay. He'd pick up Shay and X first, then Cade, who was supposed to run to the opposite corner of the parking lot. They'd decided to do it that way because they didn't know where the Molotov cocktails would spray the gas, and thought it best for the two runners to run straight away from the truck, rather than having to weave through the fires.

Shay sprinted across the parking lot, down to the far south corner, and saw the Jeep rolling onto the shoulder of the highway. She slowed when she got to the fence, changed direction until she came to a stout evergreen tree, stood on a branch near the base, got a foot on top of the fence, and vaulted over it. X, behind her, watched her go, then ran in a quick circle and hurdled the five-foot fence, clearing it by a foot.

Shay looked back: the lot was brightly illuminated both by the regular overhead lighting and by the fires. No sign of pursuit: *it had worked.*

Cade jumped from the truck when it was no more than six feet from the front door and rolling free and true. He lifted the final Molotov cocktail and hurled it through the truck's open door at the metal casing around the shifter.

The bomb exploded, and he hesitated, watching the truck as it bounced over a low step, then hit the front door, knocked it down, ripped some aluminum window supports off, and kept grinding into the building, with broken glass raining down on the dump bed.

He turned and ran along the front of the building to avoid the fire in the parking lot, and never saw the Singular man coming.

He was hit below the waist in a classic football tackle and went down on the hard asphalt. The tackle knocked the breath out of him, and as he was gasping for air, somebody else hit him in the back with a fist, below the rib cage, maybe breaking a rib, and he was stricken with a paralyzing pain, and then he was hit again, by somebody who knew what he was doing, then somebody shouted, "Lift and run. To the van. Everybody out, everybody out. . . ."

Somebody else shouted, "We've got sirens. . . . Get out. . . ."

Cade was being carried by at least four men. He groaned with pain and somebody said, "Shut up, you little asshole," and then he was thrown into a van. A door slammed and the van took off, felt like it bounced over a curb and then was running fast. Cade tried to pick up his head, but a man behind him swatted him down and said, "Stay down or I'll break your neck."

Cade felt like his back was on fire, but he could also feel, under his chest, the lump of the walkie-talkie. His hands were still free, and he pulled them up under his chest and cried, "You hurt me, I didn't do nothin'."

"Shut the fuck up," and the man slapped the back of his head, hard, and Cade felt his top teeth cut into his bottom lip. He managed to get one hand on the walkie-talkie, and he clicked it rapidly, then held down the transmit button.

"I didn't do nothin'," he cried. "Don't hurt me, man, I was just walking across there lookin' for a place to sleep, man, don't hurt me. . . . Just let me out, let me out of the van. . . ."

Twist had pulled to the side of the road, and when he saw Shay vault the fence, he popped the door on the Jeep. X jumped inside, followed by Shay, who shouted, "Okay!" She pulled the door shut and turned to Twist, who wasn't accelerating away toward the Cade pickup but was shouting "What? What?" into the walkie-talkie.

Shay heard Cruz shouting back, "They got Cade! They got Cade! There are people in the parking lot, Singular is in the parking lot. . . . I can't see them anymore."

"Cade?" Shay cried. "Oh my God!"

The fear choked her heart, and Twist gunned the Jeep past a half-dozen cars that had stopped to watch the fires. When they got to the spot where they were to meet Cade, there was no sign of him or anyone else. Twist raced to the back gates, but everything looked normal there.

"Stop! Let me out," Shay shouted. She put a hand at her hip and felt the gun butt there: she hadn't told Twist.

Twist wasn't having it. He gripped her arm and shouted, "No!"

Just then Twist's walkie-talkie erupted with a burst of call-clicks. "There he is," Twist said.

Then Cade said, "I didn't do nothin'. Don't hurt me, man. . . ." And finally: "Let me out of the van."

"Shit!" Shay cried.

The transmission ended, and Twist called back to Cruz: "What can you see? Where's the van?"

Cruz answered back, "Nothing. I don't see anything."

They were moving fast now. Shay said, "Give me the walkie-talkie." Twist handed it to her, and she said, "Yard Guy, we're coming to you."

A police cruiser flashed by, lights and sirens. Then another, and farther up the highway, they could see what had to be a fire truck, and maybe more cop cars, all headed toward them. They pulled onto the shoulder, and the fire truck went by, then another cop car, and an ambulance, and yet another cop car. Nobody paid attention to them, good citizens getting out of the way.

Shay said to Twist, "We should go up on the roof with Cruz; we need to see what happens."

Twist thought about it for a second or two and then nodded. "You're right. If the cops take a bunch of prisoners out of there, we've got some leverage to get Cade back."

"Yes!" Shay said.

They left the Jeep in a tight little residential area a few hundred yards away from the Unclaimed Freight building. The fires at the Singular building couldn't be seen from there, and there was nobody in the street.

They locked X in the Jeep and walked and then jogged back to the Unclaimed Freight building. Cruz was huddled by the base of the building with the ladder, and a moment later, they were all on the roof, crawling toward the parapet that faced the Singular building.

The scene across the way certainly suggested a disaster, cop lights and fire trucks and ambulances and, as they watched, a white media van slowing and then spewing out a cameraman and a reporter.

But no parade of rescued Singular experimental subjects. In fact, they saw nobody coming out of the building except firefighters and policemen. The fires in the parking lot were extinguished, and firemen were dragging hoses out of the building; the truck had been doused as well.

They watched for twenty minutes, the time crawling slowly by, waiting . . . and nothing changed. The firemen were cleaning up, hosing down the burn spots on the asphalt parking lot, washing away the residue from the Molotov cocktails. Cops wandered in and out of the building, and then one of the cars took off, lights flashing, for another part of town.

"What happened?" Cruz asked finally.

Twist said, "It was a trap. It was a trap and we walked into it."

20

Harmon drove a two-year-old black Mercedes ML550, a fast, powerful truck rigged out for desert travel; it had a big orange spot hand-painted on the roof, the better to help the search planes should he need to be rescued from one desert hellhole or another.

He was driving fast south on I-280 through Daly City when one of his subordinates, a former combat medic named Eric Jobair, called and told him that the "eco-goofs" had hit a secret Singular building in Stockton.

"I thought I knew them all, but I never heard that we had a place over there," Jobair said. "Anyway, it was totally empty when they hit, except for a couple of Thorne's security people. They caught one of the goofs. Some kid."

Harmon started looking for an off-ramp. "Where'd you hear this?"

"Andy Johnson."

"Don't know him."

"One of Thorne's guys, I ran into him coming out of the build-ing. He's an old pal, we used to shoot some hoops over in the 'stan."

"You say the building was empty?"

"Yeah. I guess the goofs ran a dump truck into it, set it on fire, called the cops and the fire department and the media. . . . Guess they thought it was a lab, and they'd get some publicity payoff."

"Know where they're taking the kid?"

"Didn't ask," Jobair said. "Don't think I'd want to be in his sneakers, though."

An off-ramp was coming up, Serramonte Boulevard, and Har-mon took it, beat the light at the top, went left, and slid into the turn lane that would take him onto the highway back the way he'd come.

Harmon had gone quiet, and after a moment, Jobair asked, "You still there?"

"Yeah. Listen, man, we've got a problem here," Harmon said. "I don't have time to fill you in. Don't tell anyone that you called me, okay? And don't call me again. At all. You'll know why in a day or two."

"What's the big mystery, boss?"

"You'll know in a day or two," Harmon said again. "For now, lie low, and keep your mouth shut. There's some weird shit about to go down."

Harmon had been on his way to Singular for a midnight check on what he called "sources and resources." Now he looked for the California Highway Patrol as he stood on the accelerator and the Benz blew through a hundred miles an hour. Harmon kept an apartment in a quiet building near the Lone Mountain campus of the University of San Francisco. Not the easiest place to get to in a hurry, but he liked the ambience of the area.

He had to slow down as he came up to Highway 1, and made a decision. He took a cell phone out of a lower pocket of the cargo pants he was wearing and pushed a button. A moment later, a man said, "Hello?"

Harmon: "Is this the hotel guy?"

"You bastard!" Twist screamed into the satphone.

"I know, it was a trap. Wasn't aimed at you so much as me. You were the bonus."

"What?"

"They knew they had a leak after Las Vegas," Harmon said. "They set me up, and probably a couple other guys. They leaked different locations to us to see where you'd show up. You went to Stockton—that's the location they leaked to me. I knew it was too easy. I knew there was something wrong, but that's water under the bridge, and we gotta deal with what we got. Listen: they got one of your guys."

"We know that," Twist said. "He's just a kid, a runaway. He doesn't know what's going on."

"Makes no difference. They're gonna squeeze him, and then, I suspect, they'll get rid of him."

"Where would they take him? Which direction will they head?"

"No idea."

"You gotta help us," Twist pleaded.

"I gotta help myself," Harmon said. "They're gonna kill me, too, if they catch me. How long ago did you hit this place?"

"Half hour, maybe . . ."

"Good. I got a little time."

Harmon could hear a garbled exchange on the other end, and then a girl's voice came on the line. "We need to meet."

"I don't know if I can," Harmon said. "If you call back in an hour and I answer, I'm still alive and rolling. We can talk then. In the meantime, the guy who ran this op is probably on the way to Stockton with half his people, so if you're still close, get out of there."

"Not that I trust you," Shay said, "but where's the other half going?"

"My place," Harmon said, and he clicked off.

He didn't want to get trapped in his own parking garage, so he left the truck on the street, a block away, and jogged to his apartment, slowed when he got close, and checked it out. No sign of anything unusual.

He had two separate and distinct pressures: to move fast, because they'd be coming, and to go slow, because they might already be there. But he needed his stuff. He checked around as well as he could in three or four minutes, then went in.

Nobody waiting. He lived on the top floor, the third, and took the interior stairs. The door was locked at the bottom, and it didn't appear to have been messed with. Still, he slipped the pistol out of a smooth chamois holster that he hid at the small of his back, and ran up the stairs.

Nobody in the hall.

A few seconds later, he was inside his apartment.

Weapons.

He'd built a carefully concealed cache at the back of a bedroom closet. He pulled all the clothes out and tossed them on his bed, then yanked the hanger rod out of its mounting and dropped it on the floor. The cache cover was a piece of white plywood that looked like the back wall of the closet, but wasn't. He pulled it loose. Behind it were two identical black pistols, Berettas, a combat shotgun, and an M16 with a bunch of banana clips. The shotgun was legal, but the rifle wasn't. The long guns went into an electric guitar case that had had the guts ripped out. The pistols and a dozen boxes of ammo went into a big Arc'teryx Altra backpack. His combat gear also went into the pack: boots and a Kevlar helmet of the kind issued to Delta Company operators. A bulletproof vest went on the floor.

His combat gear weighed close to a hundred pounds, as much as he could carry in a hurry. He hustled it down to the truck, locked it up, and headed back up to the apartment, keeping a Beretta in his jacket pocket with four full magazines.

Looked at his watch; if the goofs were telling the truth, it'd been fifty minutes since the Stockton building was hit. Thorne's troops were an hour's drive away, and it would have taken them a few minutes to get organized after they were called. But an hour was as much as he could risk: he had ten more minutes.

He'd seen nobody on the street except some college kids and a dog walker. He ran back up the stairs, pulled down a rolling suitcase and a big aluminum briefcase. He stuffed the suitcase with clothes, and the briefcase with necessary paperwork—insurance policies, tax returns, truck title, passport. That done, he went to his desk, yanked the bottom drawer out, and felt around the back housing until he found the envelope. Twenty-five thousand in small bills. He put it in the briefcase and was about to snap it shut when he spied his rock collection on a bookshelf. He stepped over, grabbed four or five stones, tossed them on the money, and closed the case.

Looked around. The apartment looked like he'd left in a hurry. Maybe he could come back? Maybe someday? Rent was paid for three more months. . . . Checked his watch: two minutes before his self-imposed deadline. He took the two minutes to put the cache back together and the rod back up and to rehang his clothes.

He was nearly finished when the doorbell rang. He tensed. He took the pistol out and edged up to the door, staying well to the side, and called, "Who's there?"

"Who do you think, asshole?"

Sync.

"You alone?" Harmon asked.

"Right now, I am. Won't be for long. Cartwell knows, too. He'll be sending Thorne's security people."

"You got a gun?"

"Yeah, but I'm not going to shoot you."

Harmon thought about it. Said, "Wait one."

He went into the bedroom, got the bulletproof vest from the floor, pulled it on, zipped it. Back at the door, he undid the dead bolt and backed away, the Beretta in his hand. "Door's open."

Sync came in. He was wearing a British-made suit, cut not to show the shoulder holster beneath it. He said, "You dumb-ass. How long were you talking to them?"

"A couple of times in the last week, that's all," Harmon said. "I didn't want anyone else killed."

Sync stepped inside the apartment and pushed the door shut. He looked around, saw open filing cabinets. "When did you figure it out?"

"I heard a rumor that the Stockton building was empty and knew I'd been punked. With Cartwell all swole up with testosterone and Thorne with all those gunnies, I thought I'd better get out of sight."

"You're right about that," Sync said.

"So, did they send you up here to bring me out?" Harmon asked.

"No. They don't know I'm here," Sync said. "I came to warn you."

"Really." Harmon let the skepticism show.

"Yeah, really. You saved my ass in the 'stan, when my ass was gone," Sync said. "Now I'm saving yours. You've got to get out, get far away, because you know too much. You can keep your mouth shut, but Cartwell won't trust that. He'll want your head. You keep your mouth shut long enough, maybe he'll let it go."

"How about you?"

"We're even now, so if I see you again, I will take you down."

"Ah, man . . ."

Sync shook his head and asked, "What happened, Harmon? How'd it get to this? You were one of our top guys. You had a chance to live forever. . . ."

"If you believe that, you're dumber than I ever thought you were," Harmon said. "That treatment—*if* they can get it to work—is for billionaires, not grunts like us. When the time comes, they'll put you on the table, saying you'll wake up as a twenty-year-old, give you a shot, and walk away laughing about it. Look at these people, Sync. They're murdering children to get what they want, and they can never let anybody know. You think there'll be any loose ends? Cartwell might scrape in, but not you."

"That's bullshit. We would have gotten in. I'll still get in."

"I don't believe it," Harmon said. "And I don't want it, not if it means killing children so rich people and dirty politicians can have their bodies. Nope. I won't do that."

After a moment of silence, Sync said, "You know more about the details than I thought."

"I'm an intel operator," Harmon said. "One thing I can't figure out, though, is how they roped you into it. You think buying new lives for billionaires is the American way now? What happened to *you*?"

Sync shook his head. "I'm sorry. It would have been good to sit down and work this out between us, but you don't have the time. Neither do I."

Harmon said, "West."

"What?"

"West was a good guy—as good as anybody you ever worked with," Harmon said. "Thorne murdered him. How could you support that? He was one of your own troops."

"He was a traitor," Sync said, ice in his tone.

"Traitor? What does that make you? A patriot? A patriot for a company of billionaires who murder children? Jesus, man."

"I'm going," Sync said again.

Harmon gave the apartment a last glance, and then, briefcase and luggage in hand, he went out the door after Sync, locking the dead bolt with the extra-strength strike plate behind it.

They took the rear fire stairs down, Sync in front, out of simple gun etiquette: Sync knew that Harmon wouldn't shoot him, but Harmon didn't know that about Sync, not for sure. They emerged from the stairwell at the side of the apartment building, out on green grass, edging an adjoining parking lot, on a nice California night.

"I'll head out first," Sync said as an orange tomcat, something limp in its mouth, ran past. "I wish to God this hadn't happened."

"You set me up."

"I hoped it was one of the other guys," Sync said.

"Well: good job, technically speaking."

Sync flashed a grin and held out a hand, and Harmon shook it. Sync said, "We're even. Remember that."

"I'll remember. If Cartwell sends somebody after me, make it not you."

Sync nodded and Harmon said:

"Take care, Stephen."

Harmon jogged to his truck, loaded up the last two bags, and climbed inside.

He was back at war.

He smiled as he put the Mercedes in gear. Didn't feel that bad.

Sync got on his phone and called Thorne. "I heard about Stockton, and that you got one of the kids."

"Yeah. Some punk named Cade Holt. Hadn't had that name."

"Where are you now?"

"Still in Sacramento. It was Stockton, so your guy—"

"Yeah, Harmon, that sonofabitch," Sync said. "You better get some guys moving. He knows how to run."

"They'll be at his place in five minutes," Thorne said. "I'm waiting for the call."

"Whatever you do, it's got to be quick and quiet. You don't want to take him on face to face, or he'll light up the whole neighborhood."

"We got a sniper," Thorne said. "It's all fixed."

"Call me when it's done," Sync said.

Thorne hung up and went back to Cade Holt. One of the kid's eyes was swollen closed, and his lips had been slashed open by his own teeth. His hands were cuffed behind his back; he was leaning in a corner, the wall holding him up.

Thorne grabbed his chin, dug his nails into Cade's face. "We're gonna need some information from you," he said. "Two ways we can get that: the easy way, and the hard way. You take the easy way, and maybe we can talk about what happens next. You take the hard way, we'll get the information anyway, and you'll wind up in a shallow grave out in the woods."

Cade tried to twist his face away, but Thorne tightened his grip.

"Think about it. You've got a little time. I sent a guy down to the janitor's closet for a bucket, and I already got the flannel shirt. That's the thing about waterboarding: it's so simple. Simple and sincere." He laughed.

21

When the Singular man hung up, Twist, Cruz, and Shay looked at each other, and Twist said, "We gotta get off the roof and get out of here. If Singular's got more agents around, waiting for the cops to go away, they could come back looking for us."

Shay said reluctantly, "You're right. Let's go."

Back at the motel, they packed up and were gone in three minutes, Shay riding with Twist and X in the Jeep, Cruz following in the pickup. Twist said, "We've got to contact Singular. We've got to find some leverage to make them release Cade."

"I can't think straight," Shay said. "I've got no ideas."

"The thing they might be most afraid of is that picture Cade found with the vice president and the Korean guy," Twist said. "If we called Singular headquarters and left a message for the top guy, Cartwell . . . hell, Fenfang knows his private number. . . ."

"What would we say? He'll know it's real, but he could claim it was a Photoshop job and dare us to put it online."

"But they don't know what else we have," Twist said. "Maybe

we should tell him there's also a *video* of the vice president. They're harder to fake."

"Keep talking," Shay said.

They drove north out of Stockton, talking to Cruz on a walkie-talkie. He agreed that the call was worth making. But first they called Odin and Fenfang back in Arcata and let them know what had happened. They explained their idea, and Fenfang gave them Micah Cartwell's direct line—the same one she'd used as Dash back in Reno. Twist broke out a cold phone for the call, but they got the automated message: "You've reached the office of Micah Cartwell . . . Dial zero for immediate help." Twist punched zero, and a man answered the phone after a couple of rings. "We need to speak to Mr. Cartwell or somebody who can contact him now," Twist said.

The man, with an edge of impatience, said, "You'll have to call during business hours."

"This is an emergency and we won't be able to call back later," Twist said.

"I can record the call and, if it's a real emergency, pass it on."

"Fine," Twist said. "This message is for Micah Cartwell, and he will want to hear it as soon as you can get it to him. The message is this: Not many people know about the vice president meeting with you and the North Koreans. A lot more will tomorrow, if we don't have our friend back with us. We will dump the video on the Internet."

He clicked off.

"You think that'll help?" Shay asked.

"It might slow them down," Twist said. He rolled his window down and threw the phone out.

"Not good enough. Has it been an hour? Give me the satphone

and I'll call the Singular guy back." The phone rang at the other end, three times, then four, and then the man answered.

"Yeah?"

"We have to get our friend back," Shay said.

"I'm not in a position to help you with that. I'm running myself."

"You could still help us. What would make them release him? You've got to know stuff that would let us pressure them," Shay said.

"Not enough. I'm just a disgruntled fired employee as far as any-one knows."

"Listen: we need to meet," Shay said.

"That'd be tough. You don't trust me and I don't trust you," the man said.

"What are *you* afraid of?"

"I'm afraid you're looking for somebody you could trade for that kid. That would be me."

"For God's sake, we don't know how to do that," Shay said, exasperated. "That's what you do."

"I don't know, you've shown some talent for getting what you want."

"You said when we talked before that they'll try to kill you. If we bring them down, that'll save your butt, too."

Silence.

Shay had a thought: "Hey, you said you know how to climb. Right? You know how to climb?"

"I climb."

"Could you do a 5.10?" Shay asked. The Yosemite Decimal System graded climbs on a numerical basis. A 5.10 was hard, but not a killer.

"In my sleep," the man said.

"You got a rope?"

"Yeah, I keep one in my truck."

"I'm going to steer you to a place," Shay said. "When you see it, you'll know you're safe. And we'll be safe, because we'll see you coming, and everybody around you. How does that sound?"

After a considerable silence, the man said, "Tell me what you're thinking."

"First of all, are you in San Francisco?"

"More or less," he said.

"Then head east, toward Yuba City. Do you know where that is?"

"Yup."

"Go to Yuba City and call me six hours from now."

"Why that long?"

"Because if we're gonna climb, it'd be better to do it in daylight, don't you think?"

"We're going to Yuba City?" Twist asked.

"No, north of there, to a place called Oroville," Shay said. "My foster parents took us there once. There're a couple of motels where we can crash for a few hours. I'm not sure what they are, because we stayed in a tent."

"Yeah, that's what we should have—a goddamn tent," Twist said. "Sooner or later, we're going to hit a hotel with an honest desk clerk."

Shay outlined her plan for Twist and Cruz while sitting in an all-night gas station diner.

"We need this guy. If Singular is a threat to him, and we could bring it down, he might help us—and if he's near the top of the company, he must have all kinds of information that would help us get Cade back."

Cruz said, "It sounds good, but this guy led us into the trap in the first place. He could be saying he's on the run now so we'll trust him, and then he can reel us in, too. He could just be a great liar."

"I know," Shay said. "But he warned us back in Vegas—I keep remembering that."

Twist nodded. "Tell us about the climb again—and what Cruz and I have to do to keep you safe."

Harmon probably wouldn't have gone along with the climber chick except that, first, he thought he'd like to meet her; second, the goofs were doing well enough that maybe they could damage Singular in a way that would make him safer; and third, if they were up to something crazy, like kidnapping him for a trade, he was pretty sure he could handle them.

He pulled into a rest area south of Yuba City, crawled into the back of the truck, unrolled a sleeping bag, and promptly went to sleep. His cell phone alarm woke him five minutes before he was to make the call. He took a sip of water, brushed his teeth, and spit the toothpaste into some weeds. He would have liked a shower, but he'd gone weeks without a shower before, nothing to wash with but river water or melted snow. He might stink, but he knew he'd survive.

When the time came, he called, and the climber chick said, "You need to continue north to Oroville. There's a Motel 6 there, and in the back of the parking lot, there are three orange stakes, some kind of construction thing. At the middle stake, there's a small plastic bag. Get the bag."

She clicked off.

Harmon pocketed his phone and grinned. The goofs were having the same problem that you have when you try to get the payoff from a kidnapping: you have to give instructions to the man with the money, and there's no way to tell whether the money man is repeating the instructions to surveillance specialists—FBI, police detectives, private security, whatever.

Be interesting to see what they'd come up with.

Thirty-five minutes later, he picked up the black plastic bag and looked inside. A multichannel walkie-talkie and a note that said, "Click the transmit button a few times." Interesting. No one would expect a walkie-talkie, not from a couple of tech freaks like the Rembys. And you couldn't track it, not unless you were already close by and had some really primitive equipment on hand. Even then, you couldn't track it closely.

He smiled again. Not bad. He clicked the transmit button a few times, and a man's voice said, "North on 70. Call when you cross the lake."

All right.

He drove out of town, north on Highway 70. Headed into the mountains. Into climber territory. He tried to see it from their point of view. He was on a narrow highway; if they were perched on a ridge, they could watch cars behind him, looking, say, for SUVs with several male occupants. Naive, but if they had enough watchers, it could trip up a tracking crew. Wouldn't trip up a helicopter, though, or a drone, if they were high enough.

So they hadn't thought of everything.

He called as he crossed the lake. The man came back and asked, "Are you in the black Mercedes ML550?"

"Yes. Big orange spot on the roof," Harmon said.

"Drive ten miles and then turn on your trouble lights, the blinkers. The climber will call you."

• • •

Shay well remembered the rock wall. Not a terribly difficult climb, it went straight up above the highway, with lots of cracks and edges. She probably could get up it without a rope, but somebody had bolted a beginner's crack, and the bolts would allow her to tie into the wall without doing any work.

There were two other aspects of the site that she liked: nine-tenths of the way to the top, there was an overhang, almost a cave, where she could settle in and watch the highway below. She could see straight down it, beside the river, for at least half a mile. The second thing was, the hardest part of the climb was just below the overhang. The Singular man would need both hands; she would have both free, for her gun.

If worse came to worst, and she saw several people coming after her, she could scramble out of the overhang and up the remaining rock to the top of the wall, where the forest waited. No helicopter could land up there: if the land wasn't covered by tall trees, then it was protected by a jumble of boulders.

Once she was in the trees, they wouldn't find her . . . unless they had bloodhounds.

Twist said, before leaving, "Shay . . ."

"I know."

"Don't kill yourself. It'd be really inconvenient."

He left. He'd be waiting four miles farther along the highway, at an informal turnoff used by fishermen and hikers.

When Twist had gone, Shay pulled on her pack and started up the wall, free-climbing the easy parts, tying in where the rock got steep. Twenty minutes later, she heaved herself onto the ledge under the overhang. She'd scraped the palm of her hand on a sharp rock and was bleeding a little. She pressed it against her jeans, opened her pack, and took out a pair of binoculars, a bottle of water, and her knife. She ran her fingers along the blade: now just a backup weapon, but even so, deadly as a cobra.

She slipped it back into its sheath, pushed it under her waistband, took out a cold phone, and dialed.

Cruz answered: "He's in a black Mercedes SUV and his trouble lights are blinking. I'm a half mile behind him, but he's pulling away. I got his truck tag and called it into Odin, who says his name is Harmon. He's forty-five, and from a quick look at the Net, Odin thinks he was West's boss and is probably the head of Singular's intelligence unit . . . or former head, if he's telling us the truth."

"Holy shit."

"Yes. You think we should still go with it?" Cruz asked.

"Definitely—he's too valuable not to take a chance with him."

"Okay. He's coming fast. I don't want to chase him, because he might spot me."

"Keep watch," Shay said. "I'll call when he gets here."

Harmon wasn't sure whether the man who called was ahead of him or behind him. Behind, he decided after a while, because he was traveling too fast on the narrow highway and never overtook anyone who looked like he might be a member of the group, nor did he see anyone accelerating away from him.

Twenty minutes after he crossed the lake, he took a walkie-talkie call from the climber. "You're coming up on a tunnel. See the wall? There's a parking place off to the right, before you go into the tunnel. Park there. On the wall, you'll see a line of bolts going up: it's the beginner's crack. You'll know for sure because you'll find a black Sharpie circle on the rock next to the bottom bolt. I'm most of the way to the top."

"What if I'd had a chopper?" Harmon asked.

"Helicopter blades don't work that well in a forest," the climber said. "They tend to come off."

"So you thought of that," Harmon said as he turned into the parking area. "I don't have a chopper, by the way. I'll see you in fifteen."

"I doubt it," she said. "More like twenty-five, guy who's as old as you are."

We'll see, Harmon thought as he got out of the truck, but he was grinning again. *Guy as old as you are*—she was trying to impress him. Whoever had spotted him had gotten his truck tags and gone into the DMV and looked him up—name, driver's license, photo. From there, they could get a lot more. . . . Big whoop. Everybody and his brother was into the DMV computers.

He had a pistol in his pocket, and a long folding knife, and a second pistol at the small of his back. He got his rope and a daypack with water, found the first bolt, ignored it, and started up. Twenty minutes later, he looked up and saw Shay ten feet above him. He was tied in now, balanced on a four-inch ledge. The climb hadn't been hard, but it was definitely a place you could get hurt, if you screwed up.

And looking at Shay, he thought he might have screwed up. He was using both hands to balance himself; she was nonchalantly looking down at him, relaxed, almost lounging on the rock. She had a pistol pointed at his head.

"So," she said, "you're Harmon."

"Yeah," he said. "I was the intelligence director at Singular."

"I know. I'm Shay."

"Yeah. Hello, Shay. Got a new hairdo. Your friends around?"

"One guy up the river, one guy across the river. The guy across the river is on that yellow thumb of rock. You might be able to see him; he's got a rifle and he's pointing it at your back. He said to tell you it's an accurized .308."

"Since I'm here, you might as well tell me now—are you trading me, or are we dealing?"

"We want to deal—you gotta know everything about Singular," Shay said. "First we want Cade back, but the only way we'll all be safe is if we can take the company down. You could help with that."

"Great idea, but I don't think it's going to happen," Harmon said.

"We might be more effective than you think. Right now, we need to figure out whether we can trust you."

"I'm thinking that helping you get your friend back would prove I'm trustworthy. I'll tell you, though, they lost me when they murdered West."

Shay's face went dark. "How'd they get away with it?" she asked. "I talked to him after he was shot, and he said he'd be okay—he made us leave him. Our vehicles were too far to carry him, but if we'd thought they'd murder him, we would've tried. . . ."

"When he was shot, he was down in the basement, where the prisoners were. He was still alive when they got there, so they took him up to the lobby, along with the guy he'd shot, and executed him. They sold it to the cops as a straight-out gunfight in the lobby, so the cops never went down in the basement."

"Who shot him?"

"Guy named Thorne."

Shay's mouth turned into a grim line. "We know about him. He tried to shoot my dog in Twist's hotel."

"That's the guy," Harmon said. Then: "Look, you mind if I come up? I'm starting to feel like a fly."

Shay made him hang a bit longer for her answer, then said, "Wait ten seconds, then come up. Don't try to get close to me."

Harmon could see that the route to the overhang was a series of small steplike faults and breaks, and he walked up them and twisted onto the ledge. Shay was on the opposite side of the overhang, sitting, her arms across her knees, pointing the handgun at him. "Don't shoot me," he said. "Every time somebody does that, it really, really hurts."

"If you have people watching this or monitoring this, you should know I can be in the woods in five minutes, and they'll never find me up there. You, of course, will be dodging rifle bullets. I was also supposed to tell you that our guy is shooting solid-core military ammunition, so it'll bounce around a lot in here, even if you find a place to hide."

"Kid: there's nobody out there."

"Just sayin'." She twitched the pistol barrel, saw herself doing it in the reflection of his mirrored aviators.

"Would you mind not pointing the muzzle directly at me? Could you move it over just a wee bit?"

"No, I'm comfortable like this."

"How about taking your finger off the trigger?"

"Nope," Shay said.

"You really don't want to shoot me, because I think I figured out how to get your pal back. What's his name again?"

Shay hesitated, then said, "Cade."

"Cade. We'd have to move fast. It'd be just you and me, so your other friends can stay out of sight," Harmon said. "But I think we can do it. I think I figured it out."

"You say 'I think' a lot," Shay said.

"Nothing's sure in this business," Harmon said. "The minute you think something's a sure thing, it'll bite you in the ass every time."

"But you think you can do it."

"Yes. If we're going to pull it off, it'll have to happen tonight. In San Francisco. In a really ritzy hotel."

"Let's hear it," Shay said. She pointed the pistol at the roof of the overhang and clicked the safety back on.

22

Micah Cartwell, the Singular CEO, got the message from Twist at seven o'clock in the morning. The man who'd taken it down hadn't understood it—it sounded crazy—and so he passed it along as a voice mail to Cartwell's secretary with a note: "I don't know if this means anything, but it came in after hours last night."

Cartwell's secretary had a bad feeling about it and called Cartwell at home, catching him just before he was to leave for the office. He stood with his head down, listening, then said, "Thank you, Jean. Call Sync and play this for him. I don't know what it means, but they clearly intended it as some kind of threat. The vice president? What vice president?"

When she'd rung off, he punched up Thorne's phone number.

Thorne answered instantly, although he'd been up all night. "Yeah."

"Anything on Harmon?"

"No. He could be halfway to Arizona by now. That's where he'll be—Arizona, New Mexico, Utah, Nevada, somewhere down there.

Problem is, he apparently hangs out at some of the Indian reservations, where they'd notice strangers. He could be hard to get at."

"What about the kid?"

"We spanked him a little last night, then left him to think about it. We'll get him going soon."

"Hold off on that. We've got a problem. These goddamn goofs, I don't know where they get it, but they've picked up a piece of intel that they should never have gotten."

"Probably from Harmon," Thorne said.

"I don't think so—more likely from Dash or Janes," Cartwell said. "They're going to want to deal for it, and we might have to."

"Can't be that important," Thorne said.

"Do what you do, and let me worry about how important it is," Cartwell snapped. "I'm telling you, it's a problem. I'd have had Harmon all over it, if Harmon was still with us. So: lock the kid down, and tell your guys not to mess with him until I call."

"You still want me to come this afternoon?" Thorne asked.

"Yes, unless something blows up. You and Sync need to find a replacement for Harmon, and I don't want some pussy who's going to sell us out. I need a heavily vetted hard case, and I need him now. We'll talk about it before the reception."

Shay and Harmon went up the rock wall, instead of down. "It's an easy walk down, once you're on top," she said. They were on top in five minutes, and Shay got on the walkie-talkie and said, "I'm with him. We'll follow the routine."

"What's the routine?" Harmon asked.

"A precaution," Shay said. "If I can't follow a set routine, then my friends will have to, mmm, provide some correction."

Harmon chuckled. "Provide some correction. I like that."

The back side of the rock face was simply a forested hill, with a few outcrops. They walked down it, to Harmon's Mercedes, and got in. Shay was no longer pointing the pistol at him, but she still had it in her hand, the hand next to the door, where he couldn't simply slap at it.

"Back to Oroville," she said.

On the way back, Harmon gave her a quick rundown of how he'd been set up and of his run-in with Sync the night before.

"You lost a friend," she said.

"No. He lost himself."

In Oroville, Shay pointed him at a restaurant parking lot and said, "In there." When he'd parked, she said, "Open the back hatch."

Harmon pushed a button, and the back hatch lifted up. Cruz had been walking across the parking lot, like another customer, a daypack on his back. When the hatch went up, he swerved over to the Benz, crawled inside, and brought the hatch down again. Cruz pulled a gun from under his shirt and said to Shay, "I got this."

Shay popped her door, and Harmon asked, "You're not going to stay?"

"I have no interest in seeing you naked," she said.

"What?"

She got out of the Mercedes, and Cruz said, "You're changing your clothes. We don't know what kind of tech Singular could use to track you. Track us. So you change."

"All right," Harmon said. "You must be Perez, huh? You get the dog bites fixed?"

Cruz never flinched.

"No dog bites," he said. "I'm wearing the cast because it's good in a fight."

$\bullet \quad \bullet \quad \bullet$

Seven minutes later, Shay got back in the car. Harmon had been wearing cargo pants and a heavy T-shirt and climbing boots. Now he was wearing jeans, a black golf shirt, and sneakers.

Cruz said, "I couldn't find anything in his clothes. I've been all through the car, couldn't find anything. His cell phone could be rigged somehow."

"It isn't," Harmon said.

Cruz ignored the comment. "He was carrying two guns and a folding knife that could gut a moose. He's got all kinds of military equipment in here, including electronics. I don't think it's bugged, but what do I know?" Cruz said. "The question is, do we take it? Or leave it? The car itself could be rigged."

"It's not. And given the people you're dealing with, you'll need the gear."

Shay told Harmon to drive again, and when he'd started the truck, she pointed across the parking lot. "Right by that old yellow car."

Harmon asked, "Why?"

"You'll see." Harmon drove over, perhaps a hundred yards, and parked. Shay said, "Okay, let's get out."

As they got out, Twist pulled up in the Jeep. "In the front," Shay told Harmon. He got in the passenger seat, and Shay and Cruz got in the back, with X between them. X sniffed at the back of Harmon's neck and growled: not threatening, but not happy, almost like a dog's version of a grumpy comment.

"Careful with the dog," Harmon said.

"You be careful," Shay said.

Twist drove two hundred yards to a greenhouse and pulled into a space facing the restaurant parking lot, where Harmon's Mercedes was still parked.

Harmon said, "So if you see somebody cruising both spots . . ."

"Yeah."

"You guys are really paranoid," Harmon said. "That's good."

"How are we going to get Cade back?" Twist asked.

"You'll have to trade somebody for him. If you hadn't already used up Senator Dash, she would have been a possibility. She's got guards, now, and they're good. Dr. Janes would have been a possibility, too—although they're now so desperate to get you, I'm not sure they'd trade for him. Not if your guy can give all of you up."

"We've left a message for Cartwell," Twist said. "We have something else he might be willing to trade for."

"Extremely unlikely," Harmon said.

They regarded him a bit impatiently, and then Twist said to Shay, "Reach me that bank box, will you?"

They'd brought paper copies of their evidence against Singular with them—just as a protection against Mindkill getting shut down or their computers getting hacked. Twist thumbed through some papers, found the photo he wanted, and passed it to Harmon.

Harmon looked at it for a moment, then another moment, then breathed, hardly above a hoarse whisper, "Is this real?"

"Yeah."

It was the picture of the vice president and Senator Charlotte Dash meeting with Singular and the North Korean officials. Harmon licked his lips and said, "I recognize this one guy. Chung Il Park. He's the head of their intelligence directorate."

"This other one is Ch'asu Kim Lee Pak, the vice marshal of their army staff," Twist said.

Harmon looked up and said, "This won't work as a trade."

Shay asked, "Why not?"

"Because you could have a million copies. I assume this is a print-out from a digital file, right? They could never be sure there wasn't just one more file. They'd have to make you talk about where those other files might be, and then they'd have to kill you to make sure you don't talk. Also . . . even if it did get out, they'd find ways to discredit it, because, to tell you the truth . . . I mean, I'm looking at it, and I believe you guys, but I can barely believe this photograph. I don't want to believe it."

Cruz said, "He's right."

Harmon stared at the photo and shook his head. "Sonofabitch . . ."

Twist took the photo, put it in the box. "Okay, then, how do we get Cade back?" Twist asked. "What do we trade?"

"This will freeze your feet," Shay said. "Tell him, Harmon."

Harmon explained his idea for recovering Cade, and when he finished, Twist said, "That's crazier than the attack on Dash."

"Nah. It's about the same," Harmon said. "And it's the one time I know for sure where he'll be."

"He'll have guards, they'll have guns," Twist said.

"They won't dare use them, not at a big event like this," Harmon said. "Any one of those people gets shot, it'll make headlines all over the country."

Shay said to Twist and Cruz, "We need to talk . . . alone."

The three of them walked away from the Jeep to talk where Harmon couldn't overhear. Shay said she believed him and that his plan would work. Twist asked, "You believe him? Or you just want to believe him?"

"I believe him," she said. She looked across the street to

Harmon's black Mercedes. As far as they could tell, nobody had tailed him. She said, "I'll do it. We've got to take the chance."

"Not you—me," Cruz said.

Shay shook her head. "If the plan works, we need you and Twist to pick up Cade. But going into the event . . . a girl is safer. People don't worry about waitresses—they barely even see them."

San Francisco, the sky going pink in the west. It would soon be dark, or as dark as it ever got in the ritzy part of town. Shay and Harmon sat in the Jeep in the basement parking garage of the Flavian Hotel, two blocks off Union Square.

Shay was dressed in a crisp black cotton shirt, ironed to within an inch of its life, equally well-pressed black slacks, and sleek black boots, all bought for cash at Barneys New York, a few blocks from where they now waited. The most expensive clothes she'd ever owned, for thirty seconds of playacting.

She also had a fashionable silver ring in her left nostril—not a real one, but a clip-on, bought at a street kiosk—and some styling crème in her hair to look like a dreadfully hip member of the hotel staff.

"The room is a half flight above the main restaurant," Harmon said.

"I know, I know, we've gone through it fifty times."

"So this is fifty-one," Harmon said. "When you walk through the kitchen, you have to keep moving. Don't let any of the other waiters or waitresses look at you too long. You follow me up the stairs. I go left, you go right. I'll point you through the doors, pick him out, he should be right at the head of that table to your left as you go in. You give him the message, then you lead him out the door. . . ."

They talked it over, and then Harmon gave her a last, appraising look and asked, "You think you can do it?"

"Yes. But if this is a double cross, somebody's gonna get shot, in a really public way in a major hotel."

Harmon had been in the hotel twice before, checking security for other events hosted by Cartwell. Recruiting events posing as VIP banquets, bringing together politicians and tech leaders from Silicon Valley who might like to become immortal. The first touch by the company. This one had been on the calendar for weeks, and Cartwell wouldn't miss it.

In the slightly stinky freight elevator, Shay checked out Harmon, who'd been transformed himself. He wore a blue workman's uniform, bought that afternoon at Sears, and carried a canvas plumber's bag.

They emerged on the lobby level, in a back hallway, down from an employee entrance to the kitchen of the Vespasian, one of the most exclusive restaurants in San Francisco. Harmon led the way: the kitchen was chaos, with cooks and waiters and waitresses hustling about the place, shouting orders and obscenities, rattling dishes and pans. Nobody gave them a second look. Shay followed Harmon through the throng and up a back set of stairs to the mezzanine level.

They stopped inside the door, and Harmon asked, "You've got the paper?"

"Yes."

"Don't slouch. Stand up straight and proper. Don't linger—in and out. The top security guy will be there, he's seen your photo, but only with red hair, and the facial features weren't that clear. He won't recognize you."

"I got it."

Harmon said, "All right. Pull the rip cord."

They went through the door, Harmon went left with his bag, Shay went right. Straight ahead, she could see the closed mahogany doors to the private room where the dinner party was happening. To her right, over the railing, a half floor down, was the restaurant's sumptuous main room, filled almost to overflowing with people eating, drinking, and laughing.

She kept moving, came up to the mahogany doors, slipped inside.

As promised, twenty people were seated along both sides of a twenty-foot-long dining table covered with a gorgeous strip of white linen. Dinner was well under way, the diners chatting with each other, flush with good wine, reaching for another roll.

Shay looked to her left, and there was Cartwell at the head of the table—and at his left hand, her blond hair lacquered into its signature flip, Senator Charlotte Dash. Shay almost turned to run, but smothered the impulse: she'd worn a mask the whole time she'd been with Dash. She forced herself to turn toward Cartwell, and when she reached him, she bent forward and whispered, "Mr. Cartwell?"

"Yes?" He looked up at her with no recognition in his eyes. Next to him, Dash forked a piece of Wiener schnitzel into her bruised mouth.

Shay said, "You have a call on our house phone. The caller said it was extremely important." She handed him a folded piece of paper. Cartwell opened it and saw the name Jimmie Stewart and the words *extremely urgent.*

The company's top lawyer wasn't one for hyperbole. Cartwell asked, "Where's the phone?"

Shay: "We have one just down the hall. There's a little nook where you can have some privacy."

"Show me."

He stood, and Dash turned back toward him, but Shay led him away, through the doors and down the hall to the restrooms. In the short hallway was a yellow cone that said OUT OF ORDER, and there was a note on the women's restroom door: "Please use first-floor restrooms."

There were no phones.

Cartwell said, "Where?" and turned in confusion toward Shay, and then Harmon was there, stepping out of the women's restroom with a gun.

"Inside," he snapped, and jerked Cartwell backward into the restroom. Shay followed and locked the door.

"You sonofabitch," Cartwell sputtered. "You're a dead man."

"Shut up. You're wasting air and you're gonna need it," Harmon said. He put out a leg and half tripped the other man, spinning him facedown onto the floor while wrenching Cartwell's arm behind him. Shay was there with the handcuffs Harmon had bought earlier that day at a sex shop: Cupid's Toy Box.

"You've got no chance. . . ."

"Shut up." When he was cuffed, Harmon gestured to Shay and said, "Let's pick him up. Third stall. Don't let him kick. Watch his legs."

Cartwell wasn't light, probably two hundred pounds, but Harmon was powerful, and Shay was strong from climbing, and they lifted him and carried him into one of the stalls, and Harmon said, "Stand on the toilet bowl."

Cartwell tried to put his feet down on the rim, finally found some balance, and Harmon let him go and quickly slipped a noose around his neck. The noose was actually a loop in the middle of a fat yellow nylon rope that had been tied to the corner supports of the stall where they met the ceiling.

The rope was loose, and Harmon reached up, pulled it tight, and tied a knot in it, which effectively shortened the rope.

Cartwell was beginning to panic, his Italian loafers moving on the slippery white porcelain.

Shay asked, "You know who I am?"

"God, you can't do this," Cartwell cried.

"You tortured my brother. You waterboarded him and beat him so badly he's almost crippled." This was a small lie, but it was also how she felt, and it came out in her voice. "Now you've got another friend of mine. The penalty for this is . . . well, look up."

She reached out with a foot and pushed it against the side of one of his legs, and Cartwell had to do a tap dance to keep his balance, the noose pulling at his throat. "Don't," he said, "please don't."

"Shay here, she wants to do it," Harmon said, almost conversationally. "I don't, because I'm afraid somebody would talk and I'd wind up in prison. But I gotta say, I can see it her way, too."

Harmon reached into Cartwell's inside jacket pocket and pulled out his cell phone. "If I wanted to call the people who have Shay's friend, how would we do that?" Harmon asked.

"I don't know, that's Thorne—"

Shay put some weight on the side of Cartwell's leg again, and he was forced to awkwardly shuffle to one side of the toilet bowl rim; he nearly fell off.

Harmon said, "If you fall off, we can probably lift you back up before you choke . . . unless the fall breaks your neck."

"There's a number for Sac. *S-A-C*. Ask for Gretsch," Cartwell groaned.

"Where is this? *Sac* is Sacramento?" Harmon asked. Twist was waiting in Sacramento, while Cruz stood by in San Francisco; they were hoping that Cade was being held near one or the other.

"Yes, Sacramento . . ."

Harmon's eyes clicked over to Shay, and he gave her a tiny nod, then held up the phone. "Hey, passcode."

Cartwell moaned, "Four-eight-three-nine."

Harmon found the number, then said, "You'll have to tell them to let the kid go right now. And tell Gretsch to give him a cell phone and this number. We want to talk to the kid."

"Ah, you're gonna kill me," Cartwell cried.

"Not if you make this work," Harmon said.

Harmon called and put it on speaker. At the other end, Gretsch seemed reluctant, and Cartwell screamed at him: "Let him go, you idiot. If you don't let him go, they'll kill me. They're gonna kill me right now. Do what I'm telling you, you silly shit. Now! Now!"

Harmon ended the call.

Gretsch ran. A moment later, the phone in Harmon's hand buzzed and Cade was on the line, saying, "Who is this?"

Shay said, "It's us. Get out of the building, as far and fast as you can, and then hide. Watch behind you. Stay on this line, and if they chase you, tell us. 'Cause if they chase you, there's a guy here who's gonna go right in the toilet."

There was a shuffling noise and a door banging, and Cade said, "We're going down a hall, I'm going down some stairs. They're not coming with me. I'm in the stairwell, I'm coming out of the stairwell, I'm by myself. . . ." Breathing harder now. "I'm in a lobby, I'm outside. . . . I'm outside, I'm running. . . ."

They waited three minutes, listening to his labored breathing, then Shay asked, "Are they following you?"

"I don't think so."

"We've got to go. Keep running, find a place to hide, then call Twist." She gave him a number, adding, "He'll come get you, wherever you are."

"Okay. Okay."

"Hanging up here," Shay said.

Harmon took the phone and dropped it in the toilet. "We've been eight minutes, we've got to go."

"Don't leave me here, you can't leave me like this, I could fall," Cartwell said.

"I hope not, then we'd have to start all over with the new CEO," Shay said.

When Cartwell didn't come back, Dash looked down the table to Sync and caught his eye. She curled a finger at him, and Sync nodded, dabbed his mouth with a napkin, said something to the woman to his right. He walked around the table, and bent over the senator.

"A waitress came and gave Micah a note, something about an important call on the house phone, which seemed a little odd, you know, that he wouldn't get it on his cell," she said. "He hasn't come back. And while paranoia is for crazies, there was something about the waitress. . . ."

Sync felt a chill. "What about the waitress?"

"She reminded me of that girl at my house . . . her figure. And maybe her voice. The longer I sat here and thought about it . . ."

Sync was already moving. Thorne was sitting at the far end of the table and Sync pointed a finger at him and Thorne stood up and they both headed to the doors, where Sync muttered, "They might have Micah."

"Jesus . . . How?"

"Shay Remby . . . if it's real."

They were out on the balcony over the main room. "Couldn't have taken him downstairs," Sync said.

At the same moment, they both turned down the hall toward the restrooms. Sync rounded the corner, pushed open the door to the men's room. "Here," said Thorne, nearly tripping over the yellow cone. He pushed open the door to the women's room, and Cartwell cried, "Help me."

They found him still standing on the toilet.

"They left thirty seconds ago, Harmon and the girl," Cartwell said. "You might catch them. But don't leave me, don't leave me like this. . . ."

Sync said to Thorne, "Go. I'll cut Micah down."

Thorne went down the hall, down the stairs, caught the numbers of the hotel elevator going down to P1, then P2 and P3. There was a fire door at the end of the hall, and he ran down the stairs, moving as fast.

• • •

At the bottom, at P3, Thorne pushed through the door, quietly as he could, and stopped to listen.

And heard feet on concrete. He went that way, running lightly, on the edges of his shoe soles, and saw Harmon climbing into a Jeep. He pointed his pistol and screamed, "Freeze."

Harmon froze. Thorne edged slowly toward him, the pistol never moving from Harmon's back. "Where's Remby? Where'd she go?"

The female's voice came from right behind him: "I'm pointing a gun at your spine. If you do anything except drop your gun, I'm going to shoot you."

Thorne stopped walking, but said, "I don't believe you."

Harmon had turned slowly, and Thorne saw that he had a pistol in his hand, but his hand was at his side. "Heard you coming. You gotta learn to run a little more lightly," Harmon said.

"I don't think she's got a gun," Thorne said, but didn't look back, because if he did, even for an instant, it would give Harmon an opening.

Thorne's pistol was still pointed at him, and Harmon said, "She can prove it to you, but it will hurt."

"She won't shoot me even if she has a gun," Thorne said. "She's one of those animal rights activists. They won't even squash bugs."

"You got the wrong Remby," Shay said.

"Put your gun down and you'll get out of here without being hurt," Harmon said, his voice quiet. "I really don't want to get anybody hurt."

"I still don't believe—" Thorne began.

Shay put the pistol two inches off the back of his right ear and pulled the trigger. The shot sounded like a cannon in the confined space. Everybody lurched and Harmon screamed, "No, no . . ."

Thorne reeled away, his pistol pointed at the floor, and Harmon's came up and he shouted at Thorne, "Drop the gun, drop the god-damn gun, you idiot."

Thorne's gun clattered on the concrete, and he put his gun hand to his ear and it came back bloody, and more blood ran down his neck. "She shot me," he said, shocked. "She shot me."

"Got to get going, somebody will have heard the shot," Harmon called to Shay. He was walking toward them, his gun never leaving a point on Thorne's chest. Thorne turned to Shay, the shock gone now, and snarled, "You better hope you get killed when I come for you."

"What's that?" Shay said. "You're gonna torture me?"

Her hand was shaking a little, and Thorne sneered at her—*Amateur*—and said, "That'd be the least of it. Ask your brother. . . ."

Harmon was there. He picked up Thorne's gun, put it in his pocket, and said to Shay, "Get the leftover rope out of the trunk. We'll tie his foot to a car. That'll slow him down long enough for us to get out." To Thorne he said, "Assume the position, asshole. Over here."

He pointed Thorne to a concrete pillar, and Thorne leaned against it with one hand, his other covering his wounded ear, spreading his legs. "I never thought you'd go this far," he told Harmon. "We're coming for you."

"Come ahead." Shay had gone to the Jeep, snagged the rope from the backseat, and hurried back. Harmon said over his shoulder, "Mr. Thorne does all kinds of karate and Krav Maga and all of that, so keep your gun on him while I do this. I'm going to hook this rope around his ankle."

Shay blurted, "Thorne? This is the guy who shot West?"

Harmon said, "Easy. . . ."

Shay said, "Forget the rope." She was standing directly behind

Thorne and she kicked him in the crotch. She kicked him like an NFL punter would kick a football, like a German soccer star would shoot on goal. She kicked him so hard that, for a split second, a black patch flashed across her eyes from the impact.

Thorne gagged and went down, and Shay shouted, "Come for me now!" and wound up to kick him in the head, but Harmon hooked an arm around her and dragged her to the Jeep, and a minute later they were rolling. Thorne remained curled on the floor, his mouth open, his head back, one long, long silent scream.

Shay was still breathing hard when they exited the parking structure. Harmon caught two lights in a row, and then blew through a red, and they were gone, lost in traffic.

Harmon slowed and said, "Kinda lost your cool there."

"It happens," Shay said.

Harmon grinned. "I've seen guys kicked in the goolies before, but I've never seen anything like that."

Shay said, "I'll take that as a compliment." Then: "You think Cade's really loose?"

"Yeah. If he's got the sense to really hide himself."

"He's been on the street in L.A. He can hide."

They came to a red light, stopped. Harmon glanced at her, the traffic light picking up the red glint in her hair. "How old are you?"

"Sixteen."

"Did you mean that shot to frighten Thorne? Or did you mean to shoot him?"

"I meant to shoot him; I figured that'd frighten him good."

Harmon said, "Jesus. You're a little scary, kid."

"Can we move faster?" Shay asked. "I want to find out about Cade."

Cade lay under a tree, behind a wooden-slat fence, and said into the phone, "Nineteenth Avenue crosses some train tracks. Wait there, I'll come to you."

"Pull the battery on the phone," Twist said.

Twist found the place and, two interminable minutes later, saw Cade limping toward him, his arms wrapped around his body as though to keep his lungs inside himself, struggling to keep moving. He popped the front door and Cade was in.

Twist accelerated away and asked, without taking his eyes off the narrow road, "You hurt bad?"

"I think they busted some ribs. Hurts to run, hurts to cough. I haven't been laughing a lot, but that'd probably hurt, too. Oh, yeah, they hit me in the eyes a few times, and I can't see too well out of the left one."

"Gotta get you to a hospital."

"We gotta get away from here first. . . . Just try . . . to take it easy. . . ." He gasped for air. "Doesn't hurt so much when you don't hit those potholes."

"I don't want to insult you . . . but did they ask about where we're hiding?"

"Yeah. I told them that we move every day, because we're so scared. I think they believed me."

"You are one tough little street rat," Twist said. "I think I just shed a tear."

Cade involuntarily laughed, then gasped, then gasped again when Twist hit another pothole. Twist said, "I'm trying, man."

"Yeah, don't worry, keep going." Cade half turned his head to X in the backseat, said, "Hey, dog."

X gave his swollen eye a lick, and Cade turned back to Twist and said, "I don't know what you did, but it freaked out the guy who gave me the phone."

"Where's the phone?"

"Left it by the tracks. You gotta get rid of yours, they'll have that number."

"Right." Twist took the phone out of his pocket, threw it out the window. A minute later, they took a left onto a wider street and eventually merged onto a freeway. "I think we're good," Twist said. "Never saw anyone behind us."

Cade groaned. "Man, that asshole who had me . . . Thorne . . . he was the leader of the guys at the hotel. . . . Last night, he said they were gonna kill me. But then they ignored me today."

They hit a highway seam that Twist hadn't seen coming, and Cade gasped again.

"Sorry, sorry. . . ."

"Keep going . . . tell me what happened, distract me."

Twist told him about Harmon and the meeting on the face of the cliff and the plan to grab Cartwell. "The last I heard, he was standing on a toilet bowl with a rope around his neck."

Cade laughed, then groaned, then said, "Jeez, laughing does hurt. Don't say anything funny."

"I'm not feeling all that funny," Twist said. "I haven't heard from them. . . . I should have heard from them."

"You threw the phone out the window, dummy."

"Aw, we've got more phones than—"

A phone rang in his pocket and he fished it out and said, "Yo."

He listened for a second, then said, "I got him. We're clear." He turned to Cade and said, "They're out."

Back to the phone: "He's got some broken ribs. I'm going to take him to an emergency room, see what they can tell us. It was the same guy that our new friend told us about."

He listened again and then said, "I don't want to make our boy laugh, but I'll tell him anyway. We'll see you up there."

He clicked off, turned to Cade, and said, "Don't laugh."

"Tell me."

"They caught Thorne, put him up against a wall, you know, like the cops do when they're searching you. Then Harmon mentioned that he was Thorne, and Shay punted him in the nuts. Harmon says she kicked him so hard his balls are probably in orbit."

Cade laughed, then groaned, then laughed even harder.

Harmon and Shay ruminated over Singular's possible reaction to the attack on Cartwell, but neither had much idea of what Singular could do that they weren't already doing. "And they have a handicap," Harmon said. "I'm no longer working for them."

"How big a handicap is that?" Shay asked.

Harmon smiled. "Well, it's something. My boss—everybody

calls him Sync—is former CIA. He's as good as I am, but he's got a lot of other stuff to do. So, they'll have to find somebody to fill my job. That'll take a while."

"You're sure Sync is *former* CIA? There's no possibility he's still working for the government *and* for Singular?"

The question took Harmon by surprise: he didn't reply for a moment, then said, "I think I would have spotted that he was reporting in two different directions. And when I talked to him last night . . . No. He's purely Singular's guy now."

Over the next fifty miles, they talked about climbing: Shay about rain, about snow, about rotten rock, Harmon about dry heat so bad it felt like you were in a toaster, about times when you could burn your fingers hanging on to a ledge, and both of them about the feeling after clearing the last obstacle and looking down at where you'd just come from.

"If we get out of this, I'll take you climbing down in Arizona or New Mexico," Harmon said. "There's some strange stuff down there. Take you climbing in a slot canyon."

"I'd do it," Shay said.

A while later, Shay asked, "Why'd you really ditch Singular? It couldn't all have been West. For one thing, you didn't do it right away."

Harmon looked at her, then back over the wheel, thinking about how to answer. After a minute, he took a stab at it: "I joined the army when I was just a little older than you are now. I was in Iraq, and then a few other places, and then Iraq again, and Afghanistan. Stayed in, because, you know . . . I was a"—he waved an arm, as if what he was about to say might seem silly—"a patriot, I guess. I was good at it, but I eventually got tired. I had my twenty years in, and then Sync came and talked to me about being an intel guy for a private business for way more money. I took it. It was mostly just fending off hackers, doing corporate anti-espionage, and a little espionage as well, to tell the truth—keeping up with the competitors.

"They were doing good work with prosthetics. I guess I knew there was more, but I didn't know they were killing people. After you guys hit that lab up in Eugene, everybody started freaking out and I started digging—didn't like what I found. I mean, when I went private, I didn't change what I basically believe. I'm still a"— he waved his arm again—"an American."

Shay nodded. "I get that."

They got to Danny's at two o'clock in the morning, Harmon driving, Shay pointing down the various switches along the entry road. Harmon said, "This is what I call a hideout. I couldn't find this place with a satellite."

Danny came out on the porch, alerted by the driveway chime. Shay got out of the Jeep and shouted, "Shay and a friend."

Danny waved from under the porch light and went inside. Harmon said, "I don't want to sound the least bit critical, but . . . was he carrying an M16?"

"I don't know the model, exactly, but he's got quite a few guns," Shay said. "Danny's what you might call an entrepreneur."

"Of a particular kind," Harmon said.

"Exactly," Shay said. "He gave me my gun . . . but he really doesn't know much about them. I could use a few more lessons."

"You guys have more resources than I'd guessed," Harmon said as they walked through the rock-maze fence.

Odin came out on the deck a few seconds later, with Fenfang a step behind. Shay told Harmon, "You'll want to take a long look at Fenfang without the wig. You'll see what you guys were responsible for."

Up on the deck, Odin looked at Harmon, then at his sister, and said, "This is a mistake. We don't need him."

"Without him, Cade might be dead," Shay snapped. "We're trying to bring Singular down, and I'll take any help I can get."

"Whoa, whoa, whoa," Danny said. "Everybody relax."

Shay went inside, and Harmon nodded at Odin. "Odin. Nice to meet you." He caught Fenfang's eye and tipped his head at her before following after Shay.

As they walked into the kitchen, Shay muttered, "You have to understand what Odin's been through. . . ."

"Not a problem—I know what Thorne and his people did to him, and I didn't stop them. I didn't like it, and I told Sync that I didn't, but I didn't quit over it."

Fenfang said to Odin, "Try to be good. People can change."

"That doesn't make him innocent."

"I know," she said, and stroked his hair. She turned and went inside, and Odin and Danny followed her into the kitchen. Shay got two bottles of orange juice out of the refrigerator and handed one to Harmon without asking if he wanted it, then suggested that everyone move into the living room.

As they all settled onto a pair of couches, Shay nudged Odin and said, "Sorry. It's been a long couple days," then looked at Fenfang and asked, "Would it bother you to take off your wig to show Harmon?"

Fenfang looked across Danny's cracked glass coffee table at

Harmon, who was wearing his mirrored aviators and didn't look inclined to take them off. He took a swallow of juice, then set the bottle aside and folded his hands in his lap.

Fenfang said: "I never saw you at the prison."

Harmon shook his head.

"Did you ever see me?" she asked.

"No. But that's no excuse."

She nodded and looked him over a while longer. "All right," she said, like a declaration. "I will show you my head."

Dropping her chin, Fenfang peeled the wig off from the back to reveal the dozens of tiny gold-colored knobs scattered over her scalp, and the maze of threadlike wires. Harmon stiffened—Shay felt the couch cushion shift—and said, "I have a photo of you, but . . . it's not the same as seeing for myself what we did."

"No, it's not," said Odin.

"We'll show you an X-ray," Shay said, "but the knobs are actually connections to wires that thread through holes drilled in her skull and go down into her brain. They tried to put Senator Dash in there. They partially succeeded: sometimes the Dash personality will try to take hold, and then Fenfang has a seizure."

"Hasn't had one for two days now," Odin said. "The antiseizure drug is working, I think."

Shay said, "That's great."

Fenfang spoke directly to Harmon: "Sometimes I can still feel her there. She tries to come out, but she is weaker now."

The driveway chime sounded. "That'll be Cruz," Shay said. "He wasn't far behind us."

She walked away from the group, down the deck stairs, and across the dew-covered lawn to meet him. He got out of the truck and asked, "Is everybody okay?"

"Twist took Cade to an urgent care clinic, and we know they left there, so I think he'll be okay."

Cruz stepped closer. "I mostly meant you."

"I know," Shay said, and stepped right up to him, hooked three fingers over his belt buckle, and kissed him on the mouth. She let it linger for a moment, then stepped back and said, "How you doing?"

Cruz answered her with another kiss.

Twist, Cade, and X arrived at five-thirty, as it was getting light. Shay had gone to bed, but Cruz rapped on her door and said, "They're coming in."

She got up, pulled on her jeans and a sweatshirt, and hurried out to the deck. X practically leapt into her arms, and she knelt down and hugged him as Twist and Cade made their way up the lawn. Cade was walking stiffly, like the Tin Man in *The Wizard of Oz.*

When they started up the steps, Shay stood and called down, "How bad?"

Twist answered for Cade: "He's got cracked ribs on both sides and in back. No blood in his urine, so they probably missed his kidneys."

Cade said, "Hey, Danny: I could use some medicinal attention."

"Not a good idea," Danny said. "They probably got you high on painkillers already."

"They do. He hardly complained at all on the way up," Twist said. "Before that, it was all, 'Don't hit the pothole, don't hit the pothole.' "

When Cade reached the top of the stairs, Shay looked at his face and said, "Oh, your eye . . ."

"I'd wink at you, babe, if I could," Cade said.

Shay: "Can I give you a hug?"

"Maybe next month," Cade said. His entire face was badly bruised and he had a fat lip. Shay patted him on the butt, and he smiled.

"Didn't lose any teeth," she said.

Harmon showed up, barefoot, in jeans and a gray army-style T-shirt. He nodded and said, "Twist, Cade: I'm Harmon."

Cade said, "Thanks, Harmon," and extended a hand.

They talked for an hour, everybody's version of everything they'd done since the night on the roof across from the Singular building. Cade said that he thought Thorne would have killed him, and would have enjoyed doing it. "He's that kind of guy, I think." He tapped eyes with Harmon. "How'd that work, between you and Thorne?"

Harmon drew a breath and said: "I was the intel guy—my basic job was trying to keep hackers out of our computer system and checking out people who were perceived as possible threats. I didn't have anything to do with the research or tracking the research, or with direct security. Singular is carefully compartmentalized. You only know what you need to know. I had no idea until after you attacked Eugene that they were using human subjects, that these people had been captured, that they would die. When I started looking for Storm, I listened in on a conversation that I wasn't supposed to hear between Singular's boss and a new client they were recruiting for the immortality program. That's when I began to understand. . . .

"Thorne is not intel. He's in charge of direct security—building guards, physical security procedures, moving the experimental subjects around. When you got through the fence up in Eugene, it was

Thorne who took the rap. It was his security that broke down. When we couldn't find you later, I began to get the heat, because that was my side of the job. I have to tell you, I enjoyed it. You guys were interesting opponents. Then, you know . . . it started to go south."

There was a long silence in the room, then Harmon turned to Fenfang and said, "If you don't mind me asking, how did you get here?"

Fenfang said, "When I came here, from Korea, I came on a ship, in a steel box. There were four people in my box, all separated by iron bars. We could not tell exactly how it worked, but they had a crane that lifted up those big boxes—"

"Shipping containers," Twist said.

"Yes. They had layers of containers, and we were down at the bottom. I am not sure about this, but I think the other containers were filled with clothes. New clothes, from China. They gave us drugs to make us sleep. Every day—maybe every day—they would take us out to the bathrooms to get cleaned and use the toilet. Always with supervision. Maybe a day or two before we got to America, they put more boxes around us, so the doors to our boxes were hidden—maybe in case the ship was inspected? We could not go to the toilet anymore—they put a pan inside to use. And the drugs, there were no more drugs. When the boat stopped, they took us out and put us in trucks and took us away."

"How far in the trucks?" Harmon asked.

"Maybe . . . one hour. Or maybe one hour and one half. Then we were taken out of the trucks and put in the cells."

Harmon said, "They took you directly to the research lab in Sacramento, right?" Fenfang nodded. "So if you were traveling for an hour, or an hour and a half . . . they could have come into Oakland,

Vallejo, Richmond, Benicia . . . any place in the Bay Area. It could even be in Stockton: they get ships all the way in there. So . . . no help there."

Odin asked, "How can they keep it so secret? A huge company like Singular?"

"That's where you're wrong," Harmon said. "It's not a huge company. Most of the employees are researchers, sequestered in labs. The total workforce, including janitors, is no more than three hundred."

"That almost seems . . . like we could take them," Twist said. "We're not exactly talking about Apple or Microsoft, with nine million robots working for them."

Harmon hedged: "Yes and no. It's less about size than about what resources they have and how far they're willing to go. After what we did to Cartwell, they'll kill you on sight."

"You too," Twist said.

"Yeah. Might take a more creative approach there."

"Like what?" Cruz asked.

Harmon shrugged. "One time in Iraq, there was this radical Islamic Arab guy who we knew was involved with the terrorists, but we could never get hold of him. Even if we could, we couldn't prove it. Sync got tired of him and found a guy who looked just like him and staged a holdup, three guys robbing a bunch of pilgrims on the way to Mecca, sexually abusing a young woman. Filmed it with a handheld camera so it'd look like it was filmed secretly, kind of shaky and badly exposed, and then got it on the local TV stations as a news report. The guy disappeared. Never heard exactly what happened to him, but it probably wasn't good."

"You think?" Cade asked.

Harmon shrugged again. "Somebody holds up a bank. Wears a

mask, but generally looks like me. Maybe wears a belt buckle like this one"—he tapped his silver-and-turquoise belt buckle—"and then you tip the feds. Give them a story about how I was fired and was angry, how I'm a wing nut of some kind who likes guns. Next thing you know, the whole FBI is looking for me."

"One more reason to take Singular down, before they can do any of that," Shay said through a yawn.

"Bed, everybody," Twist said. "Sleep late, if you need to. Then we start again."

Before Shay went to sleep, she thought about the kiss, and smiled. She had surprised Cruz and surprised herself, too. The idea had been in the back of her head for a while, and it felt good to get it out there. She had no idea what might happen next.

That afternoon, sitting around Danny's living room, they got caught in the whole loop of what to do next, what would expose Singular in a way that couldn't be denied.

Shay turned to Harmon. "Can you get into Singular's main-frame?"

"Not anymore," Harmon said. "Now that they know I'm working with you, I can guarantee that they're ripping out every bit of access I ever had to the system, probably sealing up every outside entry point, all the way across the system, until they can set up a whole new security apparatus."

"Sounds right," Cade said.

"We failed in Stockton, but we had the right idea," Twist said. "If we can find where they keep the prisoners . . ."

Cade said to Harmon, "Wherever they've got those people, they've got to feed them, and they've got to move them back and forth from Sacramento . . . if they're still using that lab."

"Sacramento's the biggest and most sophisticated lab. I don't think they could move out, not quickly," Harmon said. "But I don't think they'd risk using it as a prison again."

"If we watch the place, maybe we can track them to wherever they have the prison," Cade said.

"That would be tough," Harmon said. "They'll probably have countersurveillance, and from what I saw of the place, the way they'd get people in and out—down the lower-level delivery ramp—even if you could get close enough, you wouldn't be able to see what was going on: which trucks were delivering people, and which were delivering candy bars for the vending machines."

"West found Sacramento by following the food trail. The people, the experimental subjects, still have to eat," Odin said. "Maybe that could work again."

"What's that about?" Harmon asked.

Shay explained that West had found the Sacramento lab and its basement-level prison by following food orders issued by the Singular logistics office.

"Half of my job was running a computer group to fend off hackers trying to get into our system," Harmon said. He smiled at West's ingenuity. "The logistics office was specifically excluded from the management and research systems to block off any access from that direction. I don't think it ever occurred to anybody—certainly didn't occur to me—that hackers would sort through purchase orders or personnel records. Or that they could do any real damage if they ever did."

Cade sat up. "Do you have access to logistics?"

"Yes, I do," Harmon said. "But you should maybe think twice about trying to access from here. . . ."

Odin said, "We're accessing from a board in Sweden."

"Blackjack?"

"No, that's too easy to get around," Odin said. "We're members of Pitealve."

Harmon's eyebrows went up. "Really."

"Have you broken it?" Cade asked.

"I don't think it can be broken," Harmon said. "It's run by a single crazy man who has all the encryption code in his head. How'd you guys get on board there?"

Odin said, "Trade secret."

Harmon smiled and said, "If we can go in through Pitealve, I can get you into logistics."

Odin: "Good. If we run West's files against the current files, we should be able to filter out just the stuff added since the raid on Sacramento."

"Gonna be up all night," Cade said. He looked happy.

As Odin started tapping on his laptop, Shay asked Harmon if he thought Singular might have killed the prisoners she and West saw in the cell, to keep the police from finding them.

Harmon shook his head. "No way. They're too valuable."

Odin looked up and snorted. "Valuable? They're not treated like they're valuable. They're treated like . . . I don't want to say animals. . . ."

"But that's what they were treated like, I think," Harmon said. "Like extremely valuable lab animals. When they shipped them here, I don't think they intended to injure them on the way—they just didn't treat them any different than you'd treat a lab rat. A really valuable rat. They'd kill you to get Fenfang back. They'd kill you to get the *dog* back. Singular didn't bring those people here to torture them; they brought them here to test them. To examine them. To see where they were getting with their experiments. There's nothing more valuable to them."

Shay: "Since you thought they were moved to Stockton . . . you don't have any other ideas where they might be?"

"No. The only guys who know exactly are Thorne and a few of his men. What I know is, they almost panicked when you hit Sacramento, but Thorne held it together. They literally remodeled the basement overnight, in case you guys convinced a cop, or the FBI, or somebody, to take another look. The experimental subjects were taken out of there in recreational vehicles, rented and driven by Thorne's men. They were moving around from one campground to another, wherever they could hide out without attracting attention. Maybe they still are. They might not have picked a new permanent place until they found the leak. With that settled, they could be on the move now."

Twist stood up, put his hands in the back pockets of his jeans. "Finding the experimental subjects—that's still the way we beat them. What we can't do is screw it up, like we just did. We have to know it's a prison, we have to know what the cops will find when they go in."

Harmon looked squarely at Twist and nodded. "You've maybe got one more chance. They'll be coming for you, and even this place won't be safe forever."

"How much time do we have, do you think?" Shay asked. "Twist thinks we might have only a few days."

"Be lucky to get that," Harmon said. "Really lucky."

Cade cleared his throat and said to Harmon: "Why don't you get us into that logistics computer now, then?"

25

Harmon had gotten Cade and Odin into the logistics office computer, but by the next morning, they were still looking for anything that might point them at a new prison. Both Cade and Odin were getting cranky with each other, but in a way Shay had seen in every group of hackers she'd ever encountered: just part of the culture, and though it was often personal, it wasn't serious.

Shay ate some oatmeal and poured a second cup of coffee, feeling at loose ends: not much for her to do. Nobody's ear needed shooting, she thought. Harmon picked up on that and eventually asked her, "You wanna go shoot?"

Shay said, "Sure."

Harmon retrieved his military gear from his truck and transferred it to Danny's six-wheel utility vehicle for the drive out to the backwoods range.

• • •

"Guns are the ubiquitous tools of the twenty-first century," Harmon said as they bounced along. "If a Martian were watching our television shows, he'd conclude that guns were more common than hammers. They're not evil themselves—they're tools—but everywhere you go, bad people have them. It behooves the righteous to at least know how they work."

They had Harmon's M16 and four different pistols, including Shay's small Beretta. Harmon set up a hundred-yard target and worked Shay through the M16, which was the easiest of the weapons to use. Then he set up a ten-yard target and began working through the pistols. He was harsh, and she said so.

"I'm harsh because you could be good at this," he said. "If you were just another newbie, I'd be gentle and patient."

"I don't actually see that in you," Shay said.

They practiced firing a last shot and reloading. Reloading while standing up, while walking, while running, while running toward the target, away from it, and sideways to it.

"Your arm is the shock absorber, the gun floats out there—don't let it take every little jiggle and shake," Harmon shouted. "Shoot and reload. . . . Float the gun! Float it!"

Every fifteen minutes or so, they'd sit on a rock and he'd give her pointers about bullets: about .22s, about .380s ("Never trust .380s—they look good, they can kill, but you can't trust them to stop a guy") and 9-millimeters and .357s and .40s and .45s and the differences between hollow points and solid cores and their various effects ("With a few exceptions, you can't trust a pistol bullet to reliably hit somebody sitting behind a windshield . . .").

He liked Shay's gun, the one given to her by Danny. "A fine piece of machinery," he said, turning it in his hands. "It fits you. I'd be happier if it was a .40, but a 9 is fine. Most people can't tell the difference, if you shoot them in the heart."

"You might have gotten the wrong idea about me, because of Thorne," she said. "I was trying to scare him, not kill him."

"You did that," Harmon said. "But I don't think I have the wrong idea about you."

When they got back to the house, all the others were gathered around Cade and Odin at the dining room table. Odin had his feet up on the table, straddling his laptop. "You found something," Shay said.

Cade shook his head. "We found a lot of stuff about Sacramento, we've got the payroll and all that, but nothing that points to a new location for the prisoners. The food deliveries West found have just stopped."

Shay looked at Harmon. "You said the prisoners were being taken around in RVs. Did Singular buy them? Or rent them?"

"They had them early the next morning, the morning after you hit the building. . . . I assume they rented them."

She thought about that and leaned over Odin's shoulder. "There can't be that many places that rent RVs. They've all got to have websites. Could you get into them, find out who rented them?"

Odin shrugged. "Maybe. But how's that going to help? We drive around to eight thousand campgrounds between Seattle and Los Angeles and look for them?"

"They can't be that spread around, they've got to keep them close to—" Shay began.

Harmon slapped his forehead. "Stupid! Stupid! I should have thought of it! Thorne has a whole bunch of guys working for him. Some of them are serious operators. But some of them are guards and drivers—and they'll be the lowest-paid ones. If you've got the payroll, we should be able to isolate those guys."

"We can do that," Odin said.

"And if you've got the payroll, we should have their home addresses. . . ."

"We do," Odin said.

Harmon said, "Then, if they're staying at their own homes between shifts . . ."

"We could track them to the RVs," Shay said.

"That's it," Cade said. He poked Odin with his elbow, wincing at the impact. "Fire it up. Let's get some names up there."

The payroll listed three hundred names in a dozen different sections of the company. There were thirty names in Thorne's division; twice the size of the intelligence unit that had been run by Harmon. The names had weekly salaries posted next to them, along with night differentials for late-shift work. Harmon ran his finger down Odin's laptop screen ("Hey, you're muddin' up my screen") and picked out four likely candidates.

Cruz: "More surveillance?"

Harmon nodded. "A little more complicated than what you did at that booby-trap building. I'll show you how we'd do it, if I was still Singular. . . ."

Harmon borrowed a drawing pad from Twist and sketched out various ways to run a "box" surveillance on an unsuspecting subject. Ideally, they should have more cars than they actually did. Harmon's car was unusable, and the Jeep might be too distinctive, but they could manage it.

"We can use my Volvo," Danny said. "Volvos are fundamentally invisible."

They'd need more cold phones—they'd bought so many of them

that it was hard to keep track, but the cost was low. They'd take the two video cameras, too, in case they ran into something dramatic.

Harmon suggested three teams: he, Shay, and X; Twist and Cruz; Danny, Odin, and Fenfang. Cade simply wasn't mobile enough to come, so he would remain at Danny's and act as a switchboard.

"What you do is put up a satellite map of wherever we go, and when we start tracking a guy, you follow him on the map," Harmon told Cade. "You have three cell phones sitting in front of you, all of them on speaker, so we can keep you up to date, and you can talk to all of us at once. If it looks like the guy we're trailing might be getting suspicious, you'd bring in another car. You'd watch for all the places he could dodge us. You'd be directing the traffic, telling us what we couldn't see from the ground."

"I could do all that," Cade grumped. "I'd rather drive. . . ."

"But you're great at running tactical operations," Shay said. "Twist relied on you to run his political actions, didn't he? You don't choke."

"Yeah, all right, you're right," Cade said.

Harmon continued: "People working at Singular are on regular shifts. They go seven o'clock in the morning until three in the afternoon, three to eleven, and eleven at night until seven o'clock in the morning. Best time to pick up a guy is either leaving for the eleven o'clock shift, because the darkness would help hide us, or the seven o'clock, when he's just gotten up and might be a little sleepy and less wary. If we want to go tonight, we'd have to be in Sacramento by nine o'clock or so. We've got to get organized. . . ."

Driving to Sacramento again.

Shay felt as though she were now living half her life on the freeways. Once they were across the mountains and driving south on I-5, there was not a lot to look at; even the mountains were simply featureless blue streaks on the horizon.

"I don't mind that," Harmon said about the flatness of the land. "I like driving long distances: it gives you space to think. Pardon me for being old, but checking in with fourteen friends every minute of the day doesn't give you time to think."

They were in three vehicles: Shay, Harmon, and X in the Jeep, which they called Car One; Odin, Danny, and Fenfang in Danny's traveling car, a blue Volvo sedan, Car Two; and Twist and Cruz in the Toyota truck, Car Three. Cade would be called Zero.

They'd scouted the homes of the four Singular agents on the night shift, using Google Maps, MapQuest, and the real estate site Zillow. One of the agents, Dale Adams, had recently bought a town house, and Zillow had comprehensive photos of the interior of his home.

"Pretty useful piece of burglary information right there," Twist said.

"More evidence of your criminal mind," Cade said.

Another Singular agent, Ward Leonard, owned a small single-family home in a suburb north of the city. The other two agents had apartments in large complexes.

"Spotting the guys coming out of the apartments would be a matter of luck," Harmon said. "We should focus on Adams and Leonard, and hope that at least one of them is working the RVs."

"That's a lot of hope," Odin said.

"Yeah. It is," Harmon said. "I wish I had more to offer."

Odin looked at him, sighed, and picked up his laptop. In sixty seconds, he had car registrations for both men from the DMV: each drove a metallic-colored SUV, one silver, one champagne.

• • •

The three teams were in touch by telephone. Leonard's house was the closest, and not far off I-5, so Cars Two and Three cruised it, while Shay and Harmon continued south toward the Adams town house.

"There's nothing going on here," Twist reported as they rolled by Leonard's place. "No car in the driveway, not a single light, inside or out."

Shay and Harmon got to Adams's town house and found it was also dark. "Could mean that they're sleeping, but if they're working the overnight shift, they'll have to get up soon," Harmon said.

Twist and Danny parked their cars as far as they could from Leonard's house while still being able to see it, and settled down to wait.

Adams's town house complex had visitor parking to one side, and there were a half-dozen cars and a U-Haul truck in the twenty-spot lot. These other vehicles gave them some cover, and from there, Shay and Harmon could see the front of Adams's place, including the double garage.

An hour in, and they'd seen nothing but a few passing cars and a kid on a skateboard. Another ten minutes, and a cop car rolled by, but both Harmon and Shay had seen it coming and slid down in their seats. "One way to spot cop cars is that they're big and they move either too slow or too fast," Harmon said.

"I spotted it because it was mostly black and had a white door on it that said POLICE," Shay said.

"That works, too," Harmon said.

At nine-thirty, to the minute—maybe a bedside alarm had gone off—a light popped up on the second floor in Adams's town house.

Harmon got on the phone. "We got a light."

"We got nothin'," Twist answered.

"If you've got nothing in fifteen minutes, come this way," Harmon said. "If your guy is there, he'll have to get up soon to make an eleven o'clock shift."

Fifteen minutes went by, and Twist called: "We're leaving. No movement at all. Danny'll be right behind us."

Ten minutes later, Twist called again: "We're in a deli parking lot, both vehicles, twenty seconds away from you guys. Doesn't feel real secure, though, we're kinda exposed. What do we do?"

"Let's get Zero going," Shay said.

Cade was sitting at Danny's computer desk with three phones, all on speaker.

Cade said, "Two and Three, I've got you on the map; I can see that deli. You should get out of there, you're too visible. Go north on Lighthouse. Just past Fountain Drive, there's a dirt pull-off on the right side of the road, with trees around it. One of you could go back in there. The other one of you should keep on going until you get to Douglas, then take a right; there's a parking lot there with more trees, you could hang there for a few minutes, and you'd have him bracketed. . . ."

"Doing that," Danny said.

Harmon jumped in: "Scout out those turnoffs, but don't park just yet. Zero, take them around a few blocks, never too far away, for a few more minutes. We see no lights on the bottom level yet, and we should see that before he leaves."

"Got it." Cade directed the other two cars in loops around Adams's neighborhood. Shay was looking at the target house with binoculars and said, a few minutes later, "Got a light on the first floor. Light on top floor is out."

Harmon, on the phone: "Go to the turnouts. No big rush. He could still be eating his Wheaties."

Cade guided the other two cars back to the turnouts. Three minutes passed, then five . . . and the door went up on the town house's garage.

"Okay, he's coming," Harmon said. "We're going to drive out of sight."

Before Adams could back down his driveway, Harmon pulled the Jeep out of the parking spot. Shay watched through the back window with X as Adams backed out and turned in the other direction.

"He's headed east," Shay called.

Cade said, "That's you, Three."

"On it," Twist said.

Shay still had a view of the vehicle. "He's turning onto the road that goes to Lighthouse. He'll be at the intersection in a minute; he'll probably turn east on Lighthouse."

Harmon: "I'm heading toward Lighthouse, but we'll be pretty far back."

Twist: "We've got one silver Chevy Tahoe coming. We're pulling out. We're two blocks in front of him, he's still coming."

"We're coming up as fast as we can," Danny said. "I think we see him, but I'm not sure."

Then Odin, riding shotgun beside Danny: "That's him. We got him."

"Stay well back, Two, don't catch him, but don't be too obvious about staying back," Harmon said. "We're coming around the corner, we're probably two blocks behind you."

They tracked Adams east and then south. At the on-ramp for I-305, Twist went straight, but Adams turned up the ramp, headed east, and Danny called, "We're following him up, but he's going right at the speed limit, everybody else is going faster."

"Then pass him and keep going, or he'll spot you," Harmon said. "We'll be right behind him. Three, where are you?"

Twist and Cruz had made a U-turn and were headed back toward I-305. They hadn't gotten there yet when Harmon went up the ramp. Twist read a street sign to Cade, and Cade said, "One, they're about two blocks behind you."

"We're going up the ramp now," Harmon said.

Shay added, "We still see you, Two."

Danny said, "He's about six cars ahead of us, but we're catching up to him, we're gonna have to pass."

Cade: "He has to get on I-5 or go straight. Take the one he doesn't. . . ."

"Do it," Harmon said. "We'll move up."

Twist called: "We're coming up the ramp onto 305."

"He's taking I-5 south," Odin called. "We're going straight, gotta take him, One."

"We got him," Shay said.

They traded places a dozen times, taking off-ramps, waiting, then going back up onto I-5. On the tree-lined highway, there wasn't much to see in the dark, except other cars. Adams drove too slowly for ten minutes, then finally began to speed up as he got farther south on I-5. "He was looking for a tail, but he didn't see us. He thinks he's clean," Harmon called. "Still south on 5."

"Okay, there's a campground called Fiddlers' Green coming

up," Cade said. "Farther south, there's Happy Family RV Park, and even farther down, there's Oakdale Travel Park. . . . There's more of them farther south; I'll call them out as you get closer."

With Adams on I-5, and a limited number of exits, the tracking cars could stay well back, his taillights barely in sight. Adams was moving faster now, and drove more than thirty miles before turning west on Highway 12. There were fewer cars there, and they would be more easily spotted, so Cade would guide the closest tailing car onto a side road every few minutes, while the second and third cars slowly moved up, a kind of hopscotch pattern that continued to the intersection with Highway 160. They followed him south on that, still hopscotching, and then Cade called, "Whoa, sports fans. He's not going to an RV park. I think he's going to a ship. He's going to a ship channel."

Fenfang spoke for the first time, distressed: "They are bringing more of us in. He's going to a ship to get more of us."

Harmon said, "Or the new holding facility is mobile—that would be a smart move."

"What do we do?" Cade asked. "Call the cops now?"

Twist: "No. We gotta see what's there. Gotta be sure this time."

Shay: "I agree with Twist."

Harmon: "So do I. Everybody stay cool."

Twist and Cruz were in the car closest to Adams, and Harmon said, "Zero, get Three off the road. Three, fall in behind us when you can turn around, but do it quick. We need to change headlights behind him. There's just not enough cars around."

"Turning now," Twist said.

They followed the silver SUV across a river and then onto the Wilbur Avenue exit.

"I'm looking at a fairly rough riverside landing of some kind,"

Cade said. "Looks like an abandoned wharf—I don't know if it's abandoned in real life, but Google doesn't show anything on it. But that whole area looks pretty open: you gotta be careful."

Harmon said, "Everybody slow down. Let One do this. . . . Okay, he's off Wilbur."

Shay, excited now: "Zero, it's a huge vacant lot. Can you see that? It's dark, but there's something back there, there's lights up in the air."

"That's a ship," Harmon said.

Twist called: "Hey, there's another big SUV coming up from behind us. Moving really fast, he's gonna pass us, could be more Singular guys. . . ."

Shay was still watching Adams's car. "Yes! There's a ship back there, I can see it in his headlights. And another car, maybe two."

Danny: "One, you've got to move out, this guy's coming up really fast, he's going to see you hanging around."

Harmon: "We're going."

He accelerated away, and Shay, looking out the back window, said, "I see him, he's a few blocks back."

"If he goes in there, we'll see him," Danny said.

And a few seconds later, Odin said, "And there he goes, he's getting off. . . ."

Twist asked, "What are we doing?"

Shay: "It's too open back there, but we're coming up to something. You guys close up on us, we'll find a place to stop."

"We're going past the ship, there are three cars already parked there, this last guy will be the fourth," Twist said. "They're putting down some kind of ramp from the ship . . . like for getting off an old airliner, but longer."

"There," Shay said, pointing. "Turn there."

Harmon braked hard and turned into a short, poorly lit entrance for a storage facility. It was off on the right side of Wilbur Avenue, out of sight from the ship, but no more than a few hundred yards west. "We've found a spot to hide. Everybody . . . it's just past the open spot, you'll see a bunch of Dumpsters near the side of the road, three big white ones, we're just past that, down a paved drive."

Harmon added, "When you turn in here, turn off your lights."

He hit the lights and parked at the side of the drive, and a minute later, Twist and Cruz pulled in, and a minute after that, Danny with Odin and Fenfang.

"Stay here one second," Harmon said to Shay. He jumped out and jogged to the other vehicles, said a few words, then got back in the Jeep and pulled around in a circle. The other two vehicles followed, and when they stopped again, they were all pointed toward Wilbur Avenue, but tucked out of sight.

Shay got her camera, pulled it on. Twist joined them, and she saw that he was carrying the other video camera. A minute later, the group was following Harmon up a ten-foot-high dirt berm. There were several lights on the ship, and the headlights from one of the SUVs played against the side of it. The ship was long, low, and brown, with a white towerlike structure at the stern, which Harmon said would contain the bridge—the ship's control center—as well as the crew quarters.

They got to the top of the berm just in time to see a man walk down the gangway, go to the SUV with its headlights on, and get in the passenger side. A moment later, the SUV drove away. With their eyes now adjusted to the darkness, they could make out the three cars still clustered at the bottom of the gangway.

"There's got to be a guard at the top of the stairs," Twist said, keeping his voice low.

"Or something," Odin said. "Maybe a camera that they monitor from the bridge?"

As they watched, another man walked down the gangway, carrying a bag. He threw the bag in the back of another SUV, got in, and drove away.

"Somebody's got to be watching it," Twist said. "It's like the cheese in a mousetrap."

There was nobody in sight, either on or off the ship. They moved in closer, staying in a tight clump behind the berm, until they were a hundred yards out from the ship. They could see now that the ship was tied to a pier that ran parallel to the river—and the only way onto the pier was across a short walkway, where the gangway came down from the ship.

And the whole area around the walkway was an open concrete slab.

"It's a friggin' fortress," Harmon said. "Okay. I'll scout the bow of the ship."

"The two of us," Shay said.

"All right, but you stay behind me," Harmon said. "Danny, you've shot that M16 of yours a few times, right?"

"Yeah, but I don't want to shoot anyone," Danny said.

"Don't have to. If we get in trouble and yell, point the gun at the side of the ship and pull the trigger. It'll make a hell of a racket and freak out anybody on board. While he's doing that, everybody else get back to the cars. Shay and I will run for it and hide, and you can pick us up later."

"That's pretty freakin' iffy," Twist said.

Harmon laughed. "Everything we're doing is freakin' iffy," he said. "That's what makes it so much fun."

"I'm coming," Cruz said. "The three of us."

Harmon: "Both you guys are swimmers?"

Shay nodded, but Cruz conceded, "Not so much."

Harmon said to Cruz: "I'd love to have you, but there may be some water involved in this. Shay, you'll need that black jacket. In fact . . ." He looked down at his cowboy boots. "I gotta change myself."

They gathered around the Jeep's driver's seat as Harmon pulled off his boots and changed into a pair of black Nike sneakers.

He said, "Twist?"

"Yeah?"

"If I get killed, put my boots back on me."

X made a sound deep in his throat, not quite a growl, and Twist said, "Well, X thought it was funny, anyway."

Harmon stepped over to the Volvo and asked Danny to pop the trunk. Danny did, and Harmon took his M16 out of a nylon case, slapped a magazine in place, and hung the rifle over his shoulder. Another magazine went into a lightweight camouflage backpack he wore over his military-style black nylon jacket. Danny's identical rifle was in a hard plastic case, and Danny fished the case out of the trunk and carried it to the Jeep.

Twist looked skeptically at Harmon's rifle and asked, "You think you'll really need that?"

Harmon: "Like the NRA says, it's better to have a machine gun and not need it than to need a machine gun and not have it. I think they said that."

"Yeah, well, the NRA can kiss my ass," Twist said. "The *whole* NRA."

"Something I'd pay to see," Harmon said.

Afteer a few last-minute words and warnings, Twist said, "Okay, before we do this . . . what's the point?"

Shay: "The point is, we think we know what we've got, but what if the ship's empty? What if it just got here? You said it yourself, Twist: we have to be sure the test subjects are here. A quick look—"

Harmon: "A recon."

Shay: "A quick recon and we'll know whether to call the cops now or wait."

Ten seconds later, Shay told X to stay and followed Harmon into the darkness.

26

Shay and Harmon walked stooped over, straight toward the river, across rough ground. Enough light was floating around that they missed big obstacles, like mounds of dirt and bushes, while tripping over small ones or stepping into shallow holes.

The riverbank dropped steeply to the water, down perhaps six or eight feet, and was muddy. At the water's edge, the light from the ship and the street was cut off, and the darkness became inky. From there, they had to feel their way forward.

Shay whispered, "God, I hope there are no snakes."

Harmon said simply, in another whisper, "Voices carry."

She shut up.

Harmon was carrying his combat gear in the backpack, the rifle on a shoulder sling, and a pistol on his belt. In addition to the camera on her arm, Shay carried the pistol that Danny had given her, with an extra magazine in each of her front jeans pockets, and her knife, which rode where it always did, down her back. When they got close to the ship, Harmon reached back, gripped one of her arms, and pushed down. They huddled behind some brush, and Harmon put his mouth close to her ear and said, "The bow overhangs the edge of the pier. If we get under there, they won't be able to see us."

"What are we going to do when we get there?"

"I want to take a look at the hawsers," Harmon said.

"The what?"

"Hawsers. Ropes. The ropes used to tie off the ship. Put on your mask. Faces shine."

He pulled on his own black ski mask, then turned away from her and began duck-walking along the waterline, toward the ship; she followed. Every few steps, one or the other of them slipped on the muddy bank, plunging their feet into the cold water. The under-water part of the bank felt radically steep, as it would have to be, Shay thought, to accommodate ships. The mud smelled of dead fish and chemicals. Oil, maybe.

After five minutes of slow, cautious approach, they got to the end of the pier. The pier actually stood several feet away from the riverbank, the outside pilings plunging into deep water. The inside pilings, made of rough concrete, sank into the dirt bank. Another minute of duck-walking got them under the end of the pier and directly below the ship's hull. The waterline was right at their feet.

Just above their heads, a pale green hawser, as thick as Shay's forearm, stretched toward the bow, where it disappeared through an opening below the rail. Judging from the water towers she'd climbed, Shay thought the hull of the ship was probably fifteen or twenty feet high.

Harmon whispered, "If we climbed the hawser, could we get over the bow from there? That hole might be too small to get through."

"Let me run up and take a look," Shay said. "I can get up there in ten seconds."

"You think?"

"Yes."

Harmon said, "If you hear anyone above, don't hesitate, slide right back down, but stay under the bow. If they see us here, we're kinda screwed."

"Got it," Shay said. She liked the fact that Harmon didn't doubt her capabilities.

"If that hole's big enough for me to get through, snap your fingers at me," Harmon whispered. "Finger snaps don't sound like voices."

They both stood up, moving slowly: neither one could see over the pier to the parking lot. The pier was six feet high, and Shay reached up and grabbed the edges with her hands. Harmon said, "I'll make a stirrup."

She felt his hands by her ankle, and they both poked around until her foot was cupped by his hands, and then he stood up, and Shay's head and torso rose over the end of the pier. She could see now: nobody on the pier, nobody in the parking lot, unless they were in their cars.

The hawser leading to the bow of the boat was right there. Shay pushed herself up onto the pier, staying behind the mooring post, then straddled the hawser and began pulling herself along it with her hands and arms, while her thighs, calves, and ankles gripped the rope below her. The climb got steeper as she went, but she shinnied up the last few feet and pulled herself through the two-foot-high opening in the bow and onto the deck. She was behind a pile of shipping containers.

She couldn't see anything, but nobody could see her, either, she thought. She snapped her fingers at Harmon. Two minutes later, he pushed his backpack through the opening, then squeezed through after it.

They were on the ship, at the very tip of the bow, in a deep shadow cast by lights on an overhead crane.

"With only two cars, there can't be too many people on board," Shay whispered.

"Except that a few people might actually live here," Harmon said.

"Wouldn't they have cars?"

"Not if they travel with the ship."

"I'm going to tell the others. . . ." She tapped out a text message—"On board"—and sent it to Twist. "Now what?"

"Turn on your camera," Harmon said. "Then let's see what we can see."

They walked from the bow toward the stern, along the riverside of the ship, past stacked shipping containers that rose like a wall beside them. Halfway down the length of the ship, Harmon stopped, and Shay, who was walking behind him, nearly bumped into him. He whispered, "Stay here. I'm going to climb these containers and take a look at the crew quarters, see how many lights are on."

"Careful."

Harmon jammed a sneaker into the narrow space between two containers and began to climb—and forty-five seconds later, climbed down again.

"Nothing," he said. "Everything's dark."

He'd left his pack on the deck, and now he picked it up, slipped it back on, and took his pistol out. He whispered to Shay, "If you take your pistol out, which I don't recommend at this point, don't get excited and shoot me in the back. Okay?"

" 'Kay."

They started moving again, and as they got close to the tower that housed the crew quarters and the wheelhouse, they slowed: they could see more easily in the illumination cast from an overhead light on one of the cranes.

Then they could hear voices. Two men, Shay thought, laughing about something, then simply chatting. And faintly, so faintly that Shay at first thought it was an illusion: she could hear another sound, higher pitched than the men's voices, almost a buzz, like a hornet's nest. The hair rose on the back of her neck. She touched the knife at her back—habit—then went for the pistol grip at her side, but didn't take the gun out.

Harmon stopped again, leaned past her cheek so that his mouth was only an inch from her ear, and said, "Two guys. There must be an open door. And something else. Do you hear that?"

She whispered back, directly into his ear, "Yes. I don't know what it is."

"Maybe the crew," he said. "One thing at a time. Do we take the two guys? If we do that, they'll know we were here."

Shay had to think for a moment, then whispered, "We still don't know what we've got. And we can't search more if we don't take them—right?"

Harmon cocked his head, as though he might not entirely agree, then slipped out of his backpack, patted her arm, and said, "Don't come up too close behind me. I might need room. Bring the pack."

He began moving again. They got to the end of the container stack, and Harmon peeked around the corner, then stepped back and waved her up. Shay peeked. One cabin, right on their level, but closer to the other side of the ship, where the ramp came up, was lit up. The cabin door was half open, and the voices were apparently coming through the opening. A few seconds later, headbanger music came on, some old Motörhead song.

One of the men in the room laughed about something, and what sounded like an aluminum can banged off the cabin wall, and somebody said, "Two!"

Harmon stepped around Shay, moving more quickly now, right up to the door. Shay moved up behind him, but not too close, and put the backpack on the deck. She pulled her pistol.

Harmon looked at her, nodded, peeked inside through the open door, then pushed it all the way open with his gun, and said, "Everybody sit quiet."

One of the men said, "Hey! Hey!"

"Jim," Harmon said to the man directly, "I'm warning you . . . quiet."

The other man shook his head, as if clearing his ears, and said, "Harmon? What are you doing, man? What's with the mask?"

"Don't move, because I really don't want to shoot anybody, but I will if you try for a weapon. You know that." Harmon raised his voice and called through the doorway, "Send that girl in with the cuffs. Rick, put the SAW between the last two containers, and cover the crew quarters. Larry, take the gangplank."

Cue the girl. Shay picked up Harmon's backpack and carried it into the small cabin, where two men stood with their hands at shoulder height. They were wearing cargo pants, golf shirts, and athletic jackets, and both had close-cropped hair and well-developed biceps. One was fairly tall, the other a head shorter.

Shay carefully put the pack on the floor while keeping both her pistol and the video camera pointed at the short man. Neither of the men was wearing armor, and in the twelve-foot-long room, she could hardly miss.

"I heard you'd turned," the tall man said to Harmon. "I didn't want to believe it."

" 'Cause they're killing children," Harmon said. "They're wiping their brains so some rich guys can have them. Honest to God, Jim."

"That's bullshit, Harmon, they're doing—"

"Shut up," Shay said. "I get tired of listening to it. Why do you think they hired you? To guard this piece of junk? You think they're doing legitimate medical research in a rusting tub?"

The tall man—Jim—asked, "Is this the chick that ruined Thorne?"

Shay, with the crazy act: "I should have shot him in the head. If I'd known he was the guy who tortured my brother, I would have."

Jim blinked: he now believed she'd shoot.

Harmon said, "Turn around, move very slowly. Drop into a push-up position. Both of you. Feet together, body up in the air. We're going to put some ties around your ankles, then we're going to cuff your hands. We really don't want to shoot anyone—that's not why we're here."

The men turned and knelt, then got into the push-up position. Jim said, "Thorne's gonna kill you."

Harmon said, "I don't think he's got the balls for it."

The short man grunted, "Very funny. He's in the hospital."

"Eyes straight ahead, Butch," Harmon said. And to Shay: "The white ties first."

The white ties had a plastic snap lock on them, like computer cable ties. She bound their legs together, then Harmon said, "Jim, go flat, hands behind your back."

He went down, and Harmon, cuffing him with thicker black ties, said to Shay, "If Butch makes a move, shoot him."

"I will," she said.

"She's nuttier than a Christmas fruitcake," Butch said, not moving. "How'd you come to hang with the crazies? You're the guy everybody looked up to."

"Quiet," Harmon said. "This is hard enough."

"Take her gun away, man. They'll let you come back."

"I don't want to come back," Harmon said. "And I'm not sure I *could* take her gun away. What I want is for you guys to quit them. If you don't, you're going to Leavenworth for the best part of your lives. I'm not joking. The storm is coming, boys. It's gonna be a hard rain."

"Ah, bullshit."

Harmon cuffed the short man, then said to Shay, "Stand by the door, keep a lookout. I'm gonna put some tape on them." A bit louder, he called, "Rick, put the SAW on the hallway from the castle."

Shay peered out the door at their phantom comrade as Harmon took a roll of black gaffer tape from his pack and taped the tall man's ankles. He had trouble ripping the tape with his hands, so Shay took out her knife and passed it to him. He cut the tape, and then did the tall man's wrists, and then went to work on the shorter man.

"They're strong enough that they might beat the ties, but they won't get out of the tape," he explained. He cut two more pieces of tape, then passed the knife back to her. With the two men helpless on the floor, Harmon patted them down, took away their guns and three sets of keys, and put the guns and two sets of keys in his pack.

Shay squatted by their heads. "I want to tell you guys something, and I want you to pass it around Singular. We have proof of what's going on, and we're going to put it out there. You've got exactly one chance, and that's to go to the police before the police come to you."

"Thanks for the speech, sweetheart," the short guy said.

Shay persisted: "You said everybody looked up to Harmon. Think about why he's with us now. Not for his health, huh? He's a tougher guy than you are, but he's got brains, too. Think!"

Harmon slung the pack over his shoulder and gave the men his last words of advice. "Think about West and what Thorne did to him. West had a silver star, Jim, and Thorne shot him like a dog. We're not asking you to just go on what we say—think about the people you've been guarding. North Korean medical experiments? Are you kiddin' me? You spent half your life in the SEALs, and now you're working with North Korea? Does that seem right to you? I'll tell you what—someday soon, if you don't get out of this, some lawyer's going to point a finger at you and say, 'Treason,' and you won't even be able to say, 'Innocent.'"

The men on the floor said nothing. Harmon shrugged and used the last pieces of tape for their mouths. They stepped out of the room, and Harmon said, "I think these keys should work. . . ."

He tried one in the cabin door; it went in, but wouldn't turn. He tried two more, and the third one turned, locking the two men inside. He left the key in the lock, put his hand against the side of it, and pushed it hard back and forth until it finally snapped off.

"They'll have to drill it out," he said, and Shay nodded.

"Okay. What's a SAW?"

"A squad automatic weapon. Like an M16, but with a little more ass to it."

Shay was standing on the deck with her gun still in her hand. "Listen. You hear that? What is that sound?"

It sounded almost human, a low humming, muted by the steel of the ship.

"We'll go look," Harmon said. He peered at the crew quarters looming overhead: still nothing but a stack of blank, unlit windows. "I wish I knew if there was anybody up there, on the high ground. Not really a good way to check, though."

"I need to tell Twist what we're doing," Shay said. Without thinking, she walked over to the rail next to the gangway and sent a text: "Two guards secure, searching hold." She couldn't see anyone at the dirt berm, but as she started to turn away, a silvery streak suddenly crossed it and sprinted for the boat.

X had seen her and was coming to help: he covered the hundred yards from the berm in five seconds and was up the gangway and at her knee.

Shay said, "Good doggy."

Harmon touched the dog's nose and said, "Glad to have you." And to Shay: "We need one last backup before we start looking around." He jogged back to the bow of the boat, with Shay and X following. They found a light hawser coiled on the deck. Harmon tied one end to a capstan, then tossed the other end over the bow. "Always set up a second exit if you have time," he said.

They went back to a stairway leading into the bowels of the ship. X sensed the mission and led the way down. At the bottom of the stairs was a steel door, painted gray. Locked. Harmon took out the key ring, tried a few keys, found the right one, and they went through.

They were in another stairwell, which appeared to go all the way to the bottom of the hull. Dark. Shay found a light panel outside the door, flipped a switch, and a dim overhead light came on in the stairwell, barely enough to see the steps as they worked their way down.

The humming now almost seemed to be a chant, though still low in volume and deep—deep, perhaps, because only the deeper tones were getting through the steel plating that was everywhere. "What the heck is it?" Shay asked.

"I'm afraid it's bad, whatever it is," Harmon said.

At the bottom of the stairway, they found another door, and another light panel. Shay tried a switch, and the humming, the chanting, stopped instantly. "Was it electrical? It didn't sound electrical, it sounded more human."

"Maybe a radio, and the switch is plugged in here. . . ."

Even as he said it, the sound came back, but at a much lower volume than before, and then it began to swell. Harmon tried the keys again, found one that worked, took his pistol out of its holster, and said, "Stand back. . . ."

He popped the door: everything inside was in darkness, but the sound again switched off. Harmon reached back to the light switch and flicked it on.

And they found themselves in hell.

Fifteen human beings, all Asian, and dressed in loose blue uniforms, were shuffling through the hold of the old ship. Like zombies. Everything stank: at the far end of the hold was a row of portable toilets that apparently hadn't been recently pumped. All of the people were young, all but three were male, and all but two had shaved heads. Most of their heads showed the same kind of golden beads that covered Fenfang's, while the skulls of the other two were covered with carefully fitted metal plates.

Shay stood frozen and unbelieving for two seconds, five seconds. Then X yipped and jolted her out of her trance. She had the presence to be sure her camera was filming.

The three of them went forward. The victims began humming again—the noise now resolved not into song, but into a shared groan of despair. They turned wide, blank eyes on their visitors and started shuffling forward in eerie unison.

Harmon was stunned. "Oh, sweet Jesus . . ."

Shay said, "We gotta get some help here, we need help. . . ." She looked at her phone: no reception in the steel hold.

"We've got another door," Harmon said. He was pointing across the hold at a smaller, squatter door. There was no light switch next to it.

Harmon found a key for the door, opened it: the other side was in total darkness. He pulled a powerful LED flashlight out of a cargo pocket and turned it on: inside the next hold were a series of short container boxes, turned so that their doors opened into the hold where Shay, X, and Harmon were standing.

The doors on the containers were held shut by simple swing latches, iron bars that dropped into hooks. Harmon stepped over to one and pulled up the latch and opened the door. They could make out the ends of a mattress, and the stink of human waste washed over them. A few seconds later, a man crawled toward the door. He was white, European or American, and he said something that sounded like English as he looked up at them, said it again with more fervor, clear enough that Shay understood:

"Please kill me, please . . ."

The man reached out and grabbed hold of Shay's ankle as she filmed, but his grip was weak and she shook her leg and he let go, collapsing onto his stomach at her feet.

"I'm sorry, sir, I'm sorry," she said, and bent to touch his shoulder, his scalp all beads and wires, and he turned up his chin, pleading again for death. "We're here to help you, we're going to get you out of here. . . ."

Shay turned away and ran, through the first hold and up the stairs, looking for a cell phone signal. About two-thirds of the way up, the first signal she got was from Twist: a series of missed calls, spaced only seconds apart. She ran a few steps higher, and the phone rang.

Twist was screaming.

"Get out of there, get out of there, there's a whole convoy coming, you gotta get out of there. . . ."

27

Twist was screaming, "Get out of there, get out of there. . . ."

He could see the convoy a block away, closing in fast. Danny, at his shoulder, said, "Too late to come down the gangway; they've got to go down that rope."

Shay was trying to say something, but it was garbled as Twist talked over her: "Too late to come down the gangway. Go over the side, go over the side. . . ."

Then she broke through. "They're here! Prisoners! Like zombies . . . Total cut-up zombies, Twist, it's awful, you gotta get somebody here!"

Twist: "You gotta get off!"

Odin was there, one hand gripping Fenfang's upper arm, and Fenfang turned to him, asking "What are these zombies? What are these zombies? Zombies are in movies. . . ."

"They found . . . test people," Odin said. "Jesus, they've got to get off the ship."

• • •

Shay and Harmon, crouching by the rail, watched as three RVs the size of Greyhound buses and four more SUVs rolled into the parking area. A half-dozen men and a couple of women were getting out of the SUVs, and one of them called, "Ladder's down."

Harmon said, "Too late to try the bow rope—they'd see us from down there."

"How about pulling up the gangway?"

Harmon dropped to his knees, crawled over to the rail, opened the gangway control panel, and pushed the power button. The gangway started up, slowly, and they both heard a heavy, meaty impact. Shay risked moving up and saw that one of the Singular security men had jumped on the bottom step and was riding the gangway up.

"Guy on the gangway," Shay called to Harmon. "He's got a gun."

During their exploration of the ship, Harmon had rolled his mask up, wearing it like a watch cap. Now he rolled it back down, and peered over the rail. He shouted, "Get off the ladder. Get off the ladder."

The man lifted his pistol and fired a single shot through the space where Harmon's head had been a split second before. Harmon poked his pistol around the rail and fired three quick warning shots. Risking another look, he saw the man bail: he slid to the bottom of the stairs, then jumped back onto the pier and ran for cover behind the RVs.

"He's off," Shay called. Harmon pushed the power button again, and the ladder started up. When it was too high for anyone to jump on, he crawled backward to Shay and said, "We gotta go."

At that moment, lights began blinking on in the crew quarters.

Harmon looked up at the lights and said, "There is some kind of a crew here. They'll be coming. If they've got guns . . . from up there . . . they'll kill us."

Twist and the others heard the single pistol shot, then three fast shots, and saw the Singular security man jump down from the gangway and run off the pier. As that was happening, a group of chained men had shuffled off the RVs.

Fenfang: "Some of my people! There are some!" She pulled free from Odin and suddenly bolted to the top of the dirt berm and screamed, "Liko! Liko!"

A shaved head popped up on one of the chained men, and everybody looked at Fenfang as she screamed, "Liko!"

The chained man seemed to call back, a raven-like croak, and began moving toward her until one of the security men grabbed him. Twist was screaming, "Get down, stay down," and Cruz and Odin were scrambling toward Fenfang, trying to stay below the brush line, and then—

BANG!

A single gunshot from the direction of the vehicles.

Fenfang didn't blow backward the way the bodies do in Hollywood: she simply folded up like a broken kite.

Odin screamed, "Fenfang!" and broke away from Cruz, running out in the open toward the fallen girl. At the same instant, Danny opened up with his M16 on fully automatic fire. Bullets rang off the boat, and the Singular troops scattered and ran for their lives.

Odin got to Fenfang and picked her up in his arms, standing upright, calling to her, then to Twist and Cruz. There was a sudden silence. Danny's gun stopped, and Twist shouted, "Run! Run!" and Odin turned and ran back over the berm, toward the cars, Fenfang cradled in his arms.

Twist shouted, "Put her in the Jeep, in the back of the Jeep. . . ."

Odin shouted, "No key, I got no key. . . ."

"I got one, I got a key!" Twist shouted back.

Cruz held the Jeep's door, and Odin put Fenfang in the back, and Twist jumped into the driver's seat as Danny fired another burst of bullets at the RVs and the ship, and then they were moving, with Fenfang and Odin in the back.

"I can't wake her up, I can't wake her up," Odin cried.

Twist wrestled the Jeep onto the main road, took out his phone as they sped away. He punched up Cade's number and said, "Zero, Zero, we need the nearest emergency room, get us to an emergency room."

"Which way you going now?" Cade asked, his voice low and calm.

Odin shouted, "Headed west from where we were at."

"Wilbur hits a T-intersection ahead of you. When you get there, turn left."

"Left, yes . . ."

"Turn left and stay on that."

Harmon had said, "They'll kill us."

Shay: "Can't let that happen. We've got to go up."

At that moment, they heard Fenfang: "Liko! Liko!"

They both reacted without thinking and stood up to see the Chinese girl bolt from the cover of the berm, and then the single shot. *BANG!*

Fenfang went down and then Danny opened up with his M16, the bullets pounding in a steady stream off the side of the ship. They saw Odin get to the fallen girl and carry her back across the berm.

"Oh, jeez, oh, jeez, they shot her," Shay groaned. "My God . . ."

"Focus! Focus!" Harmon said. "We can't help her, and if those guys up on top see us . . ."

"But they—"

"Yeah, that happens sometimes," Harmon said. "Let's go."

In the exact middle of the ship, there was a hallway that appeared to go through the ship's castle to the stern. Off that, a stairway went up. "Got to do this fast, if we're gonna get off," Harmon said.

"I'll watch our backs," Shay said. And to X: "C'mon, dog."

Nothing on the second level. On the third level, a sign said BRIDGE, with an arrow pointing down a hallway. As they crossed the top of the stairs, they heard the gangway moving below them. Harmon said, "Must have controls up here, too. When that gets down, they'll be coming. Gotta hurry."

They ran light-footed down the hallway, and as they got to the end, a short, thin Asian man stepped into the hall, talking on a cell phone. He saw them only at the last instant and tried to get back through the door of the cabin he'd come from and slam it in their faces, but Harmon got there as the door was closing and hit it with his full weight, barreling into the cabin, knocking the Asian man down. Shay stepped over him, her pistol leveled at two additional Asian men in what turned out to be the glassed-in bridge.

She shouted, "Lift the ladder! Lift that ladder!"

One of the men said, "No understand," and she twitched the pistol to the side of his head and pulled the trigger *BANG!* The bullet smashed through the glass on the bridge, and the man ducked and the second man reached behind the first and hit a switch. Down below, the gangway stopped extending.

Harmon was back on his feet with his gun, and he waved it at the three men: "Go down, go down. . . ."

They had their hands over their heads, and they let Harmon hustle them to the main deck. From there, he pushed them along the through-passage to the stern, and when they got there, he said, "Jump!"

They did, one at a time, dropping into the deep water on the river side of the boat, then swimming toward the bank.

At the turnout, Cruz shouted into his phone, "Where's Shay?"

Cade said, in his calm voice, "She's not coming—she says you'll have to pick her up later. Right now, get out of there. Get out of there."

Cruz cursed and jumped into the truck and rolled out after the Jeep, and Danny fired a last burst from the M16 at the ship, ran back to the Volvo, and followed the others out to the main road and west.

Both Danny and Cruz could hear on the open phones Twist talking to Cade, and Cade directing traffic, and then Cruz shouted, "If they come after us, we'll separate and lead them away from the hospital. Danny, stay close."

Twist took them left at the T-intersection and onto Highway 4, and Danny called, "Nobody's behind us, I think we're okay."

"Keep coming," Twist called back. And he called out streets as they crossed them so Cade could track them.

Cade guided Twist under a freeway, they never noticed which one, but the street they were on got bigger and wider, Cade's voice calm all the way, calling out directions. Odin was crying, saying, "You gotta go faster, she's hurt bad. . . ."

Danny shouted, "Zero, where's the hospital?"

Cade said, "You should be right on top of it, it's off to your left. . . ."

There it was. Twist made the hard turn into the hospital and Cade guided him through the parking lot around to the emergency room and Twist said over his shoulder to Odin, "We've got to leave her. She's been shot, the police will be all over us. We've got to leave her."

"Can't leave her," Odin cried. "Can't just dump her."

"We have to," Twist said. He jammed on the brakes immediately in front of the emergency room doors. Cruz and then Danny pulled in behind.

On the boat, all the lights came on. "Dammit, we missed someone," Harmon said, looking up toward the ship's castle. He, Shay, and X were crouched by the rail at the bow of the boat. They couldn't see the bridge from there, but then, whoever was on the bridge couldn't see them.

Shay, on her phone, told Cade, "We're stuck here. Tell everybody to keep going, they can get us later. Tell Cruz, make sure you tell Cruz, or he'll try to hang back."

Shay said, "Okay, Harmon, what now?" As she said it, a searchlight at the top of the mast, apparently controlled from the bridge, burned across the boat and, from there, probed down the riverbank, and then into the open water of the river.

"Looking for us," Harmon said. "Don't think going for a swim would be a good idea. Not right now, anyway."

"And so . . . ," Shay said, like a kid waiting for the magician to pull the rabbit out of the hat.

Harmon had nothing. "There's a saying in the Special Forces," he said. "When in doubt, hide."

• • •

Shay called Cade back and said, "Call all the cops! Has anyone called the cops yet? We're gonna hide."

Before she hung up, Harmon said, "Tell him if we're down inside the hull, we won't be able to use our cell phones. Tell the cops we're down there—don't shoot us."

Shay repeated that and then said, "Gotta go," and punched off.

Twist ran across the sidewalk to the hospital entrance and held the door for Odin and Cruz to carry Fenfang though. As they passed, Twist looked down at Fenfang. Her eyes were closed, and a small bloodstain had soaked through her shirt, immediately over her heart. Cruz glanced at Twist and gave a terse shake of his head.

There was a nursing station inside the door, staffed by a single nurse, and Odin cried, "She's hurt bad, she's hurt bad."

The nurse hurried out from behind the station and a few feet down a hallway, got a gurney, pushed it toward them, and said, "Put her on this, put her head on this end. . . ." As Odin did that, she picked up a phone and pushed a button and asked, "What happened?" and Odin said, "She was shot. Somebody shot her."

The nurse spoke into the phone, and they heard it come from overhead: "Dr. Rice to ER, code blue. Dr. Rice to ER. . . ."

Cruz said quietly to Twist, "Hold the hospital door open, then open the back door on the Jeep and stand by to close it." Twist nodded, understanding, and Cruz walked up behind Odin, wrapped his arms around him from the back, pinning Odin's arms at his sides, then picked him up and staggered back toward the door as Odin kicked and spit and fought against him. The nurse said, "Wait, you can't go, the police—"

Twist said to her, "Take care of Fenfang. X-ray her head. You'll see."

His tone stopped the nurse in her tracks, and he said, again, "X-ray her head. Call the newspapers, call the police, show them what they've done to her head." The nurse looked back at Fenfang on the gurney. The wig had slipped partly off her skull, and the gold electric knobs winked in the overhead lights.

Odin was twisting, fighting, crying, but Cruz ground on through the doors. Danny was there, and Cruz yelled, "Get the door on the Jeep." Danny popped the back door open, and Cruz stuffed Odin inside, then climbed on top of him and held him down.

Twist was in the car two seconds later, said, "Okay," and Cruz hopped out and slammed the door before Odin could sit up, and Twist peeled away. Odin got upright and tried the door handle, but the Jeep was out on the main street and moving too fast. "You gotta let me stay!" he shouted at Twist.

"Can't let you stay, Odin!" Twist shouted back. And then he was on the phone to Cade: "Get us out of here!"

Cade's voice, still calm and clear: "You're heading toward the freeway, Highway 4. Go west. . . ."

They drove west, listening to Cade. He told them that Shay, Harmon, and X had been trapped on the ship and that they were hiding, waiting for the police to arrive.

"Shit," Twist said, fear clutching at him again.

After they'd driven a handful of miles, Cade directed them to an exit, and they pulled into a closed Chevron station, Twist and Odin, then Cruz, with Danny coming up behind. Odin virtually fell out of the backseat of the Jeep. He sat on the concrete, head between his knees, and began vomiting. Cruz went over and sat next to him, putting an arm around his shoulders.

Danny looked at Twist, the question written on his face. . . .

"We think Fenfang's gone," Twist said. "She had a bullet wound right over her heart."

Danny staggered away, pulling on the dreads at the sides of his head in grief.

Twist called after him, "Cade called the cops, told them about the shooting and the prisoners."

Danny turned back, looking down the freeway. "Where are they, then? I never saw a single cop car coming here."

"Maybe there's a faster way from wherever they're at," Cruz said. "We gotta get back there. We gotta help Shay."

Danny: "Nobody ever saw our vehicles. One of us . . . or all of us . . . could drive past there, see what's going on."

"Let's do it," Twist said. And to all three: "I told the nurse to X-ray Fenfang's head. We should call them now, and tell them that she was executed by the same people who used her like a laboratory animal. The same ones who were holding those poor people on the ship."

Odin lifted his head. "Put that out on Mindkill. Some people will see it. Get Cade to bring it back up, put it out there. Make it impossible for them to get at her . . . make it impossible for somebody from Singular to claim her body and hide it. Put her movie out there, the interview."

"We can do that," Twist said. He looked around at everybody. "I can't believe this. I can't believe this happened."

"If the cops moved fast, they'll get them all," Cruz said. "Let's go, I want to see it."

They piled into the cars and drove back to the freeway, retracing their route to the ship.

Twist led with Odin, followed by Cruz in the truck and Danny in the Volvo. As they got closer, Odin said to Twist, "Shouldn't there be more lights?"

"I don't know. I don't know what's happening," Twist said. Danny, on the phone, said, "Don't slow down when we go by. Keep it moving."

They passed the turnoff where they'd parked the cars, and then they were at the open concrete pad where the RVs and SUVs had come in.

And they saw a single cop car, with flashing lights on the roof, and a cop walking back to it. He got in the car and killed the flashers.

Behind him, the pad was empty. No RVs, no SUVs.

And the ship . . .

The ship was gone.

Deep in the hull of the ship, toward the bow, in a niche made by three supporting beams, Shay and Harmon crouched in the dark. The ship was moving: not quickly, but steadily, the engine turning with a powerful hum. Above them, in a den-like cove where the two sides of the ship joined to make the point of the bow, X lay quietly, watching the space behind them.

So far, there'd been no lights, no search parties.

"Wonder where they're running to?" Harmon said. He had been digging in his backpack and now came up with an LED flashlight. He turned it on, twisted an adjustment ring, which dimmed the light to a thin glow. He took the rifle off his shoulder for the first time, pulled the magazine, checked it in the light, slapped it back in place.

Getting ready for combat, Shay thought. *But there were so many of them. . . .*

"Once they've got the test subjects all corralled, they'll probably do an inch-by-inch search of the ship," Harmon said. "Did you see how many of them there were?"

"No, but there were three big RVs for the prisoners, got to figure three or four guys each, that'd be, maybe, twelve? And four SUVs with two guys each, that'd be eight more. So maybe . . . twenty?"

"Twenty is about eighteen too many, plus they'll cut Butch and Jim loose. . . ."

Shay was quiet for a minute. "One good thing."

Harmon: "Tell me."

"We got 'em cornered."

After a few seconds, Harmon started to laugh.

DON'T MISS BOOK 3 OF
THE SINGULAR MENACE

RAMPAGE

COMING IN FALL 2016

Harmon slowed and grabbed Shay's shirt. "Getting close to the street. We need to call Twist again."

"Not yet," Shay whispered. "Somebody's coming behind us."

Harmon turned, listened, then pushed her shoulder down. "Lie flat. It's one of the guys from the ship."

They froze in place, beneath a boat, with an axle between them and the approaching man. He'd chosen the same route they'd taken, for the same reasons: it was open enough to move quickly, and yet still provided cover.

The man came on and, just as he got to the boat, dropped into a crouch, looking ahead . . . and then his eyes turned toward them.

Harmon said, "Freddy, I'm pointing a pistol at your head."

"Goddammit, Harmon, that was you, wasn't it? Back on the ship."

"Yeah. Where're you going?"

"A long way from here. I'm done; so are some of the other guys.

Ginsburg and me are hooking up and heading for Mexico, and then maybe further south. Maybe go to Africa. There're some jobs there."

"How'd that happen?"

"The ass is falling off the company," Freddy said. "And we've all been talking about you. When we signed up, we didn't know what we were getting into. But there's some bad shit going on and Thorne's lying to us. It ain't legal—no way."

"No way," Harmon agreed. "You got a ride out of here?"

"No, we're running. Man, I walked through Baghdad in the dark, right in the middle of the war, so I won't get caught here . . . if you let me go."

"You got a gun with you?"

"A nine."

"Keep it in your pocket. You try to ambush us further up the line . . . well, we got the dog with us, he can see in the dark, and he'll tear your face off. I'm telling you, Freddy, he'll kill you."

"I'm not messing with you anymore. I'm out of it."

"Go, then," Harmon said.

Freddy started to move away, but then stopped and said, quietly, "I appreciate this, letting me go. So I'll give you something. There's another Singular base that you guys don't know about. It's in the desert, a little less than two hours by private jet, southeast of San Francisco. Mostly south. Might've been Arizona, or New Mexico? There's a good private landing strip, but not much else, wherever it was. I flew it four times as security, and to pass out drinks and keep an eye on the passengers. The passengers going down were normal, but coming back up, most of them had had some kind of surgery done on their heads."

Shay asked, "Old people? Rich people?"

Freddy said, "Didn't see you back there. You the chick who shot Thorne?"

"Yes."

Freddy chuckled. "He is *really* pissed. You won't want to spend any time with him, you know, in private."

"I wasn't planning to," Shay said. "So, old people? Rich people?"

"Yeah, I'd say so. Wrinkles and bling."

"Who were the pilots?" Harmon asked.

"Two guys named Walt and Barry. No last names. Got a feeling they flew for the agency at some point. Hey—gotta go. You guys take care. And, honey—stay away from Thorne."

Freddy faded into the dark.

They gave him a minute; then Shay pulled her own gun and said, "I got this. Follow me."